The Shadows of Kiln

Hidden From Destiny
Book One: The Shadows of Sorban

The Demon's Curse
Book One: The Shadows of the Amazon
(Late 2011/Early 2012)

Chapbooks
The Heroes of Kiln Volume I

Hidden From Destiny

The Shadows of Kiln
Book One: The Shadows of Sorban

Micaela Fischer

Book design by Amber L. Campbell
Cover Art by Gary McCluskey
Cover Design by Tiara Lynn Agresta
Back Cover Description by Vincent Costa

To my children - You bring light to the darkness

To my husband - You are my forever hero

ACKNOWLEDGEMENTS

Every story has a start. This story started with a character for a Dungeons & Dragons game. I wanted to base a character on Aramis from Disney's The Three Musketeers. I had not read the original novel by Alexandre Dumas, but I had seen the classic movie. I fell in love with Charlie Sheen's portrayal of a man who had lost his faith in the church, but never in God. From there, Serpé came to life. Thank you to the wonderful group of players who spent their Saturday nights playing the adventure, and to the Dungeon Master who laid the trail before us. Rob, your gift for storytelling still amazes me.

To the many instructors and students of Writer's Village, your words of encouragement and criticism helped so much.

Mary Rosenblum, thank you for keeping the story on track. Without your help, I would have put this one away and never allowed it to be seen by anyone else.

November is my month for hiding behind my computer screen, thanks to Chris Baty and the National Novel Writer's Month crew, also called the Office of Letters and Light. After learning about Nanowrimo from a fellow writer, I signed up immediately. With the help of this wonderful group of people, by way of encouragement and a deadline, I completed the original manuscript. And I go out of my way to participate every year now.

The musical inspiration for this story comes from Queen and their music for Highlander. "Who wants to live forever" became a motto for Serpé. Each song from the movie reminds me of a different part of her life. Thank you so much for the music you brought to the world. I wish it had never truly stopped.

To Jo A. Wilkins, thank you for asking the questions and helping me to make the story the best it can be.

To Maxwell Alexander Drake, thank you for showing me that no one else can make the important decisions about my manuscript.

To Vincent Costa, Vinnie, for your encouragement, your attention to detail. Your suggestions are truly appreciated as well as your criticism.

Tiara Lynn Agresta, thank you for your quick and amazing work.

Gary McClusky, thank you for bringing Serpé to life.

To my parents, thank you for bringing me into this world and for your support, in the many different manifestations that only parents present. To Diane, I know it wasn't always easy to deal with me and the ordeals you lived with, but I appreciate everything you did.

To my children, your encouragement has given me hope. Your love makes the hard times easier. Thank you so much for helping bring my stories to others.

To my husband, you encourage me, you support me and you love me. Thank you so much for helping me to realize that this is truly what I want to do.

And to you, the reader, thank you for making my dream come true.

Micaela

Chapter 1

923 - Spring

Serpé struggled to stay on her sweat lathered horse. The pace she and her companion forced from the animals was dangerous—one misstep could send rider and horse to the gods with a broken neck. The sound of crushed leaves and snapping twigs echoed in the night and her ears. Tree branches reached out, tangling leaves into her hair, and grabbing at her loose clothing and cloak that flapped in the wind. The snorting of the horses echoed in the darkness, and she realized no forest creatures sounded out in protest to their presence.

Her gaze met that of her companion, and she saw her terror reflected in his eyes. Instead of staring at him, she flicked an anxious look around. Because of the race forced from the already travel weary beasts, she no longer controlled the reins of her horse. He had taken them from her earlier. No matter how hard they pushed the animals, he made it clear their pursuers would eventually catch them. The hope that they would reach safety before this happened kept her from falling into the tears that threatened.

The spring night cooled her skin. A light mist formed in the moist air around her. Ignoring it all, she kept her attention focused on staying mounted. The darkness of the trees gradually lightened until, at last, the horses burst out of their shelter.

Bathed in moonlight, their pace slowed somewhat, though the man in front of her continued to pull her horse with him.

A building materialized on the plains before them, then a second just behind the first. Plowed fields, full of tall stalked plants waiting to be harvested lay beyond the buildings. The two riders raced toward the structures, pulling to a halt in the fenced yard. The house stood in front of them and Serpé strained to see the roof.

The wood building stood outlined against the moonlit sky. Windows on the second floor reflected light from the moon and stars. Light escaped from between shutters to shine on the grass that danced in the breeze.

Still struggling to catch her breath, and control the fear that gripped her, Serpé turned to question Bennan. Before her question came out, the front door opened and light from inside flooded the yard. As quick as it appeared, the light was blocked by a figure in the door. Serpé's eyes scanned the shadowed body of the new arrival. Her traveling companion dismounted, then helped her from her horse. She straightened her clothes, her hands smoothing and rearranging the material several times while Bennan strode to the door and extended his hand in greeting.

"Well met and good eve, Kian." His deep voice echoed in the night. "It's good to see you received my message. We had to leave sooner than planned."

"It arrived earlier," Kian informed him. Turning his attention to Serpé, he nodded. "Child, Bennan asked that you stay with me for a time. I assume you have brought clothing with you?"

Kian's deep voice comforted her, despite the 'child' reference, but she forced caution into her thoughts. *You don't know this man. Do not trust him too quickly.*

"Ye…yes, I have." Her attempt to control her emotions failed to keep her voice calm.

"Good. Come inside and we will talk," Kian instructed. Stepping aside, he moved so there would be no contact as she passed over his threshold.

Inside, the warmth of the house wrapped her in a comforting embrace. Glancing around, she recognized the kitchen to her left and the common room to the right. Stairs led to the second floor and, she assumed, bedrooms.

Peeking into the common room, she found a warm fire

and four lanterns lit the area. Books filled shelves, but no knickknacks adorned the tables or the fireplace mantle. The sparse decorations and furniture made it very clear no woman lived in the home.

Turning back to the entryway, she found the men still stood outside, staring at the plains that lay between the farm and the trees. A window in the common room faced the tree line she and Bennan just left. She saw no movement in the trees or on the plains, but still shivered at the thought of those who followed her. Restless, she waited for the men to enter, finally stepping closer to the door to hear their hushed conversation.

"When did you leave, Bennan?"

"Three days ago. We've barely stopped for more than a couple hours at a time. The Religious Guard has been behind us by only hours the entire way. They should be here by morning, at the latest." Bennan turned and bumped into her, holding her tight to keep her from falling.

"Then we need to leave immediately," Serpé squeaked, pressure increasing in her chest.

Kian stepped away from the door and took her by the arm. "Come with me."

He guided her into the common room and pushed her into a chair, standing over her while he studied her. Without a word, he poured tea into a cup and handed it to her, his hand reddened by the steam. Blowing over the liquid to cool it, she looked up at him and her breath caught in her throat.

In the light of the lanterns and fire, Serpé took a moment to look at the man who welcomed her into his home. *He's older than me. Eight or nine winters at least.*

Her cheeks flushed under his gaze and warmth radiated through her. She wiped away an unexpected sheen of sweat. *Why does his look embarrass me so?*

The kiss of the sun had darkened his skin and his green eyes glowed bright against his tan. His strong jaw clenched, but she saw he tried to smile. Muscles rippled beneath his shirt. *He's not the prettiest man I've ever seen, but he is handsome.*

"Kian, you need to get her into hiding." Bennan's voice broke into her thoughts.

"You are making the child nervous, Bennan." Kian's face relaxed and his smile became more natural. "Now, what is your name?"

"Serpé Navran. That is the second time you've called me 'child'." Straightening her back, she returned the cup to the table. "I am not a child. I have seen eight winters under the tutelage of The First and eight winters in the arms of my mother."

Kian's quiet laugh made her cheeks flush again. He sat across from her. "My apologies, Serpé. I am Kian Donwell." He glanced up at Bennan. "My friend, the pouch you sent with your message is on the counter in the kitchen. Would you please retrieve it for me?" The bigger man nodded, dropped her saddlebags on the floor near the stairs, and went into the kitchen. "While we wait for him, tell me how you came to be with The First."

"My father was unhappy with a marriage proposal he received for me. Mother and Father contacted the church of Azar and within a week, I was taken to the church and my studies began. The First took me as a private student and when he moved up in the ranks of the priests, I moved up through the ranks of students and acolytes. His advancement gave him the contacts to be chosen to replace his predecessor, Most Holy Korewyn."

Bennan returned to the room. A leather pouch dangled from his hand, which he dropped into Kian's waiting palm.

Kian nodded, his eyes focused on her. "I was captain of the Religious Guard and Most Holy Korewyn's personal protector until six months before his death. I left the Guards and the city to work on my farm." He pulled a golden necklace with a sapphire the size of a gold coin from the pouch. The pendant hanging from the chain's length caught Serpé's eyes and held her attention. "Bennan sent this for you, when he told me you would be coming. I understand blue is your favorite color." He leaned forward and placed the chain around her neck.

The touch of his fingers on her bruised neck—warm, but painful—made her flinch. Before she and Bennan left the capital, she hid the marks with her hair and a scarf. Now her movement called attention to the pain The First had inflicted on her.

"What is it?" Stepping closer when she moved away from Kian's touch, Bennan's hand on her shoulder sent waves of comfort through her.

Lifting her hair from her neck, Kian sucked his breath through his teeth and looked up at Bennan. "Apparently, someone decided her neck needed these lovely purple and red bruises." Returning his attention to Serpé, he asked, "Who did this to you?"

"The First, three days ago, when he found my diary. Right before I contacted Bennan." Pulling her hair from his grasp, she fanned it out over her neck again. "What's the necklace for?"

She felt Kian's eyes on her before he answered. Embarrassment filled her at his intense gaze. *If he had the chance, would he attack The First for what he did to me?*

Kian cleared his throat. "The stone is magically enhanced to provide a shield for you. While you wear it, and the stone is intact, no one will be able to find you using any kind of magic. Ever."

Sitting next to her, Bennan rested his arm around her shoulders. "It will be all right, Serpé. Kian and I will protect you."

Instead of looking at her, Kian poured fresh tea into her cup. "Why did you contact Bennan and leave Reicholt?"

"I collected bribes for The First, though I didn't find out that's what they were until later. I thought the money was donations to the church. One day, while collecting the money, two men attacked me and stole it." Serpé sniffed, rubbing her face. "They left me without my horse, food or water. Fortunately, I was not far outside Siladan, so rescuers found me easily, once The First realized something was wrong. Two days later, the men were found and hanged in the town square."

She paused, her throat tightening at the memory. That was the first hanging she ever attended. The First did not give her a choice, forcing her to stand beside him until the men were dead.

Lifting her cup, she sipped the liquid, relieved the warm liquid relaxed her throat so she could continue. "Bennan met me that night, while I wandered, confused, through the city. He told me to question why this happened. I questioned the guards who had been at the hangings. Only one answered me truthfully. I found out that the men were separated from their families because they didn't pay their tithing to the church. The men who were hanged only stole the money because they were hungry. The Guard told everyone it was because they owed taxes on their crops. Either way, their wives were placed into prostitution in a house owned by The First and their children sold into slavery." She shivered, her hand caressing her throat.

"If I had kept my mouth shut, instead of following Bennan's advice, instead of asking so many questions... If I had ignored the things that were wrong, I wouldn't need your help or protection. I wouldn't be here." *Did I make a mistake by listening to Bennan?*

Kian nodded. "I won't lie to you, Serpé. That is probably true. If Reicholt feels you're a threat to his plans, he will stop at nothing to find you. We also have evidence that he is responsible for the death of Most Holy Korewyn." He pointed at her new necklace. "If the mage who enchanted that sapphire did his task correctly, you will be protected. Eventually, I am hopeful Reicholt will forget you."

"How is that supposed to comfort me? I know him. When he discovers he's lost me, he will want to find me even more." Her throat tightened, tears threatening to moisten her cheeks. "I will spend the rest of my life hiding from him."

Bennan stood and extended his hand toward her. "Come with me, dear. I'm sure the room Kian has prepared for you will be comfortable. After the Religious Guard arrives, and their search finds nothing, Kian will teach you what you need to know to start a new life, away from the church—away from Reicholt."

Retrieving her saddlebags from the floor, he led her up the stairs. The room he took her to lacked even the sparse decoration of the living room. Minimal furniture left most of the room empty and only one lamp lit the darkness.

"Stay here until Kian comes for you. He will deal with the Guard when they arrive. I won't be here when you wake. I will take the horses and make it look as if we left together." He placed her saddle bags on the floor next to the door, chuckling when she threw her arms around him in a tight embrace. "It will be all right, Serpé. Kian and I won't let any harm come to you."

Serpé nodded and shut the door after he left the room. Turning to look at the room again, she scrunched her nose. "How long is this supposed to be my 'home'?"

On the dresser, a wash basin sat empty and next to it stood a pitcher of water. She poured the water into the basin. Using a washcloth, Serpé wetted her face. Her reflection in the mirror caught her eye and the washcloth fell back into the water.

I look horrible. I need more than just a basin of water to look normal. She touched the bruises on her neck.

Her honey-brown hair, hanging over her shoulders by half a finger's length, needed to be washed and brushed. She removed two leaves that stuck out of her hair, but even running her fingers through the length did nothing to clear the knots. Bruises under her green eyes were the most obvious sign that she had not slept since leaving Siladan. Bennan had given her one of his shirts to wear and the length made it a very short skirt. Thankfully, the breeches she wore had kept her legs warm. A brown robe had kept her arms warm as well.

"I am dressed inappropriately for an acolyte of the church, and I look like I live on the streets. What would my mother say?"

After retrieving her brush from her saddlebags, she threw the robe on the floor and tackled brushing her hair. "She would probably say I had made a very poor decision in going with Bennan." She placed the brush on the dresser. "I think I would have to agree with her."

Bennan quickened his pace, anxious to complete his task before leaving. The Guard would arrive soon and he could not be there when they did. He needed to ensure they thought he and Serpé had left Kian's home together.

"How is she?" Kian asked, meeting him at the bottom of the stairs.

"Are you concerned because she's scared, or because you don't think you can handle a woman in your home?" Bennan returned, watching Kian shake his head.

"She's sixteen, Bennan. What am I going to do with a girl that age? Why can't I just give her some money and send her to Tushin or Valen or someplace else?"

Bennan smiled at the frustration he heard in his friend's voice. "Because she knows nothing of life outside the church. All her needs have been provided for by Reicholt. He tried to kill her, Kian. He'll do worse if he catches her." He rested a hand on Kian's shoulder. "Of all of us, Kian, you are the only one who has kept Reicholt's attention off you. You are the only one who has a stable home. She must learn to depend on herself and she must find a path in life other than religion. You can help her find that path."

Kian laughed, slapping Bennan on the back. "Always have an answer, don't you? You need to leave, my friend. May the Mother or whichever deity you choose to worship, guide and protect you on your journey." Together they walked to the front door.

"Protect her well." They shook hands and Bennan made his way to the horses. Taking the reins of Serpé's horse, he rode off into the moonlit night.

When he was sure Kian had closed the door, Bennan turned back to the farmhouse. Pulling energy from around him, he directed the power toward the ground where the horses had stood. The hoof prints that appeared clean in the dirt changed from a neat line to the farm and away, to a mess meant to confuse a tracker into thinking no one had dismounted and the horses had not been allowed to rest. His and Serpé's footprints disappeared while only Kian's only remained in the dirt in front of the door.

"Azar's blessings upon you both." Magic flowed through him again, sending his blessings on the wind to surround the home.

Kian stood at the door until his friend rode out of sight. After extinguishing the lanterns in the common room, he sat in the chair Serpé had occupied.

I'm not sure how I feel about having a young, attractive woman in my home. Children should be raised by people who love them, not sent to live with strangers.

Without realizing it, he again placed Serpé in a child-like category. It was easier to see her as a child than as a young woman who would have needs he was not prepared to deal with.

I am going to have to speak to Bennan again. She can stay here. But I will deal with it after the Guard arrives.

A cool breeze entered the room through the open window and brushed his cheek. "I'll just stay here until the Guard comes."

The chair relaxed him and he allowed his eyes to close, telling himself that he would only sleep for a short time.

A loud pounding on the front door woke Kian from his restless sleep. Mumbling, he stumbled to the door, smiling at the two men who stood in front of him. Their red surcoats identified them as members of the Religious Guard, as well as the five other men who waited behind them, still astride their horses.

The morning sun had not risen yet, but its glow peeked over the horizon.

It took them longer than I expected to arrive. How did Bennan get so far ahead of them?

"Morning, travelers. How can I assist you?" Kian's calm voice was husky with the thickness of sleep.

"We are looking for a man and a young woman. Their tracks lead here." The man on Kian's left spoke, pointing at the hoof prints on the ground where the horses had stood earlier.

Amused, Kian noted the man's rank insignia of sergeant shined, untarnished with use. *He's recently been promoted, probably right before the hunt for Serpé began. He's young, and familiar, but I don't recognize him.*

Kian nodded. "And, if your men haven't destroyed them, you will see their tracks also lead away from my farm. They came after the midnight change, begging for a place to sleep and hide. I sent them away as soon as they said they were running from The First." He smiled again. "As the former captain of the Religious Guard, my loyalties lie with The First and the church."

The guard stared at him and then motioned for his partner to move away. He bowed to Kian, saluted him and remounted his horse.

"Please accept our apologies, Captain. I did not recognize you without your uniform." The guard saluted him again, the others following suit.

Kian watched them ride away, following Bennan's trail. *These tracks are clearer than I expected. What did Bennan do to make them so obvious?*

Turning away from the yard and shutting the door, he walked up the stairs to Serpé's room. He did not want to intrude, but her training would have to start immediately. *Though the necklace is intended to protect her and I trust the mage who created it, The First is a powerful man. His service to a god could be the advantage he needs to find the child.*

Serpé's door remained unlocked, and the latch opened without a sound. Kian walked the short distance to the bed, to see if she woke from his presence in the room.

We will need to work on that. She must be taught to feel danger, even in her sleep. He took a deep breath. *I criticize her for not waking, yet I told her she would be safe here—that she would feel no danger. Do I expect too much from her already?*

Watching Serpé sleep, Kian knew Bennan made the right choice in bringing her to him. Though Kian had friends who would help with her safety, none had the knowledge he did about their enemy.

But she knows Reicholt better than even me. I just don't know how using a sword will help her against the priest.

He reached down and shook her shoulder. "Serpé, wake up. It's time to start your training and we have chores to do."

Serpé moaned while she stretched the sleep from her muscles. "But the sun isn't up yet."

Kian resisted the urge to smile. "It is, just not as high as you are probably accustomed to. You have five drops of the water clock to get ready and meet me downstairs."

"What kind of training?"

"You will learn to defend yourself, the same way I will defend you when I'm around. But you will not always be with me and you must learn how to protect yourself." Her pulling the blanket over her head did not surprise him. Considering where she had grown up, it was better than he had expected. "Hiding under the blankest will not change this. Now get up."

She huffed and threw the blankets across the bed. "Fine. But I don't see why I have to help with chores. Don't you have men who can do that?"

"Did you see a place for others? Do you think I have a group of farmhands living in my home to help me? I do all the work here myself. You will help me if you want to eat and not sleep with the animals." He was done with her whining, even though it had been brief. Instead of waiting for another complaint, he grabbed her arm and pulled her from the bed.

"What are you doing? I am not a child to be dragged around." Serpé struggled against his grip and he almost laughed at her weak attempts to pull away.

"This is exactly what I mean. You can't even defend yourself against me and I'm doing nothing but pulling you out of bed. Quit your complaining and get dressed." He released her. "You now have 3 drops."

Kian left the room, not surprised to hear the door slam behind him, though the lock did not latch into place. *Stubborn child.*

"Get up! Do you think Reicholt will give you a chance to regain your footing so you can attack him again?" Kian's angry words reverberated in Serpé's ears.

The rocks cut into her hands from where she fell from Kian's sweep kick. The estoc he gave her when they started rested just a few inches from her hand. She did not want to pick it up again. *Why is he doing this to me?*

"Do you hear me? Or did you hit your head?" he shouted.

"I don't understand. Why do I need to do this? Aren't you supposed to be protecting me from The First? Not torturing me?" She did not want to cry, did not want him to think she was just a little girl that still needed her mommy and daddy.

"I *am* protecting you. Do you think I will always be around to save you or raise my sword to defend you?" He toed the sword closer to her hand. "While you are with me, you will learn how to defend yourself. I will teach you everything I can, everything I know."

Serpé wrapped her fingers around the estoc's hilt. Lifting her gaze, she glared at him. *And to think, I thought he was good looking. I should have known this wouldn't be easy.*

She stood, bringing her weapon up to block Kian's before it reached her arm. It still came close to her skin, but she stepped back before he cut her. His blade slid off hers. "Fine. If this is what I have to do, then I'll do it. But I don't understand why."

His brief smile disappeared before Serpé recognized it. "Good. We'll start with the basics." Kian gestured at her feet with his sword. "Put your feet here and here. Try to follow my movements. Let's see what comes to you naturally."

Azar help me. Kian's going to kill me teaching me how to use a sword.

Chapter 2

"What do you mean, you lost her?" Eion Reicholt, Most Holy of Azar, struggled to control his urge to strike the mage in front of him.

"I mean, she was taken someplace outside of the city, through the forest, and when she left the trees, she disappeared. I cannot locate her with my scrying spell." Mage Stein's voice conveyed his frustration.

"You follow her through the trees. She leaves the trees and you lose her? What is so special about that area that you are now so incompetent you can't find her?"

"I do not know. Maybe another mage is interfering to make a point." Stein shrugged his shoulders.

Stepping closer to Stein, Eion's eyes narrowed. "And just what would that 'point' be, Mage Stein?"

"I am sure I do not know, Most Holy."

Eion stared at the mage. Stein refused to meet his gaze and dry washed his hands. *He knows something. He was the one following her. He's lying to me.*

"If I find out you are hiding *anything* from me, I will crush your hands myself. They will never help you cast another spell." He pushed a finger into Stein's chest. "Do I make myself clear?"

Mage Stein flinched. "Yes, Most Holy."

Eion stepped away, turning his back toward him. "You will do whatever it takes to find her. Assign one of your students to scry for her daily. Notify me immediately if she leaves whatever magical protection she has found."

Mage Stein bowed at his waist, his gaze on the floor. "Of course, Most Holy."

Eion left the mage's tower, slamming each door he walked through. Even the praises and adoration of the faithful he passed in the street did not please him.

Serpé has escaped me for now. But I will find her again and my plans will progress while I wait for her to be returned to me.

Chapter 3

Heat seeped from the food on the table while Serpé waited for the man in front of her to again give permission to eat. The small knife she had held no longer thrummed where it stuck in the wall. The sound, though, still echoed in her ears. Her head and lip throbbed from his slap, but the pain developing behind her eyes concerned her more. She lifted her hand to her lip to check for blood, but he rewarded her with another slap. Biting her lip controlled the tears threatening to wet her cheeks. She focused on the pain and turned a look of devotion to the man. After years with him, she knew showing Most Holy Eion Reicholt the devotion he craved was the quickest way to cool his volatile temper.

"Don't make me repeat myself, Serpé. You know how much I despise that," The First growled. He grabbed her jaw in a tight grip, fingers pushing her already tender flesh painfully against her teeth. "Tell me why you are asking about the donations you're collecting for me? And why were you seen near the prison and the slave caravans outside the city?"

Despite his grip on her mouth, she struggled to answer. "Don't know what you mean."

"Don't lie to me." She cringed at the spittle of his scream landing on her face. Yanking her from her seat, he threw her to the floor.

"Surely you have nothing to hide, Most Holy," she cried, struggling to control the emotion in her voice. "No reason why those insignificant actions should give you a moment's concern." In the past, she always waited out his waves of anger in silence. This time felt different though, more charged, uncontrolled—deadly. *I do not think silence will assuage his anger.*

The rustling of robes masked her rapid breaths, until a small leather bound book slid across the floor, coming to rest between her hands. She recognized her own diary and a quiet moan escaped her. *He read it all, written by my own hand.*

"I know what you 'think' you've discovered about me." He emphasized his growl by kicking the book into her knees, the corner cutting into her skin.

"I can explain, Most Holy. It's not what you—" His hands closed on her throat.

"You have no idea what I think. Do you know what I've done for you? For the people of this city? This kingdom?"

She tried to shake her head, but his grip tightened. Her vision darkening, she realized he could kill her if he wanted. The pure hatred and anger in his eyes made her wonder if he meant to.

Her vision darkened until she saw only his face. Then, everything went black.

A scream shattered the silence of the night, scaring Serpé until she realized it was hers. She stopped, her throat sore. Sitting in the dark, she struggled to slow her rapid breaths. Her nightshirt clung to her, sweat sticking the material to her skin.

A knock at the door sounded while she tried to calm herself. The door opened before she could say anything. A low burning lantern cast its weak light into the room and on the man who held it before him.

"Serpé?" Kian's whisper broke the silence. "The dream again?"

"It's still a nightmare. Even four years later," she breathed. Taking another breath, she felt herself calm. "I'm fine, Kian. Honestly. Thank you for coming so quickly."

He crossed the distance and caressed her cheek. Her skin flushed, a brief reminder of her unspoken feelings for him. Whenever she needed him, he always came.

What would I do without you?

"You haven't had the dream for almost a year. Why now?"

"I don't know. Maybe Azar wants to remind me of what a horrible man The First is. Keep me alert." She watched him nod, the lantern glow giving his face an odd orange hue in the dark. His expression remained thoughtful.

Turning, he retreated to the door. "Get some rest. We should be able to finish the harvest tomorrow."

Serpé stared into the darkness that filled the room after he shut the door. *Azar's mantras have always helped me to sleep before I came to live with Kian. Perhaps they will help again now.*

Sleep did not return easily and when it finally did, Serpé saw only The First's piercing eyes in the darkness. His eyes comforted her when she was eight. They impressed her when Eion Reicholt had been named as The First of Azar, the highest ranking priest for the church in their kingdom. But when he found her diary, The First, also known as Most Holy Eion Reicholt, turned eyes on her that scared her. She had hoped to never see them again when she was granted refuge on Kian's farm, but the nightmares never allowed her peace.

Finally she gave up on sleep and pulled herself from bed. After washing her face and taking care of her other morning needs, she dressed, and went downstairs to get a cold muffin from the day before.

She ate while gathering items from the kitchen she would need for her chores. The sun had not risen yet and she did not want to go outside in the dark. Kian had laughed when she first made that confession. But she knew because of the creatures she had seen at the Mage's College in Siladan, that the stories told by mothers to keep their children indoors at night were true. Some of the creatures were not as sinister as the stories claimed, but they were scary enough.

Serpé waited until the first rays of the sun lit the eastern sky. When the rooster crowed its wake-up call, she left the kitchen.

The early morning chill sent a shiver through her. Fall held the land in its grip on the land, despite the days of warmth they still experienced. She and Kian were in the last days of the harvest, the task taking longer than on the other farms in Sorban because it was only the two of them. After four years of working the land with Kian, she knew their fields would soon be covered by the white of the first snow.

When the harvest was complete, they would go into the

small town nearby. Kian handled the selling of their harvest while she bought the supplies needed for the winter.

Serpé looked out over the fields before bending to fill a bucket with feed for the chickens. Scattering the feed on the ground around her, she returned her thoughts to the items they would need.

Most important was the Solen gifts. Solen was the day of the winter solstice when gifts were exchanged by friends and families. It celebrated the end of the old year and the start of the new one. On their first holiday together, Serpé gave Kian a dagger with a black pearl hilt. Before purchasing the weapon, she had tested the balance. The small grooves, hills and valleys of the black pearl handle warmed to her touch when she rolled it between her hands. That morning, Kian's eyes grew wide when he opened the gift and her heart pounded with joy at his smile. But the best part came when he embraced her. That was the first time she thought they could be happy as a couple.

Serpé's feet carried her to the barn while her mind wandered. She stood staring at the animals. They returned the stare, no forgiveness apparent in their looks of hunger.

"Haven't you fed yourselves yet?" None of the creatures answered her question, so she stepped farther inside to do the chores.

Pressure increased on her neck and though she rubbed to relieve the ache she felt, it remained. *I'm going to have bruises, again.*

She avoided the mirror in her room after her first night on the farm, not wanting to see the bruises The First gave her again. A parting gift that she barely survived. And the nightmare of his attack remained her constant companion for her first three years on the farm.

Her throat tightened. Drawing breath against the pressure felt like trying to churn butter in the last stages before it solidified. Coughs filled the silence around her while she worked. She loosened first one tie, then another on her shirt. Reaching for the third, she stopped when the pressure disappeared.

"Strange." Her voice sounded normal, but the pressure was in the same places she remembered from the original attack. That time, days passed before she could speak normally.

What's happening? Why do I remember the pain with my throat and not just my mind? The scratchy sound when she cleared her throat did not answer her questions.

Chores took her to the back of the barn where hay stood stacked for her to feed the horses and other animals. The pitch fork lay where she left it the day before, and when she picked it up, she found the grooves her fingers had worn into the wood.

Closing her eyes, she spun the tool around her body, the hair that had fallen out of the braid into her face stirred from the breeze she created. She continued the movement until it matched her breathing and the tool became an extension of her body. She opened her eyes and added footsteps to the dance.

Each step took her closer to the practice dummy Kian kept in the barn. Though it was movable and went outside when they trained, she and Kian had not used it for almost three weeks because of the harvest.

Kian made the practice dummy for her a week after she arrived. The burlap sack and hay were replaced numerous times each year from the damage done to it while she practiced.

It will need new sacks and hay after the harvest.

The dummy looked innocent enough, but it reminded her of the scarecrow in their field. She hated that scarecrow.

"Defend yourself, demon spawn," she declared loudly. Snapping the pitch fork against her palm, it stopped mid cycle. Her shout filled the barn as she drove the tines into the dummy's straw belly.

The dream has played games with my mind and proven my weakness against The First. She pushed the fork deeper into the dummy, until it met the resistance of the wooden center. *I do not like being reminded of my weaknesses.*

Turning from the dummy, Serpé gave a forkful of hay to each of the animals. After hanging the pitch fork on the barn wall, she focused on the cows. Kian would milk all of them when he came in from the field, without argument, except one. He had allowed her to purchase an animal that did not like him, with the understanding that she alone would milk the cow. No exceptions.

Putting her cold hands on the udder, the cow mooed in protest and kicked the stool Serpé sat on. The stool flew out from under her, and she landed on the hay covered ground, pain shooting through her back and legs. Looking up, Serpé found the cow's large head close to her face.

"T'was not necessary, Mora. You are too difficult."

Mora winked at her, then nipped at her chest. Alarm filled Serpé and she threw herself back farther. Looking down, surprise replaced the alarm at the welt developing between her breasts. "Damn you, Mora. You broke my necklace."

Glancing down again, Serpé glimpsed a sparkle in the hay. Before she could reach for it, the cow moved toward her, its hoof landing on the sparkle. Instead of the muffled step Serpé hoped to hear, a sickening feeling gripped her at the loud crunch that came from under the hoof. The stone from her necklace had survived Mora's bite, but thanks to her weight, it could no longer be saved.

How am I going to explain this to Kian?

Kian gave her the necklace the night she arrived at the farm and told her the magic infused into the stone would protect her from magical scrying. The First had many mages at his disposal and none would refuse his demand to search for Serpé by magical means. The stone's destruction brought doubt to her mind. *I can only hope that in the four years I've been away, he has found someone else to hold his attention.*

"Move, Mora." Serpé pushed her shoulder into the side of the animal, forcing her to move.

When the cow moved her foot, the pieces of the shattered sapphire caught the sun light that snuck in through the cracks in the barn. Picking up the bigger pieces, Serpé ignored the smaller slivers. She stared at the sapphire until the black and white cow mooed at her again in frustration. Removing the chain from her throat, she glared at the animal.

"Don't complain to me. I was trying to relieve you of your milk and to thank me, you broke my necklace. As if I didn't already have problems enough trying to wring milk out of your tough teats." Knowing her sarcasm was wasted on the beast, she shook her head, her hand clenched tight over the sharp shards.

"Talking to the cow again, Serpé?" Kian's deep voice thrummed through her, making her stomach clench and her breath increase.

If only you knew how your voice affects me. But if you knew, would it bring you pleasure or frustration?

Serpé turned to smile at Kian. His skin glistened with sweat from working all morning in the fields, but his smile showed no weariness. He would be ready to finish his work after they ate morning meal. Knowing he would be uncomfortable with the gesture, she could only use her imagination to brush his dark brown hair from his eyes. His hair, usually kept short, was among the many things she loved about him. Longer hair did not make the men her age more attractive. It only proved that they did not understand how it could be used against them in a fight. She would have to cut Kian's hair as soon as the harvest was done.

Four years ago, when she saw him for the first time, she had not been so eager to stay under his protection. Now a stronger, more confident woman than that girl of sixteen winters, she no longer felt threatened by his rough exterior. Within her, a deadly warrior had waited for Kian's strong hands and firm teachings to hone her skills with the elegance of an estoc in her hand. Cornering him with his own favored moves brought tears of laughter to them both.

But with war, there must also be peace and money had to be made. Trade was good but wouldn't always provide everything they needed. Caring for the land, coaxing grains, fruits and vegetables from its bosom had to be learned as well. Kian woke her early that first morning and every morning since so lessons in farming became part of her life. Days of rest were rare during the growing seasons, but the off-seasons left her wishing for the activity.

Turning back to the cow, Serpé hid her smile from him. "Mora is stubborn and looks at me as if to complain when I milk her."

Kian's quiet chuckle filled her with warmth. Comfortable silence surrounded them, but then he touched her shoulder and the blood began to pound in her ears.

Don't look at him. You are not as good at hiding your emotions as he is.

"Serpé, we have a problem. You need to be honest with me." The quiet of his voice did not hide the hint of an order.

Her previous concerns gone, she looked up at him again. His gaze did not meet hers, but instead focused on her chest. Too late, she tried to hide the bite and the tender skin that already began to swell.

"Have I ever lied to you?" The muscles of her throat clenched, stealing the confidence from her voice.

"Never. Where is your necklace?"

Embarrassment washed over her and she wanted to look

away, but his brown eyes refused to release her gaze. "Mora bit me, pulled the sapphire from the chain, and then stepped on it." She opened her hand to reveal the blue pieces of stone and the gold chain. "I was going to tell you after I finished my chores."

"You shouldn't have waited, Serpé." He paled under his summer tan, picked up the half filled bucket of milk he brought with him and hurried from the barn. Anxious to hear the explanation behind Kian's sudden change, she followed him. "I think we have four days to get our plans in order before Reicholt's men reach us," he called over his shoulder.

"But, Kian." Her hand on his arm stopped him, forcing him to turn toward her again. "Surely I'm safe by now. It's been four years."

The fear in his eyes, his clenched jaw told her otherwise. Panic gripped her and the fear she worked so hard to forget crashed into her, bringing the nightmare from the night before fresh to her mind. *I'm not safe. I never was. I trusted him and he's lied to me for four years.*

"I didn't tell you because I knew you would be scared and might run before you were ready." A deep breath shook him and she watched as he tried to bring himself and the situation under control again. "Bennan has been feeding Reicholt false information about your location. But, Reicholt never stopped looking for you, not even for one day."

Her eyes widened, and her hand fell from Kian's arms. The pieces of the sapphire and necklace fell to the ground. Turning from him, she stumbled the rest of the way into the house.

Kian stared at the area where Serpé stood only a heartbeat before. Unmistakable fear and betrayal had marred her face, his own world ending when the sparkle faded from her green eyes. Heaving a sigh, he followed her into the house, leaving the bucket of milk by the door out of habit. Her door on the second floor slammed shut, echoing through the house and he raced up the stairs to hear Serpé lock the door against his intrusion.

Four years. She has never locked the door in all that time. What have I done? The closed door sent a stabbing pain ripping through his chest. *I took everything I helped her build from her in a single breath.*

He touched the door, caressing the wood, and tried to open it. Even though he knew it was locked, his heart almost burst when the lock resisted. *I should say something, convince her to open the door, discuss this with me.*

But nothing he said would make what he had done go away. Finally, he turned. Returning to the yard, he searched the ground for the pieces of sapphire and the chain.

Without its magic, I can do nothing to protect her from Reicholt's search.

He fell to his knees, rocks jabbing into his flesh. Fear still gripped him, made worse by his own sense of betrayal. Serpé had found safety on the farm and made it feel more like a home instead of just a farm and house. Failure crashed through him, overwhelming him, filling the emptiness left behind by the loss of her trust.

I have to send her away. I'm not ready.

He held the remains of the necklace against his chest and closed his eyes. *Mother of All, please let me be wrong. Let Reicholt have forgotten about her and leave us in peace.*

Lowering his head, he stood again, but he found no comfort in the prayer.

Chapter 4

Eion Reicholt rushed through the city. His excitement blinded him to the people he bumped into and the havoc he caused.

Captain Marcin will take care of any who think to protest my pace. It is his duty.

Captain Marcin spoke to any who complained quickly, advising them the priest was hurrying to complete church duties. Eion heard murmurs of understanding, but continued without stopping.

Their pace soon brought them to the Black Scale Tower, home to the mages of Siladan who worshipped Azar. First Mage Stein and the other ranking mages lived within the tower with the church's favor, and in turn, The First's. The lower levels contained the school and library, with the upper levels providing living quarters for the mages in order of rank, with Stein at the top.

Eion stared at the tower for a moment, before he stormed through the door without knocking. Marching up the stairs, he did not pause until he reached the laboratory First Mage Stein occupied. Again, he threw open the door without an invitation, revealing the alchemy and magical implements the mage used.

"Well? What do you want?" the shout came from deeper inside.

Searching the room, Eion found the mage, his back toward

the door, in front of a large table. Stepping farther into the room, he demanded the mage's attention. "Show her to me."

Stein spun around to glare at the newcomers, then his body shook from a deep breath. He bent forward in a brief bow. "Forgive me, Most Holy. I did not realize it was you."

Moving around the table, Stein revealed a mirror framed in black wood. Vials of liquids cluttered the table top, which he reorganized with care before he waved his hand over the mirror.

The First watched clouds reflected in the glass surface part to reveal an attractive woman of twenty years. She stood in a barn, though the setting was difficult to discern since he only saw the immediate vicinity. Her brown hair rested in a braid, but several strands had come free and fallen over her face. The green of her eyes gleamed bright, accented by her tan. Letting his gaze drift over her features and delicious neck, Eion's breath came in gasps while he drank in the sight of her smooth skin and the cleavage of her breasts.

Serpé never showed her breasts to me. Not even a small amount of cleavage. And her hips, the curves in those tight breeches. I want to feel her stomach clench under my touch.

Shaking his head, he pulled his attention back to her face and her quivering lips. *She's crying? She forces me to have inappropriate thoughts for a man of my station and she's crying?*

"Where is she?" He recognized the sound of desire in his voice and glanced at the others to determine if they heard.

"I have been able to trace her to a farm three days journey from The Dragon's Forest." Appearing not to notice the tone of Eion's voice, Stein passed a rolled hide to him without a glance.

The First took the hide and turned to his captain. "Bring her to me. Quash anyone who stands in your way or who may have given her refuge these past years." Nodding, the man reached for the map, but Eion grabbed his hand and pulled him close so only he could hear the whispered command. "Make sure no harm comes to her, or it's your head, Captain Marcin. I would hate to see your captaincy come to an end so soon."

"I understand completely, Most Holy. No harm will come to her." Pulling his hand from the priest's grip, the captain studied the mirror before he left the room.

Eion returned his attention to the mirror, ignoring the door closing door Marcin. Serpé now lay across a bed with her face buried in a pillow.

"First Mage Stein." His voice was better controlled now, but he felt certain too much of his desires had already been revealed. The mage moved closer to him. "I want this mirror showing her at all times. I want to know where she is until she is brought back to me."

"Understood, Most Holy, though it will be difficult. I will do my best." Stein lifted the mirror and stepped away from the table. "Please leave me to my task."

"Of course."

Soon Serpé will be in my grasp again and my plans will progress as they should have four years ago. Grinning, Eion led his entourage from the tower and into the crowd of people making their way toward the market square.

Chapter 5

Hours after her necklace broke, Kian stood outside Serpé's room again, listening to her whispered words and quiet movements. Curiosity filled him. In four years, she had never spent so much time in her room alone. His heart ached. He could not help with whatever kept her occupied.

I wish her necklace had not broken. And I wish the Religious Guard would not arrive in three days. He rested a hand on the wooden door. *No amount of wishing will change what is going to happen. She should go someplace safer. No one knows why Reicholt still searches for her or why he is so infatuated for her.*

The first time he saw Serpé, fear marred her beauty. His first instinct was to comfort her—to make everything better. That initial reaction had not gone away. It grew into something more, something he did not want to admit to her or anyone else.

I am her protector, her teacher. Nothing more.

She struggled to control her fear until he placed an estoc in her hand. Confidence grew over time, replacing the fear. She learned to defend herself from those who wanted to harm her.

She was clumsy when we started. Only my patience and experience helped both of us through the difficult times. My military service to Sorban and my training ensures she will have no rival, save me. I have trained no one else. My training, a combination of so many instructors, and passed to only her, will make it unlikely that she will ever combat another with my abilities.

Her capability to learn quickly showed early on. On one particular occasion, when they were attacked by a group of slavers, Serpé defended herself, showing a new confidence in her abilities. Surrounding them, the slavers apparently thought the couple an easy target. He smiled at the memory. *Their surprise was very satisfying.*

He returned their attacks, but when Serpé joined in, the battle turned against them. Later that day, when the two of them arrived at his sister's tavern, his ego swelled with pride hearing her relay the story to Denai.

The noises inside Serpé's room quieted and he pulled himself away, striding down the hall to his weapon room. Closing the door, he surveyed the room's contents. Most of the weapons had been packed into crates already with the plan to send them to Marmion and Valen. Bennan supplied scrolls to magically transport everything so when the Religious Guard arrived, Kian could leave without the loss of the weapons he would need.

I will transport the crates in the morning. No reason to delay.

After a moment, he lifted an estoc with a black pearl handle from the crate he had placed it in. Most Holy Korewyn gifted the weapon to him on the day of his promotion to Captain of the Elite Guard, the personal guard for the leader of the temple of Azar. Kian swore he would never use the weapon again the day Korewyn was laid to rest, after his murder.

The magic of the weapon will help Serpé in the times to come since I cannot be with her. The enhancements will keep the blade sharp and its cuts deep. A grim smile lifted his lips. *I have fought many glorious battles with this estoc in the protection of Sorban and my friends.*

Kian slipped the blade back into the black scabbard. With a final glance around the room, he left to make evening meal.

Chapter 6

*B*acon and biscuits. Did Kian make eggs as well?

The appetizing scents lured Serpé from the memories revived by her sleep. Stretching against the morning stiffness, her stomach grumbled, reminding her of the skipped meal the night before. Instead of going downstairs immediately, she went to her window and looked out over the farm.

Bennan made a good choice in bringing me here. Kian gave me safety and comfort, a chance to grow. I had hoped I gave him something he needed as well. Obviously not, since he is sending me away so easily.

That first look, the first time she had seen Kian in the light of his home. The age difference was obvious, and even back then, she did not care. The kiss of the sun darkened his skin and his green eyes glowed bright against that tan. Chiseled features with a strong jaw clenched tight, but he tried to smile. His muscles rippled under his clothes and she remembered how she wondered what it would feel like to have his arms around her.

Bringing her gaze to the porch, she allowed her mind to conjure memories of the time they spent together after chores. Though they sat in silence, happiness filled her.

Now everything is destroyed.

Mora and Loafer wandered through the closest field, bringing a smile to Serpé's lips. Helping Loafer's mother give birth to the calf had been her most satisfying experience the first year with Kian. The cows would miss her, but not as much as she would miss the animals.

Loafer. What a ridiculous name for an animal, but she's been lazy since birth.

Wiping away a tear, she turned away from the window and looked over her room. Shaking her head, she pulled on a pair of breeches, tied the top of her nightshirt and left the room.

A fresh wave of breakfast scents filled her nose and she decided to move past her anger toward Kian until she had eaten. Thankful that he would still cook her morning feast, even though she overslept and missed the morning chores, she rushed down the stairs and into the kitchen. Kian glanced at her, hiding a smile that normally would have melted her anger away and gestured at the cupboards.

"Since you missed your chores, you can set the table." She smiled at his gruff order.

"I apologize. I did not sleep well." Without waiting for a response, she pulled plates from the cupboard. While he finished the food and delivered it to the table, she set the plates and other pieces out. When they were both done, they sat across from each other.

Reciting the usual morning prayers, Serpé invoked Azar's blessing upon their food. Kian served himself first, a habit she never questioned.

Quiet filled the kitchen while they ate, until the sound of tapping against the window drew their attention. Kian opened the window, allowing a white bird into the room. More a mass of white smoke given substance, the bird brought a chill that filled the air around Serpé. Fighting a shiver, she rubbed her hands together.

"Is it from Bennan?" She bit her tongue for asking such an obvious question. *No one else sends messages to Kian using the Smoke Bird spell.*

Taking a small tube from the bird's leg, Kian nodded, distracted. The spell melted away with the removal of the tube, the smoke drifting out the still open window.

She watched him read the note, impatience warring with the manners her mother taught her. The food became cold and the comforting scents faded from the room.

She picked up a piece of bacon and nibbled at it while she waited. "Well?" The salt of the bacon still covered her tongue when she demanded an answer.

"Reicholt is sending the Religious Guard. They left day before yesterday, in the afternoon. You need to pack your bags so you can leave. I'll make sure you have a few places to go, a few of my friends who can help you." Cold, his words left no room for discussion.

A sudden wave of nausea gripped her. "But I don't want to leave. There has to be a way I can stay with you."

Serpé sighed in frustration when a look of discomfort crossed his face. *Why can't I tell him how I feel? Why does he see me as a child instead of a woman of twenty winters?*

Kian cleared his throat and looked away. "Tomorrow, after morning meal, you'll leave. Adrastos will go with you. I'll have directions and a list of trusted friends for you as well as letters of introduction."

"He's your horse, Kian. You should keep him." Her quiet words sounded forced. *Already he's isolated me from him, with so few words.*

"He is a trained war horse. He likes you and he'll do what he can to protect you. Just remember, he likes to bite stable boys." His smile did not reach his eyes. "He won't bite you. He hasn't yet and I doubt he'll start now."

"Please rethink this. Surely we can leave together," she cried out in distress. *Again, my weakness gets the better of me.*

"Stop, Serpé. Getting upset will do neither of us any good. We need to be in separate locations now. Bennan and I have made plans specifically for this situation and your presence here will only cause problems." Though she bristled at his words, he took her hand in his. "If you're with me, you'll be in danger."

"Safe is not what I want. I want—"

He lifted his hand, stopping her. "No, you'll go and I will send for you when this is over, after Reicholt has been killed."

"You can't kill him. He is the chosen of Azar. To kill him would be an affront to the god and might bring his wrath down on you." Despite her fear of Reicholt and her need to be free of his attention, she did not want Kian hurt.

He stood and began clearing the dishes from the table. "I can't make any promises. I don't know what the future will bring."

He paused, waiting for a response, but she clenched her jaw and kept silent. Glancing at her, he sighed, then turned back to the wash basin of dishes.

"All right, I will try not to kill him, but only because of you. His actions will determine his fate."

He's promised me nothing. I have no reason to believe he will allow The First to live if given the chance to kill him.

Serpé watched Kian fill the basin with rinse water. Each heartbeat brought her closer to the time she would have to leave. *I need to tell him how I feel—now—before I leave.*

Clearing her throat, she made her way across the kitchen to stand behind him. Lifting her hand, she touched his back. He spun to look at her, shock on his face. Together, they glanced down at the knife he held in his hand. The tip of the blade brushed across her shirt.

"What? What do you want?" He tried to hide his surprise behind the gruff tone to his voice. The knife returned to the basin with a splash.

Instead of answering him, she reached up, placed her hands on both sides of his face and kissed him. For an instant his lips resisted. Then they softened and he pulled her hard against him as she molded her body against his. The world faded for that moment and she was aware only of his mouth on hers, his hands on her body, and the taste of him. His departure was sudden and she stared as he took a determined step back.

"Why did you stop?" Her breathless question revealed too much to her own ears.

"We shouldn't. This changes nothing. You can't stay with me." His words came out in a rush. He turned from her.

"How can you turn away after that?" It would have been easier if he had slapped her. "Does what I feel mean nothing to you?"

They stood in silence while she waited for him to answer. Moments passed, but he kept his back toward her.

Yes, it is best that you don't look at me. My tears will not move you.

Frustration building, she stormed from the kitchen and up the stairs to her bedroom.

Slamming the door stretched the muscles of her arm painfully and she pulled it close to massage the pain away. "Damn him. All this time has meant nothing to him. I've been an inconvenience and he's happy to see me go finally."

She glared at the room, finding nothing in particular to take her anger out on. "Since I have to leave, I should probably pack. Nothing I say will convince Kian otherwise."

She picked up the wooden jewelry box Kian gave her as a birthday present and sat on her bed. Inside rested the golden locket her mother gave her the day she left for the church. The locket no longer shined as bright as it once did. Remembering her mother's tears as she placed it around her neck brought tears to her own eyes. Her chest tightened and her throat burned with pent up emotions. She hung the piece of jewelry from her neck once again, the cool metal comforting against her skin.

Near the place her locket had lain for four years, she found the signet ring that bore her family crest. Until the day she left Reicholt's estate she wore the ring on her right ring finger. Fear that someone—anyone—would recognize the ring had forced her to hide it. Without thinking, she placed the ring upon her finger. Her skin tingled as the minor magic contained within attuned itself to her once more and the metal shrank to fit her finger comfortably.

Concentrating, she smiled when she felt the magic of the ring connect with the magic of her parents' rings. *They both still live.*

She knew the contact of the ring on her skin would tell her parents that she lived as well. Only three rings were made for each family of merchants that sat on the merchant council. One ring, usually worn by the member who served on the council, held a link to the other two rings, worn by the spouse and the heir to the family's businesses and fortune. The link allowed the wearer to know the others were alive, or at least wearing the rings. The rings were attuned to each family member and the magic could not be activated by anyone else, until it was passed on.

Before closing the box, a sparkle caught her attention. Diamond earrings rolled to the front of the box when she moved it. Kian had bought the earrings for her as a Solen gift. She studied them, rolling the pieces in her hand, before returning the box and the earrings to her dresser. *I will not take him—them—with me. I have enough to remind me of what I've lost. I don't need more.*

Serpé turned to her cedar chest. Dresses, books and embroidery were set aside without a second glance. Picking up one of the discarded pieces of embroidery, she laughed. The stitches were uneven and loose. *I never was very good at this.*

Tossing the material aside, she reached into the chest again. Her fingers touched silk and she pulled out a doll her father had given her at the same time she received the locket. Yellow stains and cracks marred the doll's porcelain face. She wore a faded, blue silk dress with browned lace edging. Serpé touched the doll's face, then laid it on the floor next to her with exaggerated care. Wiping the tears from her face, she continued her quiet contemplation of the items in the chest.

Chapter 7

"By the gods, she's frustrating!" First one plate, then another clattered into the sink. "Why must she be so childish…?"

Through the frustration and denied desire, realization washed over Kian. Gripping the counter, he lowered his head.

She's not being childish. She's acting like a grown woman who knows what she wants and I'm denying it while she embraces it.

He straightened, turned his back on the sink and stared at the archway she disappeared through only moments before.

It would be so easy to go after her.

He should have seen the changes long ago. There were the physical changes in her, the obvious ones he ignored. Her brown hair was longer, reaching her mid-back. She wore it braided when they worked on the farm, loose when the chores were done or holidays. When she arrived, she was slim, but there were still areas of child weight on her. Now, with the constant work on the farm, and the training she received, the little bit of fat had turned to muscle. Her womanly curves would not have been missed by any other man, yet he chose to turn away from them. Her eyes, though, bright green, still shined with desire and tenderness. He loved when she gazed at him with those eyes.

In the four years she had been with him, Serpé had grown, become more beautiful. By keeping her on the farm, he prevented

her from meeting others who would develop relationships with
her.

But I've protected her from Reicholt. How can that be so wrong?

Struggling to deny it, another truth emerged. Serpé's recent
words flooded his mind and the desire in her voice became more
apparent than before. Instead of accepting her unspoken desire,
he pushed the knowledge away—treating her as a spoiled child
throwing a tantrum.

*She'll get over it and move on. She's suffering from a child's
infatuation that she'll outgrow in time. It's best for both of us.*

Returning his attention to the dishes, his hand gripped the
knife he had turned on her. Bringing the knife up, ignoring the
water dripping from it, he eyed the tip of the blade.

*Would I really have hurt her? Would I have stopped before anything
happened?*

Worse than not knowing if he would have hurt Serpé with
the knife was the knowledge that he hurt her the moment he
told her she had to leave. Nothing would heal that pain.

Chapter 8

The next morning, Serpé carried her bags to the barn without asking for Kian's assistance. While she groomed and saddled Adrastos for their journey, Kian arrived at the door to the stall. Watching her, he stood with his hands hidden behind his back. When she finished saddling the war-horse, she turned to look at him. "What's wrong? Shouldn't you be preparing for your own departure?" The need to stand defiant against his decision filled her and she crossed her arms over her chest.

He stepped closer to her, drawing a sword from behind his back. The black scabbard and black pearl handle were easy to recognize.

His estoc, awarded by Most Holy Korewyn. He never takes it out of the house and he only touches it when he needs to clean it.

"Do you intend to kill me instead of exiling me?" She knew Kian would not hurt her, but her anger fueled her sarcasm and the angry question.

"Stop acting the angry child, Serpé. It doesn't suit you." Turning the estoc's handle toward her, he smiled. "I want you to have it, to protect yourself. You've a great talent and it would honor me if you used it." He placed the weapon in her hands.

"I can't, Kian. This belongs with you." She tried to give it back to him with a shake of her head.

He squeezed her fingers around the sword and pushed it

against her stomach, their eyes meeting. "Please, Serpé, keep it. I'll feel better knowing you have it since I can't be with you."

She breathed deep, searching for control. The hilt fit her hand comfortably and pulling the blade from its scabbard, the metal sang with its freedom. She admired the craftsmanship before returning it to its protective sheath and buckling the belt around her waist.

"The blade has magical properties," Kian explained. "Wounds made by the weapon will bleed worse than normal and no healing spells from a priest will help. Even touching the edges with the slightest pressure will cut you. It can cut through armor easily, unless a mage has enhanced it, but it will not cut through a blade. I'm not sure how that magic was done, but it can be helpful."

She nodded at his explanation.

He nodded as well, then looked at the ground. "Be careful. Travel with the Mother's blessings and Azar's guidance."

"And you as well." She grabbed him in a fierce hug, smiling to herself when he returned the embrace.

Together, they walked out of the barn, Serpé holding the reins of Adrastos. Kian helped her into the saddle, though they both knew it was not necessary. His hand guided her foot into the stirrup, lingering on her calf. Her leg warmed from his touch and her breath caught in her throat.

Does he realize what that does to me?

"Good luck, Kian." Instead of looking at him, she stared across the fields.

He squeezed her leg. "To you as well."

His last words left her empty and with nothing left to say, she kicked Adrastos into a run and they thundered away.

Chapter 9

Kian watched Serpé and Adrastos disappear into the horizon, before turning to walk back into the house. The ghosts of past conversations echoed around him as he made his way through the quiet house. Things had not really changed since Serpé arrived, but he never realized how empty it would be without her. *Being alone has never bothered me before, but with Serpé's absence, I have to admit, at least to myself, I was happy with her.*

Retrieving the bags from his room that he packed the night before, he walked down the hall for the last time to Serpé's room. After packing in such haste, books, clothes and other items lay scattered around the room. She never left her room in a mess before.

I can't even imagine what she thought or felt while going through her things.

A bar of soap stood out from the bottles of perfume left on the dresser. Abandoned, it waited for Serpé to return. He drew in a deep breath, his senses flooded with the remembered scent of her perfume.

I love the scent of her after a shower, when she walks through the house, her skin still damp and the smell of her perfume trailing behind her.

Opening his eyes, pain gripped his heart, threatening to rip it from his chest. *I made a mistake. I denied everything, refused to acknowledge what she offered to share with me—I am a fool.*

Bile rose in his throat. If given the chance, Reicholt would destroy what innocence she retained. Already she had seen too much pain and suffered too many lies because of the priest. Kian knew he had to keep her from that fate. Not only because of his own feelings, but because the priest would make her a slave, to his own whims—or to the highest bidder. The bruises her neck bore when she arrived with Bennan were obvious marks of Reicholt's anger. With her stories of women and children being sold into slavery and prostitution, he felt sure Reicholt planned worse for her.

Her jewelry box lay open, next to the perfumes. Kian lifted, caressing the wood. The movement sent earrings rolling to a corner inside. Removing a small cloth pouch from his saddlebags, he placed the earrings inside, closed it and returned it to the larger bag.

Glancing around the room again, he caught sight of a doll in a faded blue silk dress. With a gentle touch, he picked it up. *I don't remember seeing this before. It looks so old. She must have possessed it since childhood.*

For a moment, the doll held his attention. Finally, he put it in his saddle bag and left the room.

Returning to the stable, he added the final bags to those already in the stall with the horse he intended to take. He opened the gates to the yard, allowing the other animals their freedom. The neighboring farms would revel in the free additions to their stock.

"Oh, they'll find a home all right."

Kian turned to the unexpected voice and grinned. "Always sneaking up on me, Bennan." Reaching a hand toward his friend, he pulled him into a quick embrace. "Good to see you. You missed Serpé though. She left awhile ago."

"I'll see her again soon enough. But how are you?" Bennan waited for Kian to step through the gate before they both walked into the house.

"When you brought her to me four years ago, I thought you had spent too much time talking to your gods. You were crazy to ask me to take care of her, teach her, and protect her." The two men laughed. Taking a deep breath, Kian closed his eyes for a moment. "She didn't take her perfumes with her and I can still smell her."

"Remember it. No telling how long it will be before you'll have her around again." Bennan dropped into Serpé's favorite chair.

The careless action irritated Kian and he forced himself to unclench his fist. *Bennan doesn't know about the chair.* He sighed in resignation, his breath catching in his throat. *It doesn't matter anymore. She will never sit in it again.*

"So tell me, what has Reicholt done since he found out?" Kian's question came as a whisper, despite his pained thoughts.

"Nothing, other than to send the Guard here." Bennan waved his hand nonchalantly. "I think he's waiting to see what happens. Serpé's family now has a contingent of guards 'protecting' them. The First was extremely interested in her father's recent reaction to his signet ring."

"Serpé put the ring back on?" The news stunned him. *I told her not to wear her signet ring again, but after everything that happened, she must have decided it wasn't important any longer. The magic the ring shares with her parents' rings will tell the she is alive.*

"She must have. Anthoine could hardly wait to tell Eisa. Reicholt continues to warn of an approaching war with Tushin and pushes every day for more authority over the Guards so he can send troops to protect our borders. Many of the smaller merchant families support him and they speak loudly against the larger ones." Bennan stretched, a yawn opening his mouth wide. "If he could declare himself king, he would, I'm sure."

"But none of that explains why he still wants Serpé!" Kian demanded.

"No, but I'm sure the young man about to knock on your door can answer that." As if evoked by Bennan's words, a loud knock resounded through the first floor.

"I hate when you do that. You have too much magic for a warrior." Kian's grumbling followed him to the door.

"Did you send a chest with your weapons to Marmion?" Joining him at the door, Bennan's question made him pause.

"Only the ones I wouldn't need. Couldn't face the coming guards empty handed." Kian grinned at his friend, indicating the sword on his hip.

The man on the other side of the door stopped his pounding. Instead, he shouted, "Kian Donwell, open this door! In the name of Most Holy Eion Reicholt, you are under arrest for harboring a fugitive."

"Impatient, isn't he?" Bennan smiled with his playful question.

Kian nodded. Opening the door, both he and Bennan stepped to either side of it, clearing it for the guards charging through. Thrusting out his foot at the same time Bennan did, two of the intruders went down. With a brief thought, he called his sword to his hand, thirsty for blood. One of the men struggling to his feet went down with a groan.

Kian smiled at the feel of his muscles stretching when he brought his sword around to block a clumsy attack. Instinct guided him to reach his hand around to grip the main-gauche he kept at his back. *This feels good.*

Locking up the guard's hilt, he twisted and caught the man in the throat with the point of the dagger. The other man stumbled forward, forcing Kian to duck from the spray of blood. He taught this move to Serpé, but her skills did not match his. Not yet. With a grim smile, he beat a foe's blade aside, burying his blade in the man's chest.

Bennan left his back. Experience told him the other man moved into the room with the others who slipped past them. As another man tried to dodge around him, Kian slipped the smaller blade past his defenses and slashed the man's forearm open.

"No. You'll stay here." Kian punched the intruder with the hilt of the sword, forcing the man back down.

Again letting instinct guide him, Kian spun to block an attack from behind, grinning at his new opponent. The bloodlust of battle rose within him and he thrust hard, the point of his blade taking the man beneath the chin. The grin left his lips when the man fell backward, gurgling.

The sound of combat stopped. Kian could feel Bennan's and the remaining Religious Guard's eyes on him. He brought his gaze up from the dying man and sought out their commander.

I let the bloodlust take over again. That has not happened for years, not since I left the Guards.

"Captain Donwell, their deaths weren't necessary." A new man entered the house, no marks of combat on his flesh or clothes.

"Then you shouldn't have entered my home with weapons drawn." Kian felt calm replace the bloodlust and recognized the danger it represented.

This is not good. My training is too complete and it is too easy to lock the emotions away that might have saved them. We may be outnumbered, but these men will not survive if they push the attack. Three men remained, not counting the man who stood in front of him.

"I'm aware we made a mistake. I am also acutely aware of your reputation, Captain. It is unfortunate my lieutenant did not believe me." The man wore a tunic with the insignia of the Religious Guard, but the rank markings denoted him as the Commander of the entire Guard. A second insignia also marked him as the Captain of The First's Elite Guard. He knelt, gazing into the dead man's eyes. "You believe me now, though, don't you?"

Kian watched the exchange, squinting with recognition. "You're the man, the sergeant, who came looking for Serpé four years ago."

"Yes. Though now I am the Commander of the entire Guard. Strinnal Marcin, at your service." Bowing, the other man's gaze stayed on Kian. "My father served under you when you were captain of the Religious Guard for Most Holy Korewyn. He served with you for only a year, but his respect for you and your leadership is matched only by his love for my mother." After standing straight again, Strinnal gestured to his remaining men. "Search the second floor. Bring me any evidence you find of her."

Kian laughed and after a moment Bennan joined him. "Do you really expect to find her?"

"No, not really. But I have my orders, Kian." The commander gazed at him, patience evident on his face, and another emotion Kian could not place.

Something is wrong. He doesn't want to be here. Why would Reicholt send someone who does not support him? Unless he doesn't know.

With weapons returned to sheaths, Kian and Bennan followed Strinnal into the front room. Bennan did something magical to the lanterns in the room, and flames sprang to life on the wicks. Kian would have laughed at the gesture if the situation was different, but Kian knew the lanterns would be the final ingredient to their plan.

"Commander, or is it Captain?" Strinnal indicated the title didn't matter with a shrug of his shoulders. "Perhaps you can tell me, why does Reicholt still want Serpé?"

"The First," Strinnal emphasized the title, "seems to have some plan for her. He thinks controlling her will give him the throne."

"Reicholt doesn't deserve the respect of that title. Anyway, his idea is ridiculous. Everyone knows there is no heir to King Navrinar's throne." Kian glanced at Bennan, who shrugged his shoulders.

"Maybe he thinks her family's position within the merchant houses will give him what he wants. And remember, she *is* the only unmarried daughter of those houses." Strinnal stopped his inspection of the common room, coming to stand near Kian again. "Are you going somewhere? Things are missing, if the dust markings are any indication."

"I'm sure you'll figure it out, Captain." Before Strinnal could turn, Kian hit him on the head with a crystal decanter from the table next to him. The man fell to the floor, unconscious. "I'm sorry, Strinnal. I have nothing against you, just the man you serve."

While Bennan dragged the unconscious man out of the house, Kian knocked over the lanterns. He watched the flames as they started to feed on the rug and wood, then he left the house as well. He considered yelling for the others to leave, but decided against it. They had plenty of time to leap from the windows and that should keep them too busy to pursue.

Bennan stood outside, holding the reins of their horses. The big man stared at him with a glint in his eye that Kian always thought meant he knew more than he said.

Instead of questioning his friend about his thoughts, Kian decided a different approach would be better. "Is the captain safe?"

"Yes. He'll wake after we've left and may even be able to save his soldiers."

The two men mounted their horses, nodded grimly at each other and forced the horses into a gallop away from the farm.

Chapter 10

A warm breath caressed Strinnal's cheek, waking him. Pain shot through the back of his head, threatening to drag him back into unconsciousness. Rolling to his side, rocks dug into his cheek and grass tickled his ear. He ignored the sensations, instead focusing on the flames that danced through the windows of the first floor of Kian's house.

One of his men walked past a second floor window, and then reappeared in it, looking down at him in confusion. Strinnal stood and waved at the man, receiving nothing but a wave in return.

The idiot doesn't understand.

"Get out! Get out! The house is on fire!" The glass would not be thick enough to prevent the sound from coming through, and finally the soldier nodded and turned away.

Strinnal raced around the house, looking for a way his men could leave the doomed building. There was a back door and he could see no sign the fire had reached it yet. The metal of the handle was still cool when he touched it. Opening the door, he shouted the names of his men.

Do I run in and put myself at risk? Or do I wait to see who comes out?

The door, yanked from his hand, slammed against the wood that had begun to warp from the heat of the fire. Soldiers stormed through the back door, almost knocking him off his feet.

Turning back to the house, Strinnal backed away from the engulfing fire. *The fire waited for them to leave before reaching this door? What kind of magic is controlling this? Kian never worked with the mages of the armies before. Why would he be working with one now?*

Looking around, Strinnal could not find Kian or the man with him. Further inspection of the ground around the house revealed the hoof prints of horses, along with cattle and various other animals.

"Did you figure out which way they went?" One of the soldiers asked, coming up behind him.

He turned to stare at the man. "Do I look like a tracker? Flon was the tracker and the idiot was the first to fall to Kian's blade." He knew his anger was unwarranted, but his frustration was beyond control. "Mount up. We need to report to The First as soon as possible."

Strinnal waited for the other men to tie the reins of the riderless horses to their saddle horns. When they were ready, he led them from the farm.

For three days, Strinnal pushed his men to hasten their return to Siladan. Had their escape from Kian's home been luck? Even now, he still did not know how the fire had waited for his men to leave the burning building.

Despite their injuries and the loss of three men, Strinnal was not thankful to return home like he should have been. His rushed travel did not allow much time to decide what he should tell The First. He did not doubt the priest would be angry and may demote him.

When they arrived in Siladan, Strinnal led his men to the military barracks. Slow moments passed while he waited for the handlers to take the horses from his men.

"Get them to the healers," Strinnal yelled at the nearest handler. He waited for his order to be acknowledged before remounting his horse. "I must speak to The First." He galloped back into the main part of the city before anyone could protest.

Strinnal heard voices raised in song streaming out of the temple when he rode closer. The sound washed over him as he dismounted and handed the reins of his horse to one of the pages tending to the carriages and horses of those already inside. Stepping into the building, after making sure the door closed behind him, he surveyed the room and the throng of people standing inside.

Worshippers sang their praise and offered up prayers to Azar. Uncomfortable with the display, Strinnal adjusted his weapon and took in a deep breath.

Services never brought him the enjoyment and pleasure others found. His mother forced him to attend when he was younger and he always fought against her need to be in the church. His interest was more focused on why a kingdom of merchants worshipped a deity that controlled the magic of mages. Despite his questions, no one had ever been able to give an explanation that satisfied his curiosity.

Tapestries of Azar's great deeds adorned the walls. Despite the crisp and vibrant colors, the scenes of a god fighting another god or a dragon or other creature gave the imagination of a boy seeds to grow nightmares with.

This temple has always scared me and still does. My childhood fears have even found a way into my duties as an adult.

Strinnal studied the statues that lined the walls of the main area. The statues of the god and his chosen frightened him more than the temple. He thought their stone eyes watched his every move through the temple. They even watched Most Holy Reicholt's movements and gestures.

Holy rites continued to ring out until, in a final display of power, The First summoned small balls of glittering light over the worshippers. Gasps of surprise and excitement filled the room as the people reached to touch the lights.

Strinnal smirked, sour bile burning the back of his throat. *They are filled with so much faith that they are willing to believe these lights are a gift from Azar. Would they be disappointed to find out The First summoned them with a spell?*

Strinnal watched until the lights faded. When the crowd of worshippers filed past The First, the captain moved into the main aisle so he could better see the altar.

Despite how much I hate this place, I enjoyed the times Serpé accompanied The First. Each candle she lit brought a light to my day. Even the collection bowl for donations made the services tolerable. But it's her smile, more than anything else that I miss.

"Captain Marcin, you have news for me?" Eion Reicholt's voice broke into Strinnal's thoughts.

Strinnal turned to look at the priest. Recently he attended a celebration for The First's seventieth summer, only then realizing the man's true age. Gray dominated his once dark hair. Opulent robes and gold rings adorned his fingers, obvious displays of the riches he enjoyed in his position.

"Most Holy, I was unsuccessful in finding Serpé. She left the farm before I arrived. The farm house was destroyed along with anything that might lead to her location." Strinnal's humiliation made it difficult to form the words of his brief report.

"And the person who kept her from me?" The First asked, his voice quiet, though anger flashed in his eyes.

"Captain Kian Donwell escaped."

The First stared at Strinnal before storming away, toward the vestibule doors. "Pray you find her soon, Captain. And pray I find it within myself to forgive you for your failure. Now come with me. I would show you something."

Strinnal buried his desire to go home and followed The First out of the temple. Since only his horse remained outside, and the carriage The First normally used had not been prepared, they traveled through the bustling city on foot.

Their path did not enter the main part of the city. Instead, The First led Strinnal to the outer wall, by way of the council hall. The captain recognized their route and he clenched his fists in frustration.

Why is he leading me to the prison? This man surprises me in new ways too often. Frowning, Strinnal continued to follow the priest. His hand played with the knot on his sword, but his gaze remained alert to anyone who might step close to them.

When they reached the large prison complex, the guards made them wait outside the courtyard gates while the prisoners were forced back into their cells. Strinnal studied the wall in front of him while they waited. He was uncomfortable standing next to The First and did not want to engage him in conversation. The walls of the prison were built from rocks pulled from the fields outside the city. The aged and weathered appearance told the story of how old the building was. Wives and family who had cried outside the walls for those imprisoned inside had smoothed the rocks of the walls with their hands.

After a time, the gates to the courtyard opened and a man,

shorter than Strinnal, exited with a handful of guards behind him. His belly hung over his breeches and the captain saw stains from his midday meal on the shirt. The shirt, still wet from an attempt to remove the stains, clung to him.

"Most Holy, how gracious of you to honor us with your presence today. To what do we owe this unexpected, but exciting visit?" The sound of the man's voice echoed in Strinnal's ears. Each word brought him pain, like a dagger scraping a rock.

"I'm here to finish the business we discussed only three days ago, Warden. Have you forgotten?" Contempt laced The First's words.

When the warden glanced at Strinnal, he thought the man would refuse The First's request to enter the prison. A heartbeat later, the warden nodded and led the way into the courtyard.

"Of course. Come with me. They have been separated from the other prisoners." The warden escorted the two men through the courtyard with a monologue of chatter about the daily activities of the prisoners.

His constant chattering and adoration for The First is making my head hurt. Strinnal rubbed his temples in an effort to relieve the growing pain he felt.

The screams of prisoners echoed through the corridors of the dungeon while they descended into the lower levels. Men filled crowded cells, some hanging by chains from the walls and ceiling. Shadows danced eerily from flickering torches, reminding Strinnal of stories he heard of the prison being haunted by the spirits of those executed for their crimes.

The First's casual movement between the cells concerned Strinnal. His frown deepened when the priest deftly avoided the grubby hands that reached for him through the bars. He marveled at how easily the other man ignored the pleas for food, water, and release from earthly pain. At one point, Strinnal thought he heard laughter from The First, who remained unaffected by the plight of those around him.

Finally, the three men stopped in front of a cell that appeared no different than any of the others. Strinnal studied the occupants, also three men, and wondered what Reicholt could want with them.

"Have they agreed to assist us with the cleansing?" The First asked, his words loud over the cries of the prisoners.

"They have." The warden's squeak again drove daggers into

Strinnal's head.

"Excellent. Make sure they have whomever and whatever they need to accomplish their task." The First grinned at Strinnal.

The warden nodded, and then rushed away. Strinnal turned back to the priest, a question upon his lips.

"Aren't they perfect?" Reicholt stopped his captain's questions. He gestured at the men who returned his excitement with bland expressions.

"For serving their sentence in this cell, yes," Strinnal mumbled, squinting at the men in the torch light. He recognized them, recalling the crimes they committed to earn their place in prison. "How can an assassin and two mercenaries help with anything a holy man such as you might need?"

The First pushed him back in the direction they had come, then took the lead. His shoes clacked on the stone floor. The prisoners they passed quieted their pleas for salvation, sensing the anger emanating from the priest. Strinnal followed in silence until they reached the courtyard again.

"How dare you speak to me in such a manner! You are bordering on disrespect, Captain. If it continues, you will be replaced," The First screamed, his face close to Strinnal's.

Strinnal straightened his back and lifted his chin at the barrage of words. "It is my duty to protect you, Most Holy. In all things."

Reicholt smiled, his lips twisted into a grin that made Strinnal's stomach turn. He immediately calmed, his anger replaced with an expression of smug satisfaction. "Yes, it is. Now ask your questions."

"What do you plan on using those men for?" Strinnal chose his words with care, trying not to enrage the priest again. He watched The First's expression fall from his face, to be replaced with a blank mask.

Though it appears he has forgiven me, underneath that smile, I know he's planning some kind of punishment for me. Strinnal clenched his jaw, increasing the pain in his head.

"Those mercenaries will attack the merchant caravans, orchestrate attacks on their estates and cause panic and concern among the commoners. The assassin will take the lives of key heads of families of the merchant houses. He will also make sure anyone who opposes me is dealt with swiftly." The First smirked in satisfaction. "Through it all, my hands remain clean. The people will beg me for guidance and protection."

"They have seen your face, heard you speak to the warden. What if they are captured? They will talk," Strinnal tried to be a voice for reason, knowing his words fell on deaf ears.

The older man laughed and the trust Strinnal once held for him made the discomfort he felt in his stomach become a knot. "Who would believe them?"

"The right person." Strinnal waved a hand at one of the gate guards. Waiting for the gate to open, he turned once more to look at Most Holy Reicholt. "This is a bad idea, sir. A very bad idea." He left the priest in the yard, refusing to turn at The First's shouted demands.

Chapter 11

Serpé had not traveled alone since she was attacked while collecting donations and bribes for The First. Her journey to Forest's Edge should have been invigorating, a release from the confines of the farm. Instead, it was marred by the pain she felt at being forced to leave the home she loved.

She worked hard to find the person within herself that Reicholt tried to suppress and control. The struggle to gain an identity separate from the priest had been difficult, but well worth it. Kian helped with the transformation, through his training and guidance.

Two days after leaving Kian's farm, she finally let herself enjoy the beauty of the land around her. The land swayed with the gentle breeze that blew across the tall grass and through her hair. Animals scurried from her path as Adrastos made his way through the plains. Fall had settled completely on the land and she could feel the change within her. The cold bite in her muscles made sleeping on the ground uncomfortable. The chill in the morning air turned her breath into a light mist. She knew that in two months the plains she traveled through would be covered in snow. There would be no way for her or Kian to travel to each other.

On the fourth day after leaving the farm, Serpé rode into the village, Forest's edge. Kian's instructions included the name of a tavern and after she guided Adrastos to the tavern, she paid the stable hand to feed and brush him down. When she made her way into the tavern, a nervous knot gripped her stomach.

Though Kian had taught her to defend herself, he had never taken her into a tavern. His concern that someone loyal to The First would see her left her now unprepared for the world she was forced into. Stepping through the door, she stopped, her sense assaulted by the noise and overwhelming smell of alcohol.

Lanterns hanging from the ceiling lit the interior and a large fireplace drove away the autumn chill. In addition to the light from above, on each round table sat a smaller lantern in the center. One or two of the patrons wore the garb of mercenaries, but most looked like local farmers and business owners. A long bar ran the length of one wall and patrons crowded against it. A barkeep moved from one end of the bar to the other, serving mugs and cups to those who demanded his attention.

Serpé moved to the bar and pushed her way through the crowd to stand against it. After several tries to get the barkeep's attention, she realized the others around her had the right idea with their brash behavior.

She took a deep breathe, steeling herself against the unfamiliar. *This is but one step in my journey away from Kian. I have to remember he will not be here to help me.*

"Barkeep," she shouted over the noise in the tavern, pounding her fist on the bar.

The barkeep stepped toward her, his hard scrutiny making her uncomfortable. "Waddya want?"

"I'm looking for a man called Fenwer." Her words rushed out and with them, her pent up fear.

The man shrugged his shoulders. He leaned forward and pointed. Serpé followed his gesture to a darkened corner of the room. A lone figure sat at the table, surrounded by shadows the lantern light could not penetrate. She nodded her thanks, and after tossing the barkeep several silver coins, she made her way through the crowd of tables to the one she wanted. As she moved closer, a barrier forced her to pause. Pushing past it, she felt as if she had crossed a threshold and entered a different room. Though Serpé knew it was not possible, the sounds of the tavern diminished.

The man was more than she expected. Kian's instructions

had made no indication she would be dealing with a mage.

"Excuse me," she said, her voice echoing around her. "Are you Fenwer?"

With deliberate movements, the individual pulled the hood of his cloak from his head. Excitement filled her when the man revealed himself to be an elf.

He gazed at her through slanted eyes. "Why do you seek Fenwer?" he asked, caution in his voice.

Serpé heard his quiet voice clearly in the unusual hush that surrounded them. Before she answered, she tried to remember if she had ever experienced anything similar while she had studied under Reicholt.

Is it a natural magic or a spell that prevents others from hearing our conversation?

"I was sent to find him—to seek his help. I also have a message for him." She considered pulling the letter from Kian out of her pack, but decided against it. *Not until he proves who he is.*

"I would be happy to take the message to him." The elf held out his slender hand.

Despite how polite he was, she fought to control her growing impatience. She shifted her feet to allow herself time to bring her frustration under control. *He's trying to distract me. He doesn't want me to know who he really is.*

"No. I need to speak to him myself. I was told he would help me and I will not be forced to sit and wait while you decide whether or not to reveal yourself as Fenwer."

"You are a smart one." Fenwer's musical laughter filled the area. "I am Fenwer, the one you seek. May I now have the letter you spoke of?"

She nodded, swung her backpack off her shoulder, and pulled out a bundle of scroll cases tied together with a leather strap. Kian had marked the end of each case with the name of the person she should give it to. She untied the leather and selected the one with Fenwer's name, then placed it in his hand.

While she watched him read, she realized the light around the table had brightened. She always enjoyed watching how effortless magic came to elves.

The first time Serpé met an elf was at the School of Magic in Siladan. Remembering her lessons at the school dedicated to learning the arcane arts her god had power over, brought a pain to her chest. Kinnard, her instructor, had been angry when Reicholt forced him to take her as a student. He morphed her into a tiger at the beginning of her first lesson. Leaving her in that shape for so long, she feared she would never be returned to normal. The changes continued—everyday—until she developed a resistance to it. Then he moved on to other forms of magic.

Over time, they developed a friendship. Only after Serpé learned of Reicholt's misdeeds, did she understand why Kinnard was relieved she did not have the same moral faults as Reicholt. She had not seen him since Reicholt ended her lessons.

"Serpé," Fenwer interrupted her thoughts. "Kian has asked that I assist you in your journey to a place of safety. While I am not planning to return home yet, my daughter will be traveling to Valen. There, you will meet others who will assist you in a new beginning. My daughter will meet you at the stable in two changes to begin your travel."

A moment of silence passed between them before Fenwer motioned for her to sit across from him. "Sit. Have a meal. Enjoy a few moments of rest before you begin your journey again."

Serpé nodded her thanks and sat in the chair. The sounds of the tavern washed over them as Fenwer dropped the spell blocking the sound with a quick wave of his hand. When a barmaid came to the table at Fenwer's summons, Serpé ordered a large meal and ale. Though her companion remained silent until he left to make arrangements, she enjoyed the sound of people around her and the music of a bard who arrived shortly after she began to eat.

Chapter 12

Tired and weary from the travel, Kian rode his horse toward the town of Marmion. It would take less than a change to reach the buildings of the town. Bennan had returned to Siladan two days after they left the farm, leaving him to make the rest of his journey alone.

He adjusted in the saddle, trying to find any area on his backside that was not saddle-sore. *I need the distraction of a tavern. I've had too much time alone to think.*

His usual distraction would be a woman, but he had not brought one to his bed since Serpé arrived at his farm. She never said he could not, he just did not want to make her uncomfortable. And after the kiss they had shared, all he really wanted was the chance to taste her lips again, despite the plans he and Bennan had made for her.

A large group of men, tents and horses outside the town surprised Kian as he rode closer. No flag or standard flew over any of the tents, but he saw a small number of the men wore the tabards of the People's Army of Sorban, a military force larger than the Religious Guard. He had served in the Army and rose in the ranks there before transferring to the Religious Guard.

Three men separated from the rest, mounted horses and rode toward him. Before they reached him, they stopped, waiting. When he had moved closer, Kian sighed, and pulled his horse to a stop. *What now?*

"What do you want?" he grumbled, wasting no time on pleasantries.

They need to let me pass without a fight. I'm too tired to pull my punches and someone will get hurt.

"Captain Donwell, I am Blackette. The group of us," Blackette gestured to encompass the entire group of men watching them, "has been waiting for you."

"What for?" Kian knew he could take a few of the men, but the entire group was too much, even for a man of his skills. Straightening in his saddle, he brought his hand closer to his sword. Despite the numbers facing him, the idea of combat pushed away his weariness.

"Bennan told us you will need men to fight against the Religious Guard and The First. We have either been forced to leave our positions in the army protecting the people, left the army by choice or have a bounty on our heads because of taxes or other crimes," the younger man tried to explain, straightening his back.

"So, deserters, criminals, dishonored soldiers and commoners. And you expect me to lead this army? What makes you think I'm going to start a fight?" Kian watched Blackette's jaw tighten at his words.

Now we'll find out what kind of men Bennan has sent me. If they aren't insulted and defensive, I don't want them. If they are, then they'll fight harder to change my mind.

"Bennan said you would be resistant and would try to make us leave by insulting us. He also said you would change your mind eventually," Blackette said, lifting his chin in defiance. "We'll wait."

Kian took a deep breath and turned his full attention to the larger group of men. Though he and Bennan had discussed a resistance to Reicholt's injustices, forming an army had not been part of it. The idea seemed reasonable. Something had to be done to pull Reicholt's attention from Serpé. A war would be noticeable and would draw The First's wrath, but keeping the priest occupied could be just the distraction needed to keep him from her.

Deliberate in his actions, Kian nodded and looked again at the three men in front of him. "I'll think about it—consider my options. We'll see what time brings us." He moved his horse closer to Blackette and the other two men. "I'll be at the inn. Bring those you feel can help lead this army and I'll hear what you have to say."

Blackette opened his mouth to speak, but Kian held up his hand to stop him. "I want to eat a meal and drink a tankard of ale before I see you. My horse needs to be cared for and I want some clean clothes. If I see you or any of the others before these things are done, I will personally hand you over to the first Religious Guard patrol I see. Do I make myself clear?"

Blackette smiled, then nodded. "Perfectly, Captain."

Hiding a smile, Kian rode his horse past the three and then the larger group. *It will be good to be called Captain again. Maybe I can lead these men.*

Chapter 13

"I still don't understand the reasons for this *Protector?* Why would the forest need a Protector like that? And doesn't his wife have any say in this?" Serpé had asked these questions twice before, but she still did not understand. Or maybe she was being stubborn. Even she thought she was being too difficult on Tamar. She could not stop the pity she felt for Fenwer's daughter.

When they first met, Tamar had been unwilling to speak to her, but Serpé had not allowed that to stop her from trying to become friends. Though she never had friends away from the church, or any friend other than Kian, she decided she needed someone to call friend. She talked and asked questions until Tamar gave in and the conversation became more than just one woman talking to herself.

Tamar took a deep breath, obviously preparing to explain the social structure of The Dragon's Forest again. "Shou-Lung is a chosen of Crystalline. This forest is hers, and it is only natural for her to want it protected." Serpé nodded in understanding. "He and his mate were chosen to protect the forest. There is a clan of elves, Shayanna's own people, who also protect the forest with him."

"Were they chosen by Crystalline as well? Or were they already here?"

"They were not here. They came with the Protectors. Other elves were here already, my people. We help Shou-Lung by dealing with minor threats, with the help of the humans who are willing to live in harmony with us and the forest."

"So when Crystalline asked, or selected, Shou-Lung for this, Shayanna and her people were selected as well?" Serpé asked, defensive. *Why am I being so difficult? There is nothing wrong with a woman choosing to be with her mate in everything.*

"Do you have a problem, Serpé? Haven't you ever loved someone so much that you were willing to be with them, no matter what the danger or cost?" Tamar's own defenses showed themselves.

Serpé brought her gaze to meet the elf's. "I have and he sent me away." Before her companion could press further, Serpé pushed on. "Are there any farms? What will I do for a home? Food? Something to keep from being bored?"

Finally, after a moment of silence, the elven woman blinked and nodded. "There are farms. Some food cannot be provided by the forest, but Crystalline allows areas to be cleared for the farming. I'm sure her blessings will provide for the rest of your needs." She cleaned the remains of their meal from her bowl.

Serpé watched the way Tamar avoided meeting her gaze until she decided their conversation was done and she began to clean her bowl of the meal.

In the morning, the two started the last part of their four day journey. By mid-afternoon, they arrived in the forest town of Valen. Serpé stopped Adrastos to look around her. The way the town was embraced by the trees, yet still independent of them, surprised her. In particular, a tree that grew through a building held her gaze.

"They built that shop, about fifty summers ago," Tamar explained. "The tree sprouted before the construction was complete. They just incorporated it into their shop. Adjustments are now made for size as needed." Serpé smiled her thanks and followed her new friend when she moved away.

At the other end of town stood a tower, but they turned at an inn called The Ranger's Rest, before they reached it. Serpé handed Adrastos' reins to the stable hand after delivering a brief warning to keep his hands away from the horse's mouth. Grabbing her saddlebags, she followed Tamar into the inn.

She wanted to stop at the door to study the room, like Kian had taught her, but Tamar pulled her along. "Everyone is a friend—you'll be safe," she promised with a smile.

The three long tables were almost full and Serpé marveled at the different occupants, despite Tamar's rush. They stepped up to the bar and while Tamar spoke to the barkeep, Serpé pretended to enjoy the smooth feel of the wood. When the man walked away, she followed his movement with her eyes, careful to keep her observations subtle. He spoke to a woman with a plump figure and a motherly look about her, who glanced at Serpé when he gestured in her direction. Leaving the barkeep with a smile and a nod, the woman wove her way through the crowd to join the new arrivals.

"Tamar, good to have you home. Who is your friend?"

"This is Serpé Navran. She was sent to us by Captain Donwell. She needs our help," Tamar said with a smile, resting a hand on Serpé's shoulder.

Serpé retrieved a scroll case from her pack. Kian's list had only one woman in Valen. She hoped this was her. "Are you Jalena Winterwood?" She waited for the woman to nod. "Then this is for you." She handed the case to Jalena and waited while the contents were read.

Finally the older woman lifted her gaze to Serpé again and studied her. Her long scrutiny became uncomfortable, but Serpé forced herself to remain still. Both Jalena and Fenwer had stared at her like this after reading Kian's letter and she decided to read one before handing it to the next person she met.

"So you are the one that has lived with Kian these last four years. I can see why he took so much care not to reveal you to any of us. I have something for you as well." Jalena walked away, through a door, and returned before Tamar finished ordering a glass of winter wine. "This came for you yesterday. The accompanying letter indicated I would be seeing you before long."

Serpé took the folded parchment from Jalena, the sounds of the tavern no longer pounding in her ears. A sharp pain filled her other hand when the woman pressed a room key into it. The gesture that followed sent Serpé upstairs to the room number etched into the metal.

She had not expected to receive a letter from Kian so soon, and she wanted to believe that he had sent for her. Her mind told her he had not, that he only tried to send her some small comfort in her exile. *That is what he has done—exiled me to a place I don't know, placed me with people who are forced to show me pity and take me into their homes. This is not what I wanted in my life.*

She had wanted to be a priestess until she left the church. For the last four years, the desire to be safe from Reicholt had been her driving force. But since leaving the farm, she realized that what she really wanted was to be with Kian and whatever that would bring her. That obviously was not going to happen now, at least not while Reicholt still wanted her.

Like Kian, the letter was short on words and to the point. He had burned their home, so anything she had left there was gone. He did not want her to return to Sorban until he sent for her because he wanted her safe. There would be other messages in the future, but no indication of how often. *My exile is permanent.*

Her body jerked in surprise at an unexpected knock at her door. After a deep breath, she moved the wooden bar that barred her door from opening. She stared at Tamar and the tray of food she held before stepping aside and allowing her to enter.

"Jalena thought you might be hungry," Tamar said, quiet, putting the tray on the table. When she turned back to her, she reached up and touched Serpé's cheek. The tear she wiped away moistened Serpé's skin. "Are you all right? Is there anything I can do?"

"I'll be fine, in time. I just don't know what to do now."

"I need to return to my patrol in the militia." She smiled at Serpé. "Why don't you join us? It will give you something to do and Lord Draven takes care of his people."

Serpé remained quiet while she thought about Tamar's proposal. Lord Draven was on her list as well, so she knew he would be someone she could trust. But would he accept her based only on Kian's note and her four days travel with Tamar?

Before the smile faded from Tamar's face, she smiled in return. "That could be interesting. What's the worst that could happen?"

In the morning, Serpé followed Tamar and Jalena to the tower she noticed the day before. The steward announced their arrival, but asked her to wait outside the council room while the other women spoke to the lord. Before they left her side, though, she pushed the scroll case meant for Draven into Tamar's hand. The door to the room was left open a bit and she heard heavy booted footsteps as someone inside paced the floor.

"What do we know about her?" a deep male voice demanded, reaching her easily through the open door. She assumed it belonged to Draven because of the tone of authority it held.

"That isn't important, Lord. Kian asked us to help her. He's never asked anything of us. This is a small thing we can do for him. He's come to our aid whenever we needed him. Now it's our turn." Jalena's words surprised her.

She glanced at the door. *That explains where Kian went the few times he traveled away from the farm without me.*

"True. She stays. She will be accepted into our community. If Kian trained her to be half as good as he is, then she will be an excellent asset for our militia. And Tamar, what did you find out about her? Anything we need to worry about?"

Serpé took a deep breath, and crossed her arms protectively over her chest. *I want to go in there. But I want to hear what they say about Kian more than I want to defend myself.*

"She's running from Eion Reicholt, though I do not know why. And, she has feelings for Kian, but he has not returned the sentiment."

Serpé straightened in frustration. *It isn't any of their concern what has or has not happened between Kian and I. Tamar is supposed to be my friend, but I could have been wrong. We've only known each other for a few days. My loss and pain must have clouded my judgment.*

"It's good to hear someone cares that much about him." Jalena's voice stopped her from charging into the room.

"I think they would both be happier if they were together. But he seems intent on keeping them apart. So we should stay out of that part of it and just keep her safe." Tamar's words returned Serpé's confidence and she forgave her as quickly as she became angry. Their growing friendship was something that could be counted on and she would protect it.

"I agree. We stay out of it. Let her do what she wants with who she wants. We will focus on keeping her safe from this Reicholt person." Jalena's voice grew louder when she came closer to the door and Serpé rushed to a chair to sit before she was discovered listening. "Now, Lord Draven, shall we extend an invitation for Serpé to join us?" Draven's deep chuckle made

Serpé smile and she turned that smile on him when he opened the door all the way.

He pulled her close to him when she tried to shake his hand. She allowed him to guide her into the council room and shut the door behind them. "Welcome to Valen, Serpé. Please come in."

Chapter 14

"Are you sure? Do you trust your source?" Strinnal asked, forcing calm into his voice while he studied the man in front of him.

"Yes, sir. There is no question. I saw his body myself." The man combed his fingers through his greasy hair. "I'm sorry, sir."

The captain waved his hand, dismissing the soldier. Alone, he rested his head in his hands.

The man was a guard for the Marcin family, the one assigned to protect his mother. He had brought news that someone assassinated Strinnal's father. His mother had to be restrained to keep her from hurting herself. The description of the assassin matched that of the prisoner The First had released to fulfill his plans.

My father was a minor merchant, not even serving on the council. Our businesses are minor, my grandparents had only small businesses to leave my mother. But his death was not about the power The First could gain. It was my punishment for failing to find Serpé and for questioning his plans.

The longer he sat in silence, the more he wanted to vomit. He had followed in his father's footsteps by joining the Religious Guard and had excelled. His father had always been so proud of him and now he was dead because his son had forgotten to never question Reicholt.

I made a stupid mistake.

Serving The First became more difficult every day. Strinnal spent more time trying to cover up events and decisions The First was involved in than actually performing his true duties of protecting him and the church.

But some would consider that to be my true duty.

Again his stomach rebelled and before it became worse, Strinnal stood from his chair. After buckling his sword belt on, he left the room. Ignoring the men around him, he made his way out of the barracks and to the street.

He walked without purpose until he stood in front of the temple. He stared at the building for a moment before heading inside.

Again his feet seemed to carry him without thought. He felt numb as he walked the hall that led him to The First's office. He stopped in front of the door, unsure of why he'd come. When he opened it, he stepped into the empty, elaborate room.

I need to find something that will show what The First still has planned and what he has already done.

Strinnal glanced around the room, deciding to start with the obvious places. Within minutes, he'd examined the desk and the shelves behind it.

The First is not an idiot. He wouldn't leave anything out in the open.

Frustrated, he stepped over to the bookshelves and fingered the binding of each book as he read the titles. They all appeared normal and expected for a man of The First's beliefs and apparent lifestyle. He read the titles again; The Teachings of Azar, The Holy Word of Azar and Azar's Holy Sanctioned Manuscripts. And then an unusual title caught his eye.

Strinnal pulled the odd book from the shelf to examine it. A book of poems, but more surprising was that they were about love and romance. He remembered seeing a similar book at Kian's and one in Serpé's room four years ago after she ran away.

Of course, it makes sense. The books all belonged to Serpé.

Inside the front cover of the book, he found Serpé's name written in the feminine loops and swirls he had seen her use in other writing. Rubbing his fingertip over the ink, he could not think of any reason for the priest to still have the book.

A brief breeze blew across his check, followed by the crinkling sound of parchment in a brief breeze drew his attention to the space he had opened between the books. Looking closer, he found that several scrolls had been hidden behind the book.

"What's this?" His whisper rang out in the silence and he glanced around to ensure he was still alone.

Reaching into the shelf, Strinnal felt around the scrolls. His search was rewarded when his fingers touched another leather cover. Careful not to pull other books off the shelf, he struggled to bring the hidden book into the light. Finally giving up, he made the opening wider by removing one more book.

With the other books returned to their original positions, and the hidden one resting in his hand, he opened it. The First's elaborate scrawl covered the page and a glance at the words revealed the man's ego. Instead of reading each page in full, Strinnal slipped the book into his shirt and straightened the shelves again.

Get the scrolls too.

The First could return at any moment and Strinnal did not want the priest to catch him. *No. Not right now.*

As if his thoughts summoned the other man, the door opened. The captain straightened his back and turned to face Most Holy Reicholt, who in turn stared at Strinnal in surprise.

"I've been waiting for you, Most Holy," Strinnal kept his voice cold.

"And you thought my office was the most appropriate place to do it?" The First's words dripped with anger. Strinnal winced at the tone, but stood strong against it.

"It has never been a problem before, and I needed guidance from the texts for my mother and me." He hoped the lie would not be obvious, especially with the play upon The First's beliefs.

The First failed to hide his surprise, but soon took on his normal benevolent look and held his hands out. "Of course it isn't a problem. You may always seek guidance from Azar's teachings in my absence. May I ask what has happened that you need comfort?"

"I just learned that my father was killed yesterday. I was hoping there would be something to comfort my mother and me in our time of loss."

"That is a horrible and unfortunate loss, Captain." The First stepped farther into the office and walked to his desk. After sitting in his chair and making himself comfortable, he studied Strinnal. "Do you need time to arrange for the funeral and see to your mother's needs?"

"Yes, I will need to take care of everything and arrange for my mother to stay with family. But I do not want to leave you unprotected," Strinnal answered, clenching his fist to restrain his anger. The longer he stared at The First, the more he wanted to reach across the table and strangle the man who had ordered his father's death.

I can't believe he can sit across from me and act like he has no knowledge of what happened.

"I am sure your guards are capable of protecting me in your absence, Captain. You have ensured they are all trained appropriately, I'm sure."

"Of course, Most Holy Reicholt." He bowed slightly, ignoring the sarcasm in the other's voice. "If it would be acceptable, I would like to come back and study the texts more. Perhaps you could set some aside for me to read."

"I will admit I am surprised to see you taking such a sudden interest in Azar's teachings. But if you truly wish to seek comfort in Azar's words, I will gladly select some texts for you."

The two men watched each other and Strinnal found himself having to force his legs still when they tried to move. The feel of the leather book against his skin made him nervous and he was certain the priest knew he had it.

"If there is nothing else, Captain, I need to prepare my next sermon. And, I have a council meeting soon as well." The First gestured at the door, dismissing him.

"My apologies, again, Most Holy. I will return to my duties as soon as I am able." Bowing once more, Strinnal left the room, shutting the door behind him.

He walked down the hall to the entrance of the temple, worry that The First would come after him carrying him faster than intended.

If I can make it out of the temple without being stopped, I'm sure he will not call me back.

Instead of returning to his office, he went to his parent's house. The family friend who had offered to stay with his mother left soon after with a promise to return in the morning. After putting together a plate of food, he relaxed in a chair where he could watch his mother rest. He pulled out the book he had taken from The First's office. With a nervous glance around the room, he opened it and read.

The next morning, Strinnal returned to Reicholt's office after hiding the journal in his bedroom at his parents' home. The words he read the night before had left him cold and disillusioned. Again, the office lay empty, but Strinnal had watched The First go into the chapel after receiving the priest's blessing to enter the room.

I've always known The First was involved in questionable activities, but I never expected to learn that he'd orchestrated Serpé's pre-arranged marriage, its cancellation and her subsequent joining of the church. I'm surprised he boasted about it in the book, though I'm sure no one else ever read it, or was ever meant to.

A stack of books sat on the table in the corner, The First's attempt to provide his captain comfort in his time of loss. Instead of going to the table, Strinnal returned to the book that belonged to Serpé and the secret it hid.

Still hidden behind the books, the parchments waited, evidence that The First felt secure in the hiding place he had chosen. One by one, ten scrolls in total, Strinnal pulled them out, though he could feel several were thicker than the others. The books on the table were pushed aside to make room so he could take a brief survey of everything he found.

He opened the largest scroll first. As he read, his slow descent into a nearby chair went unnoticed. The unrolled parchment revealed the most detailed family line he had ever seen. Even Strinnal's own line, documented in a tapestry hanging in the family's dining room, had branches with no information, the members lost for one reason or another. This parchment held dates of birth and death, as expected, but each death had the cause noted below the date. Even more disturbing, the most recent deaths, within the last thirty years that were not noted as natural causes, had the name of the individual who perpetrated the death.

The First's name appears at least five times with the cause of death. What has he done?

Only four names were listed as living, Serpé, a brother he did not think she had ever met, and her parents. Stunned, he stared at the family name, and the truth behind Serpé's family line.

This explains The First's fascination with her and his obsession to possess her.

Strinnal sat back, staring at the parchment for several moments before shaking his head to clear his thoughts. The other scrolls would have to wait until he returned to his parents' home. Today's service would not last much longer.

Fear gripped his chest as he glanced at the door.

I can't believe it. He actually scares me. His name next to so many dead in Serpé's family line makes it clear The First will do anything to get what he wants.

With careful, but hurried movements, Strinnal rolled up the scroll and slid it into his cloak, followed by the others. After placing the book back on the shelf in its appropriate place, he returned to the table and thumbed through the books left for him. The marked passages did nothing to calm his fear or comfort the pain he felt at the loss of his father. Instead a question formed and he felt sure the answer would affect the performance of his duties.

How can I believe in a god that allows his priest to commit such evil?

Chapter 15

The drink did nothing to dull Strinnal's mind or the knowledge he wished to forget. The sounds of the tavern only served to amplify his own voice in his head repeating everything over and over. With a moan, he covered his ears in a futile attempt to quiet the voice and the noise.

It's not working.

"Too much to drink, Captain?" A deep voice broke through the noise in his head.

The captain looked at the newcomer, the pain in his head blurring his vision. Sudden recognition cleared his sight and his hand went to his sword.

"You're Kian's friend," Strinnal's voice sounded harsh in his throat, but he kept it at a whisper to prevent unwanted attention from others.

"Yes, I am, and I recommend you take that hand from your sword. I have more friends than just Kian and not all of them are impressed with your rank," Bennan said, laughter in his voice. He gestured at others in the tavern and Strinnal noted quite a few heads nod in return. "I'm Bennan. I hope the others with you were able to get out of the house, alive, as you did."

"Yes, no thanks to either of you."

"Don't be so sure of that. There are many things at work here that you do not know about and will never understand.

Remember how strangely the fire acted?" Sipping from the mug the serving girl placed in front of him, Bennan winked at her, bringing a deep blush to her cheeks.

"What do you want?" Strinnal mumbled. He drank deep from his own mug, thankful that the voice in his head had quieted.

"You are suffering, and considering your recent loss, I offer an ear for your pain."

Strinnal scoffed at the older man. "What do you know of my loss or my pain?"

"I, too, have lost someone I cared for and loved, but by his own actions, not those of another." Strinnal squirmed under the intensity of Bennan's gaze. "I also know how painful it can be to lose faith in someone you've believed in."

"What I've learned affects others more than me. My loss, while painful, is minor compared to the loss another has suffered in the past or will suffer in the months to come." Despite Bennan's intensity, Strinnal felt his fear and nervousness calm. The urgency to tell him everything nearly pushed the words from the captain's throat, but he kept his voice under control and his words contained.

"I can help you get this information to someone who can assist you. It will be used to protect the person you are so concerned about. That is your main concern, isn't it? Protecting her?" The big man smiled.

"How do you know it's about a 'her'? I didn't say that," Strinnal said, sitting back in his chair and studying the other man.

Something about this man is not right. He knows too much, speaks too freely with me, when he knows who I serve.

"Because I still have faith in the one you do not, even if he doesn't deserve it. Because I am closer to everything than you would believe." Bending over, Bennan lifted a sack onto the table. "Now, you must trust me for this to work. In this sack are scrolls of different sizes. Place one of the appropriate size next to whatever you need to copy. Take the copies back. He will need them soon and if they are missing, he will know you took them. There is also a journal. Do the same as with the scrolls, one page at a time."

"How do you...?"

"I walk with Azar's blessings. He guides me to those who will help his chosen warrior. You do intend to help her, don't you?" Again Strinnal squirmed over the intensity of Bennan's gaze, but with a deep breathe, he forced himself to calm.

"I will help her, especially if she can make him suffer for all the evil he's done. Does she know about this? About you?"

Bennan leaned back and again sipped from his mug. "Not yet. Her path is still unclear before her. But she will and when she does, Azar's fury will be felt by many." At the end of his statement, the counter under their mugs trembled. Glancing at others in the tavern, Strinnal was surprised no one else noticed.

"Good." He continued, "When can I see the one who will help her?"

"Return the documents tomorrow. Meet me back here at two changes before sundown. I will send you to him."

Strinnal nodded, finished the contents of his mug and stood. After throwing the bag over his shoulder, he looked down at the man.

"Tomorrow," Strinnal confirmed. When Bennan nodded, he left the tavern.

Chapter 16

The sound of the door opening, quiet as it was, still jolted Kian awake. Soft footsteps moved closer, revealing the intruder was smaller than a man, more likely a woman or an older child. Gripping the dagger under his pillow, he waited until the dark figure drew close.

I'm safe here. I have men everywhere. Who would be bold enough to intrude on me with so many ready to defend me?

Reaching to touch him, a hand appeared near his face. Before the hand came closer, Kian grabbed it, yanking the person over him onto the bed, his dagger now at the intruder's throat.

"What do you want?" His voice grated in his ears. Terror wafted off the slight person in his grip, and sobs now filled the room.

"I apologize, Captain." Kian recognized the still maturing voice of Marren, the boy who had begged to serve as his page. "Blackette told me to wake you."

Releasing the boy, remorse filled Kian. He returned the dagger to its place under the pillow. Marren hurried away, pressing his body against the door jam.

Waiting for him to speak took too long, leaving Kian no choice but to push for more information. "Well?"

"Bennan has been contacted and someone wants to meet with you. He says this person has information about The First and

Dame Navran. The man will be here tomorrow at sundown," Marren stuttered.

"Thank you, Marren. Go back to bed," Kian muttered. He watched the boy bow before he ran from the room.

I will have to apologize to him in the morning. Right now though, I'll leave him thinking twice about waking me in the middle of the night. No one is supposed to know where I am though. Bennan and I agreed on this before separating.

What information could this person have that would be so important, Bennan needs to send him to me? I do not like anyone having information regarding Serpé, no matter what kind of information it is.

The light of the new day had not yet brightened the room, but a fierce yawn shook him.

I can wait for a few more changes before beginning my preparations—or I can sleep more.

A heartbeat later, he decided sleep was more important.

Planning the meeting had been easy and all his men sat in place throughout the tavern when Kian strolled through to the table he had chosen. More men waited outside, in places where they watched the entrance. Amused at how each of the men inside failed to be inconspicuous, he decided there was nothing he could do to help them.

They are soldiers first. Citizens and spies last. Anyone who walks into this tavern will know they are not normal farmers.

A mug of warmed ale waited for him at the table. Placed in the middle of the room, surrounded by tables still far enough away to give Kian and the stranger privacy, his men could easily reach his table if necessary. Sitting, he took a small sip of the ale, savoring its hint of cinnamon and other spices.

The warm liquid filled his mouth and the scent wafted into his nose. The spiced ale had been a favorite of his since his first days in the military.

Then he shared it with Serpé. Two days after she came to his farm, Kian gave her the first mug she ever had of the spiced drink. They sat together in the common room after finishing the day's chores and her training. She complained about being sore and he thought the drink would help her relax.

He watched her sip the ale and her cheeks flush with the warmth and alcohol. Her eyes brightened with pleasure. When she fell asleep, made sleepy from the alcohol, he spent several minutes gazing at her.

I wish we could go back to that time, when she believed I could protect her.

The appointed meeting time came and went and no one walked through the door. Just as Kian prepared to dismiss his men, a shadow passed across the window and the door opened.

A figure stood in the door frame, obviously male by the large stature. Even across the room, Kian struggled to see past the thick cloak that covered him from head to foot. He saw no obvious weapons, but he knew a trained warrior would not come unarmed.

Kian watched the man walk to the table, attempting to gauge his strengths and weaknesses with each movement. Something about the new arrival seemed familiar, but there was nothing for Kian to connect him with a former ally.

Standing next to the table, his face shadowed by the hood, the man looked down at Kian.

Forcing his jaw to relax, Kian decided against saying anything that might send the man away. Instead, he motioned for him to sit at the table.

The silence between them stretched until finally Kian cleared his throat, his patience gone. "You called for this meeting. State your purpose or leave."

"I apologize. I am still unsure about my actions." Though his voice came out muffled from behind the hood, Kian heard him take a deep breath. "First, Reicholt is hiring mercenaries and assassins to attack and kill merchants, their caravans, and anyone else who opposes him."

Stunned by the news, Kian sat back in his chair. "I didn't realize his greed had grown so much. Is he really so desperate to control the kingdom that he has to take matters to this extreme? What is he thinking?"

"He seeks to keep his hands clean of blood and himself within Azar's favor. And to make himself more important to the people."

"Who is he placing in the vacant positions on the council?"

"Inexperienced sons, husbands, any male in the families that can be easily controlled. He counsels the women in their moment of weakness and mourning, tells them who he thinks should be appointed and has them sign the council papers before they can change their minds."

"Unbelievable," Kian whispered, stunned. Though he picked up his mug of ale while the man spoke, Kian returned it to the table, without taking a drink.

He undermines the core of our country and weakens the council for his own advancement.

Finally taking a deep drink from the mug, he watched the liquid swirl until it stopped. "Why does Reicholt still want Serpé?"

"That is the second reason I'm here." From within his cloak, the man brought forth a journal and scroll cases. He placed these on the table and pushed them toward Kian. "These were in his office. The large case holds Serpé's family line, in full detail. The journal, written when she was only eight winters, explains in detail what he did to manipulate her family and get her under church control."

Kian took the items, but could not open them. *I always knew Reicholt had manipulated the Navrans. But to have the evidence placed into my hands that could ruin the priest...I need to think about what I'll do with it.*

"The First has plans for Serpé." Shifting uncomfortably at the other man's words, Kian forced himself to listen. "He's infatuated with her. He wants her for himself and will destroy anyone who comes between them."

"But why? As a priest, his vows should be more important than any personal desire," Kian said in disgust.

The stranger's hooded gaze came up. "He cares only for the power he thinks she can give him. His vows mean nothing now. He will declare himself king. And he thinks Serpé can provide him an heir." The words were said in such a casual tone that Kian found himself wanting to reach across the table and choke the man.

His stomach twisted at the thought of Reicholt touching Serpé. Jealousy warred for dominance over the revulsion, forcing him to gasp for breath. *I still try to deny my feelings, but my heart knows better than my mind.*

Forcing the stranger to wait, he struggled to sort through the sudden onslaught of emotions. *I should be more concerned that it took learning Reicholt wants Serpé to acknowledge my own desire. But do I want her because I love her or because he wants her?*

"Reicholt sees her as a tool to use for his own gains. These papers you've found and her family's position in the council can be used as a way to secure a position for himself. But Serpé is not a tool or a trophy. She deserves someone who will spoil, love and treasure her. He will never treat her as she deserves." The knot of emotions within Kian relaxed with his admission.

"I would agree. If you care for her at all, you will make sure she is safe," the stranger instructed.

Silence descended over the table again as the two men stared at each other, at least Kian assumed the man stared at him.

"She's well protected." Kian finally broke the silence, his words quiet.

"I'm sure she is." The man tilted his head in agreement.

"Why are you telling me all this? Why risk your life to give me this information?"

Kian wanted to examine the journal and other documents, but he needed to know the stranger's motivation. He did not want his men arrested because of his carelessness.

"My father was the first victim on The First's list of murders. I want him brought to justice. My position will allow me to give you information on his activities and movements. You will need my information and I want to give you everything I can." The man stood, forcing Kian to stand as well.

"I look forward to our partnership." Kian held his hand out and after a brief grasp, the other man turned and left the inn.

Kian waited, then sat again and opened the largest scroll case. Spreading the parchment out on the table, he held down the corners with mugs and a plate of left over food. He traced the line from Serpé's name, past her parents, to her grandparents. Her father's parents brought him no surprise. But her mother's parents and siblings brought him to a halt. He leaned back in his seat.

"By the gods. I don't believe it."

Chapter 17

Kian rode ahead of his army, intent on arriving at Forest's Edge before the others. He had ridden for two days without much rest, and would have the time he needed before the army arrived. His horse would need attention after this if it were ever to be ridden again.

He slowed the horse to a walk as he crossed the invisible line into the small town. A familiar tavern held his attention, a comfort in all the chaos his life had become.

In all the years I've known him, Fenwer hasn't found another place to call his favorite.

After stabling the tired animal, Kian went inside the tavern. Glancing around the room, disappointment filled him at his friend's absence. He picked an empty table and informed the serving maid that he needed to speak to the elf.

"I understand you're looking for me," a familiar voice broke through Kian's thoughts while he ate the food he ordered.

He turned to acknowledge the new arrival. "I see you still enjoy sneaking up on people. You haven't found anything else to entertain yourself in three hundred years?"

"Why should I, Kian? I have plenty of time to try whatever I want. Right now, I enjoy this," Fenwer bemused, sitting across from him, and waving at a serving maid for a drink.

"I have an army a few days behind me," Kian pushed, needing

to get to the point of his visit. Pleasantries with his friend would have to wait.

"Are you being chased?" Fenwer tensed.

"No, the army is mine."

"How did you get an army?" Fenwer's eyes widened.

Kian wanted to laugh at Fenwer's surprised expression. "Bennan thought it appropriate for me to lead those who have been exiled or driven out of the military in Sorban. Some escaped from the prisons, enslavement or ran on their own."

"What was Bennan thinking?" The surprise had not left the elf's voice and Kian was not sure if he should be insulted or ignore it.

Am I not capable of leading an army? I thought I'd proven my skills long ago. Maybe it is too much to ask. I've been in retirement for too long.

"Bennan thought with my military experience, I could lead them against Reicholt. We planned to find a group of people to join us in our fight. Instead, Bennan had an army waiting for me in Marmion. They will be here in three days." The confidence he heard in his voice earlier had disappeared.

"I never thought you would return to military service of any kind, voluntary or forced. This must be pretty important for you to come out of retirement."

"It is," Kian muttered, looking down and swirling the ale in his mug.

"Why are you here?"

"Our presence put a strain on the previous town where we camped. I made the army move. When we did, we fought against the Religious Guard for the first time." He winced at the memory. Picking up his ale, he took a deep drink.

"What happened?" Fenwer's laughter had disappeared.

"Being our first time fighting together, I'd rate it adequate. I knew there would be problems with so many people from such varied military backgrounds. But we need to assign men to lead groups, learn to divide and conquer our enemies. We'll work it out." He drank the rest of his ale and pushed the mug away.

"But to bring all those men here? To the forest?"

"I need to place the army between Serpé and Reicholt. It will allow me to protect her easier. And, I need to mask our numbers. The forest will give us cover for our numbers as well as a source of food and water. Can you arrange a meeting for me with the Protector?" Kian knew what he asked for would not be an easy thing for Fenwer, but if he could, the elf would help.

Fenwer stared at him, his thoughts hidden from Kian. "I cannot promise you anything. I will speak to him, present your needs and let you know." Fenwer finished his drink and stood. "We will catch up after you speak to the Protector. You have me on a tight time restriction."

"Thank you, Fenwer. I'll be here, waiting for your return."

Fenwer had done better than Kian hoped for. Not only did he arrange a meeting with the Protector, but the man agreed to come to Forest's Edge. Immediately after telling him about the arrangement, Fenwer took Kian to a clearing a short distance from the town. Now they waited for the Protector's arrival.

"What should I expect, Fenwer?" Kian asked, tired of waiting in silence.

"He says what he's thinking. If he doesn't like you, you'll know. He may bring his mate, if she's taken an interest. But don't expect her to sway his decision. It's his forest to protect." As the elf spoke, a gray dire wolf walked into the clearing.

Unable to draw his weapon because Fenwer's hand restrained him, Kian watched the large animal. He waited for the attack he was certain would come next. As long as Kian was tall, the wolf stood the same height as a stallion. It stopped inside the clearing and gazed at the two men. When a female elf appeared next to it, her hand wound within the fur at the creature's neck, shock filled Kian, warring with the need to protect such a small person from the beast.

Watching her hand move within the fur, he realized she must have ridden the animal to their meeting. She did not step farther into the opening, but stayed next to the wolf, her gaze intent on the human before her.

From the other side of the wolf, a man stepped forward, dressed in forest greens and browns. His hair was pulled back from his face and Kian saw his pointed ears, but they were not as pointed as those of his companion. He was a half-breed, though his parentage did not surprise Kian like the weapons on his side. Kian had never seen the design before. The scabbards, slightly curved and thin, were not like an estoc or rapier scabbard. Material he could not recognize wrapped the handles and ivory glowed at the end of each hilt.

I want to see those weapons. What kind of swords are they?

"Kian Donwell, this is Shou Lung, Protector of The Dragon's Forest, Shayanna Tuellen, his mate and her companion, Silvermane," Fenwer introduced each in turn, and then gestured toward Kian. "This is the man I told you about, Captain Kian Donwell. He has been a friend for several years. I trust him."

Shou Lung studied Kian. Shifting under his intense gaze, Kian cleared his throat and met his eyes. Kian waited for the protector to speak, unsure of the protocol he needed to observe.

"Captain, I understand you need my assistance with a war that does not involve me," Shou Lung stated, finally breaking the silence. Stepping farther into the clearing, he glanced behind him at Shayanna. She moved closer to him.

Kian watched their interaction, curious, until Shou Lung's gaze returned to him. "Not necessarily your assistance. More like your permission to use the forest as our base." The longer Shou Lung stared, the more irritated Kian became.

Maybe he is trying to see how much I will tolerate before I react. It's almost like he wants to antagonize me into a confrontation.

"Why do you need the forest for your base?"

"I sent someone to Lord Draven for protection. The Religious Guard is still looking for her. I want to place my army between them. The forest will allow us to hide our numbers, give us the element of surprise and keep us close to her." Even to Kian, his reasons sounded weak.

There is no benefit for Shou Lung or any of the others who call the forest their home to help me. Serpé won't know I'm here to protect her. The only one who will know or benefit from this will be me.

Shayanna stepped closer to her mate and Kian watched her whisper something to him. Shou Lung's expression softened, for a brief moment, then he nodded, either in agreement or understanding. He fixed his gaze upon Kian again.

"My mate seems to think you're keeping something from us, but she doesn't think it is important enough to refuse your request. Keep the Religious Guard out of the forest. Otherwise, I will have to take their punishment into my own hands and you will be removed. The woman you are protecting is also my protection, but the forest comes first. Do you agree?"

Kian nodded. "I agree. My thanks, Shou Lung."

"You will not thank me if you do not keep your side of the agreement." The half-elf stared at him a heartbeat more, then turned and left the clearing. Shayanna stayed a moment longer, her gaze on Kian. Several breaths later, she smiled and left with the dire wolf, her hand again buried deep within its fur.

Taking a deep breath, Kian turned to look at Fenwer. "Well, that was not what I expected."

The elf shook his head. "Not what I expected either. I think you owe me a drink."

"I thought it was your turn to buy," Kian protested. They turned back toward town.

"Someone owes someone a drink."

"You owe me," Kian mumbled, though he knew he would buy the first round of drinks.

Chapter 18

For four months, Serpé trained and worked through the militia and was rewarded with a promotion to captain of her own troop. Tamar transferred to her command and introduced her to friends who would work with them. The dwarven cleric, Drommond, and the human druid, Aldric, also proved to be good friends for her and they spent many nights in The Ranger's Rest after they returned from patrol.

Now, the chill of the forest bit through to Serpé's skin as she led her troop through the Dragon's Forest.

Two days ago, I was sleeping in my own bed and sharing my morning feast with Striphen. Now, because spiderkin are attacking the outlying farms around Valen, I have to sleep on the forest floor. Though several men had tried to get close to her, Serpé avoided them all. Striphen, a fellow captain in the militia, was the only one who had taken the time to get to know her. Striphen never treated her as an oddity because she wanted to be a militia captain.

Serpé pulled her cloak around her tighter. The warmth of the material reminded her of Striphen's embrace their last morning together. It had been a gift from Striphen, for her birthday, the first she spent away from Kian. *I never wanted to become close to Striphen, and we aren't as close as we could be. Kian is always in my mind, despite the support and patience Striphen has shown me.*

Kian's first letter to Jalena had allowed Serpé a place to live for a month. Jalena probably would have allowed her to stay longer if she wanted, but the money Kian gave her and the money she earned from the militia let her purchase a farm. Serpé loved the farm, but it did not take long for her to realize she could not handle it alone.

I wonder how Kian did it so long without help. If I didn't have Rakel and Tomes, I would not have been able to plow the fields and prepare them for the winter months. She hired newlyweds Rakel and Tomes Newberry to help her. While she was out on patrols, they took care of the farm.

"Serpé, Jalena said you got another message before we left. Did you read it yet?" Tamar interrupted her thoughts.

She glanced over to her friend. "No, I haven't read it. Why?"

Tamar shrugged, returning her gaze to the forest around them. "I don't know. You just haven't responded to any of his messages since you got here. How much longer do you intend to ignore him?"

"I'm not ignoring him," Serpé answered defensively. Kian's messages had come to Serpé twice a month since she arrived, but she chose not to answer them. "I'll read it when we get home."

She read each letter from him, hoping that he wanted her to return. But he never asked. The letters contained information about Reicholt's use of mercenaries to attack merchant caravans and estates, assassins killing heads of merchant families and Reicholt's continued search for her, to secure his power over Sorban. But Kian never mentioned wanting to see Serpé again, so she did not feel it necessary to respond to his letters. *Perhaps I am as childish as he claimed. Maybe he is right and I should not return to him.*

"Do you think the others are having any luck with finding the spiderkin?" Tamar continued to try to have a conversation with Serpé.

Serpé's group was only one of three groups sent out by Lord Draven to find the spiderkin and deal with them. "I don't know. I'm sure they will be hard to find, since Lord

Draven thinks it has to be a small band of the creatures. Shou Lung and his people are very good at keeping the larger numbers of creatures out of the forest."

"Yes, I know. I'm going to scout ahead for a while. Keep an eye out for my signal." Without waiting for Serpé to respond, Tamar spurred her horse forward.

The sounds of the forest surrounded the troop, until Drommond rode up to fill the emptiness Tamar left next to Serpé. "It be cold and damp. I am not liking this. I should be in The Ranger's Rest, drinking me ale with me friends. Not here."

"You're with friends here. All that is missing is the ale, Drommond." Serpé was not amused with Drommond's complaint. She had grown tired of it quickly. His complaints were louder this time on patrol than normal.

"And the tavern."

He's right. It is cold and I can feel the dampness soaking through my clothes. Striphen's cloak helps and the fur in my gloves and boots keeps my fingers and feet warm. But my breath is still visible when I breathe.

Silence dropped suddenly in the forest. Her ears ringing with the lack of sound, Serpé held her fist in the air and brought her troop to a stop. She searched the trees around her while drawing her estoc. From behind her, she heard weapons drawn, the sound echoing in the silence. Pointing a finger in the air and drawing a circle, she waited for the others to separate and fan out to search for the cause of the disturbance.

Where is Tamar's signal?

"Drommond..." she began when a screech tore through the forest. Large, upright spiders charged the troop. Their upper appendages ended in two-foot long, jagged claws, almost like swords.

Serpé watched two of the monsters rush the back of the troop. Two horses, not trained for combat, reared up in fright, their riders falling to the ground. Before they could get to their feet, the horses ran away.

Serpé dropped the reins for Adrastos. Confidence filled

her, as well as trust for the horse's instincts. Kian trained her on directing her horse with pressure from her legs alone. It was a skill that he tested in combat and required her to learn it. Adrastos' training and instincts in combat made him easier to trust.

She directed the large war horse away from the slashing limb of one spiderkin. Swinging her weapon behind her, firm contact with the creature's upper segment vibrated through her arm.

Directing Adrastos in another direction, Serpé saw a creature move in front of him. The large horse lifted up and caught the monster with his hooves. Uneven steps jarred Serpé's back and the crunching sound of the spiderkin being crushed reached her despite the sounds of combat around her.

Serpé turned Adrastos again. From the trees above, two more spiderkin jumped on her, their weight knocking her to the ground. Adrastos immediately trampled one, but it curled into a ball, stunned from the impact. She rolled in the other direction, to avoid the second one. Moving to one knee, her momentum took her to her feet fully. Sliding into a defensive stance, her estoc came up ready. In a smooth movement, she pulled her main-gauche as well.

Around her, Serpé heard the others fighting. Grunts of pain carried over the clash of weapons. From experience, she knew her people would defend themselves. They were trained well and she needed to focus on her own defense.

She advanced on the spiderkin that stood to face her. She brushed aside its first attack with her main-gauche, using her estoc to block the second.

Her movements felt weighted down. The dampness of the cloak on her shoulders slowed her attacks and defense.

Another creature stepped in and tried to cut her. She kept her weapons focused on defending against the first creature's attacks. Flinging her cloak back from her arms, she kicked at the second monster, pushing it back from her.

The first creature hurried in again. Cringing, she brought her weapons up to block the double attack. She pushed the creature's appendages aside with her estoc. The second spiderkin's attack came faster than she expected. She stepped back, her weight on her back foot. Turning her body, she avoided the thrust of the jagged claw. Instead it sliced through her layers of clothes and into her flesh.

Gritting her teeth, she hissed at the sudden burn in her abdomen. She disengaged her main-gauche. "Dammit!"

The creature snickered.

The increasing burn in her abdomen slowed her movements further. Despite the pain, Serpé swung her estoc down on the spiderkin's head. Pain fueling her attack, she sliced down its head and to the bottom of its upper segment.

Ichors burst from the wound, covering her hand and arm. The creature fell to the ground and she allowed the second claw to slide off her estoc. She glanced to the side, back to the first creature. With the pain worsening, she swung up and sliced the other creature a wound to match the dead one.

"By the gods, this hurts," she cried. Serpé dropped her weapons. She knew she placed her empty hands on her bleeding abdomen, but could not feel them.

It's getting worse. Is it spreading? She took a small step back from the corpses at her feet. Glancing around her, she found the combat had ended, but none of her troop lay on the ground severely wounded.

Her knees grew weak. "Drommond…" She thrust her hand out to keep herself from falling.

Her friend grabbed her hand and pulled her close. His embrace tightened around her as he guided her to the forest floor. More spiderkin ran past them. She moved to follow, but he held her back. "No, Serpé. The others will handle them. You've been poisoned."

"Are you sure?" she whispered. She tried to look at him, but she could not keep her eyes open.

Something soft and warm wrapped around her, but she remained cold. The burning in her stomach had subsided, but it still hurt. The sensations were not pleasant, but waking to them was better than not waking at all.

Serpé turned her head and saw Drommond in a chair next to the bed, his chin on his chest, fast asleep. An oil lamp, the wick low, created a soft glow over the bed and a blaze in the fireplace drove back the chill of the winter evening.

"You're awake. That's good." Tamar's voice came from the other side of the bed. Serpé turned to look at her other friend. "Drommond spent most of the day healing your wound and waiting for you to wake. You were poisoned, so it took a little longer than expected."

"The spiderkin? Did we get them?" Talking hurt. It had been awhile since Serpé had anything to drink. Tamar must have thought the same, because she helped her sit up and held a small wooden cup to her lips.

"Yes, we got them. We found a cave they'd been hiding in." Tamar smiled. "We didn't lose anyone under your command. Lord Draven is very pleased. Rest my friend. You bled quite a bit and need to regain your strength."

Serpé gave her a weak smile before she closed her eyes.

When Serpé awoke this time, the winter sun lit the room instead of a lamp. Now she recognized the room as one in The Ranger's Rest. Aldric sat in the chair Drommond had occupied, a book in his hands.

"Blessed morning, Serpé," he said, quiet. He turned a page and continued reading.

"Blessed morning, Aldric." She stretched, cautious, even though pain no longer coursed through her.

"Lord Draven wishes to see you once you've bathed and eaten." He still kept his gaze from her. "I've requested a bath for you. I will have the water brought up immediately, as well as food." He closed the book, and left to fetch the things he had promised.

Aldric was gone only a short time. When he returned, workers from the inn followed him. They carried buckets of water to fill the tub. It required two more trips before it was filled. Plates of food were placed on the table. Serpé counted six plates in all. "I can't eat all this."

Aldric shrugged. "You should be hungry. It's been long enough."

She sighed and returned to the tub.

Aldric stood by the door and waited until she had poured scented oils and bathing milk into the water. She made certain he turned away before she undressed. After stepping into the tub, the warm water covered and she sighed in relief. A glance from Aldric revealed concern she had not expected.

The warmth of the liquid soothed her still sore muscles and as the fragrance of the oils tickled her senses, she relaxed. Aldric must have decided it was time to move because she heard the sound of a chair scrape on the floor.

"Aldric, you don't have to stay." She kept her eyes closed, afraid to see how close he was now to the tub. "Please just leave. I don't need you here."

"Tamar and Jalena want someone with you." He turned a page of his book again.

She sighed again and slipped deeper into the water. "Please, just go. I really can handle this by myself."

He must have agreed because she heard the chair scrape the floor again. "I'll send Tamar up to check on you. Don't forget to see Lord Draven as soon as you are ready."

She waited until the door closed, then dunked herself into the water completely.

One change of the water clock later, Serpé stood in the courtyard of the fort. Striphen had just left her after making her promise to meet him for evening meal. Her cheek still felt warm from his kiss and she saw him wave at her from his position on the fort walls.

Nervous, Serpé felt a lump in her throat that was painful to swallow against. *Several people have mentioned Draven's happiness with the success of my patrol, but I was injured. I didn't see the completion of our mission with my own eyes. He should not be happy.*

The steward stopped Serpé before she walked too far into the fort. "Lord Draven is in the council chamber, with First Captain Silver."

She nodded. "Thank you."

The door to the council chamber stood open and she could see Draven near a large table with a map spread out on the surface. Another man stood near him, nodding at the lord's softly spoken words. Draven looked up when she entered, his handsome features brightening. He rushed to embrace her. First Captain Silver stayed in place, though he smiled at her as well.

"It's good to see you, Serpé. I was beginning to worry." That news surprised her and he smiled. "Do you think I'm unhappy with you?"

"Yes, milord. I did not see the completion of our mission," she mumbled.

"You're too hard on yourself, my dear. Your expectations are very high. You received an unexpected injury. Your people took care of the remaining Spiderkin and kept their injured safe. They found the nest and destroyed it. I would call that a success, wouldn't you, Captain Silver?" Draven asked, glancing at his captain.

He nodded in agreement. "Yes, milord, I would call that a success."

"Good. Now that that's solved, I must ask you to excuse us, Captain Silver. I have something to discuss with Serpé." The lord's previous good nature disappeared. Captain Silver nodded again and left the room without question.

Draven waited until the door closed, then pulled a folded parchment from a hidden pocket. "This came today from Kian."

Serpé took the parchment from him, surprised to see her hand shake. *Why would a letter from Kian make me so nervous? I haven't responded to any of his messages, so he's obviously found others that will answer for me.*

"What does it say?" she whispered. The parchment remained unopened and she watched him step closer to hear her.

He retrieved the letter from her clenched hand and opened it. "Kian continues to gather men to his cause. He and his army attempt to capture the mercenaries attacking the merchant caravans and the assassins who are killing the merchants. They have also had skirmishes with The First's patrols. It seems the People's Army is decreasing in number while the Religious Guard grows bigger. Those who do not go to Reicholt either join Kian or disappear."

"What does he want me to do?" Her voice caught in her throat. *Kian wants me to run again. I am being forced to leave my home once more.*

"He wants you to stay away from Sorban and him until he sends for you. He wants you to go to the church of Azar in Sanctuary and meet with Most Blessed Tossin." Draven indicated the map on the table behind her. "Tossin will take whatever information you have to give him and keep it for future use."

Relief washed over her. *I don't have to run.*

She turned to examine the map. "May I ask for some of my command, my friends, to accompany me?"

"Of course. Whomever you feel comfortable with and trust."

"Then we will leave in the morning."

Chapter 19

Though there were preparations she needed to take care of, Serpé decided to keep her date with Striphen. She did not know how long she would be away, so she wanted to make sure certain things were settled between them.

Jalena had given Striphen one of the private rooms she kept for intimate meetings and when Serpé arrived, she indicated which one with a smirk. Serpé stopped at the door, her mouth open. Was it the heat from all the candles in the room or the embarrassment that filled her? The glow lit the food on the table and gave Striphen's face a shadowy quality.

He stepped forward and brought out two flowers. With a sad smile, she accepted the simple gift. *What I have to say is going to hurt him. But if I don't say it now, I may never say it.*

"Thank you, Striphen," she croaked through a tight throat. "You really shouldn't have."

"I wanted to." She allowed him to guide her to a chair, and then waited as he lit lanterns on the walls.

Striphen watched her while they ate, his gaze making her uncomfortable when she looked up. *Does he know? I've always been comfortable with him, but I think it was more because he offered friendship and never really asked more from me than I was willing to give.*

They both reached for the bottle of wine, their fingers

brushing. "Sorry," she whispered, though he smiled.

"It's fine." He took the bottle from her hand. "I'll pour."

His eyes hold too much love for me. In my heart, I know I can never return it to him in full. Especially now.

"Something bothering you, Serpé?" She cringed at the concern in his voice, too aware that it could quickly become hate.

"I am thinking about the morrow."

She watched him fill her glass. His words came out measured and slow. "What happens then?"

"I leave for Sanctuary. I received the message today." She brought her gaze up to meet his again. His handsome face relaxed, despite his obvious concern for her.

"Did he order you to go?" A hint of anger tinged his voice, but disappointment could also be heard.

She winced. The last time she had heard that mixture in someone's voice, Reicholt had tried to choke her. She swallowed hard, past the remembered pain in her throat.

"He?" She knew the hoarse sound of her voice removed the innocence she tried to express.

Striphen dropped his knife on the plate, the noise loud in the now silent room. Though she never thought he would hurt her, she fought the urge to draw her weapon.

He doesn't know of my past and the emotions his movements evokes in me.

"*He*—the one who sent you here. The one who distracts you when we're together. Every time *he* comes up in our conversation, you act like you don't know who I'm talking about."

She filled her lungs with a long, slow breath to calm herself. "I'm sorry, Striphen. I don't mean to be secretive. Yes, he is sending me there, to help with his task."

"Will you ever feel safe enough to tell me everything, Serpé?"

"I don't know. Maybe, when I can be sure the wrong person isn't overhearing everything I say." She watched, her pain increasing with his.

"I wish..." He stopped, searching for words to express

himself. After a deep sigh, he continued, "I wish we had met in a different lifetime, one where you weren't hiding to protect yourself and I had met you before this man who holds your heart. Just tell me what you came to tell me, so we can move on with our—friendship."

"That's it. I can't, with a clear mind, be anything more than your friend. Not anymore. It isn't fair that I can't focus on you. I need to concentrate on me and my feelings, until I am sure of myself. Only then can I commit to anyone." She laughed at herself. "I sound so selfish."

"You have that right." His hand felt warm when it covered hers. "There will always be a place for you in my life, as a friend or a lover."

She accepted his embrace without guilt, glad he could set her free so easily. She knew it was not easy for him, but he had not fought it. *Striphen really is a good man who deserves a happiness that I know I cannot give him.*

They separated after eating the last fruit tart, but she did not leave the tavern. Tamar, Aldric and Drommond waved her over before she reached the door and she realized when she sat down with them that their friendship and acceptance was what she needed right now.

"Striphen left without you. Aren't you going to his home tonight?" Aldric never wasted time on niceties and Serpé grimaced at his bluntness.

"They are no longer a couple, Aldric. Can't you see that?" Tamar answered for Serpé, the glare she turned on Aldric worse than anything Serpé could have leveled at him.

"It doesn't matter to me. I just made an observation." He sipped the tea he always drank, his face expressionless.

"As always, my friend, you are very perceptive," Serpé said, holding up her hand to prevent Tamar from saying anything else. "Later. Right now, I have something to ask all of you. I have to travel to Sanctuary. Would you like to come with me?"

She watched their faces brighten with excitement, although Aldric's reaction was slower than the others. She laughed at their quick nods of agreement.

"We leave in the morning. Lord Draven has seen to all our supplies." Their questions came quickly, but she shook her head and stood. "I will see you in the morning. I can try to answer all your questions on the way. I'm sure we will have time."

They nodded, turning back to each other to continue their conversation as she walked away.

At mid-morning, several hours later than Serpé had wanted to leave, she and her group of friends left Valen. It made her happy that her companions had not slept much the night before, because they traveled in near silence. The first night promised to be a quiet one as well.

As expected, the others retired early, and Serpé appreciated the time alone to think. They still traveled in The Dragon's Forest and the elves that helped Shou-Lung protect it had been seen while they traveled, so she felt safe enough to forgo watches.

She watched her friends fall asleep, grateful to have each one of them with her. Tamar's love of the forest and the people who lived here filled her. Because of her friend, Serpé had developed a new love for nature.

"Serpé?" Tamar's voice broke into her thoughts and she forced her hands to relax. "Are you all right?"

"Yes. I was thinking how our friendship has changed me." Serpé had forgotten elves did not truly sleep, instead going only into a meditative trance. She waited while Tamar rose and walked over to her. She wrapped a blanket around both their shoulders. "It is a good thing. I'm glad I met you."

"I am too." Tamar gestured at Drommond and Aldric's sleeping forms. "They are good people as well, Serpé. They are happy they met you too."

"I don't understand why. I haven't done anything to endear myself to them. Aldric has an almost perfect life and Drommond leads refugee dwarves of his clan. It isn't like they can't live without my friendship, Tamar."

"They probably could, but they don't want to. Drommond's mountain home was poisonous, causing the death of so many of his people. There are many who will not accept him as a friend for fear of catching a disease. Do you worry about that? That's why he likes you and calls you 'friend'. Because you don't." Tamar threw a gesture in Aldric's direction. "No one really understands why Aldric does what he does. But he stays with your patrol, came with you willingly, so he must like you."

"When we reach Azar's temple in Sanctuary, I will tell you all why we are making this journey. You deserve that. I shouldn't have waited this long," Serpé said with a sigh. *I am not proud of keeping a secret from them, but Kian taught me to be careful of whom I trust with the truth.*

"I think we can wait until then. I hope it's an entertaining secret, for us to have waited this long," Tamar laughed, stood and pulled Serpé up as well. "Now, go, get some sleep. We're protected for at least tonight."

Serpé allowed Tamar to pull her to her bedding and lay down, grateful when sleep came over her.

Chapter 20

Most Holy Eion Reicholt relaxed in the soft cushion of his chair. He surveyed the merchants in the council chamber. While they yelled at each other, a smile filled his face. His plans were progressing nicely.

Following his orders, the mercenaries and assassins had succeeded in killing five of the men who led the merchant families. He easily manipulated their successors with their eagerness to please him. The First, humble in his offer, helped each with their transition. He relished the feel of his grip tightening on the council.

This is intoxicating. He filled his lungs with air. *It tastes better than the best brandy I have waiting for me on the estate.*

The First waited until the arguing decreased before standing. The divine aura he invoked pulled everyone's attention to him. His father had once thought he should become an acting bard with a traveling troupe, and though he had a love for the dramatic, he felt a pull to the church and Azar at a young age. It was unfortunate the deity had lost appeal when he discovered how influential he could be in the decisions of the council and how much merchants were willing to 'donate' to him for his blessings.

"Please forgive the interruption. However, the information I wish to present is somewhat important." The few voices that had continued despite his aura quieted now. "Through reliable sources, I have learned our neighboring kingdom, Tushin, is preparing to move against us."

"How can you be sure? They have always been a peaceful people. Why would they attack us now, unprovoked?" As The First had expected, Anthoine Navran was the first to voice his disbelief and incite others to agree.

The First found himself slow to control his glare toward Anthoine. *It's appropriate that Serpé's father is the first to stand against my announcement.* He fought to keep his displeasure from the man. *Serpé may cause me difficulties I still struggle to master, but her father will fall victim to the assassin's dagger. One less obstacle between me, Serpé, and the throne.*

"Anthoine, those are excellent questions. However, my very reliable source informs me that all the attacks we've experienced are only a prelude to an impending war." The First changed his tone and posture. He knew he must give the impression of comfort and concern, but Anthoine's argument made it difficult. "We must put aside our differences and protect our kingdom."

"How would you propose we do that, Most Holy?"

Anthoine's voice, laced with anger and disgust, forced Eion to take another calming breath to keep from reacting. "We have two separate military groups. If we were to combine them into one force and direct their efforts to finding the assassins while we protect our borders, we should be able to prevent any further loss of life." He saw the merchants reacting to his words and was pleased to see those he controlled supporting him to those around them.

"And just who will you find to lead this new military force?" Though The First heard Anthoine's hesitation, it amused him that the man presumed to speak for the entire council. Usually that privilege fell to Tolan

"Whomever the council appoints and Azar blesses," Eion intoned, spreading his hands and arms to encompass the entire council while lifting his face toward the heavens.

"Give the People's Army to the Religious Guard," one of the newer council members shouted from his seat. "We are losing men to them anyway. Why don't we join both under one standard?"

Eion brought his hands down and covered his mouth to give the impression of deep thought. *Most of the council is coming to see things my way, though I do recognize the ones who still resist. Anthoine and Tolan, especially.* He watched the arguing increase in fervor and fought the urge to laugh aloud. Instead, he sipped at the wine his page had brought for him.

Anthoine spoke the loudest and strongest against combining the military forces, while Tolan remained silent and observant. Like Serpé's attempts and continued efforts to stay away from Eion, her father remained determined to keep the control of the military from him. The First watched through narrowed eyes. *I am curious, has the daughter been in contact with the father? It isn't possible. Anthoine and Eisa have been under constant watch ever since I learned Serpé still lived. The only thing I've seen was his curious inspection of his... Of course! The signet rings! He knows!*

Controlling himself, Eion held his arms out again to quiet the council. "The point has been made that men are leaving the People's Guard and joining the Religious Guard. It has also been suggested the two forces be combined, to which I strongly agree. I think it will be more beneficial to have them under one central command."

"We've only had one commander who proved himself strong enough to lead that type of military force. Kian Donwell has the experience and the allies to put together a force that strong and formidable." Eion's spine tensed at Anthoine's mention of Kian and his allies.

Those allies can be used against me in a war and to keep Serpé in hiding.

"Kian Donwell is leading an army of misfits and outlaws in a futile rebellion against this council. He is responsible for the kidnapping of your own daughter, Anthoine, and for the lie that she died four years ago." He waited for his deception to sink in before he continued. "Unless anyone objects, I feel only someone in a pure connection with the church should lead this combined force."

"And who do you think *that* should be?"

Eion struggled to keep from smiling at the forced tone to Anthoine's voice. "Captain Marcin is quite capable of leading such a force. He leads the Religious Guard exceptionally well. I'm sure he can lead any combined army with honor and pride." He wanted to shout in triumph, but forced himself to remain calm. *I have not yet won.*

Anthoine took a step back, almost falling down the stairs of the stadium setting of the council room. Eion held his breath, a brief spark of hope that Serpé's father would end himself and save his hired killers the trouble warming his chest. When Anthoine righted himself, the priest let his breath out in exasperation.

"That would ultimately put you in control," Anthoine's statement, though whispered, echoed throughout the chamber.

"Why, yes, it would. But who better than our kingdom's religious leader to protect the people in this time of fear and instability?" The First had practiced his response to this type of revelation. He was confident they believed him— except for Anthoine, and possibly Tolan.

He returned Anthoine's gaze, maintaining it for several heartbeats. Anthoine turned away first and proceeded down the main stairs to the floor.

"I cannot abide by any decision to give The First so much power. If we follow this path, we will destroy ourselves." Defeat echoed in Anthoine's voice and his shoulders rounded forward as he led his guards from the room.

Eion watched Merchant Tolan until the doors closed behind Anthoine. Tolan turned to address the other merchants, resistance obvious in his posture. *He must know that if he doesn't address the issues presented here, he will lose control of the council.*

"Those who want to give temporary command of the People's Army to Captain Marcin, thereby combining the two forces, raise your hand."

Eion sat silent, watching while the vote of the remaining

council members was counted. He took care to note each person that opposed him. He would handle them later. Tolan did not vote, as usual, but presented the results to The First, per a strict protocol he refused to stray from.

Tolan cleared his voice. "The council has voted to combine the two Guards and place them under Captain Marcin's command, temporarily. We expect his first task to be an end to the attacks upon the merchant families."

He listened to Tolan's demands while he imagined the man being tortured in the dungeon. *Though Tolan's death would cripple the council and his family, I am not ready to take that step yet.*

"But of course, milord. I wish for nothing but the safety of our people." Eion smiled in an attempt to smooth over his patronization of the merchant.

Tolan stared at him. He thought the merchant would change his mind, until finally Tolan nodded and ended the meeting.

Eion watched until the room emptied except for himself and the newly arrived Captain Marcin. He felt his grin stretch the muscles of his face until it became even bigger. When his upper lip tore and began to bleed, he still did not stop grinning. He wiped at the blood on his lip and swallowed the metallic tasking tasting fluid.

"My plan is coming together quite nicely, Captain. Now if only you could remedy your error and return Serpé to my bosom. That would bring about my ultimate victory." Eion laughed.

"I am working on it, Most Holy Reicholt." The sour tone to the captain's voice made Eion pause, but he did not allow it to ruin his elation.

Chapter 21

"Captain Donwell."

Glancing up from the map in front of him, Kian watched a man step into his tent without waiting for an invitation. Though he had insisted on using the large tent for his meetings with the army commanders, he still preferred when those who entered showed respect for the fact it was the place he slept.

"Well, speak, man. You are interrupting a meeting." Kian saw that his impatient order shocked the man, and he had to wait for the messenger to organize his thoughts.

"This message is for you." A scroll tube appeared in the man's hand and Kian accepted it with a nod.

Kian looked at the map again before examining the tube. *Too many more interruptions and I'll have to continue this meeting tomorrow. Another day without accomplishing anything.*

The scroll case did not carry an obvious seal, but the color of the tube revealed the sender and Kian stuttered as he tried to continue his instructions to the gathered men. He saw Blackette glance at him, concern and embarrassment tinting his face.

"Excuse me, gentlemen. I need to read this…alone." Without waiting for their response, he turned and drew the rolled parchment from the tube.

Somewhere in his mind, he heard his men leave. He also heard the questions they asked the messenger who followed them outside, but the letter held his complete attention. The color of the container had been agreed upon with Jalena years ago and her impressive and artistic letters flowed over the parchment.

I wish these were Serpé's words, her letters.

His breath escaped him in a rush and he reached out to steady himself with the help of the table.

Thoughts of her should not affect me like this. I should not feel weak when I think of her.

He took a deep breath and read his friend's letter.

Jalena again mentioned Draven's support of Kian's war against Reicholt and his offer to send men to assist. Kian had decided not to call upon those resources unless necessary. He did not want to put any of his friends' people in harm's way to free a kingdom that wasn't theirs.

He had skipped over her words about Serpé, but when nothing else remained but news of her, he forced himself to read on. Jalena and Draven were the only communication he had with the young woman who had become so important to him.

Why is she avoiding my messages? Is it because I never told her how important she is to me? Or is it because I sent her away?

At one point, he had even asked Jalena if Serpé had received his letters. Her confirmation did nothing to improve his disappointment when Serpé still sent nothing back to him.

I will not let her silence keep me from sending her letters. I want her to know I still think about her. That I haven't given up.

He stopped reading the letter, then re-read the section he had just finished. Jalena's casual mention of an injury Serpé received drew his attention again.

Draven is supposed to protect her. How could he allow her to be injured by spiderkin?

But Kian trained her to defend herself and others. Why should she not use that training to do what felt right?

At least she was only injured. It could have been worse. She could have...

He forced himself to not complete that thought. Giving

voice to what could have been worse drew his stomach into knots.

I can't think of that. How could everything change so quickly? She flourished away from me and came into her own. I must have restricted her too much while she stayed with me. Was I blind to it? I have no excuse to not treat her as an equal.

A heavy sigh shook his body. No matter how he tried to rationalize it, nothing he could do would change Serpé's anger at him. Instead of lingering on the thoughts, he slipped the letter back into the tube and tossed it onto his blankets. He walked to the tent flap and gestured for the men to return to their discussions.

Two days and I still don't feel any better. I'm distracted—I can't concentrate. This is unacceptable—it is going to cause a problem if we are attacked. I need to get my head back where it belongs.

Kian caressed the scroll tube he received from Jalena before placing it into his backpack. His thoughts had remained focused on Jalena's words and, though he knew it was not what Jalena had wanted, he had to admit to himself the affects of her letter.

Maybe I will see Serpé when we travel to Azar's temple in Sanctuary. Then I can tell her...tell her what? Tell her how I feel? So she can reject me because I rejected her first? I know I deserve it, but I don't know that I'm ready for it.

Finally he left his tent, pushing away thoughts of Serpé. Other things needed his attention, but he knew she would linger, his every action against Reicholt affecting her.

Blackette met him outside the tent, the reins of their horses in his hand. "Kian, we're ready. The patrol is about two changes away. If we leave now, we'll get there before dark."

He nodded and accepted the reins of his mount.

Before the end of this day, I will know what caused the mercenaries to attack a merchant caravan within the boundaries of the kingdom, even though it is well known that Sorban will hang any mercenary caught attacking caravans.

Two hours later, Kian and Blackette rode into an

improvised camp. Mercenaries sat a distance away from a group of the Religious Guard. He had not expected the Religious Guard and his hand crept to the hilt of his sword. None of the caravan remained.

The leader of the patrol approached Kian, his back to the captives. Kian leaned forward to hear the man's low voice.

"The mercenaries claim to be hired by someone in Siladan who knows the routes and dates of caravans and has given them specific instructions about which caravans to attack. According to the Religious Guard, they received information about where the mercenaries would attack and when. They were ordered to capture them."

"Thank you, Olian," Kian said, then dismounted. Covering the distance to the mercenaries with an easy stride, he knelt when he reached them, hoping to give them the impression he saw them as equals. "My associate's told me why you are here. Is there anything you want to add?"

"We're not talking to you or anyone else," the man closest to him said and spat on the ground.

"Unfortunate." Kian stood and turned in one smooth motion, just as Blackette approached him. The grim set of his soldier's jaw made the muscles of Kian's shoulders and neck tighten. "Maybe the Religious Guard has something to add." Without stepping away, he waited for Blackette to walk closer.

"According to the Religious Guard, they had very clear instructions. They were to find this particular group of mercenaries, specifically after they had attacked the merchant caravan. Then they were to kill them. They were to allow the attack, not prevent it. More important, the Guard captain states that they were told the group had served their purpose and should be eliminated." Watching the mercenaries, Kian let Blackette speak freely. The men glanced at each other while listening to Blackette's words.

The one who had spoken before cleared his throat. "I was released from prison along with two others. We were given gold and instructions to hire anyone we needed to complete our assignments. We went our separate ways and have received instructions every few days by messenger. Other groups have been captured and I've seen their heads on pikes outside the capital, lining the road to the main gate."

"Do you know who is sending you orders?"

For a moment, the man stared at the Religious Guard, his eyes narrowing. Then he gestured for Kian to move closer. The man's breath stank of stale ale and pickled eggs and Kian forced himself not to retreat from the stench.

Being this close to a man who collects money to hurt others is not my idea of enjoyment. But, if his information isn't worth his life, I'll be close enough to kill him.

"Most Holy Eion Reicholt," the man whispered.

Without thinking, Kian straightened, his breath caught in his throat. This was a new depth of evil for the priest. He never questioned how far Reicholt would go to manipulate others, especially after learning about Serpé's family. But he had always lived with the illusion that the priest had some level of honor. Learning he was wrong should not have surprised him.

"What else has he ordered you to do?" Kian struggled to keep the disgust from his voice.

"My group deals with a specific list of targets, caravans. Each message changes or adds to the list. The assassin takes care of the killing." With his chin, the mercenary gestured at a leather pouch attached to his belt. "My list is in the pouch."

Blackette stepped forward and retrieved a folded parchment from the pouch. Accepting it with a nod, Kian turned back to Olian and the others from the patrol that stood behind him.

"Release them." For the last time, Kian looked at the mercenaries. "Leave Sorban. The guards won't lie about killing you, even if it means they will be punished. Next time I see you, though, I will kill you."

Kian's stomach clenched, made worse by the words on the parchment he still held. Not only did Reicholt attack his own people, but he singled them out for murder.

My informant continues to be accurate. So why does it make me sick to know this is happening? This shouldn't surprise me.

When the mercenaries disappeared, Kian made his way toward the Religious Guard, Blackette trailing close behind him. He studied each man, determined to burn their faces into his memory. Finally he gestured for his own men to step forward.

"We will set you free. But you will have no supplies, no horses, only water. We will escort you from our camp, and then set you free. You can inform Reicholt I now know his game, and I will deliver my own form of justice to him and any member of the Religious Guard I see—as I deem deserving."

Ignoring their protests, Olian and his patrol blindfolded the prisoners and led them away. When the patrol returned, Kian led his group back to the main force and into the forest. He would leave for Azar's temple in two days, just as he had requested of Serpé. The army would wait in the forest while he and a small group of men went to Sanctuary.

It was time to bring all the evidence of Reicholt's treachery together in one place.

Chapter 22

Strinnal sat at the table, pushed his food around his plate and occasionally brought a bite to his lips, very little making it down his throat. He found it hard to maintain the illusion that he still served The First without question, but the less the priest suspected, the better it worked for him and those he helped.

He watched The First and listened to his description of the adoration he received earlier in the day walking through the town. The captain kept silent throughout the entire conversation, only answering direct questions.

As The First's food disappeared, Strinnal breathed in relief. His duties would soon be over for the day and he could leave. The sudden appearance of two men in the archway followed by four guards, brought an overwhelming feeling of disappointment and he pushed the plate away with a loud sigh.

The two men covered in dirt from the road looked like they had not eaten in days. They eyed the remaining food on the table. Without asking The First, Strinnal threw a roll to each of them and waved the guards back. One of the men bowed to The First and saluted Strinnal before tearing into the bread.

Strinnal waited long enough for the two men to eat the bread clearing his throat. "Explain your intrusion or the guards will escort you from our presence. Even members of the Religious Guard are not allowed to intrude upon The First like this."

"My apologies, Captain Marcin. My patrol was captured in the process of taking a group of mercenaries into custody. The mercenaries were taken from us by the rebel army that we've been hearing about," the guard who had saluted told them.

Strinnal watched The First chew slowly and swallow before asking, "Who is leading the rebels?"

The soldier paused a moment before answering, "The man leading them is Kian Donwell, Most Holy."

Strinnal scoffed at the man's dramatic display. "Of course. Kian was also the one hiding Serpé Navran, if you'll remember, Most Holy."

"Yes, I remember, Captain." The First placed his knife next to his plate and sat in silence.

Strinnal forced himself to remain still while he returned his leader's intense gaze.

"Find him, Captain," The First growled. "I want him dead. One thousand gold coins to the man who brings me his head."

Strinnal nodded, gesturing for the guards to take the two men away and stood. After thanking The First for the meal and bending in a bow of feigned respect, he left to fulfill his orders.

Outside the estate, Strinnal slowed his steps. Spreading word of the bounty on Kian was not something he wanted to do and he knew there would be no protecting the other man if he were arrested.

Things become more difficult with each day and it's only a matter of time before I am discovered.

"If your deception is becoming too difficult, perhaps you should rethink which side you show your allegiance to."

The unexpected voice surprised Strinnal and he turned to see who had spoken, his hand upon his sword.

"Bennan, in front of The First's home is not the most appropriate place for us to meet. In the future, you must wait until I return to my home or let me find you." Strinnal turned away, heading toward his home again, not caring if Bennan followed him or not.

The sound of footsteps behind him told him Bennan followed and he slowed his progress until Bennan drew even with him. They walked in silence until they reached Strinnal's home.

After ensuring they were not followed, Strinnal beckoned Bennan into his home. The bigger man followed him into the common room.

"I don't have long. The First will expect the announcement made tonight." Strinnal offered Bennan a glass of wine, shrugging when he declined. Though he didn't really want the wine either, Strinnal drank deep and quick before putting the top back in the decanter.

"What announcement?" He appreciated that Bennan waited for him to take a deep breath, but he had no reason to stall any longer.

"Reicholt has placed a bounty on Kian. One thousand gold coins, dead or alive." Strinnal watched Bennan sit in a nearby chair.

"To be expected. I'm surprised it took this long."

"After I tell the Guard, they will begin the search. They will try harder to find him now." Strinnal shook his head, words failing him.

"What brought this on?" The calm cadence of Bennan's voice surprised him.

"An attack upon the Religious Guard, or at least what is perceived as an attack. And keeping Serpé from Reicholt for years." Strinnal spun to face the larger man. "Does it really matter? Kian needs to be warned."

"No, you're right. Kian will receive your warning and we will all take precautions."

Relief washed over Strinnal. "Good."

Bennan stood. "Be careful as well. We don't need Reicholt suspecting you."

Chapter 23

The travel to Azar's temple in Sanctuary turned miserable shortly after leaving the Dragon's Forest. Serpé grumbled every time rain dripped on her head or Adrastos kicked up mud that hit her. They traveled to a warmer climate and though winter still hung in the air, the warmth had caused issues. Rain instead of snow made it hard to stay dry. Clean clothes were not an option anymore. She had stopped changing them after the third day. She could not even get the ones she washed in the river dry. They could not stay in the travel inns long enough to dry them or wait out the rain.

They traveled for almost a month before Serpé awoke to a dry morning. She changed into clean clothes and actually felt good about the decision. The change in weather seemed a good omen and she hoped they would reach their destination soon.

At high sun, a town appeared in the plains they traveled through. Instead of stopping to eat, they continued, arriving in Sanctuary by mid-afternoon. Temples for the gods glittered in the sun outside the edge of the town, each reflecting the individual deity's sphere of influence in color and design.

The people of the town waved when Serpé and her friends passed them. She returned their greetings, but did not ask for directions. Instead she rode toward a temple at the other end of town with white marble towers and spires.

The sun reflected off the marble walls of the large building. She marveled at the roofs of the towers, but it was the main part of the church that held her eye. When they turned onto the street in front of the building, Serpé saw the two wings extending from each side of the main church, their blue tile roofs reflecting the bright sunlight.

Tamar nudged her and pointed out two men in the robes of the priesthood tending to rose bushes near the main entrance to the church courtyard. As the group of friends rode closer, the priests stopped their work and stood, their faces bright with smiles.

"Welcome, travelers. We are pleased Azar's light has seen your journey safe to our humble temple," the priest closest to Serpé greeted them.

Serpé glanced up at the spires of the church, shaking her head. *Humble? I would be interested in seeing what they call extravagant.* "I have been asked to see Most Blessed Tossin. I hope he is expecting me."

The priest who spoke nodded. "Yes, Dame Navran, he is. Please follow me."

He led the group into the temple and stopped at the antechamber. "Please wait here, Dame Navran. I will escort your companions to their rooms. I will return in a moment."

Serpé watched the others leave, her confidence going with them. *What am I supposed to tell Tossin? Am I expected to tell him about The First? Is he going to believe me?*

A wave of dizziness washed over her. She lifted her hand to support herself, her palm resting on the cool wood of the wall. *I refuse to respomd to Kian's letters, but all I have thought about was being with him. I wanted to be included in what he was doing. Now he includes me and I feel like I'm going to let him down.*

"Dame Navran, will you please come with me? Most Blessed Tossin has requested you meet him in the rose garden." Serpé had missed the priest's return. "Are you well? You look pale."

She nodded.

He gazed at her, then turned away without further comment.

Serpé followed him through a service passage and into the garden of the temple. The scent of roses washed over her. She knew statues and fountains were intermingled, but she did not see them or the beauty of the garden. Impatience filled her.

"Are you enjoying the roses, Dame Navran?"

She turned toward the voice and smiled. "I'm sure they are beautiful."

"I am Most Blessed Tossin." The priest bowed to her, his smile brightening his aged features. His white hair moved in the breeze. Pale blue eyes, wide with excitement, were pronounced by white eyelashes and eyebrows. He wore the deep blue robes of the church, a silver scarf draped over his shoulders, to indicate his station.

"I am pleased to meet you, Most Blessed Tossin." Serpé bowed in return.

"You should allow the beauty of the garden to relax you. Azar's blessings can be felt everywhere. While you are with us, please visit here as much as you would like." He held his hand out for her. "For now, come with me. First High Mage Termage is waiting for us." She placed her hand in his and let him lead her into the temple.

Lanterns and torches lit the stone halls of the church. Brightly painted pictures depicting Azar's deeds hung from the walls, drawing her attention. Recreations of the paintings had hung in the church in Siladan, but did not compare to the originals.

One painting in particular held her attention until Most Blessed Tossin finally pulled her away. The scene showed Azar as he harnessed the wild magic of the stars and tied it to the world. Another portion of the painting showed the god placing two strands of magic into a man. One strand was blue, the other silver.

Serpé's teachers had taught her that blue represented priestly magic and silver wizardly magic. Only priests of Azar were granted the ability to control both types of magic, though many priests refused to use the wizardly type.

"You can study the paintings while you are here, Serpé. Please, First High Mage Termage becomes very nervous when kept waiting." Tossin pulled her with him to his office.

When the door opened, she stopped, and then stepped inside. Another man, the same age as Tossin, scurried around the room, either nervous or agitated. Tossin smiled at her. "I told you."

The nervous man stopped and turned to face them. "Oh! Excuse me. I was just..." He waved his hand at the room, unable to explain his activity.

"Yes, First High Mage Termage, I know. You found something of interest and you were trying to find more information on it." Tossin laughed at the mage. "Termage, this is Serpé Navran, the one we were told to expect. It would be most helpful if you would record everything she says into this book." He indicated a thick, hide bound book on his desk.

"Oh yes, gladly," Termage said with excitement. He directed Serpé to sit in the chair in front of the desk.

From within his robe, the mage pulled out a quill and a small vial of ink. He set the ink on the desk next to the book, then opened book. He held the quill over the first page and whispered the words of a spell. When he finished, the quill hung over the book by itself.

"It will now write every word spoken in this room." As he spoke, the quill dipped its tip into ink and transcribed his words. Termage watched until the writing ceased. When he opened his mouth again to speak, Tossin rushed forward and clamped a hand over it.

"Please, Serpé," Tossin whispered, "start at the beginning. Leave nothing out. We have plenty of parchment." He pushed Termage into one chair and seated himself across from her.

Start at the beginning? The priest wants the beginning, but of what? Does he know how Sorban politics work? The family structure? She remained silent while she decided exactly where to start.

"Women of Sorban, at least those of the merchant class, own and run the family businesses. When the men marry into a family, they take on their wife's name. They run the family, rule the council, but only the women can make the major decisions. Without their wife's consent, the men are powerless." She looked away from the quill, concerned the older men would be insulted with the matriarchal society of her kingdom. Tossin smiled at her, nodding in approval. "This system was created by the first king in the Navrinar family in an attempt to prevent corruption within the ranks of our merchants. He believed women were less corruptible, so he felt if he put control of the money into the hands of the women, there was less chance of it being used against him and anyone else in our kingdom." She shrugged. It was not a flawless plan, but who was she to question the dead king's ideas?

"I am the only child of my parents. My family is the second in line to rule the first merchant house. We lived in Parnoir, second home to the largest number of merchants in Sorban. Many merchants and their families live in Parnoir and travel to Siladan for council meetings or other business. Very few live in the smaller towns. A marriage arrangement was proposed to my parents that did not please them. They contacted the church of Azar and within a week, I was taken to the church and began my studies. I learned later that my father had created a story about my death. I have not seen them since. I was eight winters." Pain clutched her chest when she realized how much she missed her parents.

She turned the signet ring on her finger. The scratching of the quill stopped when she paused. A moment more passed before she continued. "Eion Reicholt was my mentor and guardian. When I first met him, he was within the upper ranks of priests for the temple. I was his best student, or at least that was what he told me. He pushed my studies in the priesthood and, within a short time, I rose to an acolyte. I then became his private student and only teachers who met with his approval were allowed to further my learning. During my education, he progressed through the ranks of the church, until he was one of the top three priests for the kingdom."

Her stomach clenched at the memories flooding her mind. "About three years after I arrived, he received a promotion that took him to Siladan. He took me with him. Within a year, shortly after the death of his predecessor, Most Holy Korewyn, he became The First.

"In the beginning, everything appeared fine. He lived within the limits of the money given by the church. But when he moved to Siladan, he demanded more expensive things—fine silks, exotic foods, expensive furniture. With his promotion, we moved into an extravagant estate, larger than even the richest merchant owned. He bought me the best riding horse and I received lessons from the most expensive instructor." She paused, embarrassed she had accepted the inappropriate items without question, but continued before the quill could stop. "Then I collected tributes for him. Small amounts of gold every day, under the guise of donations for the church. I always took the money to him first and the next day, I would take it to the church. If I didn't receive the money he expected, he sent out the Religious Guard. The people never refused twice. Those who tried disappeared.

"One day, I was attacked by bandits. When they were caught, he had them hanged." Her eyes stung, tears welling up. "I found out later that they weren't bandits, but poor men who were desperate to feed and keep their families together because of taxes they owed. Reicholt told me he hanged the men to make it clear who controlled Sorban." She stopped again, wiping the tears from her cheeks. The quill stopped as well.

"So I kept a record of the donations from then on, marking who and how much I collected. Each tribute I received was always more than what the church received the next day. I couldn't make the collections anymore when I learned that the people who did not give the money were arrested for petty crimes. The men were imprisoned or hanged, and the women and children just—disappeared. Later, I found out that they were either placed into slavery or forced into prostitution." Embarrassment turned into anger.

"In council meetings, where Reicholt was supposed to sit as an advisor with minimal influence, he gathered more control and power. The merchants allowed him a louder voice in all decisions. And, in all conflicts he resided over as judge, every decision fell in favor of the individual who sent a tribute the previous day. If both people had sent a tribute, he always judged in favor of the one who had sent the most gold." Serpé struggled to control her anger. "Now, he works to increase his power within the council so that on the day he announces Azar's desire for him to rule Sorban, he will have a great number of votes supporting him.

"The ruling women do not attend the meetings and rely too much on what their men tell them. When it comes time for someone to prevent his progression, the facts will be so diluted, none of the women will know the truth. No one on the council knows how the church works. They rely on Reicholt's teachings, so they do not realize Azar would never desire one of his highest ranking priests to rule a kingdom." She stopped and drank deeply from a cup of water. The quill stopped after a moment.

"Is there anything else, Serpé?" She shook her head. "If there is anything else, please let us know. In the meantime, Termage and I will spend time going over what you have given us. Please feel free to roam the church grounds as you wish." Tossin stood, moved around his desk and kissed her forehead.

Serpé stood and left the room, but before she closed the door, she saw the men bend over to read the book. Stopping one of the acolytes walking through the halls, she asked for directions to the library. She planned to spend the rest of the day buried in the texts it contained.

When she arrived, Serpé found another acolyte behind a desk, reading a book. "Excuse me, do you have any books on Sorban's history?"

He nodded, gesturing toward shelves on the other side of the room. "Over there. Each kingdom is separated."

"Thank you." She turned away and followed his obscure directions. *Was it too much to expect more specific directions? I'm sure he could have left his book for a moment to help me.*

She found the historical books for each kingdom on separate shelves. The books on Sorban history filled shelves on both sides of the aisle. Pulling several down, Serpé took them to a nearby table.

After reading three books, she pushed them away in disgust. *I already know this information. Everything in these books I learned while under The First's tutelage. What exactly am I looking for?*

Moving back amongst the books, she realized the library had darkened. A quick glance around the room showed her that the sun had set. Instead of selecting more books to read, Serpé thanked the acolyte and went to find her friends.

After evening meal and prayers, Serpé headed for the top floor of the largest tower. She and her friends had been assigned a group of rooms, connected by a common room. When she entered, she saw two sleeping rooms lay on each side of the common room. A large fireplace was set into the wall opposite the main door. Three of the four doors were shut, with the fourth door ajar. Without thinking, she stepped through the open door.

The room, dark and uninviting, confused her. She did not expect the fire in the common room to cast its light in here, but there was absolutely no light beyond the door—not even a traditional lamp was lit. She liked the practice in Azar's temples and the homes of his devout worshipers where they lit a lantern and placed it in the window of an empty bedroom. That light invited the tired, lost and faithful to a night of rest and safety. She thought it strange the priests had not lit a light for her.

Why didn't they light a lantern for me?

When she crossed the dark room in search of a candle or the lantern, an arm wrapped around her throat and another around her waist, pinning her arms to her sides. She opened her mouth to cry out, but her breath caught in the pressure against her throat. Unsuccessful in freeing her arms, Serpé settled for slamming her heel down on top of the intruder's foot.

The assailant groaned and released her arms. Now, her arms free, she drove her elbow into his ribs. Her effort rewarded her with a bone break. Gasping for breath, he loosened his hold on her. She pulled his arm from her throat, twisting it behind her attacker and pulling it up his back.

Releasing him and taking a step back, she drew her main-gauche.

He turned to face her. The fire in the common room silhouetted him. He lunged at her, a dagger or knife in his hand. Serpé met his advance, her main-gauche lowered to his belly. His dagger cut through her shirt, grazing the newly healed flesh of her stomach. Her weapon pushed deep into his belly. The blade hit resistance at first, but she pushed past it. Self preservation overpowered her need to know why he attacked her.

The new wound burned, and she felt blood soak her shirt. She watched the man lower his gaze to the blade in his stomach and the hand that held it in place. He tried to pull it from his flesh, but she pushed against him until even the hilt put pressure into his flesh. She ignored the smell of his breath, his gasps for air blowing into her face. With a final gasp, he slipped from her blade and fell to the floor.

Movement from the common room drew her attention and temporarily a sudden onset of light blinded her. She cringed when she heard footsteps enter the room. When hands clutched at her again, she batted them away.

"Serpé, it be only us." She heard concern in Drommond's voice, but she did not stop pushing his hands away until she saw him. She did not notice Tamar until the elf bent over to examine the body.

"What happened?" Aldric asked, his voice calmer and less concerned than the others.

"My lamp wasn't lit and this man waited here for…" Serpé stopped when Drommond pulled out a lighting stone. The attacker wore the robes of a priest of Azar.

"He's a priest," everyone whispered at the same time.

Tamar gasped and jumped up. "But why?" she turned to ask Serpé and her surprise became concern. "Serpé, you're hurt."

"It's not bad. I think it's just a scratch." Serpé glanced at the bloodied shirt.

"Tamar, see if the priest carries anything to tell us why he did this. I'll go tell Most Blessed Tossin and the temple knights. Drommond, take care of her wound." After issuing his orders, Aldric rushed from the room amid nods of agreement from the others.

The warmth of Drommond's healing magic tickled Serpé's wound and eased the pain left in her side. When he finished, she focused on Tamar's search. Before she could join her, the elf held up a folded piece of parchment and handed it to Serpé.

"It has a broken seal on the outside."

Serpé nodded, unfolding the parchment. She read the writing on the parchment once, twice, and still read it a third time. She recognized the elegant scrawl, but could not believe what she read.

"He paid the priest to kidnap me." She looked up when Tossin and Aldric filled the doorway.

"Who?" Tossin asked, stepping into the room and bent down to look at the body. "I do not recognize this man. He is not a priest here."

"Then Reicholt must have sent him, or he came under the guise of a weary traveler."

"We will solve this in the morning." Tamar pushed Serpé toward the bed. "She needs to rest." Tamar waited for the body to be removed and tried to usher Aldric and Drommond out when Serpé stopped her.

"No, Tamar. I need to speak to you." The elf looked back at her. "All of you."

Closing the door after the temple guards took the body out, her three friends turned to look at her.

"Well?" Aldric stood with his arms crossed, glaring at her.

"The First is looking for me. Kian thinks it is because he wants to use me to help him grab control of a dead monarchy in Sorban. He wants to take control from the merchant council. He's been searching for me for four years. Kian hid me from him, but when my magical protection was broken, I had to run. That's how I ended up in Valen." Serpé looked to each of her friends. "Do you have questions?"

Silence filled the room.

"I am sure we can think of many questions that will take too long to answer. But I will require one thing to continue my travels with you and I am sure the others can agree," Aldric spoke again, his words cold. "You have to be honest with us from now. No more secrets."

"I promise. I will make sure to be as honest with you as I can."

The promise appeared to satisfy him. He turned and left the room, with no further comments.

"Sleep well, Serpé. We will to keep you safe." Drommond kissed her on the cheek and left as well.

"Good, now that *that* is over, get some rest. I will stay with you." Tamar helped Serpé wash the blood from her side and hands.

Serpé dressed in her nightgown after Tamar left the room and closed the door. When she returned to Serpé's room, the two women crawled into bed for the night.

Chapter 24

"But why is he still searching for you?" Most Blessed Tossin asked again, confusion clouding his face.

Serpé studied the priest, sure he had been in the priesthood so long he had forgotten what it was like to be a man enticed by a woman. She hesitated to explain it to him, but there was no way around it.

"As I said yesterday, Reicholt wants to rule Sorban. He thinks that when he is made king, he will need an heir. Kian and I believe that he wants me to provide him that heir."

"And this letter?" Tossin produced the parchment they found on the man who attacked her.

"It's his seal and signature. I know them very well."

"How did he find you?" His voice changed, filled with concern.

When his face paled, she knew the priest finally understood why she ran from Reicholt. The embarrassment and revulsion over why he wanted her made her want to retch. *At least the official record contains my story now.*

"Like I said, for the four years I stayed with Kian, my location remained protected by a magical amulet. When it was destroyed, I discovered he'd never stopped looking for me. He must have someone watching me still."

"Shouldn't we create another amulet for you?" Termage,

anxious, rose and began to pace the room.

She wanted to smile or laugh at the mage, but she could not find the humor within her. "I understand the magic can be very draining. I would not want you to lose any of the time you have left because of a magical creation. I appreciate the gesture though."

"We can decide that later. Why don't you visit the library again? Tamar is there, waiting for you. She advised me that she will not leave you alone again while you are here." Tossin rubbed his chin. "Hmm, I don't know whether I should be insulted or not."

Serpé smiled despite her mood and pointed at the parchment still on his desk. "I'm sure she thinks she has good reason."

"Oh. That's right. Well, please be careful. But enjoy yourself. Try to relax. The temple knights will see to your safety now that they understand the threat."

After leaving the room, Serpé met Tamar just steps away from the door. Together they returned to the library. Though she realized that Tamar had no interest in any of the books, Serpé appreciated her friend staying with her.

Serpé buried herself in reading about Sorban again, after pushing books written in the Trade Language toward Tamar. By mid-morning, she had separated books that looked like journals from the rest.

One of the books she separated contained letters, bound together by leather covers. The letters were written in Old Sorban with a translation into the Trade language behind the original. Reading the letters, her excitement grew until she finally pushed the book toward Tamar.

"These were written by King Sernan Navrinar, the last ruler of Sorban." Her exclamation came out loud enough to draw a harsh admonition from the acolyte in charge of the library.

Tamar leaned over to look at the parchments Serpé held. "Does he say anything that will help you against Reicholt?"

"I need to read more." Distracted, she brushed the pages with her fingers while she read.

Tamar's impatient fidgeting in her chair echoed through the library and Serpé shot her a frustrated look.

"I thought elves were supposed to have more patience than this."

Her friend shrugged. "I've spent too much time around

humans. I now know what it's like to be bored, or at least I know the meaning of boredom."

Serpé shook her head and smiled, before returning to her reading. When she finished, she again looked at Tamar, putting the book between them.

"This is about the home they found after they left here. It also mentions the queen's distress about leaving something important behind in Parnoir."

"What do you think it was?"

"I don't know. I can't imagine what she would have left that was so important. No one has found anything." Standing, Serpé picked up the book. She led Tamar from the library. "Maybe someone is left there that can explain it to us." In her eagerness to show her find to Tossin, she ignored the acolyte who chased after them, protesting the removal of the book from the library.

Their pace increased until they were running to Tossin's office. When they arrived, all three burst into the room.

"They took a book..."

"This is a book of letters..."

"Was it really necessary for...?"

Tossin stared at them, a tolerant smile on his face. "Zotan, I will take responsibility for the book."

He waved his hand to dismiss the acolyte. Zotan nodded, turning a glare on Serpé. Storming from the room, he allowed the door to slam shut behind him.

Tossin turned his full attention to the women. "Serpé, what did you find?"

"King Navrinar sent letters to someone here in the temple. Those letters were bound into a book—this book." She placed the book on the desk in front of the priest. Opening to the last letter, she read, "'The new home is acceptable, but the queen remains unhappy. Having left behind something so important to her is taking a toll on her. I fear her depression will overwhelm her.' What did they leave in Parnoir?"

"The king did not live in Parnoir. He lived in Siladan." The priest glanced away, a brief look, but she still noticed it. "He only had a home in Parnoir."

It surprised her that he knew about the home in Parnoir. "Are you the one the king sent the letters to?"

Tossin returned his gaze to hers and nodded.

"Why didn't you tell me?"

"It wasn't important?" he asked.

Serpé stared at him, trying to decide whether or not to pursue her questions. Instead, she returned to the letter. "My family owns the royal residence now."

"Isn't that funny?" The priest laughed, stopping only when he realized she did not join him. "What would you like to do now?"

"I must talk to them. Someone must come back to Sorban and prevent this takeover by Reicholt."

"I see." He tapped his fingers on the desk. "You will need funding for this?"

She nodded.

"Very well. I will have supplies and funds provided. You can leave tomorrow."

She hurried around the desk to embrace him before she and Tamar ran from the room to find Aldric and Drommond.

Chapter 25

Serpé and the others arrived at a traveler's inn after sunset. The Everwood Forest hid the glow of the village beyond the inn, but their travel would not take them to the village. They settled the horses into the stable, and then went into the main building.

Serpé watched her friends sign the innkeeper's book and receive a key. She took the quill from Tamar to sign the book, but only finished her surname when the innkeeper stopped her, mid-stroke.

"Your room is already paid for, Dame Navran. I hope you will be happy with it." He counted back coins from the stack she had given him for all the rooms and placed them in her hand with her room key.

"Already paid for? By whom?" No one but Termage and Tossin knew the route they traveled.

"I don't know. He signed the book with your name. My apologies, Dame, but I have no other room in which to place you." Serpé recognized the sincerity in his apology, but he walked away before she could ask anything further. Scanning the book, she found her name several lines above her friends' signatures, but she did not recognize the writing.

He said it was a man. Maybe Kian talked to Termage and rode ahead of us.

She turned to look at her friends. "I have no idea who knew we traveled this way, or who would be here to pay for my room."

"We must find out, or you should stay with me." Tamar's concern made her smile.

"There is the chance it is someone I know, Tamar."

"Someone who already tried to hurt you once on this trip. Really, Serpé, who could have done it?" Aldric and Drommond stepped closer while Tamar spoke.

She could be right. Reicholt could have done this. But he wouldn't leave Siladan just to pay for my room.

"It is possible. It is also possible that it's someone else. A good someone." Serpé gripped her friend's hand. "You're room is across from mine. I will shout if there is a problem. Be listening for me." She led them upstairs and to their rooms.

Standing in front of her door, Serpé could feel Tamar's gaze on her. She waited until her friend opened her door, then rested her head against the cool wood.

This may be a mistake. With a deep breath, she unlocked the door.

Serpé waited for the door to swing open before she stepped into the room. She stopped, the light of a lantern showing a single man in the room.

Does Tamar see? Will she notice him or my hesitation? She had not heard Tamar's door close.

Reicholt stood in the middle of the room, next to a table. Her breath left her and her teeth clenched tight. They stared at each other through the dim light. She imagined she could feel his gaze roaming over her body.

When her breath returned, the questions rushed from her mouth. "What are you doing here? *Why* are you *still* watching me?"

Reicholt covered the short distance between them in only a few steps. "It gives me great pleasure to watch you, my dear." The too sweet, almost condescending tone of his voice oozed of seduction. She closed her mouth, breathing through her nose against the sudden nausea gripping her stomach.

"Get out." Her voice shook. *Can he hear my fear?*

"Certainly you don't mean that," he cooed. He pulled her farther into the room, reaching past her to shut the door. She stepped back against the door, her only escape now blocked. His hands came to rest on her shoulders. "There is so much I can do for you, so much I can give you, if you would only return to Siladan with me."

"I will not," she growled. She felt him squeeze, moving his hands down her arms.

"You cannot refuse me, Serpé. I will have you." He pushed his body against hers, his lips bruising the flesh on her throat. She swallowed the renewed bile that rose in her throat when he forced his arousal against her. An eager chuckle escaped his lips. He released her arms to grip her waist. "I want you, and you will be mine."

Freed of his restrictive grip on her arms, she flicked her hand and released the dagger she carried from its sheath around her wrist. She pushed the blade against his throat and forced him back a step. Watching him swallow against the blade gave her a moment's satisfaction.

It would be so easy to slit his throat and end his life. She pushed the blade harder. His blood pulsed under his skin. *What would Kian say if I did it? I begged him not to take this step. Now I want to do it?* The pressure released a small bit. *I would lose Azar's favor. I would be without a spiritual guidance I have always depended on.*

Frustrated, she pushed herself away from him, lowering her dagger. "Get away from me. The thought of you touching me makes me sick." She wanted to scream in his face, but her clenched teeth kept her voice to a snarl. *Loosening my jaw will release my fear. Releasing my fear will leave me defenseless against him. That must never happen.*

"I did not plan for our first time together to be so rough, but if this is how your passion reaches its peak, I am more than happy to comply."

She watched anger add to the desire in his eyes and his expression. *I should have gone with Tamar.*

He grabbed her arm, his movement revealed too late for her to react. He slammed her wrist against the wall until she released the dagger. Ripping her shirt open, he squeezed her breast. A cry of pain forced from her brought a fire to his eyes.

Serpé reached up with her empty hand and grabbed a handful of his hair. With her strength winning out, he bit into her shoulder. She pulled harder on his hair to force him to release her. He bit down until a chunk of her flesh went into his mouth. Again she cried out, louder than before.

Releasing her from his teeth, Reicholt met her gaze with his.

Opening his mouth to speak, he stopped when a knock came from the other side of the door. He slapped his hand over her mouth, forcing her cheek against the hard wood. "Don't even think about calling for help," he growled.

She breathed through her nose, thankful for the distraction that made him release her breast. Her eyes began to sting from sudden tears. She yanked on his hair again, this time able to get his face away from hers, then brought her knee up, into his groin. But he still refused to release her and they both fell to the floor.

His grip on her loosened.

"Enter!" She emptied her lungs into that one word as she rolled away from Reicholt, toward the door. She rose to one knee.

The door opened, the light from the hall pouring into the room. Drommond and Aldric stepped inside, moving past her. They each held weapons in their hands and for a brief moment pride filled her. Her friends analyzed the situation with just a glance. She tried to fix her clothes as they stepped between her and Reicholt.

"I didn't realize ye were entertaining guests, Serpé. Who be the visitor?" Drommond's sarcasm brought her a small amount of comfort.

"That is not what I'm doing." She flung her hand at Reicholt, though the others could not see her. "That's Reicholt."

"I think you need to leave, Reicholt." Aldric's growl made her glance at him in surprise.

Drommond stepped forward, but the sound of laughter at the door stopped all movement in the room. Serpé turned to see who else had come into the room. Her vision blurred for a moment and she realized that she had hit her head harder than she thought.

"I see things have gotten out of control." Another man stood at the door and she squinted to see his face. He walked into the room, his steps casual.

"Strinnal?" Serpé watched the new arrival nod. She had not seen him since she left Reicholt. She had not realized he joined the Religious Guard and obviously done well if he served the priest directly. "Get him out of here, Strinnal."

Strinnal stepped past her and helped Reicholt rise to his feet.

"I'll leave when I'm ready," Reicholt informed everyone, then yanked his arm away from Strinnal's grip.

Serpé stood, drawing her estoc from its sheath, the cool of the hilt giving instant comfort. Her confidence renewed, she pushed past her friends and pointed the blade at Reicholt's chest.

"Get him out of here or I will kill him."

For a moment, Reicholt looked like he would refuse and she thought she would get to wet her blade with his blood. Then he nodded and backed away from her. Maybe he had seen that in her face.

"As you wish. Captain Marcin, we will leave." Reicholt pulled a glass rod from within his robe and caressed it. "I will see you again, Serpé. Remember, you will be mine."

"Not likely."

He laughed, held out his hand for Strinnal, and activated the magic within the rod. A flash of light blinded her and she heard a loud pop from within the light. When her sight cleared, both men were gone.

Aldric turned and studied her face. "Are you all right?"

"Yes, I'm fine." She took a deep breath to steady her voice. "Let me clean up, and I'll join you downstairs for food."

"I think the blood on your shoulder says otherwise." Tamar stormed into the room. "I told you it wasn't him."

Serpé shied away from Tamar's touch to her shoulder. "It could have been." She held her friend's gaze with her own, but in her heart she felt disappointment.

"I'll stay here. The two of you go downstairs and order food for all of us." Tamar's order sounded harsher than necessary, but the men nodded and left the room, closing the door behind them.

Before the door clicked into place, Serpé sank to the floor. Tamar's gentle grip helped her until she sat on the wood. Tears that had threatened to fall during the fight now wet her face and hands. Tamar said nothing, instead holding her close and rocking her, like her mother had when she was young.

"He actually thought he could seduce me," Serpé cried into Tamar's shoulder. "That sick man shouldn't be a leader in one of the most influential religions in our world! He should be committed to one of the temples that treat unstable people."

She felt Tamar nod and hold her tighter. Fear formed a pit

in her stomach as she continued to give voice to her thoughts. "He wants me for his lover and I've done everything I can to pretend it doesn't bother me. But I can't do that any longer. Why did I let him go?" She had him at the end of her blade, twice. She could have brought an end to everything—her fear of him and his threat to Sorban. *Earlier I worried about losing Azar's favor if I killed him. I thought it would bother me if I did, but I feel...relief?*

"Because you are a good person, no matter how he has treated you, what he wants from you," Tamar whispered, smoothing Serpé's hair with her hand.

Reicholt has made me cry again. Wiping the tears away does nothing to hide the fact they were there in the first place. Or why.

"I need a bath." Serpé pulled away from Tamar, wiping her cheeks.

"What about your shoulder?" Together, the two women pull the shirt from Serpé's skin. Fresh blood flowed from the wound. "That's going to leave a scar."

"One more reason for me to hate him." Serpé picked herself off the floor with Tamar's help. "I can clean it while I bathe and if it needs healing, we can have Aldric or Drommond do it after we eat."

She walked over to the tub in the corner of the room. The scent of the oils reached her, weaker than she expected. A quick dip of her hand and she knew the water had cooled, so the bath would be rushed.

She removed her shirt, careful of the wound. "Wait. I didn't request the bath. He must have done that."

Her hand gripped the edge of the tub, dizziness making her vision swim. *The water will be just like his hands touching me.*

Putting the shirt back on, Serpé grabbed a washcloth from a stack of towels on the dresser. She folded it and placed the cloth on her shoulder. "I will have a new bath drawn after we eat." She rushed from the room, without looking back to see if Tamar followed her.

Chapter 26

"Welcome, Captain Donwell. We are pleased to at last meet the man who works the will of Azar in removing corruption from his church." Most Blessed Tossin's greeting brought a smirk to Kian's face.

His lack of faith in Azar was well known amongst the priests, spoken of by Most Holy Korewyn when he served as the priest's bodyguard. But it had never kept Kian from fulfilling his duties completely. His faith was not the reason Korewyn was killed. The assassination had not happened while he was the captain of the priest's personal guard.

"Thank you, Most Blessed. I hope I can provide you information to add to what Serpé has already given you." Kian glanced around the courtyard, looking for any sign that she was still at the temple. "Has she left already?"

"She and her friends left several days ago. She uncovered information about King Sernan Navrinar that she wanted to follow. There was something mentioned about a hidden treasure. It surprised me to learn she is a treasure hunter. Not what I expected," Tossin answered, disappointment evident in his voice.

"She's not." The priest watched him with obvious curiosity, making Kian look away. He did not know what the priest had seen in his expression, but he felt sure it was not something he wanted to admit.

"Well, come with me. I am sure you are all tired and the sooner we speak, the sooner you and your men may rest and eat." Tossin turned and walked into the temple.

Neither spoke as Tossin led the way to his office. Blackette walked beside Kian, his arms filled with a backpack overflowing with journals and scrolls.

Though they passed artwork that many would consider beautiful, it did not draw Kian's attention. His thoughts remained focused on the priest's expression when Serpé was mentioned. *Was my face filled with disappointment? Did he see how much I miss her?*

Her absence pained him. This missed opportunity to see her and the last letter he had received from Jalena left him incomplete. *I am missing a piece of me that I am sure only Serpé can fill.*

In Tossin's office, First Mage Termage waited with a quill and book in his hands. Kian could not help but return the man's wide smile. When he served Most Holy Korewyn, he had traveled to the temple with the priest several times. Though the visits were short, he had developed a friendship with both men and it continued even after his retirement and Korewyn's death.

Settling into office chairs, the priest and mage watched him when Blackette handed over the backpack. Removing the contents one piece at a time, Kian placed each item on the desk in front of them.

"These are for Serpé, if something should happen to me. These journals will give her knowledge about a spy within Reicholt's ranks and the information he has provided us so far. The spy will help her if she needs it. When it's time, he will stand with her against Reicholt. The long tube is her family tree. You should make your own copy of it for your records before you give it to her. Everything else will support her accusations about Reicholt," Kian rushed through the description of the items.

"In these books and scrolls, you will also find the evidence needed to bring the murderer of Most Holy Korewyn to justice." He stopped speaking when Tossin lifted his hand to silence him.

"You know we do not serve as justices, Kian. We can do

nothing with that evidence. You should take it to one who will deliver the justice Most Holy Korewyn deserves."

"I understand, Most Blessed Tossin. But I am hoping Serpé will do something with it. Nevertheless, you have it." Kian pulled out the last journal. Parchments filled it and threatened to fall out. "Finally, this is the evidence I have collected about the war Reicholt is forcing between Sorban and Tushin is included."

"Why don't you just give this to her now? Let her present it to the council?" Termage's almost constant smile had disappeared while he listened to Kian.

"I don't want her in Sorban, and I don't want her near Reicholt. I don't want him to have any chance of capturing her. She must stay away from him and I will do everything I can to keep her from his evil." He sucked in a deep breath. "I will deal with Reicholt, but do not give her this information unless I am killed or captured."

Tossin nodded, his face grim. "First High Mage Termage will cast a spell upon you that will allow us to know if either of those events happens."

"You have my thanks."

"We have our concerns over why he wants her so badly. We have heard her words regarding this. But we would like to know your thoughts, or if you have found out anything."

Kian nodded, but looked away from the priest and mage. *Each time I speak of this, I want to wrap my hands around Reicholt's throat and choke him, feel the life leave him. But I know Tossin needs this information, so we can protect her better. How many more times do I have to repeat it though?*

"Reicholt wants her for himself, for the power he thinks she can give him." He paused to take another deep breath. The jealousy he felt before came crashing back on him. "He thinks with her under his control, he can declare himself king and that the child he forces upon her will secure his reign."

Tossin cleared his throat, his pale face bringing a small amount of satisfaction to Kian. He smiled inside, knowing he was not the only one surprised and sickened by this knowledge.

"That is unheard of. No priest of Azar should want such things." Tossin's voice cracked. "I am not happy to hear Serpé's fears confirmed."

"Now you understand why I don't want her near him. I can't take the chance that he will get his hands on her." Both priests nodded, their eyes still wide. "We can stay one night, if you are not opposed to that. But we need to leave in the morning."

"Of course. We would be happy to have you for the night." Tossin easily adjusted to the abrupt change of topic, stood and walked around the desk next to Kian. "Anything else you will need?"

"No. I will make arrangements to send you any more information I gain." The priest nodded. He led Kian and Blackette back to the courtyard to gather the rest of their men.

Chapter 27

Serpé smiled to herself at the sounds of the forest around her. Even the shrill call of birds voicing their displeasure at intruders in their forest home was soothing. The forest floor lay shadowed, the sun's rays blocked by the ancient trees.

She felt the trees embraced her in their protective covering and made it easier to push away the memories of Reicholt's attack. In front of Aldric and Drommond, she pretended she was not bothered by what happened. But she did not sleep that night and had barely slept since. The bruises and the wound on her shoulder still hurt.

Serpé felt they would reach their destination soon. At any moment, they would break through the tree-line to see the home of the former king of Sorban. If Azar had blessed them, the king's descendents still lived there. She hoped they would help remove Reicholt from power.

She watched Tamar stop her horse and motion for everyone to join her. Serpé's heart beat faster and her hands became slick with sweat as her excitement grew. She dismounted and stepped closer.

"Just ahead," Tamar's whisper reached her. She guided the group through the last few feet of heavy forest.

The tree coverage ended and the group stepped into a bright, sunlit clearing. They took a moment to adjust their eyes to the light. When they were able to see, they stared at the manor that stood before them.

There was no glass in the windows and the dark holes gazed at the new arrivals woefully. A wood door lay on the ground several feet away from its original position in the wall. Weeds grew through a hole in the wall and the doorway lay blocked by flowers and tall grass. As always, the forest took back what had been taken from it.

"It's empty. They aren't here." Serpé stared at the dilapidated building. Disappointment and emptiness filled her, the excitement she had felt—lost. Warmth flooded her face and her jaw clenched. Tears threatened, but she held them back.

I will not cry, not again. I placed so much faith on someone in the family being alive, I never considered what I would do if we found no one here.

"Now what?" The flat tone of Aldric's voice irritated her and she turned to glare at him.

"Now we find out what happened." She crossed the clearing to the manor, entering without the others.

Serpé lit a torch and wandered through the manor. She stepped over debris and animal feces, but she could still distinguish the detail carved into the wood furniture and the remnants of pillows and cushions. The remains of tattered and dirty tapestries still hung on the wall.

I wonder how vibrant the colors were. I want to touch them, but they may crumble under my touch.

She took a mental note of each room and the contents as she passed through them. Pots still waited for a chef to return to them in the kitchen. Books filled the library, some destroyed by water that seeped through the walls, others destroyed by fire.

Footsteps entering the library forced Serpé to look up from the book she picked up to read. *How long have I been staring at it?*

Tamar wrapped her arms around her. "You need to eat, Serpé. We lit a fire outside and Drommond made rabbit stew—again." They laughed together.

"His specialty. I can't wait to get back to something other than his cooking." Serpé turned toward her. "I want to look through the bedrooms, but it's too dark."

"Let's eat, then I'll come back with you and bring another torch. We can search the bedrooms together." Serpé nodded and followed Tamar outside.

She ate the rabbit stew without complaint, though Drommond had made it every time it was his turn to cook since they left Valen. When she finished and had rinsed out her bowl with water from her water skin, she pulled two more torches from her saddlebags.

"Are you ready?" Tamar still sat eating. Serpé did not want to disturb her, but she wanted to search the bedrooms before she took watch for the evening.

Tamar nodded, grabbed her own torches and the two headed for the manor together. They were able to find the first bedroom easily.

The bed lay in pieces, hacked apart by sharp edged weapons. They found rotting clothes scattered throughout the rooms, as well as drapes and blankets from the beds. Dressers and cabinets were smashed and the wooden shards covered the floor, rotting.

They moved down the hall, stepping into each room. Furniture lay shattered, destroyed. Brown, rotted masses of material filled the floors.

When they reached the end of the hall, a closed door stopped their progress. "Tamar, where are the bones? There haven't been any remains."

"There were no graves outside either. Animals, spiderkin, who knows? It's been a few years since this happened. There's no way to know." Tamar reached for the door handle behind Serpé.

After struggling with the door, they were finally able to force it open. Serpé stepped inside, glancing behind the door. She stepped back, her hand flying to her mouth as she mouthed a silent 'oh'.

"Here's one of them." She knelt to get a closer look, Tamar walking in behind her. "Actually, two of them. She's holding a baby." Serpé stood, gesturing at the broken window across from the skeletons.

Tamar nodded. "That explains how she and the baby died. And also explains why this room is untouched."

"But not who did all this. Spiderkin wouldn't go to all the effort of breaking the window just for two more, no matter how intelligent they are. And, we have no way to know who this was or what she looked like. Bones give us nothing." Serpé began to examine the cradle.

"Only clothes to tell us she was a woman. No way to know about the baby." Tamar walked over to the dresser and rummaged through the rotting clothes.

"The baby was a boy, my son." The two women turned, both reaching for their weapons. They stopped at the sight of a third woman. Her feet floated inches above the ground, just enough to allow a space between the bottom of her dress and the floor. Her blond hair was pulled up at the top of her head, held in place by a diamond comb, the same as the comb that rested in the hair of the skeleton. She was older than Serpé, but only by a couple of years and her dress was the same as the material draped over the skeleton.

"You'll find a journal hidden in the cradle, under the bedding."

Serpé found her voice first. "Who are you?"

"Ryanne Navrinar. I am the wife of King Navrinar's youngest son, and the baby is ours." The ghost studied Serpé for a moment. "You remind me of someone, but I can't remember who. You—look so familiar."

"I don't see how that's possible. The king and his family left Sorban before I was born. At least twelve years before." She shifted from foot to foot, uncomfortable under the ghost's gaze. "Who did this to you? Was the king here? Did anyone survive?"

"The king and queen were here. They were the first killed. They were old, slower, and easier to kill." A single glistening tear streaked Ryanne's translucent cheek. "Junal put up a fight, gave me a chance to get here, for the baby. Didn't help though. They came through the window. They talked about how they had already hunted down and killed Junal's older brothers, how we were the last."

Serpé had not known ghosts could cry and she wanted to comfort her. But to touch the ghost would mean the loss of some of her life essence and she would not make that sacrifice.

"The king had a daughter. Where was she?" She was not sure how long the ghost could stay or how it was possible for her to have a conversation with them, but Serpé wanted all the information she could gather before the ghost disappeared.

"When they left Siladan, the king left his daughter in the city with servants he trusted. She should still..." The ghost turned her head away from Serpé and Tamar and new tears came in earnest. "No, she has joined us as well. Her husband is here too."

"Who did this, Ryanne? Who went to all this effort to find your family and kill you?" Tamar, impatient with the questions, pushed for answers despite Serpé's look of frustration.

"It was a priest of Azar. He let his men do the killing, then came in and gloated as our last breaths left our bodies. He had dark hair that was turning gray as was the goatee he kept well trimmed. He wore the robes of high rank. His eyes were dark brown and he had the look of a bird of prey. I do not know his name. The king left Sorban because he feared corruption within the church. Most Holy Korewyn warned him of the evil growing within an acolyte under his tutelage. He left to protect us. It was useless."

Serpé could not breathe. The description detailed a man who was younger than the last time she saw him, but the description was unmistakable. "I know who it is." She looked at Tamar and then at Ryanne's ghost. "Eion Reicholt, Most Holy of Azar."

Recognition filled Ryanne's pale face. "Yes."

Ryanne drew out the word, raising her voice louder until it reached a shriek. The ghost lifted her face to the ceiling and cried out as Serpé and Tamar fell to their knees, their hands covering their ears.

Serpé looked up when silence again filled the room. It felt empty now with the disappearance of the ghost. She helped Tamar to her feet, and they both tore the cradle apart to find the journal Ryanne had mentioned.

When Serpé's fingers touched the edge of a book, she yanked it out of its hiding place. With the book in her hands, tight against her chest, she sat on the floor and stared at Tamar.

"Reicholt killed the royal family, a baby. I had not realized the depth of his evil."

"You need to be sure the information is told to the right people." Tamar held out a blanket that was in better condition than the others.

Serpé wrapped the journal in the blanket, and they walked from the nursery. Aldric and Drommond met them in the hall, concern on both their faces.

"What happened? We heard a shriek."

"Back at the fire. I need to get out of here." Serpé followed the men from the manor. When they sat around the fire again, she pulled the book from its wrapping.

"We were visited by a ghost of one of the family. We actually found two skeletons, in a nursery. The ghost told us what happened, who killed them and directed us to the journal." She took a deep breath and help up her hand to stop Aldric's questions. "The attack was led by Reicholt. He ordered the entire family killed, even hunted down the members who weren't here."

"So where are we going now?" She could hear the impatience in Aldric's voice and found that she agreed with him.

"Back to the church."

Chapter 28

Serpé tried to read the journal she found in the king's home, but the return journey to Azar's temple was hurried. She made sure they avoided the village where Reicholt had tried to capture her. She was sure he would not try again, especially in the same place, but there was no reason to invite the risk.

So much had happened in a very short amount of time. The discovery of the king's home, the revelations of the ghost and finding the journal had her thoughts racing and she found it difficult to settle them so she could sleep at night. For the moment, Reicholt's attack was forgotten.

The worst, or best, part of the return journey was that she could not get Kian out of her mind. How would he react when he found out what Reicholt had tried? Would he even care? She needed to see him and reassure herself he did care about her. She wanted to know if he still tried to protect her. Most important, she wanted to tell him how she felt about him. And when the decision came to find him, relief filled her. She knew Termage could send her to Kian and since the mage already liked her, there should be no problem to get what she wanted.

Finally they reached the temple in Sanctuary. As they walked their horses into the courtyard, Most Blessed Tossin rushed out to greet them.

"Did you find anything? Was anyone there?" His excitement

rushed over her as she dismounted.

Serpé pulled the old book from her saddlebag and placed it in his hands. He gazed at it, reverence in his expression.

"It's a journal, and it belonged to the queen, I believe. I found it in a cradle." Her throat tightened with the memory.

"Did something happen? What did you see?"

"The princess's ghost appeared near the cradle. She told us about how she, the prince and their child were killed, as well as the king and queen, by someone they would have trusted." She stopped when he opened his mouth to interrupt her and help up her hand. "It was a priest of Azar and men dressed as bandits. But the description of the priest is the most disturbing. The man she described was Reicholt."

The activity around her and Tossin stopped as the information filtered through the priests who had come out to greet them. Tossin's face became pale at her words and he stepped back from her.

"You must be mistaken."

"I was under his guardianship for eight years and a member of his church since the day I was born. I know what the man looks like." *Why am I being so defensive? Is he only concerned about a backlash this would cause the church if this information was known by the kingdom? He needs to know, no matter how much I hate Reicholt, I would not lie about this.*

"Are you letting your emotions cloud your judgment?" he whispered the question, almost as if he thought it unreasonable.

"Most Blessed Tossin, am I *really* the source of your concern, or am I just the messenger that makes Reicholt's corruption more obvious?"

The silence between them became uncomfortable. The priest was already important to her, even after so short a time of knowing each other. To see his shock and disbelief hurt her. Finally he nodded.

"You're right. It isn't your fault. Reicholt's corruption is second nature to him." He fell into quiet contemplation. "Did you say one prince?"

"Yes, the princess's ghost only mentioned one child was there. Junal, the prince."

"But, my child, the royal family had four children. I wonder why she didn't—" He shrugged, took her by the arm, and led her into the temple. Serpé heard her friends follow her, but didn't turn to look. "We will worry about that another time."

"She said Reicholt mentioned the other princes were dead."

He stopped to gaze at her again. "But not the princess? She was the third born, before Junal. That would explain much."

"Explain what? Ryanne said…"

"Another time. I will explain later." He guided her down the hall again.

What could he have learned while I was gone about the royal family that I did not learn from their home?

Tossin guided the four back to the rooms they stayed in on their earlier visit. While the others stayed to settle in, Serpé followed the priest to his office. She again sat in the chair in front of the desk while waiting for him to get comfortable in his own chair. He used care as he opened the book to examine the pages.

"Most Blessed, I would like to have my own copy of the journal. Would that be possible?"

"Of course, my child." He studied her briefly, his fingers touching the pages of the journal with a gentle caress. "Is there anything you need while you wait?"

Will my request sound desperate? Finally she nodded. "I would like to see someone, if possible. To go where he is."

"Of course. Tell First High Mage Termage I have approved anything you want." He waited to finish speaking before returning his attention to the journal.

Serpé knew when she was dismissed, even if that was not his intention.

Leaving Tossin's office, she stopped an acolyte for directions to Termage's tower. He occupied the top floor of the tower dedicated to the mages of Azar. As she walked into his laboratory, the chaos that filled the room did not surprise her.

Rings, staves, weapons of different types, books and rods covered every table. Whatever space was available between the instruments lay filled with spell components.

When the door closed behind her loudly, Termage lifted his head from behind an extensive alchemy station and glared at her. He did not appear to recognize her and for a moment she thought she would have her resistance to magic tested again.

"Go away!" Termage's shout took her by surprise even though she had prepared herself.

"My apologies, First High Mage. Most Blessed Tossin said I could ask for a favor from you." Her words echoed back to her despite the many tables and items in the room.

He glared at her until recognition brightened his face. He crossed the room to stand in front of her. "Yes. I apologize. I didn't realize it was you, my child." He took her hand and kissed it. "What can I do for you, my dear?"

Serpé smiled, touched by the genuine love the mage showed for her. "I need to find someone I haven't seen since the fall. I would like to go and speak to him directly."

Termage nodded, then left her without a word for several minutes. When he returned, he carried a mirror, two scrolls and a crystal rod. He handed her the rod and smiled when she looked at him in confusion. He held up one of the scrolls.

"I can send you to him. When you are ready to return, just speak my name while grasping the crystal rod in both hands and you will be returned to me. You can only travel like this a small number of times during your lifetime. The number is usually not less than two and not more than six. It varies for each person. To do any more than that will cause you to age with each additional casting."

He set the mirror on the table next to her, said something under his breath she did not understand and waved his hand over the reflective surface. She watched the image change into milky clouds that moved as if blown by a light wind.

"Put your hand on the mirror and think about your friend. Make the image in your mind as clear as you can."

Serpé followed his instructions. Kian's image appeared in her mind easily, despite their time apart. A moment later, he appeared in the mirror. Termage made adjustments to the image with his magic, smiling in triumph when he finished.

"Thank you, First Mage. I truly appreciate your assistance." Her words felt inadequate to express her appreciation, but she had to try. The mage had done so much for her. He smiled in return as he read from the scroll.

"Good luck, my child." When he finished reading the scroll, a portal appeared near them. It sparkled with the magic used to create it and without further preamble, she stepped through.

Serpé stepped on solid ground and looked back to see the portal close. Taking in her surroundings, she found herself in front of trees, at the edge of a clearing near a small inn. While she looked for familiar markers, the tree-line rustled with movement. Pulling her estoc from its scabbard, she stepped into a defensive stance. She remained silent when a man emerged from the trees, glanced around the clearing, and stopped when his gaze settled on her. They stared at each other a moment before she realized Kian stood in front of her.

"Kian?" Uncertainty filled her voice, but she made no attempt to clear it. Dropping her weapon, she ran to him.

Kian caught her and pulled her close, lifting her from the ground. She felt his breath against her neck. She wanted to stay in his arms forever. Then it was gone. She found her feet back on the ground and he stood an arms length from her.

"What are you doing here? I told you not to come back until I sent for you." The brief moment in his arms had been wonderful, but now lay ruined by the anger marring his handsome features.

"I know, but I had to see you." When she tried to pull her arm from his grip, he tightened his hold. After retrieving her sword from where it lay and slamming it back into its scabbard, he dragged her into the building.

"I don't care what your reason is. You shouldn't have come."

Did he just growl at me? Before she could question him, her attention was pulled to the woman he spoke to behind the bar. *That's his sister! He is mad at me for coming, but it's all right for him to come to Sorban and see Denai?*

"Where are we going?" Kian did not answer, instead pulling her up the stairs and into a room. She walked over to the bed while he closed the door and turned to glare at her.

Slipping her hand over the crystal rod in her belt, she began to regret her decision to find him. *He's so angry, despite the embrace he gave me. Will this drive him even farther from me?*

Watching him pace the floor in front of her, Serpé noted the confidence in his posture, though she had not recognized it in him before. His eyes were more alert, but they no longer sparkled with the happiness she saw on the farm. After a sudden stop, he turned to look at her.

Shivering, she cringed away from the sharp look that pierced her soul.

Chapter 29

Deep breaths did not help. Not looking at her did not help. Kian's warring emotions held his stomach in a knot and nothing helped ease it.

How can I be mad at her when I am so happy to see her? He glanced at her and wanted to rejoice. *She smiles even though I'm not looking. Does she want to hold me as badly as I want her?*

But as quick as the happiness came, it disappeared again. Reicholt and his followers were too close. One mistake and they would find Serpé, and turn her over to the priest for the reward.

Pacing the floor in a tight path, Kian felt her eyes on him. He had forgotten how beautiful those green eyes were, how bright they glowed and how the green of the forest paled when he looked into them. *I will be lost forever if I can't control myself.*

Shaking his head, he drove his feelings deep within him. *She'll use my emotions against me and I'm not ready to have her so close to the fighting—no matter how good she is. She needs to leave and return to the safety Draven can give her.*

He stopped pacing and was about to say as much, when a knock at the door interrupted him. Still glaring at Serpé, he reached back to the door, and realized his mistake when her smile grew. Denai stood at the door holding a tray filled with the food he had asked for. Her own smile matched Serpé's and he knew any argument he had prepared for the younger woman would sound like a desperate attempt to make her leave.

I'll never get her back to Valen now.

"Thank you, Denai." He accepted the tray and nudged his sister from the room with his hand firmly on her shoulder. The door shut on her startled expression.

Taking his time, making two separate plates of food, he struggled to ignore the sound of Serpé moving around on the bed. As much as he wanted to follow the direction his mind took him because of those sounds, he had to think of something to get her away from him. After he took a long drink from one of the mugs, he turned to look at her again.

"Tell me, why are you here, Serpé?" Squinting, he tried for the stern look he had favored her with earlier. "You're not supposed to be here. We're too close to The First for you to be safe."

"Then you shouldn't be here either." Serpé returned his glare, making her own frustration obvious. "You are the one leading an army against him."

"I had business to take care of." He forced a plate of food into her hands and placed the second mug on the side table.

"Business that obviously involves Denai." She gestured at the door. "I recognized her and the inn. She looks well. How's her family?"

"It doesn't concern you," Kian barked. He took a deep breath. "I don't have to explain myself to you. Besides, you're avoiding the question. *Why* are you here?"

Staring at him, the light in her eyes faded and she lowered her gaze to the plate of food. "I'm sorry. I realize it's unimportant now," she whispered. She pushed the food around on the plate with her finger.

"That's one of the things our time together taught me. Nothing you do is unimportant or without a purpose. You always have a reason, whether I agree with it or not," he rebutted. Pulling a chair closer to the bed, he sat in front of her.

"You know me well, Kian. But there are many things you don't know, or refuse to accept. And, I've grown, changed..." Her gaze returned to his, her eyes red with unshed tears. "... since you forced me to leave."

Kian studied her while she spoke and tried to determine if her growth had been physical. Since he met her, she had matured, her body becoming that of a beautiful woman. Everything she became, he turned away from, and tried to keep her the child of sixteen winters she had been when they met.

Even at sixteen winters, though, she was far from the child I tried to make her.

Closing his eyes, Kian sucked air through clenched teeth. He looked at her again, trying to focus on the woman who sat before him. His chest tightened, fully aware of how attractive she had truly become. Tight breeches covered her muscled legs and the white linen shirt she wore barely contained her. Her skin glowed, the tan she had when he last saw her still coloring her skin.

She smiled at him, and his heart leapt. He liked it when she smiled. He wanted to caress her cheek and make her smile again. Instead, he combed his fingers through his hair.

"Serpé, please, don't make me ask again." The words came out slow and strained with his effort to keep the desire from his voice.

Setting her plate aside, she surprised him by taking his hands in hers. "I came here to tell you that I love you."

A sharp intake of breath filled his lungs. *She loves me. No strings attached, just her love and her need to be with me.*

All he had to do was return it, and he could leave his war against Reicholt, take her some place the priest would never find them. They could start a new life together, a life that included a new farm, children and the chance to grow old together.

Her family line will be a problem though. When she finds out, she will be angry with me for keeping it from her. Her bloodline makes it hard for me to even feel worthy of her. I am only a soldier. I am not good enough for her. And will there be others who will want to find her, to use her, like Reicholt?

And then he realized, no matter how far they went, or how many times they changed their names, Reicholt would never stop looking for her. Every day they would wonder if he or his men would appear at their door.

I will have to stop Reicholt if we are to ever have a chance together. I have to stop whatever plans she has to stay with me, until Reicholt has been defeated. I'll have to hurt her to make her leave. But will protecting her make her hate me? Could I lose her forever?

Pulling his hands from her grasp, slower than he had intended, he drew in another breath. He looked up into her eyes. "I don't love you." He stood and stepped away from her. "You should leave, by whatever magic you used to get here."

Watching her, his pain intensified as tears escaped her eyes. Then he turned and left the room, letting the door slam shut behind him.

My declaration will keep us apart forever. She will never forgive me.

Chapter 30

I can't breathe.

Serpé's eyes stung from her tears. The ones she had not allowed to fall. She reached up and wiped her wet cheeks. No, she failed to control them.

When she could breathe again, it came too fast. She gasped for air, but could not pull enough in. *How could he reject me so easily? Was he so happy to be rid of me? Was I just a burden?* But when she rushed into his arms, he seemed eager to hold her. And he buried his face in her neck. She still felt his breath on her skin.

I was a fool to think we could stay together. Would things be different if we didn't have to worry about Reicholt? Is Reicholt the reason Kian rejected me?

Anger filled her and she threw the only thing in reach, the wooden plate of food, across the room. It crashed loud against the wall and clattered to the floor. The action brought no satisfaction.

She wiped the tears from her cheeks again and pulled the crystal rod from her belt. Because her anger had not been sated with the destruction of the food, she looked around for something further to take out her wrath on, but found nothing. Instead, she growled Termage's name and when the swirl of magical lights and the wave of dizziness subsided, found herself again in the mage's laboratory.

"You're back, my dear. How wonderful." Termage's excitement was genuine, but surprise to see her so soon shined in his eyes. Only pausing a moment to wipe more tears from her cheek, he continued, his level of excitement the same. "Did you see your young man? Were you able to tell him everything you wanted?"

"Yes, I told him, but he did not receive it as well as I had hoped," she spat, unable to keep the anger and hurt from her voice.

The mage studied her and she cringed at the sadness in his expression. "He'll come to understand what's right, child. Give him time. I'm sure one day he'll realize he's made a mistake."

Regretting her previous outburst, she kissed his cheek. A red flush colored his face and ears, bringing a smile to Serpé's lips.

"Thank you for your help, my friend. I am grateful to Azar for bringing you into my life." She allowed him to playfully push her out of his laboratory and found that she was not at all upset with him when he shut the door behind her.

Serpé made her way to the temple garden. The flowers still bloomed in full color. The loving hands and gentle magic of the priests helped even those out of season to bloom beautifully. Hedges clipped in a precise fashion created a lush green wall along the walkways. Benches placed in strategic positions invited her to sit in front of any one of the fountains and statues.

She wandered through the maze until she arrived at the center. There, a bench sat in front of a large cluster of roses, in multiple colors. She rested on it and stared at the flowers. Leaves and petals reached out to her. In turn, she reached for them, their soft touch almost imperceptible on her skin. The light perfume from the flowers tickled her nose and she found that it calmed her emotions. It drove away the anger and sadness the visit with Kian had brought her, but only for the moment.

"Serpé, what be wrong with ye?" She had allowed the serenity of the garden to pull her into its embrace so deeply that she had not heard Drommond, in his heavy armor, approach.

She turned to smile at her dwarven friend. "Nothing that won't heal over time, my friend."

She was impressed with how quick he had been in cleaning his armor. His weapon also appeared clean. It surprised her even more to see his long beard lying against his chest, washed and combed.

"We be spending enough time together, that I've learned a thing or two about ye." He reached for her hand. "And one of the things is knowing when it be best to letting ye work yer problems out on yer own and when to force ye to be with someone. Ye be needing yer friends. Evening meal be ready, and the others are waiting for ye."

Silently agreeing on the wisdom of his words, Serpé allowed him to lead her back into the temple.

Chapter 31

The wood against Kian's back only served to remind him how stubborn he was. It did nothing to cool his anger. Something impacted the wall in the room, followed by silence. He waited for her to leave, to follow or at least plead for him to rethink his decision. His heart broke with each moment that passed in silence when she did not open the door. He had hurt her—he saw it in her face. His struggle to control his own emotions was insignificant to the pain he had caused.

"I did what needed to be done." His mouth filled with a sour taste from his words. He knew it was a lie.

Keeping her safe should make me feel better, not worse. She'd be safe with me and we both know it.

He should explain himself to her, tell the truth. She would forgive him and they could make plans for a future without Reicholt. She would understand why he had to keep her safe and she would stay away from the fight. Filled with confidence, he stepped away from the wall and opened the door.

The room lay empty.

She must have used the same magic to leave that brought her here, like I told her to. For once, she did exactly what I told her.

But that did not make his own pain any less. The lies he spoke to Serpé could not corrected now.

She will think I don't love her, for however long it takes me to see her again. I will have to stand by my decision. But can I live with it?

"The Mother tests our resolve, despite the pain it causes. Our love cannot be, not now. Maybe never." Again, his words brought no comfort.

Even though he originally planned to stay the night, he gathered his few possessions from the room, and left to find Denai. The smells and sounds of the inn's guests assailed his senses. Pushing through the crowd, he found Denai, a tray of drinks in her hands.

"Give me that," Kian ordered. He took the tray from her hands and guided her through the crowd to the bar. Out of sight of curious onlookers, he pushed a leather pouch filled with gold coins into her hand. "Take this. I need to leave."

She peeked in the pouch and smiled. "Thank you, Kian. But where's Serpé? What did she want?"

"To tell me she loves me." His sister's immediate excitement made him groan inside.

"That's wonderful! Why aren't you happy?"

"We can't be together. It's a weakness Reicholt would use against us and I have no intention of giving him anything to hold against Serpé." Bristling at the sympathy he saw in his sister's eyes, he hated himself even more for hurting Serpé.

"You'll regret that decision." She reached out to pull him into an embrace.

He slipped from her hug and stepped back. "I already do. Use that money to get out of the city. Find a safe place until this is over."

"You want my family and me to leave our home? The business? Kian, that is too much to ask of us." She looked at her husband to see if he had heard. "We are safe here."

"If that changes, I want you to leave. Take your family away. Promise me." He waited for her reluctant nod. He gathered her into his arms before he left the inn.

With his equipment settled on his horse, Kian rode out of town, intent on returning to his army. But more and more, the warmth of Serpé in his arms haunted him. He knew he would never forgive himself until he confessed the truth to her.

Chapter 32

Riding both day and night, stopping only for a few hours rest at a time, left Kian and his mount tired and worn. The horse had proven strong though and Kian made the trip much faster than expected. Following the directions Blackette sent by Smoke Bird spell, he found the perimeter of their camp, despite arriving in the dark of night.

His path lay blocked by three sentries before reaching the first group of tents. He could risk a path around them, but Blackette always followed the protocol Kian set in place. The sentries would not ask questions before they attacked, and he did not want to fight his own men. Pulling his horse to a stop, he made sure the torches the men held lit his face.

"Traveling late tonight, aren't you?" The question came from the man in the middle, and Kian thought he had seen a sign of recognition from him. Pride filled the captain at the man's attention to his duties.

"Yes, but Blackette grows impatient with my absence. I'd like to get to my tent and sleep before we are forced to fight the enemy." Kian waited for the men to nod, and then walked his horse closer to them.

"Welcome back, Captain Donwell. Blackette is using your tent for meetings right now. Continue this way. You can't miss it." The soldier indicated a path in the trees for him to follow and the men separated to allow him to pass.

Though the army kept it quieter than would be expected for a normal camp this size, the sounds of the camp engulfed him. Kian found his tent pitched in a small clearing. Blackette's tent stood next to his. Handing his horse off to one of the boys who cared for the animals, Kian walked into the larger tent.

Men surrounded a table in the middle, and all looked up when he entered. They nodded a greeting, but only one left the table to approach him.

"Glad you made it back, Captain." Blackette's voice dripped with sarcasm and Kian felt an immediate rise of anger.

"Is there a particular reason I can't take the time I need to handle a personal matter?" Kian demanded. Despite being absent, he found it easy to return to his position of authority. His renewed anger made it even easier to push thoughts of Serpé aside.

"No. The men were asking questions though." The younger man's face reddened with embarrassment.

Ignoring Blackette, Kian walked past him to the large table, and nodded at the gathered men again. A leather map lay stretched out on the surface, showing The Dragon's Forest, Sorban and Tushin drawn in detail. Colored blocks of wood rested on the map, red outside the forest, blue within.

"Tell me."

Blackette stepped closer to the table. "The Religious Guard is here, here and here." He pointed at the three blocks closest to the forest, glancing up to make sure he held Kian's attention. "They are trying to surround us, though they seem unaware of our exact position within the trees."

"Then we take the fight to them. Just like my messages have instructed."

"I've read those messages and I've shared them with the others." Kian saw each head around the table nod in agreement, though he was surprised to see concern on several faces. Blackette cleared his throat, drawing his attention again. "We are strongly opposed to those tactics, Captain. We are concerned you aren't thinking clearly. The men who have actually met with you while you traveled, the ones you've contacted to send the Smoke Birds to us, all say that you have become consumed by anger that is clouding your judgment."

I'm impressed. I've not met many men who could stand so defiantly against my anger. But that doesn't change the fact that I want to hit him for speaking his mind.

Refusing to release his second from his glare, Kian held it while he took a deep breath that did little to cool his temper.

"Your opposition is noted—and overruled," he kept his voice steady. "If you or any of the men who feel this way want to leave, I will not stop you. I won't force anyone to follow me into this fight who doesn't want to."

"None want to leave, Kian." The force of Blackette's refusal could be heard through his bark. Kian noted again the nods of agreement from the other men around the table. "We are only concerned. Even I can see, in the very short time you've been back, that you are not the same as before visiting your sister. What happened?"

Kian waved at the other men, dismissing them. "We will resume the meeting when I am done with Blackette." The men walked out, slow in their steps, but without a word of protest. When the tent flap fell back into place, Kian returned his attention to Blackette. "No man should ever have to make the decision I made, for the reason I did. I am a coward." He began to pace. Before Blackette could object, he continued. "We will continue our attacks to weaken and destroy Reicholt. I want this over, as soon as possible. I have things I need to fix and this war has stopped everything important to me. I don't want to meet with the others again tonight. Is there anything else I need to know before I try to sleep?" Kian stopped his movement, facing Blackette again, squaring his shoulders. *Say something else about it. Try to calm my anger.*

"Yes, this came today."

Accepting a message tube from the other man, Kian turned away to read it. The words he read surprised him. Barking a harsh laugh, he allowed a smile to replace his frown.

"Have you read this yet?"

"No, Captain. It was for you specifically." He ignored the renewed sarcasm in Blackette's voice.

"This is the name of our spy. And it couldn't be more satisfying."

Chapter 33

Serpé rode in front of Drommond and Aldric, but followed Tamar as they traveled closer to The Dragon's Forest. Adrastos' easy footsteps fell smooth, sure. Morning dew had settled on her eyelashes, and a rainbow of colors brightened her vision when she blinked.

She had ridden in silence for most of their return journey, and spent most of that time trying to forget everything Kian had said to her. She knew she had taken a chance in going to him, but his rejection still hurt. Instead of bringing them closer, the separation had only served to strengthen his resolve to keep her away from him.

Tamar stopped and waited for her to come abreast. "Do you see?" She pointed at the edge of the forest in front of them.

Serpé had not seen anything, but followed Tamar's gesture. A caravan, with the flags of a merchant from Sorban traveled outside the forest. Cutting across the plains to intercept, another group charged at them. Serpé saw no flags or marks to distinguish the second group.

"Mercenaries, probably Reicholt's." She urged Adrastos forward. "We need to stop them."

Serpé and her friends also charged the caravan, but kept their weapons sheathed. With two groups coming at him, the captain of the caravan stopped his advance. On his orders, caravan guards situated themselves between the unknown intruders and the line of wagons.

Still a short distance from the line of guards, Serpé stopped and held her hands up in a gesture of peace. A single man rode out to meet them while the guards turned their attention to the group of mercenaries.

"Hail, travelers. Why do you ride toward the caravan? Are you part of them?" He gestured at the group of mercenaries, who were closer, but showed no sign of stopping.

"No, we are part of Lord Draven's militia, from Valen." She frowned at the man's questions. "If I had intended to attack, would I have raised my hand in peace? We want to assist you."

"Serpé, they're almost here," Tamar advised, raising her voice.

"We don't need your help," the man admonished. Serpé smiled at him.

"Of course not. However, you do travel close to The Dragon's Forest, which is our area of protection. I am obligated to assist." As she finished, the mercenaries reached the caravan and the sound of swords clashing stopped further conversation.

She drew her sword and main-gauche and directed Adrastos past the man in front of her to the area the mercenaries attacked. She cut into the back of the first man she encountered and Adrastos pushed his heavier weight against the other horse. Adrastos, being the bigger horse, as many combat horses were, won the brief struggle between the beasts, and continued on. Serpé swung her sword, back, behind her and into the man's chest.

The closest mercenary to Serpé turned his own horse toward her. She closed the distance between them before he could, her sword ready. He swung his sword overhead and she brought her own sword and main-gauche up to block it. Bringing the shorter weapon down, she sliced across his chest. She lunged, about to bring the blade back, when an arrow embedded itself into his throat.

She did not watch the body fall. Instead, Serpé turned to see where the arrow came from and found a militia group had joined the fight. The surviving mercenaries stopped their advance, turned, and tried to escape.

Without a bow, Serpé did not attempt to follow. Tamar and three others from the new arrivals continued attacking the fleeing mercenaries until they rode out of range. Serpé growled in frustration when three still escaped her group.

"They won't come back."

She turned to smile at Striphen when he brought his horse up to hers. "Not soon, at least. Were you waiting for us?"

"Lord Draven was concerned with your extended absence. All the militia captains are on watch for your return." His own concern could be heard in Striphen's voice.

"Draven worries that I am making it difficult to keep the promise he made to someone. I won't sit on my farm letting others do all the work." She smiled, though she could not hold it for long.

Striphen nodded. "Let's get back home." He gestured to his troop and they gathered near the trees to wait.

Serpé and Striphen spoke to the caravan captain before they joined her three friends and the others. Soon, they were on their way deeper into the forest.

When they stopped for the night, on first watch, Striphen pulled her away from the others. He gazed into her eyes.

"You saw him."

"Saw who?"

"The other man," he whispered, brushing her hair from her face. "I had hoped you would give up on him." He shrugged. "But whatever happened while you were away has changed you. Despite the fact that you don't wish us to continue our relationship, I will forever be your friend."

She embraced him in gratitude. "Thank you, Striphen. Your understanding means more than you realize."

He held her for a moment longer. "Get some rest. My troop will take watch tonight."

She nodded, and walked over to her companions.

The next day, after arriving at Lord Draven's tower, Serpé and Striphen waited while the steward walked inside the chamber to announce them. When he returned, the two followed him into the large room where Lord Draven waited with Captain Silver.

"Serpé! How good to see you. I hope your journey went well. Did you find what you were looking for?" Draven's loud voice echoed in the room.

His question confused her, but she nodded. "Yes, Lord Draven.

My journey was successful."

Draven waved Captain Silver and Striphen out of the room without explanation. He went to his chair. "You were gone much longer than I had expected," he admonished.

"I apologize. After I spoke with Most Blessed Tossin, I was able to spend time in the temple library, and I found letters sent by Sorban's last king to Most Blessed Tossin. We followed the clues that were mentioned in the letters. At the end of our journey, we found an abandoned estate and what looked like a nursery. Within a cradle, hidden under the bedding, lay a journal written in Old Sorban. I gave the journal to Most Blessed Tossin. He made me a copy, and we returned home," she summarized the journey, careful to leave out her conversation with Kian and the incident with Reicholt.

He gazed at her before nodding. "All right. Take a few days. Return to duty after you have rested."

As she turned to leave, the doors to the council room opened and a messenger entered. He bowed to both of them, and then passed a tube to Draven. Serpé continued toward the door when the messenger spoke.

"This message is from Kian Donwell, milord." The messenger passed another tube to Draven.

"From Kian?" She did not rush to Draven's side, but she could not resist the need to know what Kian said.

"He's keeping me up to date on the fake war Reicholt swears is coming with Tushin, a war he created in the mind of his followers. And, because they are concerned about attacks on their own people, the Tushin king has withdrawn all merchants and ambassadors from Sorban. Tushin is increasing its military force at the borders it shares with Sorban and he requests that you..." Draven stopped and glanced at her, then folded the parchment.

"He requests I what?" Serpé demanded. She stomped up the few steps to Draven and grabbed the letter from his hand. She felt an instant flush of concern at her behavior, but ignored it. She read the letter quickly and when she finished, she glared at the lord. "He said don't tell me. 'As I have asked in prior letters, please do not tell Serpé.' How long has he made this request? Why did he want this kept from me?" Her voice rose until she took hold of herself before she yelled at him.

Draven flinched at her anger. "I've known since he asked for you to visit Sanctuary. He only tries to protect you."

"I'm tired of everyone protecting me. I am not a child. When will you all realize I do not need protection and coddling?" She stepped away from him and read Kian's letter again. "He says the ambassador from Sorban is in Tushin, negotiating peace. The ambassador is the son of Merchant Tolan, the ruling merchant family." She looked up from the message. "I need parchment and quill."

He took her by the elbow, guided her to a desk and stood over her as she penned a letter. "What are you planning, Serpé?"

"I know the ambassador, at least I did when I was younger. I'm going to Tushin to offer him what help I can." She gave the parchment to the messenger after she took a scroll tube from Draven. "Take this to Ambassador Tolan in Arcadia. Make haste. I will leave in the morning and I want this letter to arrive before I do." The messenger nodded, accepted the coins she pressed into his hand and left the room.

"Kian won't be happy about this." Draven's quiet observation upset her.

"Damn Kian!" her shout echoed back at her. "He has not cared about my feelings in any of this. He only cares that I stay safe within this cage of his making. No more—I refuse to stay within this cage and he's just going to have to live with it!" She stomped from the room, slamming the door behind her.

Serpé stormed her way through the keep until arms and hands reached out to stop her. She tried to pull one of her weapons, but the same hands prevented her.

"Serpé, calm down," Striphen's calm voice broke through her rising panic.

"Striphen, what are you doing?" She fought against him until he released her.

She glared at him and he swallowed visibly. "I heard you shouting at Lord Draven and I thought… I thought you might like to eat a meal with me."

She remained quiet as her breathing slowed to normal. "Yes, food would be good."

He nodded and guided her to The Ranger's Rest.

Chapter 34

Twice Kian traveled to Valen before Serpé returned from Sanctuary. For some reason, her return journey took much longer than he expected, and his presence in Valen at the time had been a coincidence. He planned to return to the army when he saw her ride toward Draven's tower.

She spent some time in the keep, so Kian waited for her in The Ranger's Rest. But when she arrived at the tavern, he pulled the hood of his cloak farther over his face, intent to hide himself from her. A man arrived with her, his hand on her in a way that was too familiar for Kian's liking.

Kian watched the man guide her to a table, one of the few in a corner with a full view of the entire room. *At least she is keeping an eye on her surroundings.*

Resisting the urge to charge across the room, his eyes narrowed when the man touched Serpé's cheek, and even embraced her several times as she spoke. But when he leaned forward and kissed her, Kian slammed the mug he had raised to his mouth against the wood of the bar.

How can she give herself so easily to another man so soon after declaring her love for me?

He remained where he was, the memory of the pain he had seen in her eyes when he rejected her haunting him. His heart ached more with the decision that caused her such pain.

I guess I can't blame her for finding comfort in the arms of another. But it still seems so quick. Was he waiting for her? Waiting for me to finally reject her so she would come to him, seeking comfort?

"Give me the mug, Kian." Jalena's voice reached him through the haze of his pain and jealousy.

He turned at her touch on his hand and stared as she pried his fingers from the mug. The cracks in the now useless mug surprised him.

"Who is he?" Kian asked. Jalena would know who he meant, just as she knew he waited for Serpé's return.

"Striphen, one of Draven's captains."

He closed his eyes at the sympathy he saw in her expression. "They seem close."

"They were, or at least as close as they could be with you standing between them." His eyes opened and he glared at her, no concern for their friendship apparent in the anger he sent toward her. She held up a hand, both to keep him silent and to ward off his anger. "Don't give me that glare and keep the anger for yourself. We both know Serpé will never love another while she loves you. Her feelings for you will forever keep her from finding happiness with anyone. Why must you keep your feelings for her a secret? Do you really think it serves a purpose?"

"What makes you think I have feelings for her?" His jaw hurt from his clenched teeth, but he could not relax the muscles or pull his gaze from Jalena. Looking at Serpé again would prove her words right, and he feared he would hurt the man with her.

"I've known you for years, Kian. I see the way you watch her, the pain in your eyes, and how your jealousy grows each time he touches her. Why don't you go over there and tell her how you feel?" Jalena tried to comfort him.

Sitting on the empty bar stool next to him, he gestured at the keg of ale behind the bar. While Jalena collected a new mug and filled it, he took several deep breaths to keep his emotions from his voice. He adjusted the hood of his cloak again, and then took a long draw on the ale.

"Serpé came to me while I was visiting Denai. She told me she loved me and despite my feelings for her, I sent her away. I told her I didn't love her."

"Why?" Jalena's disappointment and shock filled her next

words. "What could you possibly get from lying to her? How does that help anyone?"

"It doesn't, but there are things about her that only a few people know. She doesn't even know who she truly is. I don't deserve her and I'm definitely not good enough for her. She deserves someone more stable, someone who can give her everything she needs or wants. But seeing her with him is killing me." He must have dropped the volume of his voice because she leaned toward him as if to hear him better.

"You are who she really wants, Kian. If you walk away from her, you will regret it for the rest of your life." She rested her hand on his.

"I already do, Jalena. Don't pity me. I don't want it." He jerked his hand away from hers, knocking the stool over in his haste to leave the tavern.

Chapter 35

The bright morning light hurt Serpé's eyes, making it difficult to finish the adjustments to the saddle bags on Adrastos. The journey to Arcadia, Tushin's capital, would be long since she traveled alone, and she wanted to get an early start. She would have to stay on the road until she found a travel inn to stay in. There were not many between Valen and Arcadia, since Sorban did not allow them within their borders, but she could not change her plans now. She did not want anyone to think she was afraid.

"Lord Draven tells us you are leaving for Arcadia. Why didn't you tell us?" Tamar's voice broke into Serpé's thoughts.

Serpé straightened her shoulders and turned to see Tamar, Drommond and Aldric behind her. They blocked the exit, holding their mounts behind them. She recognized the hurt in Tamar's voice and knew she caused the pain in her friend.

"This is my battle, not yours. I don't know what I'll find in Arcadia and I don't want any of you hurt." Serpé wanted to stand strong against their disapproving glances, but their friendship had gotten her through so much already. It felt wrong to ask them to stay behind.

"It be our choice, not yers, if we want to go with ye or not. We choose to go." Drommond alone spoke, but she saw the others nodding in agreement. Even Aldric agreed without hesitation and did not offer any argument.

Relief replaced the fear nagging at Serpé. Even if Kian did not want her, these three friends did. They could always be counted on to support her. She smiled at them, eager to start the journey.

"Thank you, my friends." Serpé pulled herself into her saddle, and waited for the others to mount their horses. Once they were settled, she led them from the stable. "Let's see if we can stop this war."

Chapter 36

Kian stepped aside when the guard's large sword slice downward next to him. Locking the man's sword with his main-gauche, he brought his own sword down in an almost careless swing and cut the man's head off. Without a glance or thought for the downed man, he engaged the next guard that came at him.

The new attacker slid his legs apart, raising his sword arm above his head and his empty hand flat-palmed toward the rebel captain. Kian sighed in annoyance at his new opponent's arrogance. Instead of waiting, he stepped in under the man's defenses and impaled him with his sword. The man no longer resisted the sword holding him, giving Kian a brief moment of regret that the fight was so quick. The body slid off Kian's blade, to the ground. Looking around for another opponent, irritation swelled in him that no one stepped up to fill the space around him.

"Kian!"

Hoping that someone was attacking him from behind, he turned, his weapons raised. Instead, disappointment fueled his frustration over seeing he stood alone. Not even his men were near him.

Somehow Kian had crossed the field, ending closer to the Religious Guard than his army. He saw that his men had tried to stay with him, but they still fought quite a distance back. The Religious Guard had not moved away, but they stared at him, shock on their faces. He took a step toward them and the closest ones backed away, their shock becoming fear. Turning back to look at his own men, he saw the fear in their eyes as well.

"What is taking so long? Come and get me!" His shout hurt his throat and his lungs cried for fresh air, but he refused to acknowledge either. Swinging his arms up, he made sure the Guard knew he directed his order at them. He wanted to fight someone, to send more to the land of the dead. None stepped forward.

The order for retreat echoed from the Religious Guard, eliciting another roar from Kian.

I've been denied! Now I have to wait for the next battle.

Cleaning his weapons, he started walked back to his men, his movements automatic. Without a glance at his blades, he sheathed them. His gaze drifted between the men who had fallen to his wrath, each easily identified in a distinct line of bodies that followed his path across the field of battle. His steps slowed, the savagery in his kills penetrating his bloodlust haze.

I have never been so ruthless. I have never wanted to drive my sword through someone like I do right now.

Pain radiated through his body now, from wounds he had not realized he received. A quick glance showed cuts on his arms and he felt the ones on his torso and legs.

My anger has masked the pain of every wound.

A sudden, crippling pain ripped into his right shoulder. The pain drove him to one knee. Reaching over his shoulder, he tried to pull out whatever had hurt him.

"You have a death wish, Captain? Allow me to help you make it come true."

Kian did not recognize the voice, and the pain increased as his attacker drove the weapon deeper. Somehow, he turned his head despite the pain. His attacker stood over him, a long, thin stiletto in his hand.

It felt as if the man tried to push the entire length of the stiletto into Kian's shoulder. Each forceful push sent paralyzing pain through his body. Through the pain, he recognized the man as the last one he fought.

I should have made sure he was dead, not just accepted his fall as his death.

An arrow flew over Kian's head and embedded itself in the man's chest. The pressure on the stiletto lessened, but he still felt the length of it within his flesh. Two more arrows hit the man before he finally released the hilt and Kian could breathe again.

He could not reach the stiletto, his attempts becoming weaker as he watched Blackette and the others rush to him. Either the weapon lay too far back or the pain was too overwhelming. Either way, it hurt no matter how he moved. Trying to lift his right arm was not any better. Finally, he used his left hand to push himself back to his feet.

"Steady, Kian. That doesn't look good." Blackette slipped under Kian's left arm and they walked back to their army.

"It doesn't feel too good either." Grinning at his second-in-command, Kian was disappointed when he did not return it. "It was a good battle though."

"Except for you separating from the rest of us and this little thing sticking out of your shoulder."

"Don't get sentimental on me, Blackette. We all have to die sometime." There was no cause to be so unreasonable, but Kian's emotions were in an uncontrollable mode.

"You're an idiot if you think it's your turn. We won't leave you to fight this war on your own." Blackette stopped, and stepped away from him.

"I don't remember asking any of you to join me." He glared at his officer before he continued on toward the rest of the army by himself. Pain radiated through his body with each step, but he would not stop now. He had a point to make.

"We came out of loyalty and faith that you would stop Reicholt," Blackette shouted from behind him.

"I didn't ask for your faith or your loyalty. Just add your names to the list of lives I've ruined," Kian yelled back, his last word strangled by the pain his movement elicited.

Hands reached out to help him when he reached the camp. Pushing them away, he flinched from the pain they caused him and continued walking until a man in front of him would not move. He raised his gaze from the ground, determined to move the man one way or another.

"Get out of my…Bennan," he growled. Feeling only a need to punch his friend, instead of greet him, Kian tried to lift his right hand, but the pain in his arm and shoulder paralyzed the limb.

"How about we get that dagger out before you punch me? I'm willing to wait." His friend's attempt at humor soured in Kian's ears.

I hate when he reads my mind.

"Fine, but don't expect me to forget." Bennan took Kian left arm, forcing him to accept the offered help.

They walked in silence until they reached Kian's tent. In front of the tent, a woman waited for them, one of the clerics that had joined the army and the only female. Kian watched her eyes widen when she saw the stiletto protruding from his shoulder and the disapproving clicks of her tongue irritated him before he reached her.

"Why didn't someone handle this on the field?"

"Seems Kian is at odds with everyone today, Molena," Bennan answered and earned another glare from Kian. "He's waiting to punch me as soon as it's out, though."

"You won't punch anyone, at least not today. Maybe not tomorrow either." She helped Bennan guide Kian to his bed and sat next to him on the blankets. "Just sit back. Let me take care of you for awhile."

Kian tried to take a deep breath, but stabbing pain shot through his body. "Make it quick. I can't breathe."

"I need a moment." She put her hands on the stiletto, eliciting an immediate hiss from him. Again she clicked her tongue and leaned closer to him. "Here we go." She pulled it out.

Grunting loudly, Kian punched his fist into his thigh. The world threatened to float away, the pain overwhelming him. Then, with fervor, everything slammed back into his body. He leaned forward, supporting himself with his left arm while the warmth of gentle hands caressed his shoulder and the wound. Feeling the muscles knit together and the pain subside, he waited for her spell to end. He still felt a bruise deep inside his muscles, but at least he breathed easier.

"There. Feel better?" She moved to a kneeling position in front of him, the stiletto on the ground next to her. Helping Kian back to a sitting position, her hand lingered on his uninjured shoulder.

"Yes, thank you." He looked up at Bennan. "You get a reprieve for now."

Molena leaned close again. "I could take your other pain

away, if you would let me. I know of your loneliness, Captain."

Kian glanced at Bennan. He saw his friend waiting for him to make a decision.

I know it's been a long time since I've been with a woman, but she is not the one I want. I will not settle for another in Serpé's absence, nor ruin any chance I have of fixing my mistake with her.

"Molena, I...appreciate the concern and while it is a very gracious offer..." He glanced up at Bennan again, only receiving a shrug in response to his silent pleas for help. "I can't accept. I could never give you the attention or devotion you deserve."

"I don't need any of that. I just want to help you." Touching his cheek, she smiled at him, and he had to resist the urge to pull away from her.

"Thank you, but no. I do not want what you are offering."

She stood, a frown marring her face. "If you change your mind, send for me. Now, you need some rest and I have others to attend to." Stepping past him, she went to Bennan and caressed his arm. "Let him rest. If you need anything, I won't be far."

After watching her leave the tent, the two men grinned at each other.

Kian took a deep breath, testing the newly healed muscles. "That was unexpected."

"Almost as unexpected as you trying to get yourself killed in battle. What are you thinking?" Bennan pulled a chair close to the bed and sat, watching him.

"I don't want to talk about it right now, Bennan. Blackette's right. I am an idiot."

Self-deprecation doesn't help either. Maybe I should lie down.

"I wouldn't go that far, but I would say you've definitely made better decisions in the past." As usual, Bennan did not hide his opinion.

"I can't win today, can I?"

His friend shook his head. Kian sighed, picked up the stiletto and stretched out on his blankets.

"I think I'll take her advice and rest. Maybe you and Blackette can discuss my behavior without me." Kian knew he was being difficult, but for the moment, he did not care.

"The men need clear minded leadership from you, Kian." Bennan's quiet voice took on a melodious quality.

"Dammit, Bennan. Don't use your magic on me. I didn't ask for this. I never agreed to lead an army." Placing the stiletto that had caused him so much pain across his chest, Kian closed his eyes.

"We needed help. We both knew we couldn't do this alone." Bennan's voice came to him as if from a distance, the spell increasing in strength.

"Alone would be less painful."

"Sleep, Kian. You don't know what you're saying."

He agreed, or thought he did. He did not remember hearing his voice.

"Serpé and her friends are two changes away, by horse. They are the only ones we've seen in the forest, other than the militia, the elves and ourselves," one of the soldiers reported to Blackette the next day.

Kian listened to the report, though he was not the one the man spoke to. Avoiding Blackette and the other commanders for the day had proved easy, but Bennan refused to bring evening meal into his tent, so he had to leave his seclusion to eat.

"Two changes is farther than your patrol is supposed to take you. What's your reason for going that far?" Blackette asked, crossing his arms.

Blackette's trying hard to keep some semblance of control, considering how I acted yesterday, how I've been acting since I returned. Kian rubbed his hand over his face. *What would Serpé say if she saw this? Would she be disappointed in me?*

"We saw them pass. Shanna traveled out on a patrol of her own after they camped for the night. She says they are on some personal task to Tushin for Serpé." The man glanced at Kian, drawing Blackette's gaze to the captain as well, but neither looked for longer than a heartbeat.

"All right. Wake the next watch." Blackette turned to Kian when Bennan arrived. He gazed at both men. "Why would she go to Tushin?"

"I don't know, but I'll ask her that as soon as I see her." Kian stood from his log next to the fire, and tried to walk past Blackette. Bennan reached out to stop him.

"No, Kian. You should stay here." Bennan's hand rested on the shoulder that had been injured the day before. Pain that had been dull throughout the day flared.

"Bennan, I am going to see her." Kian struggled past the pain to keep his voice from revealing it.

"You need to stay here. Right now is not the time to see her. She will not be forgiving." Bennan pushed Kian back toward the fire.

Kian stared at his friend. *How does he know she won't forgive me?*

"More the reason I should go to her. She thinks I hate her." Hearing the desperation in his voice, Kian realized he no longer felt the need to hide his embarrassment.

Bennan refused to move and though Kian knew his friend was bigger and stronger, he still fought to get past him. He struggled for headway, but finally gave up. They stood in silence, Kian's head bowed, his hand on the shoulder of the man who had been his best friend for more years than he could remember.

"What have I done, Bennan? I pushed away the only person who has made my life worth living. All because of a man we both despise. She *should* hate me." Kian turned back to the fire and his log.

"I'll go and talk to her. She should be willing to speak to me."

Silence surrounded them and Kian felt the gazes of his men on him. He knew they waited to see the outcome of the dispute.

Would she see Bennan going for me as a sign of weakness? Another man shouldn't go to her for me—I should be man enough to face her. But if what Bennan says is true, she won't speak to me anyway.

"Tell her I love her. I think of her always and regret the mistake I made." Kian sighed, the list of things he wanted to tell Serpé made his head ache. He put his head in his hands. "Just tell her I'm sorry."

Chapter 37

They traveled for two days and Serpé could not remember when she last spoke to her friends about anything other than food. She appreciated their companionship, but she remained annoyed with them as well. That annoyance had grown between them despite her initial pleasure.

This journey is a selfish one. They should not be with me. She did not really need to see the ambassador, but it just gave her an excuse to get away from Draven's constant watch. She wanted time away from everyone, time to think and time to decide what to do next.

My thoughts are a better companion for me right now. Tamar and Drommond use every chance they can to ask me how I'm doing. Aldric has told me to just get over it and put my mind back on the task at hand. She glanced across the fire at the druid, favoring him with a glare when he met her gaze. *Sometimes I really hate him.*

"Serpé, did you hear me?" She lifted her gaze from the fire to Tamar's, not surprised to see her frustrated, again. "Of course not. I said I met with one of Kian's patrols. The army is camped close by. If you pushed Adrastos, you could see Kian before sunrise. We could stay with the army for a couple of days before continuing. I don't think that should delay us too much."

"How do you know how much of a delay it will give us?" Serpé's anger rose within her and she made no effort to control it. "How do you know what's waiting for us? How long do we have before it's too late?"

"I don't know because you won't tell me. We have no idea what we're rushing to, or what happened to make you leave so suddenly. You won't tell us anything!" The elf's own anger exploded.

Serpé stood to face her, unmoved by her friend's emotions. "Then maybe you shouldn't have come with me. I don't remember asking any of you to leave your homes this time."

Tamar's mouth twitched. *Say it Tamar. Say whatever it is you're holding back, so I can send you and the others home.* But she remained silent, just staring at Serpé.

"They came because they care about you, because they're your friends." The voice sounded familiar, but it had been months since she heard it.

Yet another person who imposes themselves on the isolation I need.

"How do you know that?" She spun to face the newcomer. "You've been away for months. You haven't even come to check on me since Kian sent me away. And now you claim to know about my friends. You don't know me anymore, Bennan. Maybe you never did."

"You don't mean that, Serpé." Bennan stepped toward her, his hand extended. She set her jaw and pushed her hands under her arms. Smiling, he nodded. "All right. But tell me, what are you really upset about?"

"I just want to be alone. There was no reason for Draven to send them with me."

Tamar moved in to say something, but Bennan held up his hand to stop her.

"She is upset, Tamar. To find the buried truth, we must deal with the outer lies." He returned his attention to Serpé. "We both know that isn't the only reason you are upset. Does Tamar know?"

Serpé took a deep breath. "No, I didn't tell anyone what happened."

"He knows you are close. The patrol that met Tamar told him. He wanted to come, but I knew it was not time yet for you to see him." Bennan laid his arm on her shoulders and she let him guide her back to the place where she had sat before Tamar came back to camp.

"I went to him, told him I love him. But he rejected me, told me that he didn't love me. He broke my heart, made me feel inadequate and unworthy of him."

Bennan's right. I am being unfair to my friends. They deserve to know what has upset me. We have been through so much together.

"I do not think that is what he meant to do. However, I am not here to find fault with your emotions or make you feel better. I just don't want you to take it out on your friends," Bennan soothed.

She looked at him in disbelief. "We would have worked it out ourselves. Does he know you're here?"

"Yes, I told him I was coming." Bennan lowered his voice, so the others could not hear.

"And he let you come? But all you tell me is that you wanted me to make up with my friends?" He gave her a half nod. "Don't lie to me. Not now. What did he tell you to tell me? What is his message?"

"He said several things that he wanted you to know. But ultimately, he wanted you to know that he was sorry. I assume it's because of what you said happened." He put his arm around her again. The warmth of his embrace comforted her and she moved closer to him.

"You delivered the message and mended my relationship with my friends. How long will you stay?"

"Until you are asleep."

She felt her body grow heavy with sleep. She tried to fight it, but the effort made her more tired, until her eyes closed. *He's using magic on me. I can feel my skin tingle from it. Why am I unable to resist it?*

"Take her to her tent. I will care for her from there." Serpé heard Tamar's instructions and felt Bennan carry her into her tent. By then, the magic induced sleep took her completely under.

Chapter 38

Their journey to the Tushin capital, Arcadia, finally ended after two weeks. Serpé sat upon Adrastos and watched the line of merchants and travelers who wanted entrance to the city. She waited while the guards searched wagons and questioned people. Even she and her friends were scrutinized because they brought no wagon of goods to sell in the market. When the guards finally allowed them past the gates, she followed directions to city hall and avoided the market square.

They walked their horses, while Tamar and Drommond marveled over the size of the city and how many people lived there. Serpé shot a quick glance behind her to see Aldric obviously uncomfortable in the city. He almost clung to his horse, shying away from so many individuals.

Where her friends felt uncomfortable or awed by the city, Serpé felt like she had come home. She loved Kian's farm, the village of Valen and her own farm, but she enjoyed the sounds of the merchants calling out their wares to passersby. Even though they avoided the main market, merchants who had opened their stalls throughout the city begged for their attention. The activity of the city comforted her.

The directions received at the front gate had been accurate and after a short time, the group stood looking up the stairs of city hall. Marble and intricately carved pillars lined the entrance above the stairs. After they handed over the reins of their horses to Tamar and Drommond, Serpé and Aldric walked into the building.

Statues of unknown people stood guard between the pillars and the outside wall of the building. Reliefs lay carved onto the wall, scenes of great accomplishments for the people of Tushin. Inside, more marble pillars connected the floor and ceiling. Large double doors opposite the ones they entered through stood closed. A man sat in front of them at a wooden desk. He looked up when the main doors closed behind them, but glanced at the doors he blocked before he gave them his full attention.

"May I help you?" His voice held a feminine pitch to it and Serpé hid the smile it brought to her lips.

Serpé waited until she drew closer to the desk before she answered. "We've come seeking an audience with Ambassador Tolan."

"I'm sorry, but that's not possible." The clerk rested his hands on the book in front of him.

"But you didn't even look in your appointment book. How can you be sure?" She calmed the desperation rising in her, and gestured at the book he covered with his hands. "Please check for me. It's very important."

"I don't have to check. I know. The ambassador has no available appointments for at least a month." He pulled his book from the desk and held it close to his chest. "Now, if you will excuse me." He stood, bowed, then left Serpé and Drommond standing there.

"I don't believe it. He didn't even try to help us." She stared at the empty desk.

Aldric followed her from the building when she pulled herself away from the desk. "So now what?"

"I don't know." The door opened and as she stepped out, the bright sun blinded her and she did not see a man entering. They bumped into each other, and she stepped back, rubbing her jaw where she hit it on the man's shoulder. "Excuse me. I couldn't see you because of the sun."

"The apologies are mine, Dame Navran. I should have waited until you left, so I did not startle you." The man bowed, before pulling a folded parchment from his sleeve. "I have come to extend an invitation to you and your companions to join my master, Ambassador Tolan, for conversation, and meals. He also offers you a place to sleep for as long as you are here."

Serpé accepted the parchment, staring at him. Aldric pinched her arm and the quick jolt made her blink. She looked down at the parchment in embarrassment.

"I'm sorry for staring. How do you know who I am?"

"My lord has spoken of no one but you since he received your message. He described you to me numerous times and though it has been over four years since he last saw you, the beauty he spoke of is wonderful to behold," the man said with wonder in his voice.

She felt her face redden.

"I have waited outside this building for the last two runs for you to arrive. May we go now? He is waiting for us."

She nodded. It took only moments to inform Tamar and Drommond of the change in plans.

They traveled through the city, until the servant led them into a portion filled with estates. The homes were not close, so each estate contained a large area of land around the buildings. Stables, gardens and servant quarters, along with private guards, were all comfortably placed on each piece of property. Tolan's servant guided them past the estates until they arrived at the last one on the road.

When they stopped, Serpé took the time to examine her surroundings and the estate they stood in front of. The land appeared twice the size of the other estates and the building towered over them with three stories instead of two. Each window shined, dressed with lace, a touch the ambassador's wife must have insisted on. Sunlight reflected off the windows, and brightened the roses that filled the garden with different colors. The first level of the house was brick, the second and third levels made from a dark wood.

As they gazed at the estate, a man stepped around a corner and walked toward them.

"This is Jorsen," their guide introduced the newcomer. "He will tend to your horses. Please leave them and follow me."

Serpé patted Adrastos and whispered to him. She did not like the idea of a stranger caring for her horse, but someone had to take him while she talked to the ambassador. After she told the horse several times to behave, she handed the reins to Jorsen and followed the others into the house.

Inside, lavish furnishings and paintings revealed the

expensive choices of the owner. Pottery, crystal vases, small statues and other pieces of fine art were placed throughout the entryway and the rooms they saw from their position. Serpé left the others at the door to examine a statue at the bottom of the stairway.

The quiet murmurs of her companions stopped, and she turned to see them staring past her, toward the top of the stairs. Following their gazes, her eyes came to rest on their host who made his way toward them.

He stood tall, as tall as Kian, and almost as muscular. His features were more squared in the jaw, and cheeks, but he still looked handsome. His brown eyes surveyed those at the door, but he did not appear to notice Serpé yet. She took a moment more to look at him without speaking. She liked how his long, brown hair was pulled back from his face with a leather thong and how the softened calfskin breeches and blue silk shirt fit him.

"Welcome to Arcadia. I hope Vinsun was able to…" He turned toward Serpé and stared at her. Serpé shuffled her feet, uncomfortable under his intense gaze before he cleared his throat in embarrassment. "Serpé, you are more beautiful than I remember." He finished his descent and stopped next to her.

"Rodin, I never thought I would see you again." She ignored his embarrassment and her smile grew larger when he pulled her into his embrace.

She saw her friends shift in discomfort when the embrace lasted longer than expected. Serpé cleared her throat, and he loosened his hold on her, but only released her with one arm. Smiling at her friends, she was relieved to see them smile in return.

"Vinsun sent a message to me as soon as you arrived at City Hall." He gestured down the hall and led them into the dining room. "And, I have had midday meal prepared for you."

The meal was a good change from the smoked meat and dried fruit they had eaten since they left Valen. Traveler's inns were not allowed within the Sorban borders, so they had not been able to eat fresh cooked food. Serpé laughed at Drommond's dramatics as he ate, his exaggerated moans of pleasure too loud to have a conversation over.

Finally they finished, but still sat at the table, and drank the tea Vinsun served. Serpé watched Rodin in silence, unsure when she should ask about the war she had come to stop. Rodin sat next to her and as he chatted with her friends about their homes, he slipped his hand over hers and squeezed.

He is so comfortable with me. Have I forgotten something? Were we closer than I remember?

She pulled her hand from his. "Rodin, what are you doing here? Is there any real concern about a war?"

"If I am successful, then it will not become real. I meet with King Malcylm and his council weekly, trying to help them understand that the Sorban merchant council does not want a war with Tushin." He tried to take her hand again, but she slid it into her lap. "Why did you come here? Your letter was so vague."

"I came to offer what help I could against The First's false war. Captain Donwell continues his offensives and since I am forbidden from helping him, I wanted to help somewhere." Serpé's stomach clenched when she told Rodin of Kian's order to not help him.

"It is good to hear that Kian is keeping Reicholt occupied on a military front while I deal with his political ambitions. Kian is a strong and talented warrior. It was a sad day when Sorban lost him from its service. Keeping you out of Reicholt's hands is important to me. Even here, you're in danger. The First has many men looking for you." The smile Rodin gave her was filled with sadness. "The First has spies even within Arcadia. I'm sure they know you are here. I can only hope they don't try anything while you are within these walls." He stood and gestured for the steward. "I had Vinsun prepare rooms for all of you. Everyone is welcome to wander the estate. I do have to ask that you stay on property, for your own safety."

Serpé nodded, and stood. "We will not leave the estate. We don't want any problems while we're here." Serpé sighed in frustration as she followed Vinsun from the dining room. *Again, someone is watching out for my safety. I will never escape this.*

Another luxury, a hot bath, awaited Serpé in the room Vinsun escorted her to. A maid also waited, and after Serpé stepped into the tub, her clothes were given to Vinsun to be cleaned.

Serpé relaxed in the hot water and allowed the lavender scented oils to wash over her senses. *The luxury Rodin lives in reminds me of how I lived with Reicholt.*

She had watched more expensive things, food, and clothing, fill Reicholt's estate as his contributions increased. Her own family's wealth had been significant, but her parents had lived modestly compared to the priest and Rodin.

When the water cooled, she left the tub to find a silk dress on the bed. Fingering the blue Sorban silk, she tried to remember the last time she had worn something so beautiful. Slippers of the same blue waited on the floor for her feet. Though Reicholt had the money, he never gave her clothes like this.

The maid helped her dress and after the last button had been hooked and the silken strands of the gown were tightened around the bodice, she worked on Serpé's hair. Her long hair was pulled on top of her head and held in place with sapphire encrusted combs. Several locks were allowed to hang free and touch her neck. Sapphire earrings now dangled like teardrops from her ears, but her neck lay bare. *Too bad Rodin doesn't understand fashion well enough to have bought a matching necklace. But for the most part, I think I can pass for acceptable.*

She walked down the stairs, careful with her steps. Before she reached the halfway point, Rodin stepped around the bottom rail, to wait for her. His eyes shined, filled with admiration, and his smile left no doubt that her look pleased him. When she reached him, he took her hand in his and kissed it.

"The beauty of the dress, the jewels—they are nothing compared to your beauty." He reached into a pocket and pulled out a silk pouch. "Maybe I shouldn't worry about this, but your neck looks—naked."

Serpé heard a hint of desire in his word, but she chose to ignore it as she watched him remove a necklace from the pouch. It matched the earrings, with diamonds that accented the deep sapphires. *Oh, he is better than I realized.*

Her gaze followed his movement, but it still surprised her when the cold stones and metal touched her neck. She sucked in a sharp breath, Rodin's warm touch next to the cold of the necklace a severe contrast. He smiled briefly at her sharp breath.

"There, now it looks complete."

Again, she chose to ignore the husky tone of his voice. *We barely know each other.*

"Where are the others?" She heard no sounds from the dining room and did not see any lights.

"They are on the veranda." He took her hand again, and guided her outside.

When she crossed the threshold of the door, her friends rose to their feet. They spoke over each other and she laughed when Tamar gave up and embraced her.

"You look beautiful," her friend leaned close to her ear to whisper. "Did he pick this out especially for you?"

Serpé nodded, then accepted the chair Rodin pulled out for her. Drommond reached over and squeezed her hand.

She smiled in return. "Thank you. It feels good to be in non-essential clothes."

During dinner, Serpé listened to the quiet conversation of the others. She knew her friends would not reveal too much about her recent activities. Since they knew little of her time with Kian, they could not tell Rodin anything from that time either.

"I meet with King Malcylm weekly." Rodin's words drew her attention and she realized the conversation had turned to the war. "He doesn't have time to meet with me daily. I have friends, and my father, who send me information about what's happening in Sorban. My friends give me more appropriate information. They aren't blinded by what Reicholt tries to pass as the truth, or by their refusal to accept the true danger in front of them. Their messages are also not watched as closely as my father's."

Serpé's food had cooled too much to enjoy, but when she tried to eat, Vinsun took the plate and replaced it with a fresh one. "What does King Malcylm say about what you tell him?" Was she more worried about Rodin and King Malcylm doing nothing or making the wrong move?

"He accepts my counsel. Extra patrols guard the border and he insists on a strict accounting of the location of any Sorban soldiers within the city. We use the information to plan against an actual war starting." She felt Rodin's gaze settle on her and she looked up at him.

"Captain Donwell leads the rebels against the Religious Guard. I don't know if they have any information that would help you. But I came here because I wanted to help. I hate waiting and not knowing what's happening." Now that she looked her reasons in the face, she doubted why she had insisted on this trip. With her immediate anger at Kian gone, she was left with only smoldering emotions that had driven her to go against Kian.

Neither Rodin nor Kian needed her help. Both were better off without her. She sat there, an inconvenience and a liability neither could deal with at the moment. *I really should go back to Valen and just wait for all of this to end.*

"Maybe we should go back home. It seems like you have everything under control here, Rodin," she whispered.

"Come to the meeting tomorrow, at least. I'm sure the king would like to meet you."

"Me? Why?" she asked in surprise. "I have nothing special to offer him."

"You never know. Stay the night. Come with me tomorrow. Then you can leave if you want," he insisted.

She mulled it over before nodding. "All right. I'll go with you tomorrow, though I have no idea what I can help you accomplish."

"We will wait and see." Rodin stood, took her hand and pulled her to her feet. "Come. Walk with me through the gardens."

He kept an arm around her waist on their walk through the garden. The summer night cooled her skin. The season had peaked in the southern lands, but here, so far north, snow still cloaked the large mountain that towered over the city. Snow touched everything, year round.

Serpé shivered against Rodin and he pulled her closer for a brief moment, then released her. Before she could protest, he produced a thick square of blue lace from his shirt. He shook the lace from its folds, refolded it once and draped it over her bare shoulders. The material itself did little to protect her from the chill, but the thought warmed her.

Finally, her curiosity won out over caution. "Rodin, why do you try so hard to show me you think I'm beautiful? Why do you look at me with so much love and desire?"

"You don't know?" Surprise filled his voice and he pulled her toward a nearby stone bench. "Not only did you play with my younger sister, but we were to be married. I was the suitor your father refused."

"That's not possible. You're the heir to the ruling merchant family, next in line to sit in your father's place on the council. A marriage between our families would not only be financially feasible, but would also strengthen our country. Why would my father refuse the arrangement?"

"You were eight. I was fourteen. My father thought I was 'wild'. I disobeyed his rules, set cattle free, got escorted home by the city patrols. I did anything to get in trouble. Your father didn't think I would ever settle down or be able to provide you with a stable home, even though we wouldn't marry for another eight years." He shook his head and a sad smile lifted the corners of his mouth. "He was right. I didn't realize how bad I'd been, or how much I hurt my father's reputation until I reached my eighteenth winter. By then, it was too late. Everyone thought you were dead. I had lost my chance to be with you. And then, I heard of the beautiful acolyte that studied under Eion Reicholt. I made every attempt to see this person, even going so far as to follow Reicholt to Siladan.

"One day, I finally saw the student that had so captivated the priests of Azar in a service. After I questioned a priest, I realized it was you. My joy overwhelmed me. I convinced my father it was you and we were prepared to approach your father when you disappeared again. This time, I used magic to try and locate you, but it didn't work." Disappointment marred his features.

"I was devastated. To lose you twice in one lifetime nearly destroyed me. Then I received your letter. I can only hope you are willing to give me a chance to prove I am no longer the boy your father knew. I know you are not mine to claim. I only ask that you give me a chance," he pleaded, covering her hand with his.

She listened in silence, but dropped her gaze to their hands when his covered hers. Finally she returned her gaze to his face.

"Rodin, I don't know what to say. I didn't know who it was that my father had refused. He never told me. But I have offered my heart to one man and had it thrown back at me. I'm not ready to take another chance like that, not yet." Speaking of Kian's rejection made her chest hurt again.

"I want to understand and in a way, I do, even with the pain it causes. This other man is an idiot for not accepting your love with open arms." Rodin pulled her close, and placed a tender kiss on her cheek. "I will always love you, Serpé, even if you marry another. I was an idiot to lose you in the first place. And, when this is all over, if the other hasn't come to his senses and taken you for his wife, I will find you again and properly court you, if you will have me."

"If you have not found another, I would be honored." She kissed his cheek as well, relaxing in the comfort of his embrace. *He seems to respect Kian. I don't want to destroy that with the truth of how he broke my heart.*

They sat together until the chill became too much for Serpé. Without a word in protest, Rodin escorted Serpé to her room. After another soft kiss to her cheek, he closed her door.

She wanted to change her clothes, but the stun over tonight's revelations stayed with her. She remembered no indication from her parents that Rodin had asked to be her husband. After her father told her the prearranged marriage would not happen, they rushed her to the temple of Azar without explanation.

Serpé closed the curtains on the windows, and turned to the dresser for a nightgown. She loosened the laces of her bodice when a knock at the door startled her. Pulling the laces tight again, she hurried over to the door. When she opened it, she stared at Rodin. He had changed into a loose-fitting shirt and breeches.

"What's wrong, Rodin?" She heard no alarms, but the look he gave her made her uncomfortable.

"Nothing. May I come in?" She stepped aside and allowed him into the room. "I do understand your feelings for this other man, Serpé, but I hate feeling like I'm letting you go without a fight."

"There is no reason to fight, for me, for us. There isn't even an 'us.' Don't you think a broken heart is reason enough to give me the time I need to heal?" she protested.

He stepped closer, pulling her into his arms, until his breath caressed her shoulder. "One night, Serpé. One night in your arms would give me the strength to wait another lifetime for you."

Rodin pushed against her, and with gentle pressure on her fingers, took the door from her grasp. The sound as it closed startled her, but he held her close to him, whispering promises into her ear. When he kissed her neck, his lips lit a fire at their touch.

Maybe from the pain Kian had caused her, or the knowledge that Rodin had proposed marriage. Whatever the reason, she gave in.

Her body molded to his and he held her tighter against him. She still smelled the scent of flowers from the garden in his hair. When his lips met with hers, they tasted of spiced wine. That taste sparked her thirst and she sought to drink in his scent— his feel—his taste. Panic rose in her. Would all the sensations fade before she was satisfied?

"How could any man refuse this? If it had been me, I would have grabbed the chance with both hands." As if to demonstrate, he cupped her shoulder with one hand and caressed her arm while he pushed the sleeves of her dress away with the other.

His words woke her from the trance-like haze that had washed over her. She wanted to be loved, needed. He offered everything she wanted. But he was not the man she wanted.

"Rodin, I can't." She pulled away from him, and surprised to find she had to grab her dress to hold it in place. "I'm sorry. I just can't. Not so soon after Kian—" Her empty hand covered her mouth. She had not wanted to reveal this, but his name came so easily to her lips.

Rodin took a deep breath to calm himself, one hand still firm on her arm. When he looked at her, she saw the pain and hurt her abrupt change of heart caused him. His smile, though, was still filled with love for her.

"I assume he was the fool who broke your heart. He's a great military man, but he obviously knows nothing of a woman's needs." Before she could protest, he kissed her again. After he left a trail of small kisses on her neck, he left the room.

She remained where he left her until her own breath calmed. *His last kiss—so intoxicating—yet so different from the one I had shared with Kian.*

"Maybe I should go back to the church. Less heartbreak for anyone who comes near me."

The words that should have followed hung in the air, unspoken. But she felt their heavy weight on her heart and shoulders.

"Less heartbreak for me."

Chapter 39

In the morning, Serpé and her friends accompanied Rodin to the council meeting. The man who refused to help them the day before sat again at his desk. When they walked past him, Serpé wiggled her fingers at him in greeting. At his shocked expression, she covered her mouth to control the laughter that threatened to escape. Rodin looked back, a question on his face, but she waved her hand to keep him moving into the council chambers.

Once inside, Rodin gestured for the others to sit in chairs set aside for guests, and took Serpé by the hand. She let him guide her to the dais where an unornamented throne waited.

"What about the others? Shouldn't we be in the gallery waiting for the meeting to start too?" Serpé glanced back at the partially filled rows of chairs.

"His Majesty wishes to see you and speak to both of us separately. We won't be taking part in the actual meeting today."

"What? Why not? I only agreed to stay so we could take part in the meeting. I want to know if there is anything at all I can do to help prevent this war, not meet with the king because he wants to see the person who escaped Reicholt." Serpé crossed her arms.

"I have not been completely honest with you. I've received

messages from Bennan and Kian about what's happening as well. Most of that has been passed to King Malcylm. The king wants to meet you because of information that has been given to him." Rodin pulled her arms apart and kissed her cheek.

He looked like he had more to tell her, but before she could push him, the curtain behind the throne moved apart. A man in royal finery stepped out. He glanced at Rodin, but his gaze rested on Serpé. She waited, nervous, as he walked up to her and took her hand from Rodin's.

"Dame Navran, it is an honor to meet you finally." He lifted her hand and brushed her skin with his lips.

"The honor is mine, Your Majesty." Serpé did not understand why he was treating her with such reverence. Even a glance behind the king to Rodin did not reveal an answer.

"Dame Navran, I understand the war that we hear of is one created by Most Holy Reicholt. And, we understand that he is doing this to gain power and control over Sorban." He pressed her hand against his chest. "We must protect our people, but we do not want a war with your country. When you are ready to make your move against him, you will have our support."

"I don't understand. Why are you telling me this? I am not the one to lead an attack on The First," Serpé said, confused. *No one has ever spoken to me like this before. I do not understand why he is doing it now.*

King Malcylm's brow furrowed. "I thought you—" He glanced at Rodin, who gave him a slight turn of his head in a negative response. "Interesting. No matter. You will be ready one day. When you are, Tushin supports you."

She stared at him. "Thank you, Your Majesty. Your support is appreciated."

He kissed her hand again before he turned to speak to Rodin. "Thank you, Ambassador Tolan. Please make sure she receives everything she needs for her return home."

"Of course, Your Highness. Blessings upon your meeting." Rodin tipped his head, then took Serpé by the elbow and guided her back to the gallery. Her friends joined them and they left the council chambers.

When they arrived outside the double doors, Serpé pulled her arm from Rodin's grip, and pushed him to a stop with a hand on his chest.

"What was that all about? What is wrong with these people?"

Confusion filled her words as the man at the desk left his chair and kneeled.

"Nothing, Serpé. We must leave. All your supplies have been restocked."

She watched Rodin wave his hand at the kneeling man, then try to hide his movement by rushing her from the building.

"'Nothing' does not answer my questions, Rodin. You and the king know something that I don't and you're forcing me to leave so fast, you're trying to distract me," she protested.

"You don't understand, Serpé. We're trying to protect you." He pushed her into the carriage and joined his driver, preventing any further conversation.

When they arrived at Rodin's estate, Vinsun met them at the gate. He ushered them into the house and into the dining room.

"Eat quickly. I've received a report of The First's men having revealed themselves. They are coming here. The city guards will delay them, but you need to leave," Rodin instructed.

"Then eating is not an option." Serpé made the statement, but Drommond had other plans. Her other companions grabbed rolls before leaving, but Drommond shoved rolls and fruit into cloth napkins and shoved the napkins into the small bag he carried. Serpé watched him, her impatience growing. "Do you have enough, Drommond? If so, we need to leave."

She followed the dwarf out of the house to the stables. Vinsun and Rodin followed, both saying something about the supplies already being on their horses, as well as their clothes and saddlebags. While they crossed the yard to the stables, they heard the commotion of a fight at the estate gates.

Six Religious Guards broke through the gate. Beyond them, another twenty men waited to step through. Serpé and the others stepped up to block the intruders. She found her rhythm easily—parry and attack, block and riposte. She was not intent on the killing blow, just in defending herself and pushing the men back.

Without warning, Serpé's shoulder burned and she almost dropped her main-gauche. Spinning to face the new threat, she raised her weapons in a defensive posture and stopped in surprise.

Her blood dripped from the man's blade, but the pain and burning in her shoulder melted away, forgotten in her shock.

Earlier that day, the man accompanied her and Rodin to the council chambers. He led the contingent of Rodin's personal guard, but she did not know his name. When they returned to the estate, he had not been with them. She assumed he left before them, to prepare the estate's defenses. Now he wore the surcoat of the Religious Guard instead of the Tolan family.

She brought her sword up again to block his next attack. Though she blocked the blow, his weight pushed her back, first one step, then another. Her sword slid down the length of his blade until the basket of her hilt caught his. Disengaging her main-gauche from the block, Serpé slashed it across his stomach. She had to be satisfied with cutting his shirt, though she would have preferred the bite of her blade in his skin. He pressed his attack and continued to push her back with his weighted blows.

When the attacks stopped, she had to move back again, not because of his blows, but because of a sword that appeared in his chest. She waited until he fell to the ground, then looked up to see Rodin pulled his weapon free. He stepped past the corpse, wrapped her in his embrace and kissed her.

"Get out of here, Serpé. These men think that capturing you will endear them to Reicholt." He kissed her again, then pushed her toward the stables. "Jorsen will guide you out of the city. Azar's blessings protect you."

She ran through the battle, her friends following her. They covered the distance and mounted their horses with skilled speed. Before she led Adrastos from the stable, Vinsun stopped her.

"Master Tolan had me put a message for Captain Donwell and Merchant Tolan in your bags. He asks that they be delivered, when you can."

"Of course, Vinsun. Thank you for your help." She urged Adrastos ahead and they followed Jorsen out of the estate through a back entrance.

Chapter 40

No children rushed up to greet them or beg for sweets. Serpé didn't mention this, but she saw that the others also knew something was wrong. The only adults they saw peeked out from behind windows and buildings.

The village lay close to the route they traveled home, and Serpé had wanted to stay the night here. But the absence of normal activity did not bode well.

Tamar brought her horse close to Adrastos. "Why are they hiding?" Her question, whispered loud enough to hear, did not disturb the quiet of the village.

"I don't know." Serpé turned at the sound of voices raised in protest. "That's coming from the center of the village. We might find answers there."

They followed the sounds until they found a large group of villagers gathered around a well. But the well was not the focus of their attention. On a white horse, his back to Serpé and her friends, a man held up an empty sack. Another horse and rider stood in front of the villagers, but he only stared at them.

"You are late in paying your tribute to the church. This affects Azar's blessings upon you and your village," the man with the sack shouted at the gathered people. Though she knew he did not speak directly to her, Serpé felt each word like a dagger striking her chest.

There had been a time when she collected tributes for the church, but the money she collected had been given willingly and without threats, at least from her. She knew there were others who collected money for Reicholt, but she never saw them or heard of questionable methods they used. That is, until today. She did not like how it made her feel.

"I thought Azar's blessings were freely given to all the faithful, no matter how much they gave in tribute or how little. You sound more like a tax collector than a man of Azar." She looked at her friends, who stared at her. The words made her feel better, despite the look of anger she now saw on the face of the collector.

"And just who do you think you are to speak of Azar with such familiarity?" he demanded.

"I was once a student of Most Holy Eion Reicholt and I am a follower of Azar's teachings." She pointed at him. "You are a thief, using Azar's name to make Reicholt rich."

"Blasphemer! How dare you make such accusations!" The collector dropped the bag he held and drew his sword. The guard with him followed suit.

Instead of attacking together, the guard charged the group of friends. Serpé drew her own sword, blocking his attack when he came closer. The collector was heavier, stronger, but Adrastos was a combat trained horse. The adjustment in her weight when the man tried to force his blade past her, the shift of her knees signaled, to the horse to sidestep the advance.

Her change in position freed the blade, and she leaned back, guiding Adrastos to step away again. The guard's sword cut into her thigh, but she ignored the pain and used it to fuel her anger. Drawing her main-gauche, she threw it.

The sun caught the metal of the weapon as it covered the short distance. Squinted from the glare, she grinned when the distinct sound of it sinking into his flesh reached her.

The collector sped his horse toward her until the twang of a bow rang out. An arrow struck his right shoulder and his look of surprise disappeared when he fell from his horse.

Serpé dismounted, took the reins of the other horse to prevent it from running and passed them to Aldric. In stepping past the fallen guard, she realized he still lived. She felt nothing when she leaned over and yanked her main-gauche from him. She continued past him to the collector. Her thigh ached from the wound she had received, but in her anger, she ignored the developing limp.

When he saw her, the collector tried to crawl away, on his back, his own weapon forgotten on the ground. Serpé followed him, sure that the look on her face warranted the fear on his. Then he was against the brick of the well, with nowhere to go.

The adults of the village separated. The women herded the children to the other side of the square. The men moved closer and surrounded Serpé and the collector. None of the men said anything, but she heard Tamar urging her to back away.

"My friend wants me to let you leave. What do you think I should do?" She twirled the main-gauche in her hand.

"Let me live. Let me go. I promise I won't tell anyone what happened here," he cried.

She leaned in, her mouth close to his ear. "I don't care if you tell anyone about this."

"When Reicholt finds out what you've done, he will have you hunted down and hanged."

Serpé smiled. "He's only found me once in four years. What makes you think he'll find me now?"

His eyes widened. "You're Serpé Navran," he breathed.

"Now you understand. Get up." She did not care if Reicholt's men knew who she was. It was time to stop hiding. "I can't kill you when you're on your back." She straightened and turned away from him.

From the corner of her eye, Serpé saw him stand, but she waited even after he picked up his sword. He lunged at her, and the moment before his weapon struck her, she swung her own sword down her back, stopping it. She pivoted to her left and pushed his blade past her.

The move brought him closer and she thrust her main-gauche out behind her. The feel of her blade burying into his flesh stopped the momentum of her swing and his weight pulled the weapon from her hand.

She turned to look at him. The looks of shock the men around her wore made her stop when she reached for the blade. Despite their expressions, she removed it and straightened her back again.

One of the men separated from the others. "What did you do? The First will just send another, with more guards."

"Not once he hears who did this." She walked over to pick

up the bag the collector had dropped. Then she returned to his horse and rifled through his saddle bags.

After she separated smaller pouches from personal items and books, she handed two pouches to the man who spoke to her. His eyes widened when he heard the tinkle of coins.

"What do you think he would have done if you hadn't been able to pay?" She watched as he lifted his shoulders. "He would return with soldiers who would have arrested all of you. The men would have been killed or forced into military service. Your women would have been sold into slavery or prostitution. And your children as well, depending on age. Can you stand there and tell me you would prefer that over what I've done?"

"No. We will have to fight when the next one comes." The other men in the crowd nodded in agreement.

"I think that would be a good idea," Serpé agreed. She put the other pouches into one bag and walked back to her horse.

"What are you going to do with the rest of the money?" The man called after her.

"The guards aren't here right now because they are probably taking another village to Siladan for the slavers. I will use it to help free as many as I can." She turned back to the villagers and the women and children who had come back. "You need to defend yourselves."

"We will. Travel safe and with the Mother's Blessings."

Tamar, Aldric and Drommond followed Serpé from the village. Without a word, she turned toward Siladan.

"Serpé, home be the other way," Drommond called to her from behind her.

She stopped and turned to see that her friends halted some distance back. She rode back to them.

"I know where home is. I'm going into Siladan to use Reicholt's money against him."

"We aren't supposed to go to Siladan. We aren't supposed to let you go to Siladan," Aldric announced, earning a glare from Tamar. Drommond lowered his head.

"You've never mentioned this. Who told you that?" Serpé already knew the answer, though. Only she had not known they were part of the deception.

Her friends remained quiet for a moment, then Tamar lowered her gaze. "Lord Draven. He said he was told not to let you go there. We were only following his orders."

"Why hasn't this come up before?"

Tamar's gaze returned to Serpé's. "This is the closest we've been to Siladan."

"I'm still going. Come if you want or go back home. It doesn't matter. I'm taking the chance to strike back at Reicholt." She paused and smiled at them, trying to take the edge off her words. "I'm sorry. It does matter. But I won't let you stop me."

They stared at each other, until, one at a time they each nodded. Serpé turned back toward Siladan and they continued their journey.

Chapter 41

They had not yet reached Siladan when they came across a slave market. They mixed in with the people there to buy slaves. Tamar stayed with the horses at the edge of camp, as did Drommond, while Aldric and Serpé went in deeper.

The lines of women and children for sale were long. Serpé walked down each line, her heart breaking. Her cheeks moistened with tears. *If I wasn't outnumbered by the guards, I would cut each one free.*

"If you want this to work, you need to stop those tears." Aldric's hiss in her ear sounded angry and she spun on her heel to glare at him.

"Unlike you, I actually have emotions." She rubbed her face dry. "This will work."

She wanted to free all the women and children, but she had not realized how many were there. Unless the slavers were in a hurry to get rid of their merchandise, she would be lucky to get away with just the children.

Serpé calculated the money she had taken from the collector, adding in the money she already had and counted the children. Unless she could keep the price down, she would not be able to free them all.

"I can get most, but getting all will be hard. I don't have enough," she whispered to Aldric.

"Tamar and Drommond gave me these. It should help." He held out two more pouches.

She took them, fingered the contents, and nodded. A quick glance around and she found the merchant amidst several other men. He sat under a canopy in a cushioned chair while those negotiating for slaves stood, blinded by the glare of the sun.

Without looking at the guards or the others who stood before the merchant, Serpé sauntered up to him and took his glass of wine from him. She sipped and with a grimace handed it back to him.

"Not a very good choice for someone of your stature. You should have a better wine in your glass." She crossed her arms and waited.

"Is that so? And just who do you think you are to charge up there, take my wine from me and tell me it is a poor choice?" he demanded.

"My name is unimportant. What *is* important is that I want to make a purchase." His eyes widened and she saw the question form in his mind. "A large purchase. I want all the children."

He nodded. "Forty gold per head," he announced without pause.

She laughed. "The youngest won't be worth that for at least three years. Ten for the youngest, five and under. Twenty for the rest."

"I thought you wanted to make a deal. I'm not in the business of giving my merchandise away."

"And I'm not in the business of throwing my gold away. These children were taken from their parents and will require extra discipline. That costs money and takes time." Serpé shook one of the pouches of gold. "Fifteen pieces flat for all."

"Thirty." Gasps and protests from those behind Serpé almost drowned his offer, but she had heard. Still, she shook her head in the negative.

"Twenty."

He glared at her, his eyes narrow. "You are hurting my profits. Twenty-five pieces."

"It cost you nothing to acquire them." She leaned toward him. "We both know where they came from. It would be unfortunate if the church found out, don't you think?"

"I don't worry about the church," he smirked.

"You misunderstand me. I mean the church in Sanctuary. I

know the church in Sorban is useless." His eyes widened. "Now, my final offer, twenty-two pieces each, flat. And I won't give your name to any of the priests or knights in Sanctuary."

The slave merchant nodded. "Deal." He gestured at the men around him. "Help her with the shackles."

She straightened and followed one of the guards. Before unshackling the first child, he accepted the gold in payment. After tying a length of rope around the waist of each child, he removed the shackles.

Serpé watched Aldric walk down the chain of women and stopped at each one that reacted to the sale of their children. She assumed they were the mothers or older sisters and she felt her heart break again at the expression each carried with them.

When all the children stood free of the chains, she led them to Tamar and Drommond.

"We must get away from here as quickly as possible." Serpé looked down the line of the children. They only had the four horses and though she could see Siladan and knew she could be there before nightfall, the children could not move that fast.

Finally she handed the rest of the money to Aldric. "You may not be able to get another horse, but you may find a wagon to buy. Get the children to Valen—my farm. I will return there as fast as I can."

"What do you mean?" Tamar turned from the child she had helped onto her horse.

"I'm going into Siladan to try and end this." Her friends protested, but she held up her hand and shook her head. "No, I understand your concerns, but you won't stop me. Get the rope off them. Make sure you get food for them when you can. Take my food and water. I'll get more in the city."

Tamar embraced her. "I do not like this. We will be in a considerable amount of trouble. Be careful."

Serpé watched them put the smallest children on the horses and leave the rope on the ground. She waited until they moved away from the slavers. Once she felt sure they were not being followed, she mounted Adrastos and rode into Siladan.

Chapter 42

Eion gazed at the crowd in front of him. The stage he stood on near the town square fountain was erected specifically for executing three of the mercenaries he had hired. Though he was not disappointed with their performance, he knew if someone was not punished for the attacks, the people would soon revolt. Previous executions took place in the prison. Today's would show the people how he protected them.

Everyone, including the town crier, made an extravagant show when the prisoners were brought onto the stage. Boos and hisses filled the square. The First stepped back and the prisoners were taken to the wooden blocks without hindrance.

With the prisoners in place, he approached the front of the stage and held up a hand. "These men are responsible for the attacks on the merchant caravans that have caused the increase in prices and the lack of items in our markets. The combined strength of our military forces captured them and brought them to justice. I promised I would protect my people. These mercenaries will be punished."

One of the men struggled against the guards holding him. "We did everything you told us to. All the attacks were on your orders."

The guard on his right punched the man in his stomach, bringing a quick end to his claims. Eion stared at the mercenary, before turning back to the crowd with a carefully placed expression of disappointment and sadness.

"Hear the lies they spread? The pain they try to cause? After all the deaths and loss of money for our kingdom, now they try to accuse your religious leader of crimes they are responsible for." He shook his head and when he brought his gaze back up, his cheeks were wet with tears.

He glanced at Captain Marcin, raised his hand, bringing it down in a cutting gesture. Strinnal immediately repeated the signal. The guards pushed the three mercenaries to their knees, and strapped them down over the wooden blocks. Three more guards came forward with axes and took position at each block. A second signal from Strinnal and the axes descended upon the prisoners. A surge of deep satisfaction filled Eion at the gasp of the crowd when the heads fell into baskets.

"Let the punishment of these criminals be a lesson to all who try and bring harm to our people." He performed a blessing over the gathering.

Silence fell upon the crowd when the heads of the mercenaries were placed on the points of pikes and carried away by the guards.

With the gruesome trophies gone, Reicholt faced his faithful. "My children, we must tell the merchant council that we will no longer sit back and accept their inability to protect us. We must demand they do whatever is necessary to protect us and unite the Guards permanently under the church's guidance."

The people in front of the stage shouted in agreement and he reveled in their adoration. *Yes, but there are those who do not join in the cheering and chanting of my name. But soon, even they will do it.* He watched the crowd move toward the council building, a satisfied smirk filling his face.

"Most Holy, I have word from Tushin." The First turned to see that Strinnal had not followed the crowd. "Serpé and her friends were at the home of Ambassador Tolan. Our men attempted to capture her, as your previous orders instructed, but she escaped and most of the Guard were killed by the ambassador's men."

"Does she know the truth about the war with Tushin?"

Strinnal nodded. Eion balked to see the man pale. "We received confirmation from our spy, before he was killed, that she does know the truth."

Eion stood silent, watching the last of the crowd disappear. Finally he returned his attention to his captain.

"You will lead a force against Kian's army. I want him crippled. Make sure he survives, and he is followed. If he knows where Serpé hides, then he will show us."

"I am not done, Most Holy. There is more."

Though he wanted to snap at him, Eion allowed the captain to continue.

"She killed one of your tribute collectors shortly before she and her friends separated. We do not know where she is now."

"This does not change what I want, Captain. If you have some concern for my safety, then contact a commander you trust to follow my orders precisely. If she returns to wherever she's been hiding, we will have her. If she comes here, we will have her." Eion grinned when Strinnal stepped back. His voice sounded malicious even to him. "Either way, I will have her."

"Of course, Most Holy."

"Now, go. Make sure your men treat the people with care. They must believe we are the only ones who have any concern for them."

Strinnal nodded, and left the priest alone. Eion stood on the stage for several moments. His failed attempts to control his anger kept him in place longer. *Serpé is not supposed to know of my plans. Now that she does, it will be more difficult for me to bring them to fruition. I must prevent her from telling anyone. Unfortunately for her, this means her parents must die.*

Eion breathed deeply, forcing his face to relax. He moved his head, the muscles in his neck loosening with the movement. Sure that his anger was well hidden, he left the square. On his way to his office in the temple, he went over the list of men who could take care of the Navrans for him.

Chapter 43

Serpé watched the guards carry the bodies of the mercenaries away from the stage. She was sure the beheadings evoked the desired response from the crowd of observers. The First practically glowed.

I never expected Reicholt to be so bloodthirsty. Beheading men as if he were drinking afternoon tea.

She waited for Reicholt to leave the stage before moving out into the street behind him. He did not look around him. People walked up to the priest and asked for blessings. She noted his distracted movements in the gestures he made over their heads. *He is not even paying attention to the faithful.*

Reicholt's journey through the city took them both to the temple. Serpé stopped across the street, and watched him enter the building.

I miss the services. The last service I attended was two years after I went to live with Kian. The two had come to the city because Kian needed to attend to some business for his parents. His father had passed away and his mother wanted him to take over the businesses they owned. Instead, he convinced her to have Denai's husband run the businesses.

His mother was such a sweet woman, so welcoming to me. The visit reminded Serpé of how much she missed her own mother. *I insisted we visit the church, and that was the last time I saw my parents. They didn't recognize me, which wasn't a surprise.*

Kian put a thick cloak over her, with a deep hood. The disguise worked perfectly. The First came me to them during the service and though he had initially been insulted that she did not look up at him, when Kian explained that she was blind due to a childhood accident, The First offered to heal her. Only Kian's quick thinking, claiming that none of the priests had been able to heal the damage, had convinced the priest not to push the point. They left the church with an offer from The First to try again, if they ever felt so inclined.

Kian was very upset with me that day. He made me promise to never insist on coming to the church again. I haven't seen it since.

She watched the doors until the sun began its afternoon journey to the horizon, then returned to the inn where she had paid for a room upon arriving. The inn was owned by a man who supported Kian and Bennan. It was also the inn where she met Bennan the night she left Siladan after The First attacked her. Taking a seat at a table in a darkened corner, she could see the entire room, as well as the door.

The barkeep came to her table, a mug of ale in his hand. "Dame, I have mutton and vegetables for midday meal. We will have stew for evening meal. The missus made bread as well."

"It all sounds wonderful. I will take a plate, but not too much. I want to be able to enjoy the stew tonight." She noticed a bard seated at a table in front of the cold fireplace. "Entertainment tonight?"

"Yes. He claims he doesn't sing, but he plays some instrument and he speaks poetry. He comes highly recommended, so I'm sure he'll be entertaining for a bit." The barkeep turned and went into the kitchen.

Serpé watched the bard tune his lyre, humming to himself while he did it. She hoped his performance would provide a distraction for the night.

Chapter 44

The scream of the alarm grew louder with each moment that passed. Kian hurried to buckle the belt with his sword around his waist. Not much time had passed since the warning came via messenger, but he could hear the patrol entering camp with the intruders now.

Stepping from his tent, Kian joined Blackette and Bennan where they waited outside. Together, they ran to the edge of camp. Three unfamiliar horses and a wagon pulled by two more horses were with his patrol, all silhouetted by the glow of the rising sun. Tapping his sword hilt with his fingers in his impatience, Kian waited until he recognized one of the riders and they were close enough to walk out and meet.

"Tamar, what in the Mother's eyes is going on?" Kian glanced at the men. *These must be the ones Draven told me about.* "Where is Serpé?" The children in the wagon begged for his attention, but he remained focused on Tamar.

"We couldn't stop her," Tamar spoke, her voice edged with panic. "She insisted on going alone, and forbid us from going with her."

Kian studied her, keeping control of his own panic. "Slow down, Tamar. Tell me the whole story." He turned and led them the short distance back to his camp.

"We went to Arcadia and met with someone named Rodin

Tolan. On our way back, we came across a tribute collector for Reicholt. Serpé killed him and his guard, took the money and went to Siladan to find slaves."

"What?" Kian's outburst stopped her and he saw fear in her eyes. "What was she thinking? What were *you* thinking?"

"We tried, but she wouldn't listen." Tamar gestured toward the children. "She bought these children from a slave merchant— to give them back their freedom. Then she sent us to take them to her farm and went into Siladan alone. She said she intended to put an end to everything Reicholt was doing. That was five days ago."

"Wonderful." So much sarcasm and anger filled that one word that fear returned to the elf's eyes. Kian turned his attention to the children. "Why these children?"

"The slaver put them up for sale to pay the taxes their families owed. But Serpé said it was more likely because the families couldn't pay the tribute Reicholt demanded."

"She's right. Take them to Draven and tell him I need them taken to Sanctuary."

Aldric stepped up to them. "That makes more sense than Serpé's instructions."

Kian glanced at him. "How?"

"Serpé wanted them taken to her farm. Shouldn't we at least consider following her instructions?" Tamar glared at the men around her.

"Draven can provide better protection at his tower than you can provide at the farm. Especially if Serpé isn't there. I'll take responsibility for you not following her instructions." They had returned to camp now, but before Kian could give further instructions, the sound of another horse entering the area pulled his attention.

The man pulled his horse to a stop so fast that dirt and leaves swirled up around their legs. "The Religious Guard is on the move. They're headed this way. They will be here in one change."

Chapter 45

Kian sent only three priests with the children and the worse of the injured into the forest. The patrol he sent with them had orders to take them straight to Valen and Draven's tower.

Kian buried the pain from his own injuries deep while he spread words of encouragement to his men. But even with that, he still had time alone before the Religious Guard began their attack.

He stood in the camp, now empty of tents, next to the campfire that still struggled to burn. *Again, too much time alone to think. My anger at my decision faded before Serpé passed us on her way to Arcadia. I fight now for the chance to go to her and tell her I lied. With my thoughts clear, my strikes are true again.* He glanced over at Blackette and Bennan. *I know they have seen the change. I see their approval, though they say nothing.*

Finding a more realistic goal to fight for gave him the focus to become the leader his men needed. He no longer sought revenge for Korewyn's death, the many crimes Reicholt was guilty of, or the loss of Serpé's love. Instead, he was determined to see justice done and to protect the people of Sorban from Reicholt's ambition, a goal he should have fought for from the beginning.

Shouting from the perimeter guards drew everyone's attention to the edge of the camp. His own weapons ready, Kian pushed to the front of his men, joined by Blackette and Bennan. No command to stand ready was needed—he knew his men would follow his example.

"Captain Donwell! You are ordered to surrender yourself and your men to the Religious Guard," the voice boomed through the space between the two armies.

Kian recognized the voice, but he had not expected to hear it. "Only you and your men will be surrendering, to us, Captain Marcin."

He waited, sure that Strinnal would make the first attack. Staring across the field, he saw flags of the other army flapping in the breeze. That cool breeze also kissed his cheek, but not hard enough to move the trees and plains grass.

"Reicholt is planning to attack Serpé. I don't know when." Again he recognized Strinnal's voice in the warning that was carried to him by a message spell on the breeze. "Serpé's parents are dead."

Kian glanced to his right, Bennan's nod confirmed that he heard the same warning. They both looked across the field when the order to attack echoed from the Religious Guard. Kian saw anticipation growing in his men, but no answering cry came from the Religious Guard as they charged forward. Instead, the distinct twang of bows releasing arrows reached them.

"Shields!" Kian released his shield from his back and raised it between him and the arrows when the rain of projectiles reached him.

The arrows hit the shield, driving him to his knees. He ducked and dodged the small number that pierced through the cover, or avoided the shield, but one still punctured his arm. Behind him, he heard the screams of his men who also sustained injuries from the assault.

I need to get them deeper in the trees. The canopy will give us better cover. But I have to keep the Guard out of the forest. I promised Shou Lung, but if we retreat, and they follow us, that promise will be broken.

"Kian!"

Kian turned at Blackette's shout from behind. He saw Blackette kneeling next to one of the clerics, panic filling his expression. The cleric did not move, not even to breathe. But Kian saw only one arrow protruding from the priest's arm.

Looking around, Kian saw all the clerics and mages on the

ground, dead, even though their wounds appeared minimal. Next to him, Bennan appeared ill. Arrows lay at his feet with blood on the tips of each, though he continued to fight.

"Retreat!" Kian ordered.

I'll deal with Shou Lung's anger if the Religious Guard follows us. I need to save my men.

Hearing another volley of arrows released, he twisted to face them. He barely brought his shield up in time to protect his head. Grunting, he realized he brought the shield up too slow and he joined the others who had been hit.

The arrows continued, volley after volley, the archers no longer held back by their commanders. Unable to keep his shield up and make an effective retreat, Kian suffered more hits from the arrows. Men around him also fell to the ground.

Arms encircled him, but he could not see who helped him into the protection of the trees. He fought the darkness gathering around him, barely making out Bennan crawling on the ground toward him. He tried to roll when he heard more arrows soaring through the air. When the next volley struck those hiding within the trees, he reached toward his friend. Sadness filled Kian when he saw the life leave Bennan and he surrendered to the darkness as well.

Chapter 46

This entire trip feels like a waste of time. Serpé swirled the ale in her mug. *I miss the spiced ale… No, I miss what it represented to me. I actually thought it represented a relationship with Kian. How stupid.*

For almost a week, Serpé wandered Siladan, watching The First. Captain Marcin had not been with him for the last two days, so three other guards followed the priest around the city in his daily activities. *I wonder where Strinnal has been.*

The day before, she paid a courier to deliver Rodin's message to his father, Merchant Tolan. Fear that the merchant would hold her and contact The First had made it necessary for Serpé to hire the courier. She did not know what the message said, but she told Rodin she would deliver it. Her task was complete as far as she was concerned.

The noon bell rang from the temple, startling her. *Midday. It's time to go to the church. Please protect me, Azar.*

The service Reicholt presented was just as Serpé remembered it. Sitting in the last pew, the comfort she felt in the church four years earlier did not fill her.

The last time I was here, I didn't feel Azar's touch either. But I did feel Kian's hand over mine and his arm around my waist as he walked me out.

When everyone stood at the end of the service, she left the main area and went to Reicholt's private office. She ignored the statues and tapestries that lined the hall to the room, then went inside before anyone saw her.

While the warming afternoon light created shadows within the room, Serpé sat in the chair in front of the desk. She gazed at the tapestries that depicted the acts of Azar and his visitations to his most devout followers. Her impatience grew as her wait lengthened. She stood, adjusted her weapons and removed her gloves, slipping them into her belt. She paced the room. Stepping closer to one of the tapestries, she ran her fingers over the colored threads that made up the piece.

When the heavy oak door to the private office opened, its hinges creaking, she removed her hand from the tapestry. Her spine stiffened at the sound of footsteps on the stone floor.

"A very beautiful piece, isn't it?"

She recognized the deep voice that spoke from behind her. "Yes, still as beautiful as it was the day it arrived at the church, Most Holy." Serpé turned from tapestry to face Eion Reicholt.

"That's right. I forgot you were still here when it arrived." He rested the candelabra on the corner of his desk and walked around to his chair. Arranging his silk robes around him, he sat. "You look well, Serpé. I'm glad to see that your life as a mercenary has treated you with kindness."

"I'm not a mercenary. I am captain in my own right in a militia. However, I'm not here to discuss my health or my accomplishments." She took her seat again and resisted the urge to smile at the sarcasm in his voice.

"Just what exactly do you wish to speak to me about?" Eion leaned back, and, with his elbows resting on the arms of the chair, brought his fingers together under his chin.

"I know what you're doing. I've seen the slaves and the women you've turned into whores…"

His deep laughter interrupted her. "You know nothing, Serpé. You misunderstand everything."

"Do I really? You demand tributes from the faithful and if they can't pay, you send them to prison, slave markets, whore houses or worse—you kill them. You take children from their mothers. Do you have any idea how much you're hurting these people? Do you even care?" She watched for some indication her words affect him.

His grin actually grew wider. "Who do you think is going to believe you? I can tell you—no one. You have no proof. All you are is a woman who left her home, left the church and lived with the man who is now leading an army against me. So the next question would be, were you his whore or did you keep yourself from him as well?"

Serpé stood, and stared down at him. When she stepped closer to the desk, the opening door stopped her. She turned to see Strinnal Marcin walk into the room. When he noticed her, she thought she recognized a flash of fear in his eyes.

"Arrest her, Captain Marcin." Reicholt's voice sounded unsteady. "I have to thank you for saving me the trouble of coming after you, Serpé. I was beginning to wonder if Strinnal would ever redeem himself for losing you."

"So glad I could help. I will enjoy bringing you to justice, Most Holy. Watching you hang will be so satisfying." She paused, thinking. "Or maybe, I'll let the women you've disgraced decide what to do with you."

He blanched, then rising from his chair, lunged at her. Strinnal stepped between them and put his hand out to stop him.

"Most Holy, I will handle this. Calm yourself. The lower priests would like you to lead the meditation. They are you expecting you before the next change." Reicholt nodded and smoothed his robes.

"Of course, Captain. Take her out the back way."

"I'm not done with you, Most Holy. Your crimes against the people of this kingdom will not go unpunished," Serpé declared.

Strinnal grabbed her arm and yanked her from the room. She went with him, sure she could free herself when they were alone. Once outside, she yanked her arm out of his grip, pushed him away and drew her estoc.

"Please, Serpé." Strinnal held his hands up. "It is only my intention to help you leave here safely. Don't you realize how much danger you've put yourself in?" He pushed her sword away from his chest. "Why did you come here?"

"I wanted to end all of this." She found no comfort in Strinnal's 'friendly' words. They were enemies and no amount of concern on his part would change that.

"You're not going to end this locked in a prison cell. That man wants you, in ways that would make the most abusive of men cower in fear."

"Don't pretend to care about what happens to me. Now, I'm going to take my horse and leave and you're going to come up with some story about how I got away." She pointed her sword at his chest again.

"Of course, Dame Navran," Strinnal said, sarcasm and frustration in his words. "But you need to know something first. Kian's army was attacked earlier this morning."

Serpé lowered her weapon. "How do you know that?"

He paused. "I led the attack."

"And this is supposed to convince me to let you go? Not exactly the wisest choice." Panic built in her chest, but she could not explain why. *Kian can take care of himself. He practically told me as much.* "How did you get back so quickly? Why are you telling me this? I can't do anything to help him."

"I don't know how many survived. Kian is most likely injured." The sound of his words rang true, but she still did not understand his intentions. "Mage Stein gave me a rod for magical travel. It is the only way I could get back here. I knew you were in the city because of his scrying."

"I'm sure Kian's fine. There are clerics in the army who can help." *If Mage Stein knew I was in the city, why didn't he tell Reicholt?* Her unspoken question distracted her.

"No. My instructions were to kill all magic users and clerics with his army. We used poison that would attack the magic within the clerics and mages, killing them. Anyone with magic of any kind was killed, by one simple cut of an arrow." Before she could interrupt, he continued. "I follow Reicholt's orders only to keep his attention away from my actions. I had no choice in this."

Anger rushed through her. Clenching her fist, she felt the skin stretch across her knuckles. She brought her fist back and swung at Captain Marcin's jaw. They connected, pain shooting through her hand and up her arm. Strinnal's eyes closed, his head turning away from her. A crack echoed around them from the contact.

Strinnal stepped away from her, his hand going to his face. He looked up, his expression filled with surprise.

"Captain, you better pray that Kian is alive. If he isn't, I will return and kill you myself."

Chapter 47

Riding through Valen, Serpé was surrounded by the quiet of the sleeping township. Flickering candlelight played behind curtained and shuttered windows. Packed dirt muffled Adrastos' hooves. The animals she passed reacted to her late arrival and their calls felt as if they greeted her. Reaching the end of town, smoke from the chimney of The Ranger's Rest drew her. She smiled, momentarily at peace.

She stopped in front of the inn and dismounted. She had missed her friends on her return journey, but this time alone had allowed her to think. On reflection, she knew confronting Reicholt might have been a serious mistake. The man never reacted well to provocation and she had no one but herself to blame for any retaliation.

After tying Adrastos' reins to the log, she entered the inn. The warmth that embraced her drove away the slight chill of the spring night.

"You're back!" Jalena's excitement washed over Serpé. The woman rushed forward to embrace her.

Serpé allowed her friend to hold her for a moment before pulling away. Pulling three scroll tubes from the bag slung over her shoulder, she studied them before placing two in Jalena's hand. The last, destined for Kian, was returned to the bag.

"This is for the temple of Azar in Sanctuary and the other is for Lord Draven." She touched each tube in turn and she waited for Jalena's nod of understanding.

"Of course. I'll send them in the morning."

Serpé noted the curiosity on Jalena's face, but her fatigue would not let her linger for casual conversation or questions she was not prepared to answer yet.

Kissing Jalena on the cheek, Serpé whispered her thanks, and left the inn. She found the road home and allowed Adrastos to take the lead. The coolness of the trees relaxed her and for a short time she tried not to think about anything but staying mounted.

When the moon crested in the night sky, Adrastos arrived at the farm. Serpé studied it with weary eyes, noting the farmhouse and worker's quarters appeared lifeless. She dismounted when Adrastos reached the barn and guided him to his stall. After filling his bin with food, she removed the saddle, bags and blanket, rushing to brush him down. He would get a full pampering in the morning, but for now, she needed to find a bed.

When she finished the task with the same care and thoroughness she would have normally taken anyway, she picked up her bags and turned to leave. But instead of being greeted by the small number of animals her farm normally had, each stall was filled with horses. A quick glance to the back of the barn revealed more horses corralled there as well. *Where did all these animals come from?* With her weary mind not cooperating, she shook her head and left the barn.

She walked across the yard to the house and into the kitchen through the door. The door gave Rakel easy access to the yard, so she could feed the chickens and reach the fields without going around the house.

After the door shut behind her, Serpé stopped mid-step to stare at the mess in the kitchen. The room was well lit, something she had not noticed before, and she was surprised to see Rakel at the wash basin, her arms wet. She stood washing the large pile of dishes in front of her. More dishes lay piled on the preparation areas, table and cutting block. A good number of chairs sat stacked against the wall and a keg of an unknown alcohol lay on the ground near the cellar door.

"By the gods! What happened?" Serpé exclaimed, dropping her saddle bags.

Rakel glanced up from the dishes. "You're home! Finally!" Wiping her hands on her apron, she rushed to hug Serpé, her smile sparkling in her eyes. "Tomes will be so happy to see you again." She left Serpé's arms, but held onto her hand, dragging her to the table. "Let me get you some ale and bread."

Serpé allowed herself to be pushed into a chair. She watched while Rakel cleared away some of the dishes and gathered the items she wanted Serpé to have.

"Rakel, what's going on?" Her friend's hurried pace served to wake Serpé from her weariness.

"We have visitors." Rakel placed the food and drink in front of her. She took the seat next to Serpé. "About six days ago, Tamar, Drommond and Aldric brought a group of children and almost an entire army to our door. The leader is seriously injured, but one of the others said that you would know them and requested aid and shelter. Tomes questioned the man and he seemed to know you well enough for him to let them stay. The healthy have helped with the farm work. Their leader is still recovering and I have tried to keep him in bed. It took me two days to stitch and dress his wounds properly. For some reason, he wasn't tended to by either Drommond or Aldric."

"But who are they?" Serpé loved the woman, but she liked to skip around the important information until pushed. Too tired to wait, she resisted the impulse to act out of frustration and took a measure breath to calm herself.

"The one we talk to the most is Blackette."

Serpé had brought the mug to her lips, but set it back on the table without drinking. "Their leader, how bad is he?" The concern Serpé heard in her voice angered her. She had not controlled it—but then, she did not expect the visitors to be part of the army she worked so hard to avoid just weeks ago.

"He's doing better. Drommond was the only cleric with them and like I said, their leader refused the healing. Blackette said that their last cleric died from his injuries before they reached us. Despite Drommond and Aldric's attempts to heal their cleric, he still died. Even though Lord Draven's priests are more experienced than Drommond, Blackette refused to send for one. Their leader is in the room across from yours. He was not strong enough for the second floor."

Serpé waited until she composed herself to stand. Her stomach threatened to revolt, contracting against the emptiness she did not have the chance to fill. The pounding in her chest made it hard to breathe and she felt her throat tighten with each beat of her heart.

I can't believe the emotions crashing through my body, and that Kian is the cause. I shouldn't feel like this. Kian spurned me. How can I still want the man who broke my heart?

Standing, Rakel reached out to grab Serpé and pulled her close. "Whatever he means to you, Serpé, and whatever happened between you, he was very demanding about speaking to you. Even when we told him that if he didn't have a cleric tend to his wounds, he may not live to see your return. He is punishing himself, I think, for something. If it's between you and him, give him the chance to explain."

Serpé felt her momentary weakness over Kian's condition disappear with Rakel's words—only to be replaced with anger. "He broke my heart, Rakel. Rejected my love when it was offered, as if I were infected and not worth a second glance. He will need to do more than suffer in silence from his injuries to receive my forgiveness."

She left the room before her friend could find her voice again. But her steps slowed walking through the common room, the clutter drawing her attention. Every where she looked, she saw the remnants of the large number of men that now occupied her home. There were no signs of the children she rescued, though, and a new fear filled her. *Rakel did not mention anything happening to them, so where are the children?*

She crossed the room and approached the hall that led to her bedroom and the downstairs guest rooms. Her steps slowed more when she walked toward her rom. She heard sounds of deep snores from the other rooms she passed.

Farther down hall, brighter with each step, a dim light could be seen from under the door across from her room. The light drew her to the room and its occupant. She stopped and glanced at her own door. Shut tight, like the others, but no light or sound came from within. *Rakel probably kept everyone from my room and kept it clean as well. She always takes good care of me.*

She turned her back on the solace and comfort she wanted. Reaching to open the other door, she did not know if Kian would be resting or waiting for her. His refusal to be healed may have been because he wanted the survivors to receive the help instead. He could have also done it to play on her sympathy. *Maybe he hoped I would return before he was completely healed. Either way, I will not allow sympathy to cloud my judgment. He made his decision and there will be no going back now.*

She opened the door, careful to keep it quiet. A lantern, flame set to low, sat on the nightstand. *At least they were smart enough to keep it dim so it wouldn't disturb him while he slept. But I can still see the bulk of his body in the bed.*

She made it to the bed, but could not remember how. She gazed at the bruises and the wounds healing on his face. Despite her promise to herself to bury her sympathy, a wave of emotions clenched within her, knotting in her stomach and tightening her throat. He moved, moaned in pain and the blanket slipped from a large dressing on his shoulder. Seeing the dressing, stained as if the wound still bled, made her struggle to keep from touching him. *Rakel did not prepare me for this.*

Despite seeing his bruises and wounds, she could not forget how he hurt her. *To forgive him just because of his wounds feels weak. I will not give him the chance to tell me that.* She pulled the blanket back over him and pushed her emotions under a blanket of their own.

"Serpé?" She accidentally touched him before she could pull her hand away. Even in his fevered sleep, he must have felt the contact. Her hand was still warm from her brief touch to his feverish body.

"Yes, Kian. Sleep. We can talk later—in the morning."

She waited for his nod before she turned away. His hand on her arm stopped her and she looked back down at his face. Her skin burned again under his touch.

"What?" Her harsh whisper made even her cringe.

"I'm sorry, Serpé," he mumbled.

"For what?" But his hand slipped from her arm. He had slipped back under the shroud of sleep, before he could answer. With a sigh, she left his room and crossed the hall to her own. Tired, she locked herself inside and crawled into her bed, barely taking time to undress.

Chapter 48

The sun had barely peeked over the horizon when Serpé awoke the next morning. She struggled against leaving the bed, begging the warmth wrapping around her to lull her back to sleep. She did not want to face the man who slept across the hall. She still hurt from his rejection. And she had definitely not had enough time to get over her anger now.

What angers me more? His assumption that he and the men would be welcome at my home or that I would ever want to see him again?

But she did want to see him, she just did not like him assuming she would. To show up on the edge of death made it all the worse. Then, to refuse any healing, almost as if he wanted his wounds to kill him. *Does he really hate me so much?*

Finally, because sleep would not return and she knew Tomes would want her help, she left the bed and dressed. No surprise, Tomes waited for her in the kitchen. Though he tried not to look impatient, she saw it in his demeanor.

They ate morning feast with men from the army, who then joined them in the fields for the harvest.

The last time Kian and I slept in the same building, we worked on the harvest together. Too many similarities, too many memories, with no one to blame but myself because I bought the farm. Maybe I tried to hold onto the familiar too tight.

She loved the feel of manual labor, the strain she felt in her muscles working parts that had rested too long from travel renewed her. The sun felt so good on her skin, she tied her shirt up, so it could warm her back, stomach and arms. One man whistled, more followed—as the volume and laughter increased, so did the grin on her face. *Maybe it isn't a bad thing Kian brought the men here to rest.*

While they worked, Tomes introduced her to Blackette. Kian's letters spoke often of his second-in-command, but this was the first time she met him. They were close to the same age, but his eyes revealed the death he had seen. For a brief moment, she was thankful for the protected life she once led.

Before she realized it, the sun reached its zenith and Rakel rang the bell for midday meal. The conversations on the way back to the house were relaxed. The men talked about the homes they had lost and the happier times they had shared before Reicholt exiled them.

Another group of men stood in the kitchen, helping Rakel. They greeted Serpé and the others and passed out plates of food to everyone. Serpé looked at Rakel, her question shining in her eyes.

"They help with everything. Each group is assigned a different duty each morning. It's been very helpful," Rakel explained.

"Well, that's…" Serpé stopped, unable to put her surprise into words. Kian brought the army to her home and did not expect them to be waited on by Serpé or her friends. Maybe she had been too hard on his decision. But it did not change how she felt about seeing him again.

"I'll take my food to my room, Rakel. Anything else planned for today?"

"No. Tomorrow we'll need today's harvest taken into town and more supplies brought home. Will you do that?" Rakel watched her.

Serpé did not understand the question. She had never refused to help with the chores or anything else around the farm. Rakel and Tomes were considered friends and companions, not servants. "Of course. Why wouldn't I?"

Rakel shrugged. "I just thought you might want to stay around here. Maybe try to fix a few things."

"There is nothing I need to fix. Tomes handled everything in my absence. Everything is running very well." Serpé turned and walked out of the kitchen.

"That's not what I meant, Serpé."

Ignoring Rakel's shouted response, she crossed the common room. The doors to other rooms were open—except hers and Kian's. She glanced at his door, but went into her room. *He does not need to know I'm in my room.*

The bed had been made and her saddle bags emptied. Already Rakel had gone through and put things away. The blue silk dress from Rodin hung in the closet. Serpé closed the door until it rested against the frame.

After she placed her plate on the window seat, she stretched out on the bed. She sunk into its comfort and after her active morning, the softness soothed her warm skin. It held her as she fell asleep.

Someone is touching my hair. A sudden move would let whoever it was know she was awake, and her weapons lay too far away. Serpé counted three breaths, grabbed the hand that still touched her and twisted to sit up. Her eyes opened, and squinted against the light flooding her room from the hall. It dulled the glow of the lantern next to her bed.

"Serpé, wait. It's me." Recognizing Kian's voice, she stopped, but waited to release his hand. She finally pushed him away.

"Kian, go back to bed." She groaned and lay back on the bed, sleep still holding her in its grip. "Rakel says your injuries are bad. You need your rest."

"You slept through the afternoon and evening meal is almost ready." He sat next to her and smiled. "It's good to see you. I've really missed you."

"Really? Why is that?" She let the sarcasm she felt creep into her voice. Sitting up again, she glared at him.

"Because I did." He looked away and studied the bandages on his hands.

"Is that the best you can do?" She waited for a response, but his continued silence made it clear he was not going to answer. "I thought so." Leaving the bed, Serpé picked up her plate of uneaten food and left the room.

His footsteps echoed behind her. With a deep sigh, she turned to glare at him. "Surely nothing is so important that you need to be out of bed."

Heaviness settled on her chest and her shoulders. A yawn

escaped her, but she knew she was not tired, at least not physically. She dreaded looking at him, but wanted to see him so badly, her breath caught in her throat. Despite the hurt he had caused her with his rejection, his injuries distressed her. No matter the past between them, she did not want to see him in pain. She straightened her back and squelched her impatience.

"Serpé, please hear me out," he pleaded, and she found herself grinding her teeth. "There are many things I need to tell you. Since I last saw you, I've fought in battles and killed more men than I can count. But we've lost men as well. Bennan died in the last battle. He tried to protect our clerics and gave his life for our cause."

She scoffed at him in displeasure. "Our cause is all for naught if the people it is supposed to help don't know or even care about it."

"That's true." Kian looked at the ground and she swore he delayed on purpose. She saw the worry crease his forehead and his deep sigh almost echoed in her ears. "Serpé, please, come back into the room."

"No. Tell me whatever you need to tell me, so I can eat."

He sighed again. "Reicholt has killed a lot of merchants, seized their homes and businesses when he found no available heir. Your parents were killed by his assassins and all your family's businesses and homes have been seized by the church."

A sudden weakness slammed into her and she pressed a hand against the wall for support. "My parents are dead?"

"I'm so sorry, Serpé."

She saw him reach for her, saw the intent of comfort in his eyes. *No! I will not be comforted by him.* She shoved his hands away and dropped her plate.

"That's what you wanted to tell me? You came to my home on the brink of death to tell me Reicholt killed my parents and Bennan?" She knew she sounded defensive, knew her home was the safest place for he and his men to recover, but her anger and disbelief made her back away from him.

"No, I also came to tell you that I'm sorry for lying to you, for telling you I didn't love you," he whispered.

She stopped and glared at him. "You break your promise to protect my parents, fail to do any of the things you said you would do for me to make sure my family and I was safe? And now you tell me you lied to me too?"

"That's not fair, Serpé. You know I've tried to keep every promise I ever made to you," Kian growled.

She had hurt him and it brought a burn of satisfaction to her chest. "Obviously you didn't try hard enough." She stepped past him, back to her bedroom door. "Go back to bed, Kian. I can't take anymore heartbreak from you tonight."

She slammed the door in his face, and found she just did not care. He pounded on the other side, calling her name. While she listened, her heart beat with each thump on the wood.

When the pounding stopped, she heard the door across the hall slam shut. Before she could step away from the door, a softer knock caught her attention.

"Serpé, are you all right?" Rakel, the best friend she could ask for, besides Tamar, called out to her.

"I need time alone, Rakel."

"I'll put together a plate and bring it to you in a few minutes. It'll be outside your door."

Serpé hoped the woman did not wait for a response. Her voice would reveal too many emotions and she did not want to concern Rakel more than she already had.

Her room brightened behind her and she turned, slow in her movements as she scanned the room for easy to reach weapons. A man stood in her room, surrounded by a glow that might have blinded someone else, but Serpé gazed at him without pain.

She had seen him before, in her dreams and in the tapestries and statues in the temples of Siladan and Sanctuary. Azar's earthly body was handsome, but she was more drawn to the comfort his presence gave her and the warmth that emanated from him.

"My daughter, you need to move past the pain you are holding on to. Either forgive Kian and embrace the love you share, or forgive him and go on without him." He held his arms out for her and she stepped into the god's embrace.

"Why must I forgive him? He has caused me so much pain. His rejection cut a deep wound in me. He let Bennan die—failed to protect my parents."

"Even gods suffer hurt and heartache because of a lover. And you are fortunate to have the love of two men. In your heart, you know you could never love Rodin like you do Kian. That same heart cringes at the thought of loving Kian. But to defeat Reicholt, you must forgive Kian, and learn to trust the one you love."

"Why? What does forgiving Kian have to do with defeating Reicholt?" She did not understand what Azar meant and did not want to figure out riddles.

"The power of forgiveness in you will be the power to defeat him."

"Can't you just take him out of power, punish him yourself?"

Azar touched her cheek. "I can only observe, to a point. Right now, I must wait for him to show just how evil he can be. I am bound by the rules of another. My justice must be delivered by someone else. And I have chosen you." He held her tight again, and filled her with warmth and fatherly love. "Remember, I love you, my daughter, and I will protect you as I can, though I may be limited in some of my actions. I am always listening to you."

She allowed him to guide her to the bed and cover her with a blanket. His soft kiss brushed her cheek and when the warmth of his breath left her skin, she fell into a contented sleep.

Chapter 49

The next morning, Serpé woke with the sun warm on her skin. Tomes had prepared the wagon already and after she dressed, she went into town without morning meal. She planned to see Jalena since the morning meals she served at The Ranger's Rest were always a treat.

The ride into town and back gave her the time she needed alone. The supplies had been waiting for her and she was able to begin the journey back to the farm before noon. Azar's words still echoed in her mind and she wanted to consider her next steps.

Serpé did not understand how forgiving Kian or Reicholt could defeat the priest. Only someone who was truly remorseful would benefit from forgiveness. She knew Kian was capable of such remorse, but Reicholt never regretted anything he did. How could she forgive someone like him?

She passed the fields, waving waved at the men. Blackette and a few others left their work, to meet her at the kitchen door. They unloaded the supplies before returning to the harvest while Serpé and Blackette put the horses and wagon away.

The two worked in silence. Serpé did not know what to say to the man and felt sure he was equally uncomfortable with her. They never met before, but Kian's letters described his second well enough for her to recognize him on sight.

Eventually the silence weighed too much on her. "Why did you join Kian and the others?"

Blackette appeared surprised by her question. He filled his lungs before answering. "The stories of Kian's prowess, cunning and ability in commanding the different military factions he's been part of are well known amongst army families." He stopped when she entered a stall with one of the horses. When she came out again, he continued. "I was moving up the ranks of the People's Army when a group of us were approached by Bennan in a tavern. The more we drank, the more we talked. The information he gave us made each of us question why we served in an army that Reicholt was slowly bringing under his control. Within a week of that first meeting, our entire group left the People's Army and went in search of Kian and his army. We waited for him because he still protected you. But, ever since the death of Korewyn, he has been a voice of rebellion against Reicholt, shouted through Bennan. We gladly waited for him to come to us. We've been with him since."

She stared at him, surprised by how much he said. She always knew that Kian commanded respect from others, though by his actions only. Never by force. It was the depth of loyalty these men showed that she had not expected.

"Come." She left the barn, pausing only to listen for his footsteps.

Silence surrounded them again while they walked toward the small pond on the farm. Ancient trees shaded the water on one side, but Serpé went to a log on the other. She indicated the space next to her with a pat, and smiled when he sat. Instead of continuing their conversation, she listened to the sound of the water where a hidden stream fed it.

Blackette cleared his throat and took it upon himself to continue their conversation. "A while back, maybe three months ago, Kian went to visit his sister after we went to Azar's temple in Sanctuary. Something happened, because when he came back to us, he had turned angry, violent and uncontrolled in his fight against the Religious Guard."

Serpé nodded. "I saw him while he visited there. I'm the reason he returned angry." *I'm surprised. I knew Kian was not pleased when we saw each other. But to take it out on his men does not seem like him.*

"What happened between you?"

"I don't think I should tell you. I thought he would be happy. He became angry with me, though." She turned away and stared at the pond.

"Whatever it was, he made it clear to me that he'd made a decision he regretted and had lost something he valued." Blackette shifted and she returned her attention to him. "He acted like he didn't care if he lived or died. He killed more than anyone else. I have never seen another fight like him, and I hope I never do again. He was injured at one point, because he separated from the rest of us. I thought we were going to lose him." Serpé watched his eyes fill with sadness at the memory.

"When we heard you were traveling past our camp, he tried to leave, to talk to you. Bennan kept him with us, though I know it wasn't easy. He was even more upset when Bennan left to find you. It took some time, and many nights spent talking to Bennan, for his anger to calm. Even when he brought it under control, he still fought more fiercely than anyone else, but with more direction."

He cleared his throat. "I listened to their conversation one evening. All Kian could speak about, besides his plans for the next day, was how much he hurt you. He said he'd lied to protect you and didn't know if he could ever get past your hatred of him."

"I don't hate him, Blackette," she breathed. "How could he think I hate him?"

"I don't know, but that's good, because he loves you, more than I think any of us realized. He lingered close to death when we arrived here. I don't want to see his emotional downfall again. Please give him the chance to fix whatever mistake he made." Blackette squeezed her hand, rose, and left her alone.

Serpé stayed for awhile longer, not sure how this changed what she felt. *My pain is still so fresh. How can I move past it? Even with Azar's guidance, it is hard to forgive the hurt Kian has caused me.*

When the sun started its descent toward the evening horizon, she returned to the house.

She sought the isolation she could only find behind the locked door of her bedroom. But when the sun fell beyond land's edge, hunger drove her to leave her room.

"Serpé." Kian's hushed voice stopped her before she had taken a handful of steps. She turned to glare at him. He held up a hand to fend off her anger. "I know, you're upset. Please hear me out. If, after you hear what I have to say, you still want me to leave, I will. I promise."

Serpé stood tall, her chin up. Warmth from her anger flushed through her chest, rushing to her cheeks. Her hands clenched into fists, her short nails biting into the flesh of her palms. Measured breaths finally succeeded in calming her impatience and anger and she nodded to him. "Speak quickly, I'm hungry and I want to take a bath." Her brow furrowed, remembering his words the night before. "Why the change of heart?"

He shook his head and reached for her hand, sighing when she pulled away from his touch. "There was no change of heart. I told you I didn't love you to protect you from Reicholt. He can't find out how I truly feel about you. He would use our love against us, as if it were a weakness he could exploit." He grabbed her hand, taking advantage of the shock she could not hide. "Serpé, as much as it pained me to lie to you, I know it hurt you more."

"You have no idea how I felt, Captain Donwell." She yanked her hand out of his grasp.

She was satisfied when she saw anger flash in his eyes. *Not using his first name did exactly what I wanted. I hurt him. Nothing like he did to me, but I still scored a win.* The satisfaction disappeared as quickly as it had come. *A small, petty win.*

Kian paused before he spoke again. She watched him close his eyes before meeting her gaze. Determination had replaced his anger and he pulled her into a tight embrace.

He crushed her with his strength, despite his wounds. Struggling against his hold, each movement made him grunt in pain. When she recognized the pain she caused, she stopped resisting him. He continued his plea for her understanding.

"I have an idea, Serpé. Draven told me of your lack of concern for yourself, of how you retreated into anger and silence, and took the war on as a personal mission. I know how you feel. I feel it too." He stopped, seemingly at a loss for words and the silence lasted for several moments.

"You told Draven to babysit me. You told him not to let me go to Siladan, like a child." She punched his shoulder, though not with her full strength. "I am not a child. I am only eight winters younger than you."

"You went anyway, didn't you? Despite my repeated attempts to keep you away." She only glared at him, but he continued without waiting for a response. "You tell me you love me, and then you come back here—to the arms of another man. You acted like what you told me meant nothing." His anger had returned, and his grip tightened around her again.

"What? I have no idea…" *He saw me with another man? But I was only here one night before I left for Tushin. Who did he see me with? When? How?* Then she realized. "Striphen. I wasn't in his arms, not in any way except as a friend. How do you know about him?"

"I came here, before you returned. I arrived only a couple of days before you and waited. I knew how long it would take for you to travel from Sanctuary. I wanted to take back what I had said, tell you why I said it." He stopped—caressed her cheek, hesitant, and with a soft touch, his thumb tracing the curve of her lower lip. "My heart ached. Every word I said cut like a knife, ripping my soul to shreds. It excited me when you said you loved me. But the thought of Reicholt using it against us made me fight my feelings and say I didn't love you."

Her resolve wavered at his words and his touch on her skin. Azar's words came back to her. It would be easy to forgive, or at least it seems that way. But to decide between loving him or leaving him, that choice is not so easy.

She saw the effort he put into saying the right thing and smiled at the confusion on his face. *Such a strong warrior, so skilled in the art of combat, but the difficulty in expressing himself to me makes him vulnerable—human.*

"You're repeating yourself, Kian," she whispered.

"I'm doing my best to explain myself to you." A husky tremor ruffled through his voice and reached within her to touch her broken heart. His lips brushed her ear. "I love you, Serpé Navran."

Her resistance and emotional walls crashed around her. Before it all disappeared, though, she grasped onto a small piece for protection; a piece to keep safe in case happiness with Kian became a temporary thing. A deep sigh moved through her throat and tears moistened her cheeks.

"I love you, Kian Donwell."

They kissed and she melted into the feel of his body against hers. He held her tight in his embrace. His hand caressed her back, a shiver following his touch. But the sound of someone clearing their throat stopped them.

Together, they sighed and turned to face the intruder, their bodies still touching. Kian only loosened his embrace enough to allow her to turn. She felt his breath on her ear.

Rakel stood at the end of the hall and Serpé saw by her smile that she regretted interrupting them. The glare she threw at her friend was met by a bigger smile.

"Pardon the intrusion, Serpé, Captain. The evening meal is ready. Will you be joining us?"

"Yes, we will be there soon," Serpé answered quickly, desperate to send Rakel away.

"As much as I would love to take you back to your room, if we don't eat now," Kian's whisper sent a shiver down her spine, "We won't eat for several hours. I intend to make this a night neither of us will forget."

Serpé's eyes narrowed with a desire that she had buried since leaving his farm. She pulled him down the hall toward Rakel.

"We'll eat now."

Serpé enjoyed the meal, though not as much as if she and Kian had been alone. Their hands touched when they reached for bread at the same time, and their legs remained next to each other under the table. Her skin warmed when he touched her and she knew she wanted more.

When they finished, and were ready to leave the dining room, Blackette walked in. She watched the two men argue for several moments before she spoke.

"Go, Kian. Talk to him about whatever is so important, everything else can't wait. Otherwise, he'll be at our door all night." His look told her he did not want to be away from her, but he nodded and led his second outside.

Rakel stood and brought another skin of wine to the table. Serpé watched her friend fill their glasses, then they both drank in silence.

"Did you forgive him?" Rakel's question broke the silence.

"Mostly." Serpé stared at the door Kian and Blackette went through, her voice just louder than a whisper.

"Mostly? What does that mean?"

"I want to forgive him completely. I can feel it, in here." Serpé touched her chest. "And, I have forgiven him. I guess I'm just protecting myself from being hurt again."

Rakel squeezed her hand. "That's the thing about love. It hurts, it heals. To make it work, you have to accept it all."

Finishing her wine, Serpé stood. She kissed Rakel on the cheek. "I think I'll take a bath."

"Enjoy, my dear."

The sconces in the hall burned low and Serpé hoped she would remember to fill the oil in the morning. Retrieving her robe from its hook in her room, she continued down the hall to the door at the end that led to the attached bath house.

I like baths, but I haven't had one since Reicholt tried to… Quick in, wash up and out will keep my mind from what Reicholt tried to do. Relaxing in the tub was not something she planned to do. Water waited, already heated and after she poured it into the tub, she added rose scented oil. Her clothes fell in a pile and she stepped into the large tub.

The warm water caressed her skin and made it easy to relax. *If only I could let my worries drown in the water.* Instead, she closed her eyes and drifted into a light sleep.

"Serpé." Kian's voice woke her. His touch on her leg sent a shiver through her.

"What took so long?"

He knelt next to the tub and kissed her. "It doesn't matter."

His shirt joined her clothes on the floor and he picked up the soap with a grin. It did not take long before he was almost as wet as her. At the insistence of her hands, he undressed, then joined her in the water.

Her stomach clenched as his fingers caressed the scar she'd received from the Spiderkin. *Will he search for all the scars I've received from different fights?*

"This scar, how did you get it?" She heard the passion in his voice and knew neither of them really wanted to discuss the wound.

"The Spiderkin that attacked the farmers." She entwined her fingers in his hair and pulled him to her. The taste of his mouth left her breathless.

She resisted the urge to touch his chest because of his still inflamed wounds. But she let him pull her closer and molded her body to his.

This was what she had waited for since meeting him. She felt his need for her and together, they strived to satisfy that need.

Chapter 50

"But, Most Holy, surely she has taken steps to protect herself again." The First glared at Mage Stein and for a moment he considered having the man tortured just because he was irritating.

"She knows the cost for such magic. She would not ask anyone to make that sacrifice for her. But if we cannot locate her, then you will locate Kian Donwell. I want to know what she is doing." He stepped closer to the mage. "You will find her and show her to me."

Eion studied the fear in Stein's eyes until the other man turned away to prepare the mirror and other spell components he needed to cast a scrying spell. Though he knew he must be patient, Eion tapped his foot in impatience. After several minutes, Mage Stein turned back to him and nodded.

He stepped forward and gazed into the mirror Stein used to cast the spell. Within the mirror, Serpé and Kian lay in a bed, moving to the beat of their love. Eion straightened, anger and jealousy warring for dominance within him. A fire ignited within his loins at the sight of Serpé's naked flesh and he longed to reach through the mirror to touch her. While he watched, they sat up on the bed, Kian pulled her into his lap and caressed her back. Eion's inner fire turned cold and he looked away from the image to glare at Mage Stein and Captain Marcin.

"How long ago did they start this?" he demanded, gesturing at the mirror.

"I have not…" Stein's hesitation told The First everything.

He's lying! Before the lie continued, Eion reached out and grabbed Stein by the throat. "Do not lie to me, Mage Stein. I am suddenly without even the smallest amount of patience I once had with you."

"They consummated their relationship last evening. I do not know if that was the first time or not," Stein struggled to speak.

"Most Holy," Reicholt turned to look at Captain Marcin, releasing Stein's throat. "Why are you so concerned about Serpé? We know she has contacted many people. She could have told them anything. If you'll excuse my being forward, you're too wrapped up in her. She doesn't want you. She has made that very clear."

"I will not excuse your being forward, Captain Marcin. I don't care what she wants. She will be mine. I will control her again, as I once did, and I will make her understand that her world begins and ends with me. And if she won't give herself to me, I will kill Kian and take what I want from her, using his corpse as a bed. Now get out!" Eion threw a gesture at the entrance to the tent, his shoulder aching from the pain the movement caused.

Eion waited until the footsteps of the two men faded away from his tent. He sat in the chair he insisted be brought for his pleasure. In a pit in the ground, a fire burned, warming the tent and his face.

After all this time, I did not expect Serpé to remain virginal, but it infuriates me to see she has given herself to Kian. The child displays no loyalty to me. ME! He smacked his fist into this thigh. *The man who raised her since she was eight winters. This newest betrayal burns worse than her escape from me four years ago. I will punish that impudent brat, I swear it.*

He sipped from the glass of wine that had waited for him on the small table next to his chair. He hoped the wine would dull the jealousy that soured his stomach. After a long draught, he leaned back, the glass tipping precariously in his fingers. His thoughts joined the seductive dance of the fire licking at the wood, flaring and dancing with a passion all its own.

The fire remained seductive, its flames reminding him of the enticing dance of Serpé's hair in the wind. As she grew from a child to a woman, he longed to touch her hair and brush it back from her face. But he restrained himself because of her age and though he planned to make her his, eventually, at the time he thought it best to wait.

He remembered seeing the image of Serpé in Stein's scrying mirror for the first time in four years. While he felt triumph at having found her again, his lust renewed, more powerful than when she lived with him. The way she wore her clothes drew his eyes to where her shirt opened, revealing just enough of the smooth skin of her breasts to make him gasp for breath at the sudden pain in his loins.

Lost in thought, he did not realize he spilled his wine in his lap until the moisture reached the skin of his thigh. He straightened, with even more pain from his desire and watched as the glass fell from his lap.

"Dephia!" He slapped the few droplets left on his robe away.

His maid appeared from the other side of the tent, where his bed lay hidden from view by a cloth wall. He stared at her as she rushed over, joining her hands with his to minimize the stain on his robe. He looked down.

If I can't have Serpé to ease my pain, I can still satisfy my lust.

He grabbed Dephia's arm when her hand touched him a second time and yanked her to her feet. Eion pulled her back toward the partitioned room. *Dephia is not as young or beautiful as Serpé, but I can still use her. And I can be excessive in the things I do to her, in ways that I fear would turn Serpé against me.* His body trembled. *Oh the pain I will cause her relieving my desires.*

"Most Holy!" Dephia's protest and the fear in her voice excited him more and he tightened his grip on her arm.

Chapter 51

Strinnal Marcin stared at The First's tent, before turning to follow Mage Stein to his own tent. Without waiting for an invitation, he pushed the mage inside, allowing the flap to fall behind him. His cheeks warmed with his anger.

Before he could say anything, Stein raised his hands between them. "Captain, I had no choice. He did not give me an opportunity to prepare before casting the spell. He demanded I perform it in front of him."

"Why can't both of you just leave her alone? His lust disgusts me. Your lack of a back bone against his demands makes me sick." Strinnal's anger carried him closer to the mage. "I don't care what his demands are, from this day forward, you will not show her to him again."

"Perhaps it would be better served for us to determine why she is still unprotected. The necklace I created for her should still be functioning."

"What? You are the one who protected her before? So why are we able to find her now?" Strinnal stepped back in surprise. "This doesn't make sense. Your magic is strong. Not even your own spell should be able to penetrate the protection."

"Something must have happened to it. I told Kian the sapphire was the source of the protection, but it was actually the chain itself. I do not understand why she would remove the chain even if the sapphire was destroyed." Stein wrung his hands in distress.

"That isn't important right now. What *is* important is that you do not show her to The First again. *Ever.*" Confusion warred with the anger Strinnal felt.

"What do you expect me to tell The First? I can't just forget how to cast a spell I've been casting for him for years," Stein protested.

"Tell him she's protected against your spells now. I don't care what you tell him, but figure something out or I'll make sure you forget how to cast that spell permanently." After glaring at Stein, Strinnal stomped toward the entrance of the tent. "Make sure you understand me, Stein. I don't want him seeing her through your magic again." Without waiting for a response, he threw the flap aside and left.

Chapter 52

Serpé enjoyed waking up to sunny mornings the best. The sun warming her skin relaxed her. This morning was different though. The warmth of the sun was not the only reason she felt at ease.

For the last two days, she and Kian had enjoyed each other, explored their needs and desires and found ways to satisfy them. They finally found happiness together.

"Good morn, Sweetest." Kian's deep voice vibrated through her and touched her deep inside.

She sat up and smiled, pulling the blanket over her chest. Kian sat on the edge of the bed, watching her.

"Good morn, Love." His smile grew at the sound of her morning voice. It only lasted a moment though and she felt her jaw tighten at the serious expression that replaced it.

"There are things you need to know, Serpé," he said, his solemn words worrying her.

He sounds like he did that morning, the day my life changed. I do not want to run again. Serpé took a deep breath, preparing herself for an argument. "I am not leaving again, Kian. I'm done running from Reicholt. If you want me to leave again, forget it, unless you plan to come with me."

"I'm not asking you to leave again. Trust me. I learned my lesson last time." He tapped her covered foot in what would have been a playful gesture if he had smiled. "Bennan didn't make it. He died in the last battle, if it could even be called a battle. It was more like a massacre. I know he meant a lot to you and I'm sorry all I've had for you is bad news."

She reached for him, but had to settle for only one hand. "You said that before, but I was still a little upset with you. How did he die?"

Kian shook his head, studying their hands, their fingers intertwined. "The arrows the Guard used were not normal. They hurt, but for the clerics and mages, they were deadly. I always knew Bennan had more magic than a warrior should have."

"The arrows?" A memory cried out for attention. *Strinnal mentioned the arrows. What did he say?* "The arrows! Strinnal told me that the arrows were coated in a poison that worked against the magic in mages and clerics. Whatever magic Bennan had, the poison must have worked against him."

"That makes sense, though I have never heard of it. If we are going to be facing that type of poison, how am I going to keep my people safe?" They stared at each other, silence surrounding them.

Serpé reached up to caress his cheek. "I'm sorry for your loss, Love. You knew him longer than I did. He was your best friend."

"You were always his pride. News of you always made him happy. He loved you like a little sister." Kian turned into her hand, kissing her palm.

She smiled, returning her hand to his. "I loved him too, Kian. When this is over, we will mourn all our lost, including Bennan." They both fell silent again, watching the movement of her fingers on his palm.

"I need to know what you did to anger Reicholt so much recently, Serpé. And why."

She looked up and met his gaze. "What do you mean?"

"I know about the children. I actually sent them to Draven. I also know about your trip into Siladan. What were you thinking?" His voice had risen in volume with a burst of emotion. She waited for him to bring it back under control.

"I wasn't, all right? Is that what you wanted to hear? I had no plan for escape and I had no idea what I would do if I couldn't threaten someone for my freedom." She did not control her emotions as well as he did and when he shook his head, she realized anger from either of them would not resolve the problem.

He looked toward their swords, the estoc he gave her and the estoc he favored, where they rested on the dresser. "What do you think would have happened to all of this if you had been captured? Or even worse, killed?"

She scoffed. "What a silly question? "What does my living have to do with the war against Reicholt? You would keep going, just as before."

"You are much more important than you realize, Serpé. Without you, we lose our edge over him. You must stay safe until it's time to bring everything you are to bear."

"Don't be ridiculous, Kian." She shook her head.

"What were you doing in Tushin?" He ignored her whispered words.

"I was with Draven when he received one of your letters. So I went to Arcadia," she evaded the direct question.

"Why?" he pressed.

"I was upset that you were keeping so much from me. You had just broken my heart. I really didn't care what you wanted. I met with Rodin Tolan, to find out if there was anything I could do to assist him. I believe he has everything there under control." She stopped, her gaze drawn to the bit of the dress Rodin gave her visible from the closet.

"What else?"

"Rodin told me that he was the one my parents didn't want me to marry. When he grew out of the pranks, he says he realized what he'd lost and that he tried to find me, but by then I'd gone to Siladan. Then when he found me again, I had gone to you." She felt her skin flush at the memory of his touch. "He swears he loved me and still does." Kian flinched at her words and she immediately wished she could take them back. "He sent a message for you. I kept it because I hoped I might see you at some time, I guess. I'm not real sure why, exactly."

She reached over and pulled a scroll case from her bag next to the bedside table. While he read it, she watched him. This time he did not keep his emotions in check. *Rodin must have said something to make him angry. His face is so red.* She leaned forward to try to read the parchment. Kian pulled it from her view and crumpled it.

"I see. It's good we have Rodin in Tushin, to keep the peace with the politics. I couldn't have done that." He pulled his hand from hers and stood, then went to the window and pulled the curtain back slightly, revealing the fields.

She threw the blanket aside and reached for her robe. After the soft garment closed around her, she stepped over to stand behind him. Putting her arms around him, she rested her cheek on his back. *What can I say to break this silence? It feels like a heavy blanket over the room.*

He took a deep breath and caressed her arms with his thumbs. They both watched the men in the fields finishing the harvest and preparing the land for its dormant period.

"I saw you with Striphen, when you came back from Sanctuary. The way you looked at him, turned into his touch when he caressed your cheek. Those should have been my looks, my caresses, my moments," Kian finally broke the silence.

"He's only a friend, and it's always bothered him. He's always felt like he stood in competition with you. I didn't do or say anything to change that." She liked the way his body vibrated when he spoke, and she tried not to move too much when she answered him. *I don't want to lose contact with him.*

He shook his head. "You shouldn't have to. I should have done something much sooner, not waited for you to come to me and refuse you, not once, but twice. I'm a warrior, Serpé. I do my talking with a blade and my fist. I'm not a romantic, or a courtly gentleman. I could never give you the kind of life Rodin can. My family lost their businesses the day Reicholt found out I led this army." He turned in her arms and brushed her cheek with his fingers.

"I know I made a mistake and I'm truly sorry I did. I've seen too many friends die. I'm stubborn, and rough around the edges. You are beautiful, and smooth, like an opal. Reicholt couldn't destroy the innocence in you when you were with him. And it still shows in your desire to protect, love and be protected and loved in return." Kian pressed his finger to her lips when she tried to speak.

"I've ridiculed myself for the mistake I made by sending you away. Since then, I learned no matter what is happening, there is never a good time to be in love and never a better time than the present. I've learned that I love you more than I ever thought possible. I want to love you, if you think the life I have to offer won't disappoint you. It won't be like the one Rodin could give you, but we would be happy, I'm sure."

"Of course I want you to love me, just as I want to love you. You are all I ever wanted." Serpé knew she loved him, despite the pain he caused her. His honestly was what she questioned.

He smiled, pulled a piece of blue material from within his shirt and placed it on their joined hands. She stared at the material, then covered her mouth with her other hand.

"This is the engagement material, Kian." She fingered the royal blue material, the silver thread woven throughout prickling against her skin. "A woman only receives this to show her engagement."

"I know. Until the wedding, she is the only one to wear it. In the ceremony, it is replaced by another swatch of material with gold instead of silver." Kian brought his eyes up to hers. "I would be able to wear the material as well, to show my marriage...to you."

"What?" *Did he say marriage?*

"I know it is difficult for us to follow the traditions of our country, considering all we've been through. But marriage isn't a tradition exclusive to Sorban." His voice shook with the nervousness she saw on his face. "I would be honored if you would become my wife."

A proposal had not been expected. She looked up at him, guilt gripping her. *He loves me, has begged for me to forgive him, and all I've been able to do is give him minimal forgiveness. Can I say yes with the memory of the pain still so vivid?*

She loved him, there was no question of that in her heart. She wanted to be with him. *Complete forgiveness will come, but I will never tell him I didn't give it to him fully the first time.* Serpé remained quiet a moment longer.

"I would be honored." Her answer felt right, despite her remaining reservations.

Kian's smile broadened and he wrapped the material loosely around her wrist. "One more thing." He went to one knee, a slight grimace marring his handsome features, and gazed up at her. "I swear my loyalty and fealty to you. My sword is always at the ready to serve you and Sorban. Not only as your husband, but also a warrior."

She watched him lower his head. *Why is he doing this? Why is everyone acting so strange around me?*

"Kian, I don't understand."

"You will. One day." He kissed her hand, then stood. "Right now, just accept it."

She nodded, still unsure. He untied her robe and pushed her back to the bed, his hands gentle on her skin. She lost herself in his touch again, his oath forgotten for the moment.

Chapter 53

Eion's knees hurt from kneeling so long in front of the makeshift altar he had brought with him. His actions since he saw Serpé in Kian's arms had been deplorable. *I should be asking for forgiveness, but I can't find it in myself to ask Azar for it.*

With the bright light of the sun fading around him, a glance up showed that despite the time of day and the sun's position, he stood in a darkening circle. Ten feet away the sun shined bright and clear. Lightning shot through the dark surrounding him and he jumped to his feet when the ground started to rumble.

Cursing, Eion tried to remain standing while the ground moved under him. A sharp pain shot up his arm when his hands slapped against the altar for support. Losing his balance, he landed on his butt hard enough to make his teeth gnash against each other.

While he watched, the area in front of him filled with silver light that coalesced into the shape of a tall man. A wrap matching his robe pulled the man's long white hair back. The blue silk robes he wore flowed around him as if blown by a soft wind. His stern, chiseled features, tight lips and blazing eyes, glared at Eion.

The First stood, hasty in his movements and took an anxious step backward. He tried to return the man's intense stare with his own, but failed.

"Azar?" The man in front of Eion resembled the paintings and statues that filled the temples.

"Eion Reicholt, murderer, rapist. You are a disgrace. I am dishonored having you as a representative for those who teach my theology," Azar's voice rumbled. The god lifted his arms.

Eion tried to move away from Azar's outstretched hands, but the altar bit into his back, stopping him. His body convulsed toward Azar's right hand, eliciting a scream from the priest. Black tendrils arced through and from Eion's body, leaping toward his god's hand. The tendrils raced toward Azar, black with corruption, fading and changing to strands of blue and silver. Pain coursed through the priest until the last tendril disappeared into Azar's hands. Eion gasped for breath, his body suspended in the air by the god's will.

"I have taken from you the powers I once granted. Your corruption will pain me no more. You are no longer one of my chosen." The deity began to glow. Strands of silver and blue lifted from his arms and body, toward the heavens, until he disappeared.

The words faded with Azar and the sky over Eion cleared. When the sphere around him disappeared, he fell to the ground.

The next day, despite the pain he still felt, Eion summoned a small number of messengers. He sat in his soft, cushioned chair, not moving. Even the chair caused him pain.

He tried cursing Azar for taking his powers, but it was a waste of breath. The god no longer listened to him. His prayers and curses fell upon deaf ears. Now it was a matter of hiding this loss of Azar's favor from his followers.

"Most Holy, the messengers are waiting for your instructions."

Strinnal's voice interrupted his thoughts and he turned a glare from the captain. "I don't need your observations, Captain. I can see they are waiting." Eion returned his attention to the messengers and forced himself to straighten his back. "On that table are scroll cases. You are to each take one and deliver the contents to the person on the case at the designated location. Do not open the cases. Do not read the contents. If you do, I will know and you will be hunted down and killed. I assume you all understand me."

After the men nodded, Eion gestured toward the table. He felt like they took an eternity to pocket the cases and leave the tent. When all had left, he sat back and closed his eyes.

"What do you want, Captain? Surely you can see I am ill and do not wish any further inconveniences."

"Yes, Most Holy. I can see that you don't appear well. Is there anything I can get you before I attend to my other duties?"

Eion did not like the tone of Strinnal's voice, but for the moment he chose not to react. "Captain, please tell me. What happened to the mirror Mage Stein had ensorcelled to watch Serpé? It was fine the last time I saw her. Today it's broken and he has no explanation."

"I'm afraid I don't know, Most Holy."

Eion did not believe him. But there was the possibility Azar destroyed it. He gazed at Captain Marcin, watching for any kind of reaction. It did not matter. As soon as they arrived at Serpé's farm, he would decide whether or not to rid himself of Strinnal Marcin. If he no longer served a purpose, the captain would die.

Eion gestured toward the door of the tent. "Those men carry messages to the mercenaries. As soon as they are delivered, the attacks will escalate. We will use the panic they cause to take Serpé, unless Kian interferes. Now leave me. I feel the need to rest."

The captain made a slight bow at the waist, turned and left the tent. Eion watched the flap settle before rising, and with a hand on his back, walked to the table holding his decanters of brandy. The liquid caught the light of the fire and lanterns while he poured it into a sifter, but he doubted its numbing effect would drive his pain away.

"Aren't you going to pour me one as well? For some reason I thought you would be a more gracious host. Perhaps I was wrong."

Eion spun, the brandy decanter dropping from his hand. A woman sat in his chair, her leg draped over one arm. She lounged across the seat more than sitting in it, and the position of her legs left nothing to dream about except what lay hidden by a single strip of cloth draped between them.

Her hand gestured toward him and he glanced down to see the brandy decanter hovering inches from the ground. As he watched, the decanter floated back onto the table. An empty sifter slid closer to it.

"It would be a pity to lose a single drop of that beautiful elixir. Pour me a glass. Now!"

Eion's heart skipped at the barked order, but he rushed to do as the strange woman commanded. He felt her eyes upon him as he poured and capped the decanter. His hand shook delivering the glass to the woman.

She watched him while she sipped the amber liquid. Her eyes bore into him and though uncharacteristic for a man of his age or position, he shifted nervously. Finally, he stopped his movements and glared at her, or at least tried to.

"What do you want? Surely you have something more important to say to me than pour you a glass of my finest brandy." He knew better than to threaten someone of such obvious power, but his anger at her disrespect grew stronger than his common sense.

"Finally. You humans take too long to say what needs to be said and your lives are much too short to take that long." She brought her leg down from the arm of the chair, and stood. His chest tightened as she walked closer to him. "I have a proposition for you."

"Who are you?" he demanded.

"Angast, goddess of pain and deception. You are certainly a most satisfying specimen, Eion. The pain you've caused so many of those who trusted you, worshipped you. Your deception and lies made me tingle. They still do. Oh, the things you can do for me and my favored ones." She wrapped herself around him. She touched him in ways he had only dreamt of, where none of his partners had ever willingly done.

"I can't help you. My powers were stripped from me and my station will follow as soon as the church finds out." His body reacted to her caresses. There was nothing he could do, or wanted to, to stop it. Amazing. *The feel of a willing woman upon me brings so much more arousal than one forced to be under me.*

"That's the beauty of what I have to offer." He felt her guide him to the curtained area of his tent and when her hand slipped past his robes to touch him, he realized her intentions. Instead of rushing his steps, he allowed her to maintain control. "Serve me and I will give you powers you never imagined while you slaved for Azar. No one will ever know," she breathed into his ear.

"Humph, what else do you want? One man is surely not enough to satisfy your desires." When she pushed him onto the bed with enough force to leave him breathless, yet more excited, he realized his body no longer hurt. *What has she done to me?*

"How right you are. My favored will come to you when you control this kingdom. Four siblings and one other. You even know one of them. You gave him to me. You will turn everything over to them and they will let you remain in power. And, they will even help you gain possession of that little plaything you desire so much. But this kingdom and everything in it will belong to us."

He could no longer control his breathing and almost begged her to relieve the pain growing in his loins. But he forced his mind to focus on her words and the conditions she placed on him for her help. *If I agree, I will not be in sole control of Sorban. But if I serve her and her chosen well, she will most likely reward me handsomely. The first reward she offers is the one thing I want most—Serpé under my control and in my bed is worth the combined dictatorship Angast offers.*

"I will remain ruler of Sorban?" She nodded, then leaned down and bit his exposed chest. He gasped at the sudden pain. "Then I will serve you, my goddess."

She purred and climbed on top of him. He felt her dark powers corrupt his soul when she took his body. With each caress, he realized his journey down the path of darkness would never again be hindered by the light of good.

Chapter 54

Kian stood in front of the desk in the common room and stared at the parchment. He had not gone looking to find anything. He only needed parchment to write a message.

Now I wish I'd waited for Serpé.

His eyes scanned the letter again. Serpé's mother had written to her somehow. The most concerning issue was how it had been sent to her. Her parents were not given her location before they died and there was never any offer of contacting her for them.

Too many messages lately and most of them filled with bad news.

He did not tell Serpé what Rodin's message said and he probably never would. The other man gave him the most recent information about his activities in Tushin, but then he closed the letter with a threat. Rodin was unhappy to hear of Serpé's broken heart and his message to Kian was simple; treat Serpé the way she deserved or when they were done with Reicholt, Rodin would consider him the next enemy. His threat angered Kian, but it was not why he asked her to marry him. He did not want her thinking his proposal was a reaction to the threat. The question had been planned the moment he let go of his anger at pushing her away.

A soft touch brushed his arm and he jerked away, instinct taking over before he realized it. Touching him again, this time stroking his skin in a longer caress, Serpé gazed at him, concern flooding her green eyes. Fighting the urge to pull away again, he took a deep breath.

"What's wrong, Kian?"

He saw his anger reflected in her eyes, and immediately regretted it. But that did not change the way he felt. "How did you get this letter?"

There is no reason to hide it from her. If we are to be married, then she will need to know how I feel.

Without realizing why, he turned from her. His stomach knotted at her expression.

"It was delivered while I was in Sanctuary. I thought you sent it to me for my mother." Reaching around him, she took the letter from him.

He faced her again, but eased her back from him, or at least he tried to. Her eyes widened and he knew he failed at being gentle. Looking down at where his hand had been on her stomach, she opened her mouth as if to say something, but he shook his head to stop her.

"I didn't send it. First, you get a letter from your mother, and then you go to Siladan to confront Reicholt. Does my need to keep you safe mean nothing to you?"

Finally! She flinched like she understood. Maybe she would be more careful now. Satisfaction filled him briefly.

"It does mean something. I didn't ask for the letter. It just came. As for Siladan, I already told you. I wanted to try and end this," she defended herself.

"You didn't say that. You only said you went and you weren't thinking."

She huffed at him and he stepped back, his eyes wide at her reaction.

"That wasn't the first time I've seen Reicholt since I left you. When I went to find the old king's last home…"

"What? You didn't mention this before." *So she did find the king's home. Termage was right. But why is she keeping everything from me? She should have told me this sooner.*

"I found letters and followed the information to the king's home. Inside, I found a journal and spoke to a ghost about the family. It seems the queen left something back in Parnoir when they left Sorban," she explained.

As he listened, he felt himself calm. He struggled to find the anger again. *I can't let her voice calm me. I have to force myself to stay mad at her. Does she have any idea how she affects me?* "Do you know what the queen left behind?" He tried to keep his face free of emotion, but she squinted at him, her brow furrowing.

"No. Neither the ghost nor the journal said. Anyway, we stopped at a traveler's inn on the way. Reicholt waited for me, in a room he paid for. He tried to seduce me and became violent when I refused. He tried to..." She stopped, her throat moving as she swallowed and her gaze dropped from Kian's. "He only left after I threatened to kill him."

Feeling his hands shake and his heart beat faster, Kian clenched his teeth. "I'll kill him."

"You promised you wouldn't."

She pleads for his life, after everything Reicholt has done to her and her family? He doesn't deserve her pity.

"I didn't promise anything of the sort. I only said I would try. He deserves to die. I can't let him live, not after everything that's happened, everything he's tried to do to you."

"No, Kian, if you kill him, I might lose you to Azar's anger." She pulled him close. "Please. As much as it disgusts me to even know he thinks about me, the idea of losing you to Azar's wrath makes me ill. Let the council pass judgment on him."

A knock at the door interrupted him before he could respond. They stood together for a moment more before Serpé left him to answer. Kian waited, his hand on his dagger, missing the estoc and main-gauche he normally wore.

The minutes passed, and he started toward the door when she reappeared at the arch to the common room with a cloaked figure behind her. With the tension leaving his shoulders, he nodded at the figure, confident she would not let anyone into the house unless she knew them.

"It's Nosen." She gestured at the man, who lowered his hood and nodded at Kian.

"I hope your journey was safe, Nosen." Relieved that he would not have to respond to Serpé's plea for the moment, he greeted the new arrival. *Nosen may have replaced Bennan as messenger, but he will never replace the friendship we had.*

"It was." After passing Kian several scroll tubes, Nosen went into the kitchen without another word.

Kian stood in silence and read each message. Returning the parchments to the tubes, he looked up at Serpé and smiled, though it felt forced.

"What does Rakel have planned for evening meal?" His voice shook, his inability to keep it steady ringing loudly in his ears. *I don't want to leave, but if these messages are right, I have no choice.*

"What do they say, Kian?"

She heard it in my voice. I will never be able to hide anything from her again.

"Reicholt has ordered an escalation to the attacks on the merchants who oppose him. We need to add to the protection we already have in place. And I need to bring the army back together."

"What else? You sound like you're hiding something." She reached for the parchments, but he held them out of her grasp behind his back.

He waited. To tell her that Reicholt planned to arrest her might make her panic. Or, she might just try to go after the priest instead of waiting, again. After her trip into Siladan, there was no way to know what she would do. He saw her impatience grow the longer he took to answer and he finally sighed in resignation.

"Reicholt plans to arrest you. He's decided he's tired of waiting. So I need to leave a sizable force here and gather what we can to prevent him from coming into the forest."

She shook her head. "No. You need to protect the merchants."

"Serpé, I need to protect *you*. You don't understand. We can't let you fall into his hands."

"So explain it to me. Stop keeping secrets from me and just tell me why I'm so damn important!" Her voice rose with her own anger and for a moment, the sounds from the kitchen paused before resuming louder than before.

She's right. I should tell her. But will she accept it as the truth, or think it's just a story I made up to get her to stay? The only way I'll find out is to just do it. Kian took a deep breath and steeled himself against the burst of anger he expected.

"You're the last surviving member of the royal family. By marrying you, Reicholt thinks he can solidify his hold on the throne." He had not expected the laughter that immediately filled the room. Her laughter overpowered his words and he stopped.

"Kian, you sure know how to end an argument, but to come

up with such a story, I never expected that." Gasping for breath, she ignored the look of frustration he gave her.

"It isn't a story, Serpé. We have proof. Why do you think he wanted you in the first place?"

"Because he's a sick, disgusting man. Honestly, go, protect the merchants. Leave a smaller group with me if that makes you feel better. I'll be fine, though." She smiled at him, but he thought he saw a hint of fear—in the flick of her gaze from his, the shake of her hand as she brushed her fingers through her hair.

"Serpé, you could come with me. I was wrong to send you away before. I can protect you better if you're with me." She did not resist him, when he pulled her close. Even if she did not believe him about being the last royal heir, at least she realized he needed to hold her.

She shook her head against his chest. "I'm not going. We both know I'll be a distraction. I'll stay with some of the men, and protect my home. It will be better if I stay anyway."

"Then promise that you won't come to my rescue if I'm captured, especially if the message comes from anyone other than one of my commanders. They have been instructed to inform you personally. If none are able, then you need to confirm it through Jalena's message network." He still did not like the idea of leaving her. *Nothing could make me feel better about this decision. I will have to speak to Draven before I leave to make sure he has militia available to watch over the farm.*

"I understand. And if Reicholt does come for me, you must do the same. Confirm through Jalena or Draven and then keep our merchant council safe."

He heard the conviction in her voice, but her demand felt like shackles on him. *I've lost control of this conversation and she's taken control of the future from me as well. She has to know I won't keep that promise and then she'll use it as a point to argue over later.*

Finally he nodded reluctantly. "Agreed. If I hear that you've been captured, then I will confirm it first." They stared at each other, neither willing to bend. He smiled. "I won't leave until the morning. We have tonight."

She relaxed against him and he breathed in the scent of her hair. After guiding her into the kitchen so he could tell Blackette the plan, they made their way to their bedroom.

Chapter 55

Serpé tried to protect Rakel and Tomes from what she feared would come. They argued with her, but in the end they left for the safety of the town proper. She sent a message for each of her friends with the couple as well.

Though Kian left to protect the merchants they feared stood in danger, Serpé could not fight the feeling that Reicholt was coming for her. It had been too long since she confronted him in the temple. She could not believe that he had waited this long to punish her for the humiliation of her escape.

Kian's departure with most of the army left the house and the farm echoing in emptiness. He left less than a dozen men with her and those only because she could not convince him to take them all. The men stayed in the farmhand house, though they took turns on watch in the main house.

Despite feeling Reicholt would come for her, Serpé was still surprised when her common room darkened briefly by shadows moving across one of the windows.

She stared at the window before standing and walking to the door. Placing the book she had been reading on the small table near the door, she picked up a sword she kept against the wall. This habit, learned from Kian, brought her small comfort in the face of an unknown intruder. With her grip firm on the hilt, she leaned toward the door to listen for any movement from the other side.

Before she could place herself completely, the door was pushed into her with a painful thrust. She stumbled backward. The blur of movement that rushed toward her barely registered. Grabbing her by her arms, two men pushed her across the entry hall. Serpé found herself against the wall opposite the door. Her back was pushed against the wood. Her stomach ached where a shoulder had been pushed into her by one of the men. While she tried to catch her breath, she watched men in red tunics stream into her house and move past her prone position.

Serpé finally found the breath to shout out a question. "What do you want?"

"I will ask the questions, Serpé." She recognized the male voice, though she could not see the face of the figure because of the shadows cast on it by the sun.

She struggled against the men who held her. The grip on her right arm tightened and she felt the sword she held slip from her hand. Another guard stepped between the first two, his fist clenched tight. He grinned, then pulled back and punched her. The air in her lungs escaped in a painful whoosh, but the men who held her slammed her back against the wall again when she doubled over to lessen the pain. Her head bounced against the hard surface and her knees buckled, the only relief from the pain in her stomach.

Her head fell forward, her chin resting on her chest. She struggled to breathe despite the burn in her lungs. Lifting her gaze again, Serpé glared at the man before her. Her vision remained blurred, forcing her to squeeze her eyes shut several times to bring the room back into focus. Though she had tried to prepare herself, the sight that became clear left a cold lump in her chest.

"What do you want, Reicholt?" she asked through clenched teeth.

Eion stepped closer and put his mouth close to her ear. His breath on her neck made her gag and the movement elicited another jab in her ribs from a guard.

"I want you to obey me, Serpé. I want to be the center of your world. I want you to desire me with your entire being."

"Never!" She tried to kick out at him, hitting a guard instead. He grabbed her leg and twisted. She felt the muscles in her knee and hip stretch and strain painfully under the assault.

"Stop!" Reicholt smacked the guard on the back of his head. "I don't want her to be useless. Take her into the common room." The man released the pressure from her leg, but maintained his grip to keep her from kicking him again.

The guards carried her into the next room. Her resistance had been futile against their combined strength, and her arms hurt more from their grips. The furniture in her common room had been pushed against the walls. Only a single chair remained in the middle of the room. Next to the chair stood the captain of the Religious Guard, a length of rope in his hands. Strinnal Marcin almost looked apologetic and she scoffed at him while he tied her into the chair, her arms behind her.

Serpé did not watch Reicholt walk toward her. The pain from her arms, leg and stomach still blurred her vision. But she did not close her eyes, instead focusing on the window behind him. She would not give him the satisfaction of seeing fear in her, nor would she bow to his demands.

"My dear, answer my questions and we will leave. I don't want to hurt you." The First's words lacked sincerity.

"I will tell you nothing," she growled and pulled against her tight restraints. Obviously she would not escape easily.

"Show her how wrong she is." Reicholt nodded to the guard on her right. "But do try not to ruin her beauty for me."

Though Serpé kept her eyes focused on Reicholt, she saw the guard nod in understanding. He stepped in front of her and grinned. *Of course my vision clears in time to see his pompous expression.* She sighed, full of disappointment, just as the man slapped her. Still grinning, he moved so she could see Reicholt again.

The foul iron taste of blood filled her mouth when she licked her lip. *How appropriate. The two times I have experienced abuse have been at the hands of the priest I once adored. Kian never taught me how to stand up to any form of torture—neither of us ever expected me to be captured.*

"Since we met more militia patrols the closer we came to this farm, I'm sure Lord Draven knows we're here. Will he attempt a rescue? Or did you really expect your traps to keep us away? Oh, I lost a few men, but not the number I'm sure you hoped for." Reicholt smiled at her. "I'm surprised Kian didn't leave more men with you. He should have known the attacks on the merchants were meant as a distraction."

"We did. But I wasn't going to let you get your hands on Kian or more of his men." The traps were her idea and the men who stayed were eager to help with them. "We knew you wanted to arrest me. I'm not afraid."

"Tell me where Kian is camped."

"You are the reason the false attack on the merchants came to his attention. Don't you know?" Serpé liked throwing the question back at him. She wanted to make him work for anything he got from her.

"If you do not tell me, I will take you back to Siladan and torture you." His grin grew wider. She recognized confidence in his ability to obtain the answers he wanted.

"I can't wait to go back with you."

The guard backhanded her, the metal of his ring cutting into the flesh of her cheek. Reicholt grabbed the guard's hand and tore the ring from his finger. He threw it across the room, though he did not look away from the guard.

"The wound does not make me happy. Do not make things worse." Reicholt released the man's hand and turned back to Serpé. "My dear, you will tell me where Kian is because he is keeping you from me. If it wasn't for him, you never would have left me and helped him create this war."

"He had nothing to do with my leaving you. That was all your doing." She turned her face away from the expected slap, but the guard slammed his clenched fist into her stomach instead. Gasping for air again, she fought to control her tears, to regain her composure.

"I don't want to hurt you, Serpé. Where is his army camped?"

I don't believe the sympathy he has forced into his voice. She took a deep breath and glared at him, pushing her pain and emotions behind a mental wall. The same wall she had used to bury her love for Kian. *There is only one thing that will give me the strength to fight against Reicholt.*

"Azar guides us with his wisdom," she intoned.

"Don't recite Azar's teachings to me!"

Serpé smiled at Reicholt's anger, until the guard slapped her again. Her lip split this time and blood run down her chin. She moved her tongue over her teeth—one had come loose.

"*Where* is his army?" Reicholt prodded.

"Azar protects us with his love."

Again the guard punched her in the stomach.

"Answer me!" Reicholt shouted in her face.

Serpé closed her eyes against the verbal assault. "Azar helps us to choose the path of right." Her last word was garbled by the slap she received.

"How long do you think you can keep this up, woman?" Reicholt's anger grew more intense. "You will break eventually."

She did not find any pleasure in the emotion she had invoked. The pain pushed all satisfaction away. "Azar teaches us to respect the magic around us." She spoke the words knowing the punch she received to her stomach was deserved.

Reicholt leaned over and whispered in her ear, "Kian will pay for his crimes and you will be mine." He licked her cheek, sending a disgusted shiver down her spine.

"Azar teaches us to respect others." She spoke loud enough to ensure everyone in the room could hear the final devotion.

The First roared in anger at her response and stormed from the room. The guard and Serpé watched him leave, then the man turned back to slap her again.

Chapter 56

*E*ach day, it is easier to refuse Reicholt's questions. Serpé found strength in Azar's Devotions, even though each Devotion received some form of punishment. For five days, Reicholt delivered the question and punishment routine, but he never struck her himself. Not since the first time. *I wonder if he seeks a false sense of innocence in the pain he allows others to cause me. Does he think his hands are free of my blood because it is spilled by another?*

She remembered hearing messengers sent out by Strinnal, though she could not remember on which day. One messenger to Jalena, another to Lord Draven, and both returned with no response. Each had also been sent to deliver a message to Kian. It seemed Reicholt refused to wait for answers she would not give him.

When the sun set on the fifth day after Reicholt's arrival, someone untied Serpé from her chair. Dephia helped her bathe, though the woman did not speak to her and she was given clean clothes. Dephia's face held the ugly green of healing bruises around one eye and her jaw.

"Dephia, what happened?" Serpé whispered so the guards would not hear.

The servant shook her head. Unshed tears pooled in her eyes.

When Serpé finished, guards escorted her down the hall to her bedroom, now occupied by Reicholt.

She surveyed the room with a critical eye, and took note of the changes the priest had made. With her personal items no longer in view, she could only hope he had not destroyed them. *There is no reason to believe my possessions have survived. Reicholt does not care about me or anything that would not advance his ambitions.*

A table laden with food and tapered candles sat in front of the window. Reicholt stood in the middle of the room, between the bed and dresser. The guards pushed her into the room, and shut the door. She stood defiant against his gaze, though it raked boldly over her body. *His look makes me feel dirty, despite the bath. And his clothing… so inappropriate for a priest.* The silk shirt he wore ruffled with his movements and the cotton breeches rested light against his skin.

"I'm so happy you accepted my invitation, Serpé." His voice rang of honesty, like he courted her.

"I was not given a choice." His eyes narrowed and she saw the chill of her words bring an instant change of his mood.

"True." He motioned for her to approach the table. When she planted her feet and crossed her arms, he covered the distance to her instead. His fingers brushed her wet hair from her shoulder with a gentleness she had not expected. "You are so beautiful, Serpé."

She stared at him, and tightened her arms around herself.

"I'm willing to forgive your previous refusal, if you will only take me into your arms now," he whispered. His breath on her skin sent an unpleasant shiver through her body.

"I refused you before and I do it again. Especially after finding pleasure in Kian's arms." She intended her words to anger him and waited for his outburst. Serpé did not like using the happiness found in Kian's arms against the priest, but it was a potent weapon.

She did not have long to wait before he reacted, more forcefully than she expected. He stepped back and backhanded her, letting loose a growl close to that of a wild animal. Pain tore through her head when his ring of station in the church reopened the cut from the guard's ring. The blow forced her back against the door. One hand went against the door to steady herself while she wiped the blood from her cheek with the other.

Reicholt advanced and wrapped his hands around her throat. She pushed at him, but his anger added to his strength. When he squeezed, she changed her tactics and tried to slap his hands away.

By the gods! Again, he wants to kill me. He will *kill me this time, for sure, if I can't break free.* Her lungs screamed for air, but when her vision darkened, she brought her knee up, slamming it into his groin. He released her and grabbed himself. Both struggled to catch their breath, glaring at the other.

"That's twice, Serpé," he growled. "I should kill you for the pain you've caused me."

"Does it upset you to hear of my time in Kian's arms? To hear how he can satisfy me in a way you never will, Eion?" She never called him by his given name before. It made him more human, more susceptible to the temptations he never denied. He could be punished—she could defeat him. Now all she had to do was escape.

Reicholt advanced on her again. "How dare you speak to me of your time with another man!"

"You don't want to hear how much I enjoy his caresses, his kisses? Aren't you happy for me that I feel complete as we lay in each other's arms, our bodies one?" she goaded him.

He grabbed her by the shoulders. "Enough, woman! I will shut you up if I have to." He pounded her against the wall, her head bouncing against the wood.

"What will you do? Hit me again? Rape me? Won't that hurt your standing with Azar?" Her head and throat hurt, but she could not stop. Her sarcastic words were meant to anger him and he deserved all of them.

Reicholt released her suddenly. "I have lost Azar's favor and no longer serve him. I serve another now. And it's all because of you." He pulled away from her, only to lunge in and smashed his lips against hers. He forced her lips apart and when she felt his tongue near her teeth, she bit down until he released her with a cry.

"Good. One such as you does not deserve Azar's blessings." She spit on the floor between them.

He slapped her again. "Get out."

She opened the door and waited until the guards grabbed her.

"Return her to the chair," he ordered, turning from the

door.

Her laughter filled the hall as the guards dragged her back to the common room.

Chapter 57

Strinnal waited outside the common room until Reicholt retired for the night. He knew Serpé did not sleep much, since The First would not allow her to be untied at night.

I want to free her, even if it is just for the night, but The First will know if I do. He questions my loyalty enough, but I doubt she knows it. He shook his head. *I just can't risk it.*

He walked into the room, careful to keep his footsteps quiet. A single lantern on a table near the chair cast a dim light over the room. Serpé sat in the chair, her chin resting on her chest.

"Serpé?" Even though Strinnal whispered, his voice echoed around him.

Her slow, pained movements when she raised her head made him wince. The flickering light from the lantern gave her skin a sickly pallor and deepened the bruises on her face.

"Go away." Her weakened voice reached him.

He walked closer. "Can I get you anything? Some water?" His offerings felt inadequate compared to the pain he knew she had suffered.

She looked him in the eyes. "You could free me from these ropes. What are you doing here? Why are you doing this, Strinnal?"

"I can't free you. The First would have my head."

She lowered her head again. "Then why bother asking me?"

her whispered question lack emotion.

She's given up. The realization stabbed at him.

"Because I can't do anything else. My choices are not my own." He stepped around the chair and loosened the ropes on her wrists enough to give her some movement. "But my guilt in this demands I do something to help you."

"If your guilt is so strong, then do the right thing and set me free."

"Things aren't that simple, Serpé. Too much is beyond our control right now. No matter how much it hurts us, we have to let things happen, or more people will die than you realize." He wanted to touch her cheek, but kept his hand to himself.

It is not my place to touch her like that. Kian would kill me and she doesn't need to think of me like The First.

"Strinnal…we knew each other. I met you at the church. You used to watch me when I assisted Reicholt with services."

For a moment, happiness filled her voice and it lightened the pain in his chest when he heard it. "Many young men attended services so they could watch you. When you disappeared and Reicholt replaced you with another, attendance dropped significantly." He stood in front of her again, but went to his knee so she did not have to look up at him. "Serpé, I need to tell you something about Kian."

"What? Has something happened to him?" She strained against her restraints and again his chest filled with discomfort at her obvious pain.

"Not yet. When he gets here, Reicholt is going to make him choose between his freedom and yours. There is nothing I can do to stop it."

I pray this news does not devastate her, but she must know what is happening before Kian arrives. It is only a matter of time before he comes for her.

"You need to warn him."

Desperate again, her struggles increased, but he could do nothing to comfort her.

"If I can before he sees Reicholt, I will. If you don't want him to sacrifice himself for you, you need to convince him when you see him. But we both know that he will do what he wants, no matter what we say to him. He will do what he needs to, to protect you." He stood again. "One more thing. Your necklace, the one Kian gave you for protection from Reicholt finding you.

Put it back on, as soon as you can."

Strinnal walked away. Turning his back on her whispered demands pained him.

I can't risk being seen by The First or the guards that support him. Kian will do what he can to save Serpé and I have to make sure I'm with him when his sacrifice is accepted. I must make sure Kian survives. Or we will lose her and the hope she can bring our kingdom.

Chapter 58

Stubborn animal. This horse is a poor replacement for Adrastos, which is exactly why I gave the war horse to Serpé. I just don't have time to train another one, though.

Kian tightened the saddle again, his fourth attempt this morning. He pushed his shoulder into the horse's ribs until it finally fastened properly.

With saddling his horse complete, he turned to watch the army finish their own preparations. The attacks on the merchant caravans turned out to be little more than a nuisance, but he decided to continue their assault against the Religious Guard to drive them back from the border of the forest.

Blackette's displeasure with this decision became obvious in the glares he sent Kian over his shoulder. He wanted to return to the farm, but Kian thought he could keep Reicholt and the Religious guard away from Serpé with his attacks.

We still argue about this tactic every night, though I am beginning to think Blackette is right. We should return.

Interrupting Kian's thoughts, an unknown, mounted rider raced into the camp. His horse cried out in pain and displeasure when the man brought it to an abrupt halt. Dismounting, Kian's men surrounded him before he could identify himself. The soldiers refused to hear what he said and only after he waved a parchment at them, did one of the men walk over to Kian and

Blackette. The newcomer remained where he stood, awaiting Kian's orders.

"He says he has a message from Jalena, about Serpé."

Kian nodded and strode over to the group of men, Blackette close behind him.

"What's your message?"

"Five days ago, a man came to the inn. He told Jalena to deliver a message to you. Another messenger delivered the same message to Lord Draven. Jalena denied knowledge of you and your whereabouts, but he told her if she didn't get this message to you, Serpé would die." He pushed the parchment between the men to Kian.

"You weren't followed?" Blackette stepped in while Kian read, and waved the surrounding men away.

"No, that's why it took me five days to get here. Jalena and Lord Draven didn't want more than one person looking for you, so we had to wait."

Kian did not hear what the man said. *Reicholt was waiting for me to leave the farm and has taken Serpé prisoner. I gave him exactly what he wanted by leaving her. Again, I failed her.*

He crumpled the parchment and glared at the messenger. "This mentions another message. What did it say? What else do you know?" He struggled to keep the emotion from his voice.

"If Jalena did not find a way to deliver the first message, the inn would be burned, and she and Serpé would both be killed. We are prepared for an assault, though. Serpé sent Rakel and Tomes to Jalena with a request for increased patrols around her farm. The largest patrols are being led by her friends and they have been stationed at the farm since we first learned of Reicholt's arrival. However, Serpé ordered no one to move in, so we wait. There is a large force of men at the farm with two wagons, one of which we assume is The First's carriage. Serpé also ordered that no move be made against him unless he tried to take her. I don't think she thought he would want you at the time." The messenger accepted a waterskin and drank deeply.

"Probably not. His focus has been on her, for the most part." Kian wiped his face with his empty hand and sighed.

"What does the letter say, Kian?" Blackette made no attempt to hide his impatience, earning a glare from his captain.

"As I'm sure you figured out from what has been said, Serpé has been captured by Reicholt. She is to be charged with my current crimes and any others he plans to bring against me. Namely, treason for leading this rebel army." Kian succeeded in keeping his emotions under control for now, but what would he do when he came face to face with the priest? "Blackette, we need fifty of our best men and fastest horses. The rest of the men will follow when they have broken camp. We leave immediately."

"If we hadn't left in the first place, we could have prevented this," Blackette pointed out.

"True. But we can't change that now."

I agree with him. Why does he continue this argument? Is it really solving anything?

"We should have left more men at least," Blackette continued as if Kian had not spoken.

"I know! I should not have left. Now get the men I need and get on your damn horse so we can get back there." No longer caring if he offended his second, his anger rushed out of him in a wave.

Blackette stared for only a moment before he left to carry out Kian's orders.

Kian watched him leave, then leaned against his horse for support. Though there had been a small threat against some of the caravans, it really had been just a ruse.

And I fell for it. Serpé must have known. She always did know what the priest was thinking when no one else did. And she sacrificed herself to keep me safe. She's not supposed to do that. It's my job to protect her.

His stomach soured with the thought of what Reicholt could have done to her in the five days he had her. The time until Kian arrived at her side again would be too long for him. He knew too many things could happen to her.

"We're ready, Kian."

He had not heard Blackette come up behind him. They stared at each other before both nodded and mounted their horses. Once the rest of the men were ready, Kian ordered the move out of camp.

Chapter 59

The thunder of the horses charging through the forest echoed in Kian's ears and reverberated throughout the trees. He and Blackette moved ahead of the group of men, but within sight of the main group.

Kian watched for any movement in their path, but the forest remained deserted around them. The race from the encampment took taken three days, but it felt like a month had passed since the message found its way into his hands. He and his men rode hard throughout the previous night in order to reach the edge of Serpé's farm as close to daybreak as possible.

Raising his hand, he slowed his horse. Militia waited ahead of them, in their path to the farm, and though he had no intention of speaking to them, he knew their assistance would be helpful. Past the men, through the shadows of the trees, he saw Serpé's farmhouse. Moments passed after all the horses came to rest before the natural sounds of the forest returned.

After nodding to Blackette, they dismounted. With a quick gesture for his men to keep them with the patrol, Kian crept to the edge of the forest, Blackette close behind.

Sorban soldiers lounged around the farm, their horses grazing where they were tethered. The two men watched and plotted before returning to their force, now joined by the militia patrol.

"There are about fifty men outside the house, but enough horses to accommodate seventy-five. We will leave the horses here, and move toward the house. I need to get inside. I have no problem killing anyone who gets in my way," Kian informed the gathered forces.

His men nodded in agreement, many of them showing an eagerness to drive their blades into the Religious Guard. The militia nodded as well, most of them stopping though when a single man stepped forward.

Kian groaned inwardly. *Fitting that Striphen should be here to see my failure in protecting Serpé. All I need now is for Rodin to make an appearance and my humiliation would be complete.*

He waited until Striphen came within yards of his men before closing the distance between them.

"I'm Striphen. Lord Draven sent my patrol to assist you and your men. What can we do?" He stood under Kian's scrutiny without movement, almost defiant, waiting for an answer.

"You and the other patrols can add numbers to the men I've brought. Reicholt wants me. If I can't get out of this, you need to let me go. Serpé must be kept safe." Kian stepped even closer to the man and lowered his voice so no one else could hear. "I know of your feelings for her and I've seen the two of you together. You need to keep her from sacrificing herself. She thinks she's protecting me, but she cannot be taken back to Siladan. She is the only one who can save Sorban from itself. If Reicholt is allowed to gain the power he wants, no one is safe."

"It took you long enough to tell her how you feel, Kian. I suggest you do nothing that would take you from her again. I don't want to see her hurt, by you or anyone else. I will do what I have to, to make sure that doesn't happen."

The two men stared at each other in silence.

He still cares for Serpé, despite her need to be with me. It probably hurt him more than she will ever realize to see the pain she suffered because of my rejection. Maybe I should have left her alone and given her a chance at a safe relationship. I doubt she would have ever been truly happy with Striphen, though, and no matter whom she chose, Reicholt would still have tried to use her against me. At least this way, we had some time together—short as it was. Striphen will just have to get over it.

"Let's go get her back." Kian turned, gestured at the group of men and walked to the edge of the forest. Stepping out of the trees together, he and Blackette were joined by three of their own men and Striphen.

The Religious Guard on duty turned at their appearance, advancing toward them and drawing their weapons. Kian scanned the Guard out of habit, making note of the types of weapons they carried as well as the men he would fight himself. Their stances revealed weaknesses he could use if the tension between the two groups escalated into a confrontation.

Though nothing was said by either side, the Guard that faced him returned their weapons to their sheaths and scabbards, surprising everyone on Kian's side. Movement to Kian's right drew his attention and he turned to see Shanna step out of the forest with her own group of militia. Behind them, a large number of elves riding dire wolves also left the protection of the forest. Soon the farm lay surrounded by Draven's militia and the elves under Shou-Lung's leadership.

With this many, Reicholt would be an idiot if he tried to leave with Serpé. Either he has a very good plan in place, or he is the fool I think him to be.

"Don't forget, Striphen. Serpé's safety is your primary concern." The other man nodded. Kian stepped away from his men. "I will enter the house and speak with Reicholt. With or without bloodshed. Your choice."

I want one of them to attack me. It would make everything so much easier. And fifty less men in the opposing army would be a big boon to the morale of my men. He glanced at Striphen. *But I don't know what Draven has commanded for the militia's involvement and the elves are also unpredictable. Have Shou-Lung's instructions changed? Will they assist me if a fight breaks out, or just wait to see if I lose against the Guard?*

Though the Religious Guard parted to let him pass, he knew by their expressions that they did it only because they had to. Reicholt had probably ordered them to let him through, and though he took Blackette and the others with him, the Guards followed their orders precisely.

The air tingled with caution when they entered the house they called home just weeks before. The building lacked its usual comfort, and many of the things he had been familiar with were missing. The others drew their swords when they walked through the hall to the common room, but Kian waited. He wanted his hands empty and knew the magic in his sword would bring the weapon to his hand with only a thought.

Kian stepped into the common room first, stopping to gaze around him before the others could follow. Ten more soldiers stood in front of the windows and doors, each armored and marked as The First's elite guard. Through the windows that faced the back of the house, Kian saw the soldiers that had not been accounted for in his first survey of the farm.

Reicholt couldn't have moved all these men through the forest without someone noticing. He must have sent smaller groups to Serpé's home to hide his numbers. Our current numbers can't stand against this force until the rest of my men arrive.

A chair sat in the middle of the room and Kian knew without looking at it that Serpé sat there. But he was not ready to look at her yet.

I need to know every possible escape and what I'm facing before I react to what he did to Serpé. I don't trust myself to stay calm and Reicholt probably expects an emotional reaction.

Reicholt himself stood behind the chair. Kian felt his gaze on him and as soon as he brought his own to the priest's, he decided he wanted to drive his sword through the religious leader's bowels. The thought pleased him, but he kept the emotion from his face.

The priest will turn any emotion I show against me—try to convince Serpé of the opposite of what I am truly feeling.

Kian took a deep breath and forced himself to look at her. Her hair hung loose and he wanted to brush it from her face.

Blood stained her white shirt and for a brief moment, he wondered how long it had been since she changed clothes. Her breathing came with difficulty and she did not react to his presence.

They must have worked to make sure she remained unconscious for my arrival. I can only imagine the things they did to you, Serpé. I swear, I will make him pay for every mark on your body. His silent vow helped to steel him against further emotions. He knew it wouldn't last.

Clearing his throat, Reicholt waited until Kian returned his attention to him, then he reached down and lifted Serpé's head, revealing her bruised face. Blood dried at the corner of her mouth, but fresh red blood flowed from the edge of the wound. Dried blood also crusted her cheek and a red, angry line marred her perfect flesh. Grinning at him, Reicholt let Serpé's chin slip from his fingers and hit her chest.

Growling, Kian took a hurried step forward. Before he could take two steps, Blackette reached out to hold him back, his grip tight on Kian's arm. With a quick gesture, Kian saw that the Guards had placed their hands on their weapons.

Blackette is trying to prevent violence. This day will not end without blood shed, though.

"I knew you would come, once you heard of my arrival. Now, the only question I have is how are you going to save Serpé *and* yourself?" Reicholt asked, filling the silence.

Kian heard the confidence in Reicholt's voice and decided nothing would stop him. Grinding his teeth, he dragged Blackette farther into the room.

Reicholt rested his hand on Serpé's shoulder and squeezed. Even in her unconscious state, Serpé pulled away from the pain he imposed on her. Kian stopped his forward motion. Reicholt released the pressure.

He will hurt her more with each step I take. Forcing himself to take a deep breath, Kian contemplated Reicholt's question. *I know he has feelings for Serpé, even if they are demented by his corruption. What those feelings are remains to be seen.*

"Serpé isn't in danger, not from you, at least. You wouldn't hurt her, because she is the only one keeping you alive, Eion. If it wasn't for her insistence, I would have killed you long ago." Grinning at the priest, Kian believed his own declaration, and then he looked at Serpé again.

I'm wrong. It wasn't just his men who hurt her, but Reicholt laid a hand on her as well. She is no longer safe from physical harm just because he desires her.

"Not only will I hurt her, but I will watch the Master Interrogator question her. As you can see, I've already begun the questioning." Reicholt's voice dripped with satisfaction. "She resisted us well, but these injuries are minor compared to what my man will do once we return to the capital."

"You're a fool to think you're invulnerable. We will never allow you to rule Sorban, even if it costs us our lives." Kian matched his contempt to Reicholt's in every word. He even allowed a grin to return to his lips.

"Honestly, Kian, there's nothing you can do to stop me. My power is supreme. I rule the kingdom and its church. I am untouchable." Caressing Serpé's hair, Reicholt kept his gaze locked with Kian's.

Unable to prevent it, Kian swore, but stopped his forward motion again at the sound of weapons being drawn.

I will wrap my hands around his neck and squeeze, Serpé's need for justice be damned. I will make him stop touching her.

"Does it bother you, Kian?" Reicholt grinned. "I have plans for her. During her trial, she will sit at my side, for me to use in any way I want. Maybe I will find out what it is about her that attracted you to her bed."

No longer caring about the guards, Kian advanced on Reicholt. With a quick whispered command, his sword appeared in his hand. The guards at the windows rushed to stop him, his own men positioning themselves to prevent them from reaching their captain. Weapons clashed, but his men were unsuccessful in their quick attempt at protection. Kian's arms were grabbed by two Guards while a third appeared in front of them. The Guard's sword was raised, ready to run Kian through.

From his right, Blackette appeared, stepping in front of Kian. He thrust his sword into the soldier in a move Kian knew was pure instinct, not skill. Blackette was talented, but he fought with his heart, not his head.

A sudden silence filled the room, everyone staring at the injured Guard when he fell to the floor, blood seeping through his fingers.

Why doesn't Reicholt heal him?

Kian counted the heartbeats before the man's pained motions stopped. Returning his gaze to Reicholt's emotionless face, he renewed his struggles. Around him, his men continued their attacks against the Religious Guard, despite being outnumbered.

"I will put her on trial for leading this rebellion against the merchant council and against the church of Azar." Over the sound of combat, Reicholt's voice boomed, further describing his plans. "Any and all charges against you, I will transfer to her. She will be tried in your stead and will suffer the punishment that should be yours."

"You can't hold her for my crimes." Reicholt's grin strengthened Kian's struggles against the guards who held him, forcing their grips to loosen. They did not have his determination.

"If you loved her as much as you pretend, Kian, you would

have kept her out of your rebellion. You would have sent her back to me, to finish her training, where she would have been safe."

Kian watched Reicholt continue to caress Serpé's hair and knew the priest was right, in a way.

If I had been able to send her some place safer, farther away from Sorban, or had her necklace been replaced, he might not have found her. But I still think, no matter how hard we tried, Fate would have done what it wanted. And 'might' is not a word that fills me with confidence when it comes to her safety.

"You would have killed her because she knew too much about your activities. That much was obvious by the bruises you left on her neck when she first came to me." Pulling an arm free, Kian grinned when Reicholt gestured at the guards and they released his other arm.

A moan from the chair's occupant drew everyone's attention, heralding Serpé's return to consciousness. Kian rushed forward, surprising the guards, and dropped to one knee in front of her. He took her face in his hands.

"Kian, what are you doing here?" Straining to hear her hoarse whisper, he leaned in, closer to her.

"I came for you, Serpé." The tender touch he tried to use to wipe tears from her bruised cheeks still made her wince with pain. A lump formed in his throat and he swallowed against it.

"You shouldn't have come. We both agreed, no matter what happened, we wouldn't try to rescue the other until we knew it was true."

"Shh..." He touched her lips to silence her protest. "I know what we agreed to and I received the confirmation I needed. Reicholt threatened Jalena as well. I needed to come for you."

She's going to fight me, fight against the decision I have to make, but I can't allow Reicholt to take her back to Siladan.

"He came because I told him I will try you for his crimes, Serpé. I think it is rather sly of me to charge and execute you and let him suffer with your loss for the rest of his life. He will be rather miserable, don't you think?" Reicholt laughed and Kian heard the priest move around and stop behind him.

"Kian, go. Leave while you can. You are the leader of the army and they must be led against him. You're the only one who can defeat him and free me."

Kian's chest tightened at her plea. Lifting his face to hers, he rested his cheek against the heat of her face. "No, you can do it too. I need you to be free. Remember what I told you? He can't have you." Kissing her cheek, he lingered for a moment in her scent. "I love you, Serpé. I'm sorry I took so long to realize it, to tell you how I feel. I never meant to cause you any pain." He kissed her again before he stood, turning to face the priest.

The group could fight and we might get some kind of warning to the others outside, but we are outnumbered and would be hard pressed against the Guards in this room.

Serpé's safety was more important than his. She could lead the army with the training he gave her. Sacrificing himself for her freedom was the only way to ensure they had any chance of winning the war and keeping Reicholt from ruling the kingdom. Ignoring the sounds of her struggling to free herself, he took a deep breath to prepare for her outburst when she realized what he'd decided.

"Blackette, you and the men will protect Serpé. She must not be taken prisoner by Reicholt again. She will be the army's captain, but will need your advice. You will follow her orders as if they were my own." When Blackette opened his mouth to protest, Kian threw a glare at him, stopping any argument. Reaching behind him, Kian touched Serpé's shoulder. "Free her. I want to hold her before I go."

"Go?" Reicholt's mock surprise irritated him. "Where are you going?"

"You will not have her. She will not answer for my decisions or my crimes. I will take whatever punishment a *real* trial deems necessary." His jaw clenched tight. "Free her."

No one moved until Reicholt nodded. Turning back to Serpé, Kian heard the rope hit the floor. She threw herself at him, wrapping her arms around him.

"Please, Kian, don't do this," she pleaded with him. "We'll find another way." Her tears wet his cheek and neck.

Kian held her until her body stopped shaking from crying.

I will miss this. She fits me and the trust she has in me makes me feel whole.

"Blackette." Forcing himself to release her, he pushed her into the other man's arms.

I can't believe I'm letting another man take her from me. Worse, I'm letting Reicholt take me from her, again.

Holding his sword out, Kian allowed the Guard's search.

When they found his every weapon, even the small knife he kept hidden in his belt, he held his hands out and waited for shackles to be placed on his wrists. The renewed sound of Serpé's muffled sobs drowned out the sound of the shackles as they locked shut.

Reicholt watched him with a satisfied smirk and for a moment, Kian considered using the weight of the metal shackles to aid his strength in an attack on the priest. Instead, he stood still, watching Serpé despite the pain her cries caused in his chest.

"You may have me, Reicholt, but you have not won this war. Serpé will free me and bring an end to your tyranny." Guards entering the room wearing the prison insignia made Kian pause. He gave the other man his full attention. "I expect you to keep her notified of the trial and any actions she can take in my defense."

"Of course. I am not beyond giving her the opportunity to see your trial and execution." Waving his hand, Reicholt dismissed his statement as if to do otherwise would be absurd.

The prison guards replaced the Religious Guard around Kian and they pushed him from the room, through the kitchen and out the back door. Outside, the true number of men Reicholt brought with him was finally revealed. Another one-hundred men and horses waited, damaging the land where Serpé's crops would grow. They stood, exchanging glares with the elves and militia.

Those who stand in support of Serpé and me are still outnumbered. My army will not arrive in time.

Two carriages waited, four horses hitched to each. Silk curtains and gold gilding decorated one carriage, with intricately carved designs in the wood. The other resembled a box on wheels with a seat for the driver. The unadorned wood, banded with metal, held a single door as the only way in or out. Narrow slits allowed for the passage of air.

The door to the prison wagon stood open to the darkness within, giving Kian a glimpse of the bleak future awaiting him. Before he was pushed inside, he turned to look at Serpé one last time. Smiling at her, trying to convey a confidence he did not feel, he touched his fingers to his lips. He climbed into the darkness after a fierce push from the guards.

"Learn from this, Serpé." Kian heard Reicholt say as the door closed and the darkness swallowed him. "Disband this army, give up this war, find a farmer, settle down, and have lots of fat babies. If you continue the path Kian has laid out for you, you will be next."

"No, Eion, I will come for him and you will pay for the pain you've caused."

She waited before she answered him. I wish I could see why.

Reicholt's laughter echoed through the dark wagon, surrounding Kian. It lasted only a moment, until it was cut off in a cough. Kian smiled.

If she gave him the same look she has given me in the past, his silence does not surprise me. Even with the many times she has given me that look, I still don't know how to defend myself against it.

Uncounted breaths later, the wagon moved. The sounds of horses and the voices of many men reached him. They had started their journey to Siladan.

Chapter 60

Serpé watched the wagons roll away, held tight in Blackette's embrace. With her cheek still warm from Reicholt's breath, his threat sent a shivering chill up her spine.

"It doesn't matter what you do," he had whispered, "I will be back for you after I have executed the captain. Only my children will swell your belly. I'll see to that."

She fought against Blackette until he released her. Three steps and she fell to the ground. Rocks cut into her knees and the pain shot up through her legs, over shadowing the pain in her chest.

Fresh tears filled her eyes, and she laughed in spite of her pain.

"Of course. I am like a child learning to walk again. How can I expect to keep up with that wagon?" Laughter did not stop the tears, and soon her sobs filled the quiet yard.

Footsteps crunched the rocks behind her, and arms enfolded her again. Glancing up, she saw Blackette's concern through her tears. Activity and noise around the farm heralded the arrival of other allies.

"Come with us, Serpé. We must tend to your injuries."

He guided her into the house and toward her bedroom, but she stopped him before he could open the door. Her hand shook as it rested on his.

"No. I will not go in there. It's not my room, not now." She pulled away from him, toward the room Kian had stayed in.

He released her and opened the door to her room. "I don't understand."

"Reicholt used my room."

"We'll take care of it, Serpé." Tamar had come up behind Blackette and put her own arms around her friend.

They helped her inside the room Kian occupied when he first arrived, and after Tamar pushed the men out, she helped Serpé change out of her bloodied clothes. Comfortable under the covers, or as much as she could be with the blanket resting on her bruises, she waited for the others to return.

Drommond, Aldric and Striphen entered her room. "Serpé, me and Aldric will be healing ye. And we be making sure ye get the rest ye need." Drommond stopped when she shook her head.

"Do not use your magic to make me sleep."

Aldric sat on the bed next to her. He looked uncomfortable, but did not move away. He took her hand in his. "You know I'm not the person who will make you do anything against your will, but you need to let us help you. We don't know how bad you have been hurt, but for the healing to help you, you need to rest. We will talk to you each time before we cast the next spell."

Serpé looked at each of her friends, her gaze locking with Striphen's last. He nodded in agreement, his expression filled with encouragement.

"I will be here each time, Serpé. I promise."

She looked at Aldric again and nodded. "I trust you to help me. Please." She felt the little control she had gained with Reicholt's departure slipping away. Instead of waiting for the magic to make her sleep, she closed her eyes, feeling the warmth of the spells wash through her.

Two days lost because they wanted me to sleep. The sleep helped with healing the physical wounds, but the emotional ones will take more than the healing magic can do. Now I have to reach Siladan to free Kian.

Serpé moved slower than she wanted, the bruising from her two broken ribs holding her back. She packed a few things into a bag while she prepared a mental list of the things she would need before she left.

"What are you doing?"

Lost in her plans, she had not heard Blackette walk up behind her. She straightened her back, and turned to face him, her jaw clenched tight against the pain. "I'm leaving for Siladan. They have a two day advantage on me. I don't want to give them anymore." She expected him to fight her. *No, I want him to fight me on this. I need to release the frustration I feel over the delay and he's as good a focus as anyone.*

"Kian wanted us to stay together, to lead the army. He wanted us to defeat Reicholt and then free him."

She couldn't believe the man was so naïve. *Does he really think the mad priest will wait to rid himself of Kian?*

"Just how ignorant are you?" When the look on his face froze, she wondered, *Did I really say that?*

"Serpé, I understand you're upset, but that doesn't give you free reign to insult those who support you and Kian." He turned away.

Yes, I said it, out loud. And he is right, on both counts. This war had to end and it would take more than surrender from either side. Not that she would surrender to Reicholt. Nor him to her. *I must find a better focus for my anger.*

"You're right. Get everyone together. Has the rest of the army arrived yet?" When he shook his head, she went on. "We can't sit around waiting for them. We need to strike before Captain Marcin can get their army back in place."

"Damnit, Serpé. Would you stop for a moment? There are things you need to know. You're acting just like Kian. Come out to the barn without me." He held his hand out to her.

She rested her hand in his hand and allowed him to guide her from the room. Someone still worked to return her bedroom to the way it looked before Reicholt had arrived, but without Rakel, they had not yet succeeded.

When they passed a mirror, she averted her eyes to avoid her own image. The yellow from the bruises around her eyes had faded with the spells and only a pink scar drew the gaze of others when they spoke to her.

Blackette led her through the house and out the kitchen door without stopping, despite attempts by others to talk to them. They walked into the barn and he stopped her in front of a stall containing a chest and several saddle bags. He gestured toward them and followed her inside.

"These are Kian's. He had them brought here after you left for Sanctuary."

How could I miss this? I just don't spend a lot of time in the barn, even to care for Adrastos. The horse is usually groomed in the yard.

Blackette pushed past her when she did not step any closer, and knelt in front of the chest. He searched through it until he found what he needed. Standing, he turned and placed a journal in her hands.

She stared at the book, her breath slow and measured. Still silent, she opened it and glanced over the words written inside.

"We have a spy in Reicholt's ranks? Reicholt hired the mercenaries that have attacked the merchant caravans?" She looked up in surprise to see him nod. "Why?"

Instead of answering, he turned to another page and pointed. "He wants to declare himself king."

She could not hear him. The page he turned to held her attention, and the sickness that gripped her became worse the longer she stared at it.

She shook her head. "This can't be right. Kian could not have known. Surely my mother would have said something"

"Not if she tried to protect you."

"Then why send me into Reicholt's clutches?" She shut the book.

"No one knew what he was capable of back then, Serpé. They were deceived and manipulated by him, just like so many others."

She stifled a scream. "I will hunt Reicholt down and show him that I will not be manipulated. He's caused me so much pain. Kian was right. I can't just walk into Siladan and expect to end this. And, I can't let Reicholt get his hands on me again. Kian sacrificed himself to give me a chance to bring Reicholt to justice. I can't waste it." She caressed the book.

"I can't go back. Not yet. Too many things remain out of place." She looked at Blackette and knew he saw her disappointment and anger. "I have to leave Kian in Siladan until I can remove Reicholt from his position. Tell the other commanders I will meet with them immediately. We must make plans to rid our country of this bastard once and for all."

She knelt in front of the chest and with careful movements,

sorted through the items. A cry of surprise escaped her, and she pulled out an old doll.

"By Azar's Blessings, this is my doll. I can't believe he kept it." She held the fragile possession against her chest and felt the final wall within her break. The emotions she had struggled to keep under control for so long broke free and her sobs filled the stable.

Blackette knelt next to her and held her until she calmed. When her cries stopped, he pulled away. He seemed uncomfortable with the support he gave her and rushed to his feet.

"I'll go speak with the others." He did not wait for a response and almost ran from her.

Alone, she continued her search through Kian's chest. Under a stack of shirts, she found a small wooden box. In the box, resting on top of a softened leather pouch, two signet rings, matching the one she wore on her finger, glistened in the light.

"How did he get these?"

She removed the ring her mother had given her on her eighth birthday, before she left for the church. A short prayer was whispered to Azar as she placed the ring her father had worn on her finger. The cold metal warmed against her skin. *My parents felt the warmth of their rings as death accepted them into its bosom. My family was connected as long as we all wore the rings. Now I stand alone.*

She picked up the pouch with the thought of putting the other rings inside, but the sound of metal clinking from within stopped her. Careful not to let anything slip between her fingers, she emptied the contents into her hand. In the light of the barn, the broken pieces of the sapphire she had worn for four years sparkled in her hand. The chain that held the sapphire slipped from her hand into the hay. Ignoring the sapphire, she let the pieces fall into the box.

"Strinnal knew about this necklace. How?" She dug the chain from the hay and put it around her neck. Her skin tingled from the magic it still held. "Why didn't Kian know about the chain? Why would he tell me it was the sapphire if it wasn't?"

She returned her attention to the chest's boxes contents. *Why did Kian keep these things? Did he care for me all that time, but fought against it?* After reading his journal, it did not surprise her anymore why he did not feel he was good enough for her. But she loved him without knowing the truth of her birth and heritage. His lack of royal blood meant nothing to her.

I have to leave the barn. It feels oppressive. Before she left, she pulled one of Kian's shirts from the chest, then closed it. With everything held tight in her arms, she returned to the house.

The other commanders had their own ideas about how, where and when to attack the Religious Guard, and did not readily accept Serpé's command. Blackette, and then Striphen, were forced to repeat Kian's instructions until she was accepted. As they discussed their plans, Blackette let it slip about Serpé's royal heritage and the others made an immediate change in their attitudes toward her command of the army.

I do not like this change, not for this reason. It shouldn't matter who my grandparents were, or who I might have been if the king remained in power. All that matters is that Reicholt killed the king and the member of his family who were with him. And that he plans to use me to rebuild the monarchy with him on the throne.

Serpé was trying to explain this to the others when a knock on the front door interrupted them. When Striphen brought the new arrival into the common room, their discussions stopped.

"He's a messenger from the temple of Azar." Striphen paused as the others began to pull their swords and step in front of Serpé. "From Sanctuary. Someone called Tossin sent him."

"Let him pass," she shouted over the protests of the others.

A path cleared between her and the man, who sauntered past the commanders and stopped with a bow in front of her.

"A pleasure to see you, Dame Navran. Most Blessed Tossin sends his prayers and blessings." He handed her a small sack she had not noticed before.

"Give us a moment." The commanders left the room, but Blackette and Striphen stayed with her and the messenger. She considered sending the two men away, but gave up without trying. *They rarely leave me alone anymore. But their presence only serves to remind me of Kian's absence.*

She placed the contents of the sack on the table, then looked at the messenger and Blackette for an explanation. "What is this?"

Blackette spoke first. "Kian went to the temple after you did. He wanted to make sure everything that had been collected against Reicholt to that point was kept in a safe place." Blackette turned to the messenger. "He's only been gone four days. How did you get here so quickly?"

"Our magic is not limited. Most Blessed Tossin wanted to ensure Dame Navran was ready before he sent me, or I would have come sooner." The messenger focused on Serpé as if she were the only one in the room. "Most Blessed Tossin wanted to make sure Azar's Righteous Avenger knew she had his assistance. I have been placed under your command, Dame Navran."

She nodded, but did not hear what he said. Kian's documents held her attention and for a moment, there was no one else in the room with her. Finally, some of his words broke through her concentration.

"You're to help me in any way I need?"

He nodded. "As long as it does not dishonor Azar's theology."

"Excellent. We will use these documents to further our cause. After duplicates have been made, you will deliver them to those who will join us. We will lead the physical attacks while you deliver the evidence that will bury Reicholt."

Chapter 61

Darkness surrounded Kian within the prison wagon. The darkness, the sound of horse hooves clacking on stone and the hum of the wooden wheels vibrating through the tight space were the only constants while they traveled. The travel stopped only at night, but even then Kian did not see the sky. He was only allowed outside the wagon to relieve himself, and that had been limited to twice a day.

Not long after they left Serpé's farm, a contingent of the Religious Guard joined them. Strinnal took a chance telling him that men had been left at Serpé's farm. The survivors of Kian's army and Draven's militia had driven them from her land and the forest. Reicholt's rage could be heard through the wagon walls and Kian was sure his own laughter had angered the priest even more.

The pressure of darkness never broke Kian's resolve and the isolation did not give him cause to question his decision. Keeping Serpé foremost in his thoughts and her image clear in his mind gave him the strength to push away the dark that tried to turn him. He knew the isolation was only the first of Reicholt's plans to torture him. But Kian would not give the priest anything, no matter the pain he inflicted or the prison they headed toward, especially if he wanted information about Serpé.

After days of travel, the sounds outside the wagon changed. The hum of the wheels became louder and Kian heard voices cheering the Religious Guards' return to Siladan. Eventually the wagon stopped and he waited for the door to open. He could not stand in the short space, and his back ached from hunching. As light penetrated the darkness and his eyes became accustomed to it, a courtyard lay revealed. Waddling to the doorway, he recognized the prison yard in Siladan.

Placing his foot on the step outside, he glanced around the yard. He smiled, noting the guards that flanked each side of the wagon. Another step and he stood on the ground, face to face with Strinnal Marcin. He held a lit torch above his head, despite the prison yard being well lit already. They stared at each other, before Kian swung his shackled hands at him.

There was no real reason to attack Strinnal, but they had spoken briefly during the travel back to Siladan. They agreed something needed to be done to deflect Reicholt's suspicion from his captain. Strinnal blocked Kian's blow, then swung low and landed a punch on Kian's unprotected side. Kian grunted and swung again, this time making contact with one of the guards who stepped forward to help. Somewhere deep in his mind, he noted the blood spurting from the guard's mouth before turning back to Strinnal, his hands ready.

"Take him down, but keep him alive," the captain shouted in Kian's face, pushing him back into the guards.

Against his natural instinct, Kian fought the urge to defend himself. He needed to make Reicholt feel as if he had won something, but he could not be sure that the priest would not return for Serpé. Killing the guards would give him satisfaction, but Kian did not want Reicholt returning to her in revenge for Kian's actions. Instead of fighting back, Kian gave a small show of resistance until their blows drove him to the ground.

"Take him to the interrogation room. I will be there soon." Reicholt's voice boomed over the grunts of the guards. Their blows stopped. Lifting Kian from the ground, they dragged him into the prison. He heard Reicholt's chuckles of pleasure following them.

Lifting his head against the pain made it throb. After trying twice, Kian decided that examining the prison would have to wait. The ground inside lay covered with straw and dirt. A sudden turn took him into a room with a clean floor, a clear contrast to the filth in the hall.

Finally able to lift his head, Kian found a lone table occupied the middle of the room. The shelves along one wall sat filled with torture implements. Before he could protest, the guards lifted him onto the table and chained him down, his arms and legs outstretched. From the doorway, another guard came forward and threw a bucket of water on him, the shock of the cold water making him gasp for breath. Kian spit the water from his mouth, choking on what made its way down his throat. Forgetting that chains held his arms down, he tried to bring his arms in to hold his chest as the coughing wracked his body.

"I hope you still feel your sacrifice for Serpé was worth it," Reicholt said, smug, from the door.

"Yes, I do." Kian coughed again, pain raging across his ribs.

"Just how much does our precious one know about my activities?"

Kian watched the priest take a dagger from Strinnal before the captain sent the remaining guards out of the room. Reicholt held the dagger over Kian's leg, the blade glinting in the torch light, his lips pulled back in a sneer.

"Would you have done this to Serpé?" Returning the question, Kian made no attempt to hide his sarcasm.

"Do not presume to question me, traitor!" Reicholt's voice boomed, raising his arm above Kian's leg.

Unable to stop him, Kian watched Reicholt plunge the dagger into the muscle of his thigh, an uncontrolled scream escaping as metal hit bone.

"How were you able to find my men so easily? How did you know about the mercenaries?"

Blood roared through Kian's ears, blocking out Reicholt's words. The dagger was pulled from his flesh and he gasped at the release of pressure from his bone.

"Did you know that Serpé feels nothing but disgust for you?" Trying to breathe through the pain, Kian's breath came in ragged gasps. "The idea of you touching her, even thinking of her, makes her violently ill."

Kian heard Reicholt's animal-like growl of hatred over the sudden scream that filled the room again. Taking a breath, he realized it was he who screamed. The priest drove the dagger into his leg again, the pain more intense as he tried to push it through the bone. He dragged the dagger toward Kian's knee, then yanked it out.

Reicholt raised the dagger, blood dripping from the tip, as he prepared to stab Kian a third time. Strinnal reached out to stop him. Kian watched them struggle, Strinnal's face betraying the difficulty in holding back the priest's fury.

"Most Holy," Strinnal's calm voice cut through Kian's heavy breathing. "The Master Interrogator would be most upset if you take his pleasure from him. And, if you kill Kian, you will have no one to use against Serpé or to answer your questions."

Through the haze of pain, Kian saw Reicholt calm. Serpé's name appeared to be the force Strinnal needed.

"You're right, of course. Put him as far away from the other prisoners as you can. I want him in the deepest level, away from the sun. Tomorrow, the Master may begin his questioning." Reicholt strode out of the room, the bloody knife falling from his grip in a loud clatter before he crossed the threshold of the door.

When his footsteps no longer reached them, Strinnal stepped closer to the table. Producing a small vial from a pouch, he held it for Kian to drink the liquid within.

"This will heal some of your wounds and start the process for the rest. But I can't give you more without exposing everything."

Kian nodded, his eyes closed against the pain. "How much longer can you lie to him?"

"However long it takes for Serpé to free you and our kingdom."

Kian nodded again and tried to relax despite the pain. The room remained quiet while Strinnal bandaged the wounds he could. Kian waited until he finished, and when the younger man removed the bonds, he gratefully pulled his arms back to his chest. He allowed Strinnal to help him stand, leaning against him on their way through the prison.

Other prisoners stepped up to their doors, peering out to see the new arrival. Those who fought in Kian's army were the first to recognize the man who nodded at them. They chanted his name, the cries resounding through the prison. The sound followed him into the lower levels until he no longer heard their voices.

Chapter 62

It was easy for Serpé to adjust to the tactics of the army Kian had built. Being divided into units, she really only worked with the commander of each one.

Lord Draven sent most of his militia in to add strength and numbers against the Religious Guard. Striphen stood as the spokesman for the militia and Serpé appreciated that he helped without bringing up their past. Even the militia kept to their individual units giving Serpé the ease of only working with their captains and Striphen.

After a month of skirmishes to wear down the Religious Guard, Serpé felt confident that the combined army and militia were ready to launch a major assault. The planned attack against the Sorban border would push toward Siladan. If they were successful, the Guard would be decimated, allowing them to free Kian and their men from the prison.

The morning light remained dim because of clouds that threatened to rain. Exactly the kind of weather Serpé did not want to fight in. She stood at the front of the rebel army and surveyed the weather, the land and the army that stood against them.

Behind her and the army, she could feel the ancient trees of the Dragon's Forest. Though she did not follow Crystalline's theology, she felt strengthened by the forest.

It's as if the trees are presenting a defensive line against the Religious Guard. Do they feel the bloodlust and tension from the two armies as I do?

She knew, within the protection of the trees, the base camp waited for word of the battle. *Soon, the quiet the camp has had all morning will be shattered by the sounds of combat and the cries of our injured. No matter what I do, I will lose men today. No amount of planning or prayer can prevent the losses.*

Blackette stood next to her and as the commander of the Religious Guard stepped to the front of his troops, they both drew their weapons. Serpé's emotions waged their own war within her and she steeled herself against them. She buried the feelings that would weaken her in the battle to come. *I have to be free of weakness. Only those emotions that will strengthen my instinct to kill can remain free. And I will kill all who stand in my way to freeing Kian.*

A silent signal from the enemy commander sent his troops in a rush toward the rebels. Serpé brought her clenched fist up for her men to see, holding it and them in place. Her men would not move until she gave the signal. The plan was to let the Religious Guard tire themselves with their charge.

The Religious Guard came closer, and still she waited until she heard her own men shuffle in impatience. Her fist shot forward, toward the other army, her shouted command lost in the roar of the rebels as they charged forward.

The crushing sound of the armies colliding deafened Serpé. The fight had not reached her yet, but she recognized the sick sound of swords and axes slicing past armor and shields into flesh.

A guard pushed past the line, and ran toward her, his sword over his head. With little concern, she waved at Blackette. "Wait. His run weakens him." She stood patient until the man came almost upon her. When he brought his sword down, she ducked and sidestepped. Her own sword, in a reverse hold, the blade parallel with her arm, cut into his stomach, through his armor and deep into his flesh.

The man fell to the ground. Without a thought for his lost life, Serpé prepared to defend herself from the next attacker. Blackette stepped closer to her and the two began a dance that sent their opponents from one to the other until they had bodies piled up around them. The force of men continued to push at Serpé and Blackette until they were finally separated. The fighting around her lessened as the combatants moved off to fight battles of their own, around a less skilled fighter.

A new foe presented himself and she fought off his attacks with her more practiced finesse. The ease of blocking his attacks brought frustration. He grinned at her over their crossed blades and she pushed him back, striking the next attack herself. He parried it. Pushing toward her, he swung his fist at her. It landed firm in her stomach. The air rushed from her and she struggled for breath. But he only allowed her a moment and a small space between them before he attacked again.

His sword came across and she ducked to avoid losing her head. Her opponent was better than she thought. Concern crossed her mind briefly that he may injure her and she silently vowed to train more before the next battle.

A sudden burn in her arm brought Serpé's attention back to the man in front of her. His grin grew wider. She stepped into his next attack and pushed his blade away with her own. Her main-gauche sliced across his arm and delivered a wound that matched hers.

He stepped back, growling at the pain she caused him, before charging at her again. She stepped under his attack and brought her smaller blade up, across his face. He howled, his attacks now filled with fury, and despite her better skill, she struggled to defend herself.

Her blades weaved a dance between them, working to force him back. Cuts on her arms burned, evidence he had been successful with numerous attacks. His defenses had also been penetrated, but she barely had a chance to notice how the blood moistened his clothing when he disengaged from her weapons. Her gaze remained focused on his eyes, satisfaction filling them. His weapon had disappeared from her view and she still could not see it. She tried to press her attacks, then stumbled toward him.

"Die, traitor." He pushed toward her again.

She felt a pressure in her stomach. The man grinned, his expression reflecting the triumph in his eyes.

Her gaze drifted downward and a gasp escaped her. Her eyes widened. *A dagger. In my stomach. But I don't feel anything. Why?*

A shout reached her as if from a great distance. "Blackette?" She heard him scream again and glanced toward the sound to see him cutting a bloody path to her side. His mouth moved, but a loud vibration in her ears blocked his words.

At that moment, pain tore through her body. The man held up the dagger for her to see, freed from her flesh. Blood dripped down the blade, over his hand. Serpé fell to her knees. The thud of her weapons hitting the ground barely registered. She tried to staunch the flow of blood from the wound, but her weak hands faltered. The Guard reached down and grabbed her hand. After a brief struggle, he removed her signet ring and scarf. Her futile reach for his leg sent her to the ground.

Blackette finally reached her. He stood over her, his sword slashing wildly at the man who had stabbed her. The weapon ripped into the man's chest and blood dripped from the open wound. Blackette shoved him away from her. He raised his sword in a defensive posture and stood between her and the Religious Guard. The man sneered at them, clutched his treasure to his bloody chest and disappeared amongst the crowd on the battlefield.

The fighting around them stopped and she saw the armies separate. Blackette charged a retreating Guard with the tabard of a commander. His shouted challenge warned the man and he turned. Blackette held his sword in both hands like a spear and drove it into his stomach and across, opening a large wound. Silence descended on the battlefield as the man fell to the ground.

Thunder crashed through the silence, but it was the sound of horns that surprised her. "They are retreating?" Serpé whispered, struggling to push herself from the ground.

Darkness overwhelmed her, obscuring the departure of the Guard. Another crack of thunder echoed through the battlefield. Her arm shook with the strain of supporting her weight. Her strength disappeared and her head hit the ground. When rain poured from the sky, Serpé's eyes closed.

Chapter 63

The First watched the soldier before him squirm under his gaze. *Since my powers were returned by Angast, I find it amusing that no one can stand under my stare for long.* It allowed him a sense of superiority that he had not previously felt, and he liked it.

Eion stared at the man while he gave his report. The soldier had been in the recent battles between Kian's army and the Religious Guard. It was not the battles that grabbed Eion's attention, but what the soldier did in the last one that earned the priest's glare.

"Tell me again." The First kept his voice quiet and calm. He could almost smell the man's fear and made no attempt to hide a malicious grin.

"Most Holy, I confronted Serpé Navran in combat seven days ago. Through my superior talent with a blade and the excellent military training I've received, I defeated her."

Eion laughed, loud enough to make the sound echo in the lavish room. "I doubt your skills outmatched hers. She was trained by one of the best officers our kingdom has ever seen. I'm sure you were just lucky. You have proof you killed her?"

The First watched the soldier pull a blue scarf from a leather pouch. The material was laid on his desk and spread out to reveal a gold ring. He picked up the ring and slipped it on his finger, while eyeing the workmanship critically. The Navran family crest, engraved within the gold, held his attention.

Sudden anger raged within him at the loss of Serpé and the impudence the soldier showed in killing her. *I did not want to share her with Kian or anyone else, but I did not want her dead. The soldier will pay for his misguided initiative.*

The First brought the scarf to his face and caressed his cheek. "Leave me. Send Captain Marcin in so that we may discuss your reward."

Eion waited for Strinnal to come into the room, the scarf and ring again on the desk in front of him. Entering the room, Strinnal's eyes widened in surprise when Eion gestured at the trophies.

"That soldier killed Serpé, even though no one had orders to do so. I want him arrested for treason and placed in a cell near Kian. I want to be sure that the captain has access to that man. He will punish the idiot for me." His throat tightened at the thought of Serpé lying dead on the field of battle. "Have Kian brought to the courtyard. I want to tell him myself."

Eion waved his hand at Strinnal, dismissing him. The ring and scarf held his attention again. Now, only his manipulations would give him the throne. She was the only Navrinar that would give his monarchy any kind of legitimacy. When the captain returned, they walked to the carriage waiting for them outside the temple.

Chapter 64

Light…there shouldn't be any light. Light means someone is in my cell and it's too soon for me to see the interrogator or the council room. Or is it?

Kian opened his eyes, trying to shield them with his hand against the painful torch light. But the movement made his arms hurt, like knives cutting him. He squinted at the light until he had to shut his eyes.

How long have I been asleep? If I did actually sleep. I don't think being unconscious can be called sleep.

It's been long enough for my arms to go numb. The weight of his body pulling on the shackles that held his arms suspended from the ceiling made the numbness worse.

Maybe if I wait long enough, whoever it is will go away.

The light could be seen through his eyelids. He waited, and squinting, checked again.

No, the torch light is still there. Don't these people understand how this is supposed to work?

He opened his eyes completely. Three prison guards stood in his cell, the one in front holding the torch. Each wore an ugly grin on their face.

"His Most Holy wishes to see you," the one with the torch broke the silence and flashed a toothless smile at him.

I remember he had teeth when I arrived. He was the one I attacked that night.

They unlocked the shackles attached to the ceiling chains and he struggled with a deep breath to keep the moan that threatened to escape from being heard. Blood flowed back into his arms, his fingers throbbing. The pain still radiated through him as they placed new shackles on his wrists and ankles. The new chain ran between his hands and feet, with a third portion connecting everything. A slight smile came to his face. *These guards still keep a wary eye on me, they are still nervous despite my restraints.*

Kian walked as slow as the guards would allow, nodding at the other prisoners on his dungeon level. Most of them were freedom fighters, rebels, who had once been members of the Religious Guard or the People's Army before joining him in his war against The First. Now they watched him walk and he acknowledged each one with a confidence he no longer felt.

When they reached the door that led out of the dungeon into the main part of the prison, he waited for them to open it before he stepped through.

They walked through the main floor of the prison, past rooms that held devices of torture. In the month he had been imprisoned, Kian learned about each of those devices first hand. Bruises and cuts covered his body and the Master Interrogator made sure bones were broken.

Pain shooting through his leg with each step reminded him of the worst wound he suffered since arriving at the prison. The knife that Reicholt tried to push through Kian's thigh had created a wound that the Master Interrogator enjoyed reopening whenever he could.

I doubt I will ever walk without a limp again, no matter how many healers I see. If I ever see freedom again.

Rain pelted the doors that led to the courtyard. The sound made Kian realize he wanted to stand in the rain and feel it soak through his clothes. He waited, though, for the doors to open. When the prison yard lay open to him, he glanced around from habit to locate any threats awaiting him.

Strinnal Marcin stood in the rain, soaked, a look of irritation covering his face. Three guards stood behind him, another prisoner between them. Strinnal waved Kian out of the doorway, stepping aside to let the guards and the new prisoner enter.

"Remove the captain's leg shackles and chain. I don't need

him slipping and breaking his neck in the mud."

Kian heard the irritation in Strinnal's voice and for a moment he thought the captain had a plan for escape. *Too many guards are in the yard and Reicholt's carriage sits in the middle of it. An escape attempt would be asinine.*

Again he waited, this time for the chain and leg shackles to be removed. Without further instructions, the other guards and the new prisoner disappeared into the prison.

He did not waste a moment of thought on the man, his attention drawn by the bowmen on the walls, their weapons loaded and pointed at him. Ten guards also stood between him and Reicholt's carriage. They watched as he and Strinnal walked across the courtyard, stopping a few feet from the carriage. A hand pulled the curtain back, revealing The First, dry and untouched by the rain.

"So nice of you to come, Captain Donwell."

"Always a pleasure to stand in the rain." Kian filled his response with sarcasm. It gave him great satisfaction knowing that no matter how hard Reicholt tried, the priest could not control every aspect of his life. The rain cooled his skin and wounds, and he held his hands, palms up, to catch the drops of rain.

I must have a fever. I didn't realize the rain would be such a relief. I needed this.

"Are the accommodations acceptable?" The First's voice echoed with false concern.

"Not that you care." Kian shifted his weight, suddenly aware of a different kind of pain in his legs other than what he'd become accustomed to. A dark memory filled his mind and reminded him of what fostered this new pain.

The last time I was taken from my cell. The Master Interrogator beat my lower back as I hung from the ceiling. Wait? What did he say?

Kian had been ignoring Reicholt, deciding that he was talking just to hear himself. But something he said finally broke through Kian's thoughts.

"What did you say?"

"Weren't you listening?" Reicholt laughed. "The least you could do is pay attention to what I'm saying."

Kian growled, the primal reaction feeling the most appropriate, but he knew the sound was lost on Reicholt with the rain and distance. Stepping closer to the carriage, the guards behind him intervened, grabbing his arms. The ones between him and the priest moved in to block his advance.

"I said I have unfortunate news about Serpé." Reicholt smiled at Kian. "It seems she did not heed my advice and chose to continue your pointless war against me. I received word that she was killed seven days ago in a battle with my army."

The world around Kian stopped. The rain slowed, his heart did not beat and his breath caught in his throat.

"I don't believe you. Serpé wouldn't be that careless." His voice shook, the emotions he struggled to control breaking through.

"I wouldn't jest about this. Serpé is the only woman I have ever loved." Reicholt paused, turned away, and leaned forward, out of view. When he straightened, he gave a small item to one of the guards. "Give it to him."

Kian watched the guard saunter over to him, but his mind still struggled to understand everything the priest said about Serpé.

Did he really say that he loved her? In almost the same breath as he told me about her death?

Holding his hand out, Kian watched a gold ring drop into his waiting palm. He studied the ring, his hand shaking more the longer he stared at it.

"This…this means nothing. The original crest was designed in Parnoir and is well known. You could easily have had another made. You've had her followed and had time to examine it when you used her to capture me."

Am I denying what he's saying because I don't want to believe she's dead?

"Good point, but I have more important things to do with my time." Reicholt grinned, and leaned forward again. When he straightened this time, he motioned for Kian to come closer to the carriage. "This should prove it."

Kian accepted the new item, his breath catching in his throat again. His fingers caressed the silk material of Serpé's engagement scarf. Blood stained the material. He could see the stains spread as it became soaked by the rain. On his hand, the blood was washed away by the rain. Groaning, he fell to his knees, the scarf gripped tight in his hand.

"It can't be true." His heart clenched in pain. *I would endure all the tortures the Master Interrogator could think of, if I didn't have to accept Serpé is dead. No torture can compare to the pain in my chest.*

The torchlight in the courtyard faded from his vision and a darkness blacker than the night surrounded him. He heard her voice begging him to leave her in Reicholt's clutches. Drowning out the sound of the rain, it changed to the whisper she used to say she loved him when they lay in bed after making love.

I loved the husky tone of her voice in the morning. Reicholt has taken that from me, taken everything, just like I feared he would.

"It's true. The soldier who ran her through brought the ring and scarf to me himself." Reicholt leaned out the carriage window. "Would she have let him take those if she still lived?"

"No, she would have fought until her death." Kian held the scarf against his stomach. His breath did not come easily, each draw causing pain as he forced his lungs to take in air. "She can't be dead."

"She can and she is. She was warned not to continue your war against me. She brought this upon herself. I have to tell you though, the only reason I kept you alive was to bring her under my control." The sympathy in the priest's voice disgusted Kian. "I know what you're feeling."

Kian brought his gaze up to Reicholt's face. His pain fueled the anger growing within him. "You know what I'm feeling?" With each word, each articulated syllable, his voice grew louder.

Roaring, like a wild animal finally released from its confinement, Kian threw himself at the carriage. The weight of the chain and shackles on his wrists added to his anger and enhanced his strength. With his hands clasped together, he swung wildly, hitting the guards who stared at him in shock. His advantage lasted only a moment before the guards reacted to what was happening and drew their weapons.

Grabbing the window of the carriage, Kian pulled himself partway through and latched onto Reicholt's robes. He pulled the man close, until he could smell the wine on his breath and the fear he tried to hide behind his grin.

"You have no idea what I'm feeling. You tried to rape her, beat her, and then killed her and yet you claim to love her." Kian's hands moved up to Reicholt's throat and a momentary thrill filled him that he may actually kill him. The priest's skin became slimy with sweat. "Go to hell."

Tightening his grip on Reicholt's throat, he felt the guards hitting him. No weapons pierced his flesh and he briefly wondered if Strinnal had stopped them. With his ribs cracking under their assault, he lost his grip. They beat on him until they could pull him from the carriage. On the ground, their attacks changed to kicks, forcing him to protect his head until Reicholt called out to stop them.

"Leave him. He'll be dead soon, and I'll finally be rid of him. Leave him there to wallow in his misery, then return him to his cell." Kian heard Reicholt's smug words through the rush of blood and pain in his ears. "Take me home, Captain Marcin."

Looking up, past the guards, Kian saw that Strinnal had climbed onto the seat of the carriage. The younger man turned away from him, clicked his tongue at the horses and flicked the reins to encourage the animals to leave the courtyard.

Left on the ground, Kian clutched Serpé's scarf against his chest and watched the torch light flicker off the gold of her signet ring. Only then did he realize he had dropped it in his struggle to get at Reicholt. Reaching for the ring, his body screamed in pain, but he ignored it, finally pulling the ring in close.

The rain slowed when the guards finally took him back to his cell.

On the way back to his cell, Kian decided there was nothing left to do against Reicholt. He was the last of a lost cause. *With my imprisonment and Serpé's death, nothing will prevent Reicholt from becoming Sorban's king. Blackette and Strinnal may continue to fight for awhile after I die, but they will eventually be caught as well. Strinnal is closer to capture than anyone else. It is only Reicholt's lack of trust in anyone else's ability to keep him safe that keeps the younger captain alive for now. Time will change even that eventually.*

The guards gave Kian dry clothing and blankets when they arrived at his cell. Confused, he spent several moments trying to decide what was expected of him when the guards handed him the clothes and blankets. Despite his own desire to end his pain, he wrapped himself in the blankets after changing his clothes. Each movement felt automatic and forced.

Who will remember us? The battles we fought? What we fought for? My love for Serpé?

Before long, Reicholt will have everyone who knew about me and

Serpé killed. There will be no one left to remember us. No one will know she was the true heir to the throne. The queen who was hidden from Destiny.

Not that putting her in hiding had done any of us any good. Reicholt still killed her. Maybe Strinnal and Blackette can find her lost brother. There were no remarks about his death on the family tree Reicholt kept. Perhaps he still lives.

After Reicholt declares himself king, what would it matter? None of those who follow him blindly now will even care. They will know no difference, gladly bending to allow the bastard to have his way with them.

What were we fighting for, then? Serpé gave her life for people who don't care enough to look past their front doors to see how he manipulates them. Those who do realize it will find out too late to help themselves. We should have just walked away and not bothered with the fight to save them.

The faces of the children Serpé had saved flashed through his mind. *They are the reason the fighting started. Those children and all the others that have been lost and will still be lost. But they aren't the only reason.*

The children were replaced with the vision of Serpé, in the bed they had shared. The way the sun lit her face and her eyes fluttered open when he pulled the curtains back.

At least my memories are still fresh. They will go with me as I climb the gallows.

Reaching out, his fingers warmed at the memory of touching her skin. His body responded, an ache building until he fell to his knees from a need he could never share with Serpé again.

We almost had everything. But she had to go and challenge Reicholt face to face. Why couldn't she just do as she had been told? Why did she have to fight against everything I did to protect her?

His roar of frustration filled his cell, echoing back at him. It rang through the rest of his dungeon level. He and Serpé argued about it back on the farm, and now there was no point in doing it again, alone.

Wouldn't Reicholt love too know of our disagreement? That even after her death, I am still angry with her decision? I'm sure he would find some way to twist it to his advantage in the final days of my trial.

The cold of the stone floor bit into his hands. Slamming his fist against the stone sent a shot of pain up his arm, enough to clear Serpé's image from before his eyes. He was alone, in the dark of his cell, again.

It doesn't matter what Reicholt does to me now. There's nothing left.

Kian did not bother to stand, or try to find the cot they put in his cell while he had been in the courtyard. The cold of the floor against his cheek became a welcome contrast to the numbness that invaded his body.

Chapter 65

The First had commandeered the most comfortable chair in the room, despite the home belonging to Merchant Tolan and his family. He also demanded food and drinks, yet in a more subtle way so the head of the Merchant Council would think he remained in control of the meeting. Eion did not need the merchant becoming defensive. He wanted to present his demands before the man tried to refuse him.

Strinnal stood behind his chair, even though his insubordinate behavior continued to frustrate Eion. He was close to becoming the ex-commander of the Religious Guard. There had been too many questions from the captain—too many times he balked at Eion's orders. It would be unfortunate to lose him, but loyalty was rewarded with life—all traitors would meet their deaths.

"Most Holy, is there a direct reason for your visit? Not that your visits aren't appreciated. However, I have many things to take care of, what with so many new additions to the council and the death of Merchant Navran."

Eion recognized Tolan's impatience. *It is impressive that the merchant has the backbone to show such defiance to my face.*

"I have shown the people the ineptitude of the council and I have captured the leader of the rebel army. It is time to remove the council and make our kingdom a monarchy again. Only I am able to rule our people in the times ahead." The First casually waved his hand.

"What are you saying?" The merchant almost slammed his brandy snifter on the table next to him. Eion marveled at how the crystal did not break under the force.

"I'm saying it's time to declare me king."

"I can't do that," Tolan protested.

Eion sighed at the man's refusal. *I expected this. He does not want to give up control of the kingdom, but I have grown tired of his games.*

"On the contrary, Tolan. You are the only one standing in my way. Now, I can either be declared king and allow you to live, or I can remove my final obstacle." The First leaned forward. "And I will not stop with just you. Your wife and son will also be dealt with. I know a good whore house for your wife and I'm sure there will be any number of assassins who would gladly kill Rodin for a very reasonable amount of gold. Or perhaps he would be better suited for slavery."

He sat back to watch his words take full root in Tolan's mind. When the merchant's eyes narrowed, Eion knew he won. Though he still saw resistance, Tolan would do as he wanted.

"I will call a council meeting to take place in three days."

"I'm sure everything will go as planned and everyone in your family will be just fine." Eion stood, nodded at the merchant and let himself out of the house.

Things were going as planned, despite the changes he had to make and the obstacles encountered. *Though I will not have Serpé to ensure I have a legitimate heir, the throne will still belong to me.*

Chapter 66

The next morning, Strinnal returned to Merchant Tolan's home. The time had come for everyone who opposed The First to gather in one place and remove him from power. Those who could make the final preparations stood in the room with him and he saw their confusion over why he asked them to return.

He watched everyone retrieve drinks from a man servant, each lost in their own thoughts. Rodin Tolan stood near his father, already several sips into the brandy filling his snifter. Strinnal knew the ambassador had seen Serpé when she visited Arcadia and that he sent her away when The First's men attacked. Mage Stein and Merchant Tolan watched him in return. They all waited for the servant to leave.

When the servant finally left the room, Merchant Tolan cleared his throat. "Captain Marcin, are you ready to explain why you've called us here? The First's request to set up a council meeting has me quite busy."

"You need to play into Reicholt's plans, sir."

"Are you daft? He thinks he's going to be named king." The leader of the council waved his hand dismissively.

"Exactly. Be prepared to make him think he is achieving exactly what he wants." Strinnal expected the expressions of shock he saw on the faces of the other men. He waited, patient, for his statement to sink in.

"You can't be serious!" Rodin took a step toward Strinnal.

"Hear him out, Rodin," Mage Stein advised, reaching out with Merchant Tolan to stop the younger man.

Strinnal nodded at the mage in thanks. "I know I'm asking you to do the one thing we've been fighting against. But the army is ready to move against Reicholt in support of the council."

"Kian was supposed to lead the army against Reicholt. Serpé was to join him and present her evidence against him." Rodin sounded confused and Strinnal did not blame him.

"That had been the original plan. With Kian's capture, Serpé took command of the army. But recent news indicates she has been killed in battle." Speaking of Serpé's death reopened the wound in Strinnal's heart. "The second-in-command, Blackette, has taken over the army now. He has all the evidence, but we will have to do it without her."

"How are we supposed to remove Reicholt without them?" Merchant Tolan continued to stare at Strinnal, concern growing in his eyes. "They are the only ones who have been able to keep our plans moving, despite their personal losses."

"We will have to move ahead with our plans. Do we really want Reicholt to declare himself king over our country?" Desperation crept into Strinnal's voice. If Tolan did not support moving forward, Reicholt would become king and all those who died trying to stop him would have died a pointless death.

"You are asking us to place a great deal of trust in you and this new commander, someone we don't even know," Tolan observed.

Though he heard the doubt in Tolan's voice, Strinnal felt the merchant would agree by his relaxed posture.

Strinnal watched Stein stepped forward. "Before Bennan died, he and I had worked to keep communication lines open between Kian and the captain. Strinnal's information has always been helpful and accurate. If he says this is necessary, then I believe him."

The two Tolans studied the mage and Strinnal. The captain shifted under the intense scrutiny until the elder nodded in agreement. "The meeting will be called. All those who oppose Reicholt will be prepared to move when you tell us. Understand, it falls on your head if this goes wrong."

"I understand, Merchant Tolan. You will know when to act." Strinnal bowed and left the room.

Walking back to his home, the captain prayed that everyone would be ready when it was time.

Chapter 67

It's been two days since they told me of Serpé's death. Two days and I've actually been allowed to see the sun from this new cell. Reicholt must have a reason. No visits to the Master Interrogator. Just the walls of my cell and my window. And why did he let me keep Serpé's ring and scarf?

Kian had tied the ring into a knot in the material and tied the scarf to his arm. *On the day Reicholt executes me, I will take the last of Serpé with me.*

Footsteps approached his cell, pulling him from his thoughts of Serpé. He waited for the guards to walk past. No one had come for him since placing him inside. This time they stopped at his door. Someone worked the keys to open it.

"Get up, Donwell. You're going out for sun and exercise. Should feel good after being locked up in here for so long," a guard announced when the door opened.

The news surprised Kian, but he rose from the cot, and waited for shackles to be placed on his wrists.

Not paying attention to the sounds around him, Kian walked through the prison, allowing his thoughts to wander.

Things have changed too quickly. Even if they planned an execution within the next week, my confinement shouldn't have changed so drastically.

Stepping into the prison yard, Kian realized the guard had

been right. The sun shown bright and the warmth felt good as it flowed over him.

Will this be the last time I stand in the sun like this? Even if I could escape, without Serpé, there is nothing I can do to stop Reicholt's plans. Without her position, I will always be seen as a rebel.

"Not so special now, are you, Borian?" Turning away from his guard while waiting for the shackles to be removed, Kian noticed two other guards harassing another prisoner.

Squinting, lack of interest filled him, but he recognized the man they harassed. The prisoner was the same man Strinnal had brought in two days before, when Kian learned of Serpé's death.

Just another victim of the guard's perverted sense of fun.

"I am! I have done a great service for The First and Sorban." The man sounded desperate. "Just talk to Captain Marcin. This has to be a mistake."

"I don't think so. The First's signature was on the parchment for your arrest and imprisonment." It surprised Kian that one of the guards actually took time to respond to the prisoner. The sympathy in the guard's voice made Kian turn back to the scene he dismissed just a moment earlier.

"But I killed the leader of the rebel army." Noticing the guards glance in his direction, Kian became fully interested in the outbursts. "I drove my sword into her belly and then gave proof of my victory to The First. Why would he want me imprisoned? He should reward me for my service." Borian turned to Kian as if to ask for support. "Don't you agree?"

Kian did not answer. Instead, he swung his fist, taking instant satisfaction in the feel of his knuckles connecting with the man's jaw. Bringing his other fist up, he slammed it into the man's stomach, following it with the first. Borian looked at him, surprise then recognition filling his expression.

Technique no longer mattered. Kian had a focus for his anger and hatred. Though the man was not Reicholt, he claimed to be the one who killed Serpé. That was enough for Kian. Nothing would stop him from killing this man.

Kian did not care what punches he threw, where he hit, but pain in his own body brought him out of his bloodlust. Again and again, from different places, the pain shot through his body. A quick glance to his right and he found the guards trying to get him off Borian. Another swing of his fist, downward, and he realized he straddled Borian's chest. He stopped his punishment and stood, allowing the sympathetic guard to pull him away from the other prisoner.

"Captain Donwell, I'm sorry for Serpé's loss, but don't give the other guards a reason to kill you as well." The guard leaned toward Kian, keeping his voice low so the others could not hear. "I can't stop them if they want to take it too far and Captain Marcin has instructed me to keep you alive."

"Why bother?" Kian did not wait for the guard to answer. He walked past him, leaving Borian unconscious on the ground, to the guard who brought him to the yard. "Take me back to my cell."

Chapter 68

Eion sat in his soft, cushioned chair on the top tier in the council room. He watched the merchants settle into their seats in the three levels below him. His seat had been moved to the middle of the half-circle seating arrangement.

I have finally achieved my greatest ambition. This meeting, planned so quickly that no one will have had time to move against me, will declare me king. I will then give the kingdom to the siblings and their dark goddess.

I am pleased with everything I have accomplished. Kian's capture, as well as that of most of his army, helped me prove that Sorban needs a monarch again. The merchants that were killed were replaced with those who will support me and my bid to become king. They outnumber those who stand against me now.

Serpé's death had been the only significant loss he endured. *It is unfortunate they did not recover her body. I would have gladly used my new powers to restore her life. But Borian's beating by Kian, then torture by the Master Interrogator was most satisfying. His hanging this morning was truly exquisite.* The First had come from the hanging directly to the meeting. He had not even taken time to change his robes in his excitement.

Trumpets sounded and the meeting started. Last minute arrivals settled into their seats. Merchant Tolan waited for conversations to end when he took his place at the base of the seats. He turned in a slow half-circle to look at everyone, his gaze finally settling on Reicholt.

"Most Holy Reicholt, the council thanks you for joining us on such short notice." He paused when the other merchants clapped their approval. After allowing them a moment, he gestured for silence.

"Since you were given command of a larger military force, you have successfully captured the captain of the rebel army and many of its members. You were able to prevent a war with our neighbors and capture their assassins." Cheers and applause filled the room again.

The First saw the frown on Tolan's face and knew that the threat against his wife and son still weighed heavily on the merchant.

"The people have cried out for a leader. As the current ruling body of Sorban…" A loud commotion at the doors to the council chambers interrupted Merchant Tolan again.

The doors opened, with enough force to slam into the walls, and an individual entered the chamber. The intruder wore all black, with a hooded cloak that hid the face. Black shirt, breeches, boots and gloves were seen as the person strode farther into the room. The figure radiated confidence that filled the large room. Even in his seat, so far away, Eion felt intimidated by the figure as it stopped in the middle of the floor.

He pulled his gaze from the intruder to the fifteen men he had not noticed came in as well. Each one wore either the vestments of the People's Army or the Religious Guard.

Afraid, many merchants stood and cried out for their guards. Eion noted that each one was a supporter he had placed on the council. His guards tried to move forward, but the fifteen men drew their weapons and prevented them from advancing. From the doors, Captain Marcin appeared with thirty men, First Mage Stein, and Rodin Tolan. The First stood and pointed at the intruders.

"Captain Marcin! Remove these intruders." His voice echoed throughout the room, but the figure in black stood unaffected. As if trying to insult The First, the figure crossed its arms and tapped a foot on the floor.

"Of course, Most Holy." Strinnal directed his men with a small gesture, but instead of removing the sixteen intruders, the soldiers escorted the merchant's guards from the council chambers. The doors were closed and the men took up positions around the room. Strinnal then stepped closer to the hooded intruder and grinned at Eion.

The cloaked figure gestured for one of the pages in the room to approach. When the boy stepped closer, he was given a large stack of parchments, and whispered instructions.

Eion watched in frustration as the boy gave each merchant two of the parchments. When he received his own, he crumpled it in his grip, refusing to read it.

"Most Holy Reicholt, you are accused of crimes against the people of Sorban and the church of Azar." Eion did not recognize the voice, nor was he able to distinguish it as either female or male. The voice was more a mixture of many voices, not just one or two. It occurred to him that he listened to the voices of the people he was accused of committing crimes against.

"You are accused of murdering Most Holy Korewyn, accepting bribes in exchange for preferred judgments, extorting funds from the church, hiring mercenaries to attack merchant caravans and assassins to murder merchants and replacing them with people you can control..." A loud murmur rippled through the merchants and the figure held up a hand to stop them. A blue glow filled the room and those who started to protest became quiet. Eion noted, though, that the glow avoided him.

"Please allow the charges to be read in full, so that all may know the corruption of he who wishes to rule over Sorban." The glow faded and the merchants nodded. "The merchants placed into these positions did not know of Reicholt's intentions, or the extent of his manipulations. Reicholt, you have demanded tributes and placed families in prison, slavery and whorehouses if they could not or would not pay. You created a false war with Tushin to gain control of the military forces. The figure took a step back and held its arms out wide.

"But the worst of your crimes will surprise and convince even the most skeptical, including those you think you control. To gain this meeting, you threatened to kill Merchant Tolan's family. And you are the man who led a murderous attack on King Navrinar and the family that went with him. You were the reason King Navrinar left Sorban in the first place—the corruption growing within you, that Most Holy Korewyn warned our king about. Finally, you destroyed a marriage agreement between Serpé Navran and Rodin Tolan, with the knowledge that she was the last heir and granddaughter of King Navrinar. You intended to use her to give you the throne." Again, a murmur grew louder in the crowd, but the blue glow did not return to silence it.

Eion pounded his fist on the table next to him. The room quieted again, but the merchants turned to look at him now.

"Who are you? What do you want?" His voice cracked with anger.

"Shall we continue this here, or should we go someplace without so many who wish to witness your downfall?" The voices mocked him, but remained casual.

"I control them. It matters not what they hear." Again the merchants interrupted, this time in anger. Those closest to him reached out to grab his arms.

"Gentlemen, please stop." The combined voices were no louder than before, but echoed with power through the room. The merchants stopped, though they did not release him. "Reicholt, the only way to keep yourself alive is to agree to my demands. If not, I will leave, take all the guards with me and let the merchants deal with you as they please."

He glanced at the angry expressions worn by those who held him. "Are you threatening me?"

The intruder laughed softly, the combined voices musical. "No, I make you a promise. In your hands, as well as the merchants', is proof of your disgrace, the lies, the payoffs, murders, rapes, enslavements and the betrayal of our country.

"You will face justice by the people and the church. You will free Kian Donwell and his men. He is guilty only of trying to stop your takeover of Sorban. Restore his family name and remove all charges against him and his followers. Their property and businesses will be returned to them and their families."

Eion heard confidence growing in the voices. "Why would I do that?"

The intruder gestured with their hand to include everyone around Reicholt. "Because, despite these men being civilized, I am the only thing keeping you from being removed from your position and your life being taken from you."

Eion stepped forward, shaking off the hands of those who held him from his arms. "Captain, Marcin, free Captain Donwell." He returned his gaze to the intruder. "Anything else?"

Strinnal left the room. The First watched him leave, but his anger remained focused on the figure in black.

"Control your temper, Most Holy. I may become nervous with your yelling and order your death before you have the chance to correct your mistakes." The figure paced the floor. "As you can see, behind me stand members from both our military groups. More join me every day. Since you manipulated the merchants to combine the armies, the men have been unable to defend their country in the proper fashion. They have joined me and mine so that they may continue to protect the merchants and the people. The only difference is, now they are criminals for doing what they were trained to do."

"Criminals should be punished." Eion was bold in his declaration, but did not expect the laughter that came from within the hood.

"I'm so glad you think so, because as a traitor to the kingdom, you will be punished. The figure stopped at the bottom of the steps. Those who had held him before grabbed him again and dragged him down the stairs to stand in front of his accuser. "How do you sleep at night?"

"Very well, thank you."

"How did you sleep after you heard of Serpé Navran's murder?" The figure stepped closer, but still stood out of his reach.

"She was killed in battle, not murdered." His answer sounded stern, to him, as if he tried to convince himself as well as those who watched.

"Is that how you live with it? By justifying her death as a casualty of war? Inciting the Religious Guard to capture both Kian and Serpé caused carelessness. Her death is murder, by your hands. You caused it." The figure turned toward the council chamber doors as they opened again.

Captain Marcin entered the room, his arm around Kian to help him walk. The former prisoner limped and grimaced in pain with each step. The two entered and stared at Reicholt and the figure before him.

"Now that you've seen him, I am done with your games. I remind you who is in charge here, Captain Marcin. Order your men to arrest these intruders."

Strinnal shook his head. "I don't think so, *Most Holy.*"

Eion felt shock spread over his face. "You dare defy me?"

"Yes, he does." The figure's voice changed, becoming all feminine, the many voices combining into one. A voice he recognized—they all recognized. The men returned their attention to the black cloaked figure as the hood dropped back to reveal the attractive features of Serpé. Bright, radiant silver light washed over her.

Chapter 69

"Serpé?" Kian called out in a voice filled with pain and relief, but she did not turn to look at him. *If I look at him now, I will not finish what I started. I will kill Reicholt instead of serving justice.*

"The power to heal is granted to the faithful, Eion. You should remember what that was like. Do you still have it, now that you serve a dark goddess?" Even to her, her voice sounded cold and detached. The look on Reicholt's face revealed he heard the same.

"I have many more abilities now that I serve Angast. She is very gracious," he growled with obvious frustration as the merchant's protests began anew, many invoking Azar's name.

"My family line is on the parchments each of you holds. My mother was the child King Navrinar left in Parnoir with the servants he trusted. I am the rightful heir to the Sorban throne. Eion Reicholt knew this because he went to the king's home with mercenaries and killed everyone there. My mother was missing, so he searched for her until he found her." She turned her attention back to Reicholt.

"I should have killed you when I had the chance." He spat at her.

She looked at the ground where his spittle landed. "Yes, you should have. As it is, you fueled this war against you."

"Your family died begging for their lives. I personally watched them kill your mother and made sure the last words she heard were what I intended to do to you."

Her heartbeat slowed for a moment, then exploded into faster beats. She saw the men who held Reicholt in place release him and stare at her, fear in their faces. A blue fire lit her body and she stepped toward him. Her vision clouded with a haze of blue and silver.

She flipped the cloak from her arm and drew her sword. When she stepped forward again, she felt a hand on her arm, trying to hold her back.

"Serpé, don't. Remember what you said about the wrath of a god if he was killed? Do you think it will be any different because he serves another?" Kian's voice reached her through the rush she heard in her ears. He restrained her with one hand while his other came up to touch her cheek.

She saw that he wanted to say more, but everything slowed as the room filled with a bright silver light, blinding her. Kian's hand left her cheek, but she still felt him holding onto her sword arm.

When the brightness faded, it took a moment for her eyes to adjust. She looked around, not surprised to see others just as stunned as her. But it was the man who stood between her and Reicholt that made her stop.

"Bennan?" She reached out for him and fought back tears that threatened to ruin the intensity of the situation. Her hand stood empty again, the weight of her estoc back in its scabbard on her hip.

He nodded, took her hand in his and pulled her close. "Yes, my child."

Bennan embraced her, memories of the times he held her flooding her mind. Startled murmurs, cries of surprise and the sound of several men falling to their knees broke through Serpé's momentary peace. She pulled away from his embrace, determined to control the situation again. Kian stared at them, as well as Reicholt, Blackette and Strinnal. Several merchants knelt, their hands clasped and their heads bowed as if in prayer.

"What is wrong with all of you?" She looked up at Bennan, then stepped back, her own mouth open in surprise. "This isn't possible."

Bennan no longer resembled the man she called friend. He

now looked like the many depictions of Azar. The tapestries and statues, as well as her dreams, were poor visuals to what the god actually looked like. He was even more handsome in reality than in Serpé's dreams.

"I told you I would always be with you, my child. But it is not the most important thing I have ever said to you." He put his arm over her shoulder and turned with her to look at Reicholt. Warmth filled her at his touch, but the fear on Reicholt's face reminded her of the reason she faced him.

"Remember what I told you while you suffered the heartache of Kian's rejection? You must forgive Eion to defeat him. Only in forgiveness will you be able to take away his power."

"But does he truly deserve forgiveness? He has hurt so many." She glared at the priest who once served the god who stood next to her. "He deserves a slow, painful death. Not forgiveness."

Azar released her and she felt his presence step away from her. "The longer you hold the anger against him, the longer he has a grip on you and your life. Will you allow him to continue making you look for him behind every tree? Or continue a war against him that will eventually take yours and Kian's lives?"

She stared at Reicholt. *I do not want to forgive him. I want him dead.* The memory of her first night with Kian warmed her. She glanced at him. *Reicholt has hurt us so much. I want to take all his power over us away.* A brief flash and she saw Reicholt, older, broken, in a dark cell, on a cot. *He will die a lonely, broken man, the memory of his defeat at my hands his only companion.* The glow around her intensified so much she saw it reflected in Reicholt's eyes, wide now with fear.

"No, the war must end and our country must be allowed to have peace." She took a deep breath, and smiled. "It is easier than I thought to forgive you, Eion. I understand that everything you've done was purely out of greed. It falls upon me to put all of that behind me and mine and forgive you. Now that everyone knows what you've done, you will find no refuge in Sorban."

"I didn't ask for your forgiveness. I don't need it." He held his hands out at his sides and lifted his face to the ceiling. Dark smoke circled around his hands. When he brought them closer, he created a ball of smoke between them.

Reicholt grinned. The ball grew, black lightning arcing over the surface.

Serpé watched him form the ball of dark magic, calm though

she felt panic rise around her. Azar's presence still lingered nearby, but he took no actions to stop Reicholt.

As the ball grew, and he prepared to throw it at her, she brought up her own hands to stop it.

When it had grown to the size of a medium pumpkin, he brought his hands back, and flung the ball at her, the name of Angast on his lips in praise.

The ball flew at her, but a blue shield of light appeared in front of her. The black smoke dispersed over the shield. A strong wind blew past the shield and her hands, blowing her hair back.

When the wind stopped, she glanced back to see Kian and the others pushed back several feet from where they had stood. Azar had not moved, but stood with a grin that reminded her of Bennan. A roar of outrage brought her attention back to Reicholt.

"Impossible! You don't have the abilities to stop my magic. No resistance you've gained would give you the power to do that." His frustration hit her, powered by another spell he cast with only a gesture.

This time, unprepared, she moved back several feet. The blue light around her blocked the spell from affecting her, other than to push her. On instinct, she brought her hand down over her face and body and the black of his spell disappeared.

"Enough, Eion. It is time for you to be judged by those you have hurt." She threw out her other hand and blue tendrils shot from her fingertips at him. Clenching her fist, the tendrils wrapped around him. "Surrender without further actions or I will be forced to stop you."

Before he could answer, a beautiful woman, dressed only in leather strips that barely concealed her shapely flesh, stepped out from behind him. She ran her fingers down his arm. The tendrils that held him broke and faded at her touch.

"Tsk, tsk, tsk, Azar, letting your Righteous Avenger torture my newest acquisition. I cannot allow any of you to harm my pet. He'll be useful to me in the future." The woman focused her attention on Serpé. "Your brother waits to take away from you what you cannot hold, Serpé. I look forward to the battle between the two of you."

Azar stepped past Serpé, but the woman put her arms around Reicholt and they disappeared. He turned back to her.

"I apologize. I did not realize who he had turned to when I removed his favor. I could not stop her. Each of us is able to affect our Chosen without another interfering."

"He will face his judgment sooner or later." Serpé smiled, and turned to find Kian.

Though she had seen his face, she did not expect the extent of injuries she now saw. He lost weight and was thinner than even after his injury that brought him to her months ago. The layers of filth that coated his skin could not hide the cuts and bruises on his chest, arms and legs. One eye had nearly swollen shut, but the other gleamed bright when he smiled at her, his cracked lips bleeding anew. She reached out for him, but was stopped by Merchant Tolan appearing between them with a smile.

"Dame Navran, it is good to know you survived. With everything that has happened here, the merchants and I would like to welcome you and those who have served in Captain Donwell's army home. If I might ask, what are your intentions toward the throne? And what of your brother? Will you search for him?" He seemed almost afraid as he waited for the answer.

"I don't know yet, Merchant Tolan. Obviously, without the protection of the army, I am at risk. But we have been without a monarch for so long, there is concern as to how the people will react." She stepped around him to Kian and put her arm around his waist to help him. "We will discuss it, and my brother, if he lives still, in two days—here—mid-day."

"I think that is an excellent idea, Dame Navran. I look forward to helping with the transition." He bowed to her and Kian. "All charges will be dropped that have been brought against the army, in the name of the royal family."

She did not want to argue with his assumption that she would take the throne. "Two days, Tolan. Give me two days."

He nodded as she helped Kian walk over to Azar.

"I don't understand…" Kian started, but Azar's laughter stopped him.

"Even when you see it with your own eyes, you still doubt."

"It explains why Bennan had too much magic, I guess. But why make us think you—he—had died?" Kian looked at Serpé when she touched his arm.

"Kian, it is not our place to question him." Serpé shook her head.

"No, Serpé, he has the right to ask. Walking on the Prime plane allows me to see how magic is used by those who have learned to control it. This kingdom in particular, having chosen to worship me, receives a good deal of attention. You, Kian, have protected my interests here, whether you believe or not. For that, I thank you." The god rested a hand on her head and then Kian's. "My blessings, children. I will be with you always."

Before Serpé or Kian could respond, he faded from sight.

Serpé returned her gaze to Kian and frowned. Azar had used magic to clean him, but now his wounds were more obvious and the discoloration of his bruises marred his features. "We need to go home, Kian. You need to have your wounds tended to."

They turned to leave, but this time, Strinnal blocked their path. "We will have to find Reicholt, Serpé. While he is free, there's still an uncontrolled threat."

"I know, Captain. We will find him. I need time to let Kian heal first and for the kingdom to recover." His disappointment made her sigh. "Go through his office. See if you can find anything that will tell us where he went. You found out about me. I trust you to find this." He bowed, and fell in behind Serpé and Kian as they left the council chambers.

The fifteen men she and Marcin had brought with them followed as well, joining twenty more outside the council chambers. The large group made their way to the stable where Drommond, Aldric and Tamar waited. Before anyone could tend to Kian's wounds, he grabbed Serpé in a tight embrace.

"I thought you were dead." His voice was hoarse with emotion. Tears fell, landing on her cheeks and mixing with her own.

"Without you, I was dead," she breathed.

They stood in silence. She kept her arms around his waist, while he caressed her cheeks with callused thumbs. Time passed, unnoticed, except for the movement of horses and the nervous fidgeting of those around them. Finally, she untied her scarf and ring from his arm. He took the ring from her and lifted her right hand in his.

"You're wearing another ring?" He rubbed the metal on her finger.

"It's the one my mother wore." She took the ring from him and slipped it onto his finger. "You now wear my father's." The ring she wore warmed once his was in place.

"What happened?" Confusion and wonder filled his voice.

"Yours is warm too?" He nodded. "Obviously it doesn't need to be attuned to you. Now we will always know the other is alive while we wear them."

They embraced again until Strinnal interrupted them.

"I'm sorry to intrude," he kept his words quiet, as if reluctant to speak, "but the army is waiting to be brought home, and we really need to have Kian's wounds tended to."

They released each other, but Serpé kept his hand in hers. "Kian, I'm sorry. I did not give you the forgiveness you deserved, when we were on the farm. I was wrong. You didn't deserve that. I know you only tried to protect me. Next time though, when you find out I'm the heir to some throne, tell me the truth, sooner."

"I promise." He smiled at her and kissed her hand.

Everyone in the stable mounted their horses and traveled through Siladan. Serpé gaze at the city with new eyes. The people continued their daily lives as if nothing had changed, innocent in their ignorance. Reicholt no longer held the city in his grip of greed and lust for power. Next to her rode the man she loved and together, they would return the kingdom to its former glory.

About the Author

Micaela Fischer lives in Las Vegas, Nevada with her family and their zoo of animals. As a second generation native of Sin City, she always smiles and nods when "newcomer's" try to tell her about the city she has called home all her life. She has been writing for as long as she can remember and looks forward to every day when her muse speaks to her and her characters agree it's a good day to write.

You can reach Micaela at silvermanewriting@cox.net or visit her website at www.micaelafischer.com